The Songbook of Benny Lament

ALSO BY AMY HARMON

Young Adult and Paranormal Romance

Slow Dance in Purgatory

Prom Night in Purgatory

Inspirational Romance

A Different Blue

Running Barefoot

Making Faces

Infinity + One

The Law of Moses

The Song of David

The Smallest Part

Historical Fiction

From Sand and Ash

What the Wind Knows

Where the Lost Wander

Romantic Fantasy

The Bird and the Sword

The Queen and the Cure

The First Girl Child

The Songbook of Benny Lament

A novel

AMY HARMON

LAKE UNION
PUBLISHING

This is a work of fiction. Names, characters, organizations, places, events, and incidents are either products of the author's imagination or are used fictitiously.

Published by Lake Union Publishing, Seattle

www.apub.com

ISBN-13: 9781542023535
ISBN-10: 154202353X

Cover design by Holly Ovenden

Printed in the United States of America

For
Korrie,
Renita,
and Gladys,
who shared their
hearts with me.

The Barry Gray Show

WMCA Radio

Guest: Benny Lament

December 30, 1969

"Good evening, ladies and gentlemen, this is Barry Gray, and you are listening to the fabulous 57, WMCA in New York. Happiest station in the nation. I am here for you, keeping you company in the darkest hours of the night, especially on this, the last show of the year, the last full night of the decade. Tomorrow the clock will strike midnight and the sixties will be gone, and I've been lucky enough to cover it all.

"What a decade it's been, folks. What a decade it's been! The sixties brought us death. War. Revolution. We lost a president. We've lost almost fifty thousand young men in Vietnam. Some of you might say we've lost our moral compass. Or maybe we never had it. Sometimes I wonder. Dr. Martin Luther King was gunned down. Bobby Kennedy too.

"But it wasn't all bad, my friends. Five months ago, on July 20, 1969, America put a man on the moon. We put Thurgood Marshall, the first Negro justice, on the Supreme Court. I believe history will look back on these years and say this was the decade of civil rights, the decade of desegregation. The times are a-changin', as Mr. Bob Dylan so aptly put it.

"We play music all day long here on WMCA. Mine is the only program in the WMCA lineup that doesn't. The Good Guys spin the hits and tell you what's playing around the nation. All day long today, listeners heard a wrap-up of the biggest hits of the decade. Did you know the number-one song on *Billboard*'s Hot 100 in 1960 was 'Theme from *A Summer Place*' by Percy Faith? It was a pleasant little number with a full orchestra and not a single lyric. Remember that song? It isn't a song you can dance to, unless you're dancing cheek to cheek, which, by the way, is Mrs. Gray's favorite way to dance.

"I think it's telling that we finished the decade with Woodstock, a folk-music festival last August in Bethel, about a hundred miles northwest of New York City. We began and finished the sixties with vastly different music. Some might say two totally different worlds. I was there, covering the festival, as you all know, and I must say, I still prefer Louis Armstrong, Frank Sinatra, and Sam Cooke. But nothing highlights the last decade more than the shift in what, and who, we're listening to. If you want to know what's happening in a nation, look at the music.

"Now, I don't play the hits on my program. You all know this. I talk about the world. I've interviewed people from every walk of life, from leaders and activists to the biggest stars. But I don't think any of my previous guests could tell you more about the intersection of music and change than my next guest.

"You've most likely heard his name, but I guarantee you don't know his story. Not all of it. Not even close. He's an entertainer, a producer, and a prolific songwriter. Name an artist, and chances are he's written them a tune. Tonight he's promised to play for us and maybe sing a little too, and he's going to tell us about the songs that have marked his life and his career so far—the ones you know and the ones you don't.

"Welcome to *The Barry Gray Show*, Benny Lament. Let's talk."

1

Can't Cut it Out

I wrote my first song when I was eight years old, a chocolate ice-cream cone in my hand, while my father roughed up a shop owner. My song was a simple little thing with a one-line chorus and a single verse, but I never forgot it. *Pop is a scary man. Better do what he says. Pop is hurting Gino's hand. Better do what he says.*

That day, in front of Gino's, I didn't need a piano to write my song. The melody just appeared with the words. Dissonant. Ugly. Mrs. Costiera would have covered her ears. The only piano I ever got to play in those days was in her apartment, but she let me play it whenever I wanted, and she'd taught me the names of the keys and pointed out the patterns so I could combine the notes into chords.

Chords are like families. The notes go together. Like you and your father and your aunts and uncles and all your cousins. There. Hear that? Isn't that beautiful? That's an F chord. F for famiglia. *But listen . . . let's add a stranger. See? It doesn't sound so good. That note doesn't belong in the F chord.*

I was supposed to be sitting on the bench across the street by the ice-cream cart, lapping up my melting treat while my father paid his visit to Gino. I liked Gino. He'd given me a harmonica once, and I wanted to see him more than I wanted the cone. I recognized the ice cream for what it was: a bribe to keep me occupied while my father went inside the shop. My father told me to stay put, but I had my harp in my pocket, and I wanted to show Gino how good I was.

That's what Gino had called it. A harp. When I took to it after only a couple tries, instinctively knowing where to move my mouth to change the sound, Gino threw up his hands and said, "He's gonna be a harp man, Lomento. Listen to that. Kid's got a knack and an ear."

I could see my father through the window. His big back was to me, the back he carried me on sometimes, and Gino faced him over the counter. Gino's face was twisted like he was trying not to cry, and his hands were splayed wide above the display case of his watches and wares. He looked as though he was "reaching for the octave," as Mrs. Costiera called it, but my father's knife protruded from the back of his hand.

I wanted to shout, but I didn't. I was shocked, but I wasn't. I was scared, but I didn't run or turn away. I sang silently instead, the words clanging through my head, rhyming and rhythmic, the tune fully formed like it belonged with my lyrics.

When my father came out of Gino's shop, I was standing there, perfectly still, but my ice cream had melted all over my hand and pooled on the sidewalk.

Pop's face fell, just like the ice cream, and he took the cone from my fingers, tossed it into the street, and handed me the handkerchief from his pocket to wipe my hands. He didn't say anything as we headed for home, the sun shining down on our capped heads. It was warm that day, and the streets smelled like shit and sugar. It was September of 1939, and the paperboys screamed about the Germans and faraway places. But there was no war in New York City. At least, not the kind that involved airplanes and submarines.

"I thought you liked Gino," I said after several blocks. My chest felt as sticky as my hands.

"It's got nothin' to do with that," my father answered.

"It doesn't?" I couldn't imagine hurting someone I liked.

"It doesn't." My father didn't seem inclined to explain, and we walked another block before I tried again.

"B-b-but Gino's nice."

"He was nice to you. Yeah. But he was nice to you because he's scared of me."

That stopped me cold. My father walked ten paces before he realized I wasn't beside him. He turned around and came back, took my sticky hand in his, and pulled me along.

"Everybody can be nice, Benny. But it ain't real," my father said. He sounded so convinced.

"Never?" The stickiness became a tickle that warned of tears.

"No. Not never." He sighed like the discussion pained him too. "But there's no such thing as good guys and bad guys. There's just people. And everybody's rotten inside. Some are more rotten than others, and some just aren't rotten yet. But eventually, we all get a little ripe, ya know what I'm sayin'? We all have dark spots."

"Even you?"

"Especially me." It didn't seem to bother him too much. He seemed accepting of the fact. Resigned to it. We walked in silence, his big hand sheltering mine, and he didn't complain about the chocolatey residue or my slower steps. We turned onto Arthur Avenue, and the lines of laundry stretched across the side streets, from terrace to terrace, waving to us.

"I'm sorry you had to see my rotten today, Benito. I try hard to be a good father. A better father than my father was, but I'm not always a good man."

"Can't you cut it out? The dark spots, I mean. Mrs. Costiera cuts the mold off the cheese."

"I can't cut it out. No. There's too much of it. I'd bleed to death."

"Am I rotten?"

"No. You ain't rotten."

"But someday I will be?"

He sighed like he'd gotten himself into a mess he didn't know how to get out of.

"Yeah. You probably will be. It's just life." He shrugged and shook his head.

"You don't care if I'm rotten?" I squeaked.

"Depends on why you're being rotten. If you have another choice . . . then yeah. I care. Gino owes Uncle Sal money. He's been stallin'. Avoidin' me. I was patient until I couldn't be patient no more. He left me no choice."

"Why can't Uncle Sal get his own money? Why do you have to do it?"

"That's my job, Benny. I work for Uncle Sal. My job is to make sure people meet their obligations. Sal's a busy man. Runs a big operation. I work for Sal. You know that."

"What's an . . . obligation?"

"A responsibility. A duty. You know. Sal was Mama's brother. So we're family. And family is our number-one responsibility."

"Our number-one obligation?"

"Yeah."

I decided then and there, walking down the street where I was born, toward the building where I was raised, among people who were just like me, that I didn't want a family if that's what family meant. I decided the chords I liked most were the ones with notes that didn't belong. Over the years, those were the chords I kept going back to, the chords I built my melodies around, the chords that spoke to me.

"I tried to cut you out. Now I'm bleedin' to death," Izzy McQueen wailed at the mic, and I was catapulted back from the memory of ugly chords, simple songs, and the day, long ago, when I saw my pop for what he was.

"I tried to cut you out, baby. Now I'm bleedin' to death," Izzy repeated, so mournful, so convincing, no one in the audience could doubt his impending demise.

Funny. I'd written "Can't Cut You Out" for Izzy a year ago but hadn't made the connection to that conversation on the way home from Gino's until right now. Maybe I'd buried it deep like I did with so many things concerning Pop, but those lyrics were his.

I would have to write him a check.

"Can't Cut You Out" had been my biggest hit so far, and I got a little thrill every time it came on the radio. It wasn't me singing—I doubted it ever would be—but it was my song. Pop's song too, I guess. I'd been writing songs on the same theme my whole life.

"You took a little here, and you took a little there, and I've given all I can," Izzy moaned, and my hands flew over the keys. I didn't usually do this kind of gig. I was a behind-the-scenes man, but I'd been having a drink, listening, and Izzy called me up on stage, announcing me like I was a hometown hero. Next thing I knew I was backing him up.

I was hot, and I'd loosened my tie and lost my coat a few measures into the first verse. The Murray's in my hair was holding up, though, all except for the lock that clung to my brow in a damp swirl. The smoke and the music made the world soft and soundproof, where nothing and no one existed beyond the keys and the curling ring around my head.

But I was never alone in New York. Pop had eyes and ears everywhere. Especially at La Vita. So I wasn't surprised when my father sat down at a table right in front of the stage. He didn't get a drink or unbutton his coat. He just sat, listening.

I hadn't seen him in months. I'd been in Detroit and LA and Chicago and Miami. I'd been all over, writing songs for everybody from

Elvis Presley to Smokey Robinson. Smokey didn't need anyone writing songs for him; he was churning out hits for himself and everyone else too, but he said I kept his sound fresh. Berry Gordy, the president of the up-and-coming Motown Records, had taken ten of my songs for his artists just last month.

"Smokey writes light, and you write dark. Sunshine and rain. You should team up," Mr. Gordy said. "Call yourselves Smokey Lament. It could be huge." But I wasn't much of a family man, and Motown had that feel. Like family. Plus, like I said, Smokey really didn't need me.

Izzy didn't really need me either. Especially not tonight. Between his voice and his horn, the piano was an afterthought. But I was better with the "lyrics and the lamentations," Izzy said, and he liked my songs. Luckily his label did too.

There was a time, not so long ago, when Izzy McQueen headlining at places like La Vita wouldn't have been possible. I'd been in the audience when Harry Belafonte performed at the Copacabana, Sal's biggest competitor, in '58. But they wouldn't even let Harry into the Copa in the forties. They turned him away at the door. No Negros allowed. Took him a while to forgive and forget, but Harry came out on top. Nobody refused him entrance now. At least not in New York.

Berry Gordy had a whole roster of artists he wanted to book at La Vita. He asked me to arrange a meeting with the manager, Jules Patel, but I didn't know if I could do that. I sure as hell didn't do it for Izzy, though I wondered suddenly if he'd dropped my name. The thought made me sweat. I would have to talk to Izzy and set him straight. No more pulling me up on stage.

It's not that Patel wouldn't hear me out. He would. He would bring up my father and my mother—*God rest her soul. She sang like an angel, that woman*—and that would be my cue to reinforce my connection to Uncle Sal. The name Salvatore Vitale always got the skids greased. Then Gordy would get his meeting and his bookings, and I would have to pay up at some point. I tried to explain it to Gordy, but he just laughed and said, "That's how the world works, Lament. Don't tell me you don't know that."

I knew it. But I didn't think Gordy knew what paying up looked like in my family. I didn't want anyone at La Vita thinking they'd done me a favor and asking for something in return. Start calling on the family connections, and family obligations soon followed.

Pop waited until the number ended, and when I walked off the platform to greet him, he stood, impatient.

"Get your hat. I got someone I want you to meet," he said.

Just like that. No hello. No guilt. No "Where've ya been, kid?" And I was relieved. Maybe that's why I didn't argue. I retrieved my coat, straightened my tie, and picked up my hat from the girl at the coat check. Pop hurried out the front doors and into the cold air. I followed him, surprised.

"You're leaving Sal?" I asked. My father never left Sal. When Sal was out, Pop was in position. The best, most faithful guard dog in the world.

"Sal's not here. He's home. I came to find you and hear Esther."

"Esther?"

"That's her name."

"You got a new lady, Pop?" The women liked my father, but he'd never been serious about anyone but my mother. When he went sniffing, he was discreet about it, the way he was about everything else. He'd never even had a girlfriend.

"Shut your mouth," my father snapped, offended. "It's not like that."

"No? Then whose kid is she?" I was sure it had something to do with family. It always did. "You owe somebody a favor?"

Pop bristled again but didn't answer directly. "When did you get so suspicious? I don't owe nobody nothing. She reminds me of your mother. I heard her sing, and I wanted you to hear. That's all." He walked briskly, motioning for me to follow. "It's a place called Shimmy's. A few blocks over. We can walk."

"Mom was a mobster's daughter. I don't date mobster's daughters."

"Who's asking you to date her?" he snapped. "And watch yourself, kid. You're gettin' kinda loose with your tongue."

We walked in silence for ten minutes. My father's tension put me on alert. I smelled trouble, and not the usual kind. If it'd been anyone but my dad, I would have bailed. But it was my dad, and he never asked me for anything.

"How did you ever find this place?" I grumbled. There was no sign on the street, and we had to walk down a flight of stairs and through two doors guarded by men as burly as my father before I heard music. The men didn't stop my father, and they greeted him by name.

"Sal plays cards in the back sometimes," he muttered by way of explanation. But I was used to it. Everybody knew my father.

The place was packed, but a waiter rushed toward us. My father waved him off, and we found a place to lean against the wall. He pointed at the stage.

"That's Esther Mine," he said. "You're gonna want to listen."

Her hair was a gleaming cap of pin curls, and the short softness contrasted with her sharp, square jaw and bold lips. She'd painted them red, and every time they parted I saw a flash of straight white teeth. Her brown skin was unpowdered, and her eyes were unlined, but her lashes were thick, black brooms against her cheeks when she began to moan into the mic.

The sound in the room was terrible. The ceiling was drafty, messing with the mix, and the drums were too loud. The guitar was amped, and the microphones squealed. But as I listened, my chest grew tight and my eyes pricked with tears. I was eight years old again, listening to a voice that covered my arms in gooseflesh.

She reminds me of your mother.

I knew what my father meant. There was something there in the tone quality and the delivery, but my mother wasn't the voice Esther Mine brought to mind. Mom had passion, but she didn't have power.

Esther Mine sounded like a female Bo Johnson. The comparison to the huge boxer made me smile.

They call him the Bomb 'cause he's big and loud, they call him the Bomb 'cause he can level a crowd.

"She's loud . . . but she's not very big," I said, arguing with my comparison.

"She's big enough," my father said. "And don't tell her that. Women are sensitive about their size. Kinda like someone else I know."

"I'm not sensitive about my size. I just don't like people looking at me."

"They aren't looking at you because you're big. You're just ugly."

"I look just like you, old man."

I heard my father snort, but I couldn't look away from Esther Mine. She was a tiny, beautiful package wrapped in polka dots. Her wrists, her hands, her legs, all slight. She wore the tallest pair of red heels I'd ever seen, giving her some length, but even still, her head didn't reach the guitar player's chin. He cooed into the mic alongside her now and again, their heads stacked one above the other, taking the high harmony when she was belting out the melody. He was slender too, but tall, his shoulders hunched over his guitar, his long hands working the strings. The boy on the drums hardly raised his eyes, but he never lost the rhythm or called attention to his skills, which was easy to do on drums. The man on bass was a little less impressive; he wasn't as good as the other three, but he smiled more than the rest of them put together and seemed to be enjoying himself, which made him a pleasure to watch.

They didn't have a man on a horn or a man on keys. It was just the four of them, but when the lady sang "Ain't Nothin'" the audience didn't believe her. I didn't believe her. It definitely felt like something. She may have been pint sized, but her voice was all woman. It had the rasp and razor's edge of Billie Holiday and the wail and power of a trained soprano. They didn't need a horn with her on the mic.

I closed my eyes to distance myself, but somehow it made her even harder to ignore. Her voice seeped in under my lids and made my fingers twitch. I wanted to write a song for her.

"What's wrong? Why you closing your eyes like that?" Pop whispered. "She's good, isn't she? They're all good. Just as good as anybody singing at La Vita. Just as good as anybody on the radio."

When I didn't say anything, didn't even open my eyes, Pop continued. "You got a problem with her color? You been working with Negros for a long time. I didn't think that would matter to you."

It was a stupid question, and I didn't respond, but Esther Mine had launched into a new song, and I had to look at her. Her voice was a slap in the face, demanding and sharp. She didn't smile or flirt with her audience. She sang like she wanted to shove the number down our throats. Angry. Rough. Her small figure vibrated with the sound.

"She doesn't want to be up there," I said out loud, not meaning to, but Pop jumped on my words.

"She's been singing in this dump for two years. She needs a break. A big hit. Something that can justify sending her on Erskine's tour."

"Erskine Hawkins? Erskine is old news, Pop. He's big band. That stuff isn't what people are listening to anymore. They haven't been listening to that for a decade. Erskine Hawkins hasn't had a hit since *Tuxedo Junction*. Is he taking the whole orchestra on this tour?"

"I don't know, Benny. I heard that from Ralph." My father pointed at the bartender.

"Huh. How did you get mixed up in it?"

"I'm not mixed up in it. You're a songwriter. You're a big shot now. Thought maybe you could help her."

I immediately started shaking my head. I didn't want to get involved. I wouldn't do it for Berry Gordy, and I didn't want to do it for Esther Mine.

But my reluctance disintegrated beneath her rendition of "Maybe" by the Ink Spots.

It was a simple little song that shouldn't have worked with her voice. But she sang it like a threat, and it bored a hole into my chest.

"Well, damn," I whispered.

"She's good, right?" my father murmured, his mouth by my ear. He sounded pleased with himself.

"Yeah. She's good, Pop."

I stayed for the entire set, standing next to my father, but when we walked outside, I told him to go on back to La Vita without me.

"You don't want a ride home?" he protested.

"Nah. I'm at the Park Sheraton. I'll walk. I think I'm gonna go to Charley's for a bite."

"Come home, Benny. No reason to spend money on digs when you can sleep in your own bed."

"I've outgrown that bed, Pop."

He stared at me for a moment, stuck a cigar in his mouth but didn't light it, and turned toward La Vita. "I bought you a new one. Come home. And next time you're in town, don't make me hear it from Sal. It embarrasses me."

I didn't apologize, and I wouldn't go home. Not tonight. My skin felt hot, and my chest ached. I was getting sick. Elvis sang about it. About his hands shaking and his knees being weak.

"Well, damn," I said again. Pop was gone. No one was listening. All shook up or not, I would probably be back at Shimmy's tomorrow night to hear Esther Mine sing.

~

I didn't go to Charley's. I wasn't very hungry. I walked instead. There's a freedom afforded a big man in an expensive suit that allows him to aimlessly walk without worrying about the lateness of the hour or the part of town. I kept thinking of another big man, a man I hadn't thought of in years. Bo "the Bomb" Johnson. It was the oddest thing, but the rumble of his voice wouldn't leave my head. I'd heard an itty-bitty Negro singer belt into a microphone, and Bo Johnson rose from the dead—or wherever he'd ended up—to walk with me through Manhattan.

My grandfather, Eugenio Lomento, emigrated from Sicily at the turn of the century and taught my father to box by beating him to a pulp every night after dinner. My father figured he might as well get paid to get the shit knocked out of him and was only sixteen when he fought his first sanctioned bout. He was so good nobody even questioned his age. In the ring he was Jack "Lament" Lomento, and the biggest name in East Harlem.

He was the heavyweight champ for a decade and never lost a fight until Bo "the Bomb" Johnson knocked him out so cold he didn't wake up for a week. He didn't fight after that. At least not in the ring. He started working for Sal Vitale at his club in Harlem, a bouncer instead of a boxer, a fixer instead of a fighter. That's when he met my mother, Sal's sister. My father said Bo Johnson did him a favor taking his title the way he did.

"Bo knocked some sense into me," he said. "If it wasn't for him, I wouldn't have ever stopped. No Giuliana. No Benny. Just boxing."

The first time I saw Bo Johnson, I didn't know how my father ever survived that fight.

Bo Johnson was the biggest, strongest man I'd ever laid eyes on, even bigger than my father, and his voice was like the pipe organ at Mass—rich, deep, and resonant. I tried to hum the pitch, but it existed below my register.

A few months after my mother died, I awoke to that voice seeping, along with the light, beneath my bedroom door. I leaped from my bed, thinking I'd found heaven, and God was in the other room. God and my mother. The voices were a mixture of familiar and strange, high and low, and a cat was yowling. I threw open the door and stood, blinking at the light, my hands shaking as they shaded my gaze.

But my mother was not there.

God was not there either, though the stranger in my living room could have been a destroying angel. No beams of light engulfed him, but he radiated power. He didn't have wings, but his arms and shoulders bulged with muscle, and his neck was as thick as his shiny, bald head. He was sitting with his back bent, and his head was bowed between his big knees. When he raised his head and met my gaze, my feet melted into the floor.

"Bo Johnson," I stammered and rubbed my fists into my eyes, certain that I was dreaming.

"He knows who I am?" Bo rumbled.

"He knows the stories," my father replied.

"I know all the stories," I said, nodding. "I know you're the best fighter in the world. Even better than Pop. Everyone's afraid of you."

"Everyone?" he asked.

"Everyone," I said, nodding emphatically.

"I shouldn't have come. He'll talk," Bo said, turning to my father. He looked so tired. A thick blanket was folded beside him on the couch, like maybe Pop had offered him a place to sleep. As I watched, the blanket moved. A soft mewling emanated from the folds; the crying-cat sound explained.

"Go back to bed, Benny," my father said, pointing at my bedroom door.

"I won't talk, Pop. I won't talk, Mr. Johnson," I said.

"Benny. Bed."

I obeyed, shutting the door behind me, but I stretched out on the floor so I could hear them through the crack beneath the door. They were quiet—even the cat—but big men have big voices and children have good ears. I strained to hear every word, though I didn't understand any of it.

"Did you do it, Bo?"

"I didn't touch a hair on her head. But they'll blame me. They'll say it was my fault."

Silence filled the living room, and I was sure they knew I was listening and lowered their voices. But a few minutes later my father asked, "What do you want me to do?"

"Take her to Gloria. Give her the cash and the letter. Tell her there will be more. I'll come back when I can. In Harlem, she'll just be another mouth to feed. Nobody will look twice."

"Will they be searching for her?" my father asked. "Maude's family?"

"I don't think so. They wanted nothing to do with her before. Why now? They'll be glad she's gone."

I heard someone leave the apartment and ran back to my bed, terrified. Pop never left me all by myself. Mrs. Costiera watched me when he worked. Seconds later, Bo Johnson pushed open the door to my room. I pulled the blankets up over my head and pretended to be asleep.

"You don't need to be afraid of me. I don't hurt kids," he said. "I don't hurt women or kids." His voice broke, like he was trying not to cry.

"You hurt my dad," I argued softly, peeping over the top of my blankets.

"That was different. We agreed to hurt each other. We were fighting for money. But your dad's my friend. He's my only friend." His voice cracked again.

"Where did he go?"

"He's helping me. But he'll come back. I'll stay until he does. I'm tired. I'm going to sleep out there. You don't need to be afraid."

"Mr. Johnson?"

"Yeah?"

"I won't talk," I promised.

"I believe you, Benny," he whispered. "I got no choice, I guess. But if you do talk . . . it won't hurt me. No one can hurt me no more. If you talk, it'll hurt your dad."

"Will you knock him out cold again?"

"No. Not me. Not me."

"Who?"

He didn't tell me who. He just looked at me with his big, dark eyes.

"Do you know why they call your daddy Lament?" he asked.

"It sounds like Lomento. His name is Jack Lomento. Lament is a nickname."

"Yeah. But do you know what a lament is?"

"No."

"Lament means to cry. To wail. To mourn. When your daddy was boxing, his fists made grown men cry."

"But not you."

"Not me."

"Do you know why they call me the Bomb?" he asked.

"They call him the Bomb 'cause you never know when he'll go off," I sang softly.

He smiled, surprising us both. It was a big smile. A beautiful smile. And I wasn't scared anymore.

"You know the song," he said.

"I like songs," I said.

"Me too. Sing the rest."

I sang the whole thing.

They call him the Bomb 'cause you never know
when he'll go off.
They call him the Bomb 'cause his swing makes the
shingles blow off.
They call him the Bomb 'cause he's big and loud.
They call him the Bomb 'cause he can level a crowd.
He's Bo "the Bomb" Johnson, and you better watch out.

"That's right," he said. "I guess you *do* know who I am."

I yawned widely. Without my fear, I was getting sleepy. But he wasn't done.

"That's the song. But that's not really why they call me the Bomb. My mama gave me the nickname before I ever started boxing."

"Why?" I yawned again.

"I leave destruction wherever I go. Ever since I was your age. She called me the Bomb because everything I touched turned to shit. You keep singing, Benny. You sing all you want. Singing won't get you in trouble. But don't talk. For your daddy's sake, don't talk."

"Okay."

"Okay," he repeated. He turned and left the room and closed the door behind him.

I didn't talk. Not when Pop got home and woke me up. Not when Bo Johnson's name was in the papers. I didn't say anything to anyone about Bo "the Bomb" Johnson. Pop didn't either. Not even to me. He was good at keeping people's secrets. Maybe that was the reason he was so big. The weight of people's confidence is a heavy burden. He could yammer on all day about Tammany Hall or baseball, but he wouldn't ever rat out a soul. Still, some secrets find their way to the light no matter how well they are guarded.

I'd have to ask my father whatever happened to Bo Johnson. Twenty years had come and gone. Surely now I could talk.

The Barry Gray Show

WMCA Radio

Guest: Benny Lament

December 30, 1969

"You're listening to WMCA New York, and we're back on *The Barry Gray Show*. It's the last show of the year, and I'm talking to Benny Lament—singer, songwriter, native son. We talked a little about your beginnings, Benny. You were born and raised in the Bronx. Your mother sang, music came easy—"

"—the only thing that ever has," Benny Lament says.

"—and your father raised you alone from the time you were eight," Barry finishes. "He has quite the story himself. Jack 'Lament' Lomento was a heavyweight boxer back in his early years. I never saw him fight, but I knew his reputation."

"Everybody around here knew Pop," Benny says. "And he knew everyone."

2

I Don't Want to Love You

I went back to La Vita after all, but my pop was gone and Izzy was done. It was 2:00 a.m. on a Sunday morning, and the place had started to clear. Some weekends it didn't empty until four. There was no piano in my hotel room. I wanted to play and knew Terrence would let me tinker while the waitstaff cleaned and the hangers-on continued to dangle. He managed the house band and was the last one to leave the joint every night, and he'd always been good to me. Like every other relationship in my life, I wasn't sure if it was because he truly liked me, thought I was talented, or was just aware of who I was, but I genuinely liked him.

My moody blues turned into a variation of the Bo Johnson ditty. I wondered if anyone had ever recorded it. It needed some verses, some Jerry Lee Lewis treatment. I would make it something that people could dance to. Something maybe Esther Mine could sing. A fighting song from a female perspective.

"What's that melody you're riffing on, Benny?" Terrence asked, unrolling his sleeves like he was done for the night. "I know it."

I picked up the tempo and sang along. "They call him the Bomb 'cause you never know when he'll go off."

When his expression blanked, I assumed he didn't recognize it and continued, but in another measure he was sliding in beside me on the piano bench and quieting my hands.

"Shh, Benny. Damn. I didn't know that was what you were playing or I never would have asked. Man, I haven't heard that name since before the war." He looked around, nervous, and ran a hand over his smooth head.

"I saw him once when I was a little kid." I shrugged. "I used to sing that song all the time. Pop taught it to me. Told me all about Johnson. They were friends, despite the rivalry. I thought of him outta the blue. That song just popped into my mind. That's all."

Terrence shook his head, relaxing when it appeared no one was paying us—or my song selection—any attention. Stanley Tunis from WRKO was sitting at a corner booth with an ashtray and a row of shot glasses. I'd thought about putting a bug in his ear about some of my songs but decided he was too drunk to remember anything I said to him.

"You can't say that name in here, Benny."

"Why?"

He scratched at his cheek and bit his lip.

"It's just . . . it's been a long time. But not long enough. People still remember. This is Sal's place."

"So?"

"So Sal didn't like Bo Johnson. That's all. You're too young to remember. But play something else. Don't want to leave that one hangin' out there like that."

I obeyed, frowning. The song my fingers reached for was the last one Esther Mine sang in her set.

"That's better. Oh, I like that one. Haven't heard that one in a bit either." He nodded in approval. "Maaaaay beeeee," he sang, but he was still nervous.

"Me and Pop heard someone sing the hell out of this one tonight," I muttered.

"Oh yeah?"

"Yeah. Over at Shimmy's. You know the place?"

He froze again. I felt his tension radiate down my right side where he still sat, staring at my hands.

"You heard Esther Mine." He said it with finality, like he was putting all the pieces together.

"Yeah. You know her?" My question was why didn't everyone know her, and why was she singing in a dump like Shimmy's?

"Yeah. Oh yeah. Sure. It's my job to know what's what and who's who."

"Well, if you know about Esther Mine, why isn't she singing here? I've never heard a better voice, and she's a looker."

He studied my face again, like I was testing him. "She's good all right. But the boys she plays with aren't anything special. It's a family thing . . . but I don't think she'll accept a booking without 'em."

I could see where that would be a rub. It'd happened to more than one band. One member had all the star power, and the others became shackles around their ankles. It usually ended in destroyed relationships, broken dreams, and years of resentment, one way or the other. Better to not ever get involved. To look out for yourself so no one else had to.

"And your Pop took you to Shimmy's, you say?" Terrence asked, his voice conversational.

It was my turn to squirm, wondering if I'd said something wrong. He was too innocently curious. I hated this damn town. Every time I came back, I remembered why. You never knew what the sides were and what you could and couldn't say. You didn't know who was snooping for who. Everyone tiptoed around, spoke in code, or didn't speak at all. Watching your back and worrying about the double cross was a nonstop job.

"Sal plays cards there sometimes," I said, echoing Pop's excuse, and finished my song.

"Huh. Well. You can play until I'm ready to lock up. Another hour at least. No hurry."

But I was ready to leave. I was unsettled, like I'd forgotten something important or misplaced my trust. I said good night, wishing for my car, and set off at a good clip for my hotel.

~

The hotel lobby was 4:00 a.m. empty; the clusters of chairs illuminated by intimate lighting near the grand entrance were no contest for the beds in the rooms upstairs. I couldn't wait to crawl into mine. I heard a vacuum running, and the night clerk was nowhere to be seen. I strode toward the elevators when Esther Mine stepped out from the gloom, still wearing the polka-dot dress and blistering red heels she'd performed in hours before. Her curls were neat and her lipstick bright, and she carried a cloak of determination and a coat over her arm even though it was cold in the lobby and brisk outside.

"Mr. Lament?" she said. "Could I have a moment, please?"

I halted, hardly believing my eyes. Esther Mine was calling my name and walking toward me. I looked around, trying to find an explanation.

"Mr. Lament?" she said again, and the throaty purr of her voice made my fingers flex, wanting piano keys and complementary chords.

"Mr. Lament?" the night clerk called, echoing her query. He'd reappeared, his cheeks red, trailing cigarette smoke. His eyes bounced from Esther to me and around the room, like he wasn't sure if he should intervene.

I waved him off with a sharp frown. He turned away, but not far enough. He was hovering.

"He's the guard dog," Esther said softly. "He's been yipping at me for an hour. I told him I was waiting for you."

I stuck out my hand in greeting, and she walked toward it.

"We haven't met," I said. She slid her hand into mine, shaking it firmly. Her fingers felt like icicles, thin and cold, and I released them immediately, afraid I would squeeze too tight. My reaction embarrassed her. I saw it in the widening of her eyes and the tightening of her lips.

"You're cold," I tried to explain. That just made it worse. Her slim back was so stiff I rolled my shoulders in commiseration.

"I'm Esther Mine," she said. "You came to my show tonight."

"Yeah, I did," I said, not trying to hide my surprise. I didn't know how she knew, but that was New York.

"I would like just a minute of your time. Please," Esther said.

The clerk approached again, tugging at the bottom of his maroon jacket. "Can I offer you some coffee?" he asked. "Or maybe a nightcap?"

"You can leave us alone," I said. He turned on his heel and obeyed instantly.

"He's not sure how to handle me," Esther murmured. "I don't look like your type. And I'm definitely not his. He's afraid he's made a mistake letting me linger."

An attendant stepped out of the elevator, eyed the two of us, and asked, "Are you going up?"

"No," I growled. I couldn't take this woman to my room. Wrong impression. But I didn't want to sit in the lobby either. The attendant folded his hands and stepped back inside the gold box. The doors slid closed, and I looked down at the woman before me.

"Can you walk?"

Her brow furrowed.

"In those shoes. Can you walk? I don't like being on display, and I'm not in the mood to keep running people off. We'll sit in the park."

She nodded, but she didn't put on her coat. I took it from her arm. For a moment I thought she would argue, but she relented and allowed me to hold it while she slid her arms into the sleeves. It was the color of her shoes and the dots on her dress, but it was too big and the cuffs and hem were threadbare. I suddenly understood her reluctance to wear it.

"It's nice to meet you, Esther Mine," I said gently, and offered my arm. She took it, and we turned for the door. She matched my stride as though her legs weren't half as long and capped in ridiculous shoes. Her feet had to be on fire, but she didn't teeter or slow, and we walked for a few blocks without saying a word. The park was just ahead, and I veered toward the closest bench. The air was cold but perfectly still, and the park was strewn with political detritus. Tuesday was election day. It couldn't come too soon.

"Who's going to win?" I asked her, breaking the silence. "Kennedy or Nixon?"

"Does it matter?"

I kicked at a flyer with John Kennedy's smiling face beaming up at us. "Probably not."

"Everybody I know wants Kennedy. All but my brother Money. He says he doesn't trust pretty men. But Money doesn't really trust anyone," she said.

"Money, huh? How'd he come by that name?"

"That's what his daddy wanted him to have. Money."

I laughed. "And 'Esther'? Why'd they name you Esther?"

She shrugged. "Esther married a king. Saved her people. It's in the Bible."

"True. Now *she* coulda been president. I would have voted for her."

"She was a queen. President would have been a step down."

"True. But Frank Sinatra sure likes him." I sang Frank's jingle for Kennedy beneath my breath. It'd been stuck in my head for months. How could Kennedy lose when Frank Sinatra was singing his campaign song?

"He's got friends in high places. That's for sure," Esther said, voicing what I was thinking.

"They all do," I answered.

She halted, perfectly positioned beneath a streetlamp, and looked up at me.

"Do you?" she asked. "Do you have friends in high places, Mr. Lament?"

Beneath the light, her skin was glossy, her lips red, her eyes shadowed, and the moment took on an otherworldly sheen.

Suddenly, I was afraid.

Of her.

Of the quiet.

Of the oddness of our meeting.

I pulled her from the pool of light and dropped onto a bench just beyond the glow. The darkness felt safer.

"Why are you here, Miss Mine?" I asked, my voice harsh with my sudden unease.

"Ralph saw you at our show tonight. He told me and my brothers who you were."

Ralph? I searched my memory for the name. Ah, Ralph. The bartender.

"And . . . Pete overheard you say where you were staying. He told Ralph. Ralph told me," she added.

Overheard? He must have followed me and Pop up to the street. The thought made me shake my head. Damn town.

"And who did Ralph tell you I was?"

"Benny Lament. He says you play piano and write songs for all the big names. Colored and white."

"Huh. And you couldn't wait until morning?"

"When a big fish lands in your lap, you don't let him get away."

I was oddly flattered.

"Why did you come to my show, Mr. Lament?" she asked.

"My father likes your voice. You remind him of my mother."

Her brow furrowed and her red lips pursed. She didn't know what to make of that. "Did you like my voice?" Her tone wasn't flirtatious. It was blunt.

"Yes," I admitted. "You might be the best I've ever heard. But I got the feeling you don't like singing."

"I love to sing," she protested.

"You sing like you hate your audience."

She frowned. Then she shrugged, releasing the grimace. "Maybe I do."

"Why?"

She was quiet for several seconds, pondering. "I'm not sure you'd understand, and I'm too tired to explain it. It might take me a while."

"Is it just the audience at Shimmy's or do you hate everyone who listens to you sing?"

"You don't mince words, do you, Mr. Lament? Kind of bold, aren't you?"

"Says the woman waiting for me at my hotel at four o'clock in the morning."

She laughed, a deep rumbling sound that gurgled up from her chest and spilled out her pretty mouth. Her laugh was as incongruous as her voice, and I laughed too, but my laughter was from surprise more than anything else.

"So you want me to write a song for you. Is that it?" I asked. I didn't admit I wanted the same thing.

"I do. But I have some questions."

"Questions?"

"Yes," she said, and she took a deep breath like she was beginning a long recitation.

"Are you a mobster?" she asked.

I didn't know how to respond. Was I? When you are born into something—a culture, a religion, a place—how do you separate it from who you are? It was like asking someone, "Are you Irish?" or "Are you

Jewish?" You could be Irish even if you'd never spent a day in Ireland. You could be Jewish even if you'd never set foot in a synagogue. It was something in the blood. Something in the history. I could say I wasn't in the mob and mean it with all my heart. But I still . . . was.

"Do I look like a mobster?" I asked her instead.

"Yes," she said.

"Why?"

She raised one slim brow, like I was toying with her and she didn't much care for it. "You're Italian," she said.

"Sicilian." But close enough. "So you think all Italians are mobsters?" It was a common stereotype.

"Italians that live in this city and look like you? Yes," she said, nodding. "It's your hair. Your clothes. Your looks. The way you carry yourself. Your reputation. You're a gangster. I just wanted to see if you'd admit it."

"People see what they see. They'll think what they think. And I can't do a damn thing about it."

She studied me for a moment. "Why would you want to? Gangsters like you run this town. Especially the clubs. They decide who works. They decide who doesn't. For whatever reason, they don't like me. I can outsing anyone. But no one will book me."

"You got a pretty big opinion of yourself for someone so small."

Her eyes blazed and her back stiffened, and I thought for a moment she was going to abandon her mission, whatever it was. But she took a deep breath and let it out so slowly I could have had a cigarette while she exhaled.

"I can sing, Mr. Lament."

"Yes, you can, Miss Mine."

"I look good. I sound good. And I work hard. I don't do junk. I don't even smoke."

"Good for you." I searched my pocket for a cigarette just to be contrary. A pack usually lasted me months. Everyone smoked, so I tried not to. I didn't like being dependent. On anything.

"I could make you a lot of money," Esther said.

"How, exactly?" I lit the cigarette and took a deep drag.

"I want you to be my manager."

I gaped at her, smoke billowing from my lips. "I write songs. I don't manage talent."

"You manage yourself, don't you? You manage your own talent. You don't have a manager."

"How do you know?" I got the feeling she was guessing, but she was right. I didn't have a manager, and I didn't want one.

"I just can't imagine anyone telling you what to do," she said.

"You're sure trying to," I shot back wryly.

Her mouth quirked, but she was too busy negotiating to smile.

"You know the business. You know the players. You have contacts," she said.

"But . . . I might be a mobster," I argued softly. She met my gaze, big brown eyes solemn, and realization flooded me. That was why she was here. She *wanted* a mobster.

"I won't cause you a minute's trouble. I'll be a blessing. I'll sing, and I'll dance, and I'll do whatever you say. I'll be the best investment you ever made," she said, her voice firm, eyes clinging to mine. "I don't want to sleep with you. Or anyone else, actually. But I'll even do that."

"And we're done here, Miss Mine," I said, standing up and grinding out my cigarette beneath my toe. I'd been intrigued. Now I was just insulted. She was bold. She was beautiful. But she was terrible at persuasion.

For a moment her back bowed, and her chin hit her chest. Then she straightened and rose to her feet. The girl who didn't want me to see her tattered coat had just propositioned me. It didn't make much sense.

"How old are you, Baby Ruth?"

"Baby Ruth?" She glowered at the nickname, but I wasn't deterred.

"Ruth. Esther. Both Bible names. Babe Ruth was the Sultan of Swat and the King of Swing. You can be the Queen of Sing. It's a compliment. How old are you?"

"I'm almost twenty-two."

"You don't look it. When were you born?" I was trying to trip her up.

"1939."

"When's your birthday?"

She shrugged. "I like cake and presents all year round, if that's why you're asking. But I am old enough, I assure you. I graduated high school five years ago, and I've been trying to get someone to take me seriously ever since."

"Does your daddy know where you are?"

"Excuse me? Does your daddy know where *you* are?" she shot back. "I don't have a dad. Or a manager." She emphasized the last word.

"What about your band? Are you negotiating for them too?"

"My brothers? I can't help them if I can't help myself. I can't get them work if I'm not working. I need a manager who can get us work."

"I don't want to be your manager. That's not my thing. I don't need that kind of responsibility."

"Okay," she said, folding her arms. "And how old are *you*, Mr. Lament?"

"Older than you are."

"You don't look that much older. What are you, thirty?"

"Almost."

"But you don't have a wife?"

"I don't have a wife."

"A girlfriend?"

"No girlfriend." I didn't do relationships. I was terrible at everything but the sex part. Maybe I was terrible at that part too. I hadn't gotten any complaints . . . but I hadn't gotten many compliments either, come to think of it.

"No kids?" she persisted.

"No. No kids."

"No family who depends on you at all?"

"Nope." Just my pop. And a string of Vitales, but I wasn't going there.

"So no responsibility whatsoever?" she asked, letting a note of disgust creep into her question.

"None," I said.

"Well, it's time you take some."

"Some what?"

"Some responsibility," she snapped.

"You're no good at this, Baby Ruth," I said, shaking my head. "I am not interested."

"Yes, you are," she insisted. "Pete told me you stayed for the whole set. He said I blew you away. I can sing. You know I can."

"Maybe you *better* sing. Because you sure as hell aren't going to shame me into this."

"Sit down, please," she said. "Please . . . just sit. Okay? I'll sing for you again." She put her hands out, gesturing for me to wait, to halt.

I groaned, but I didn't leave. She centered herself beneath the streetlamp like she was on a stage, under the spotlight. When she began, I laughed out loud at her choice. It was one of mine, a song I wrote for the McGuire Sisters called "I Don't Want to Love You." She sang like she was willing the world to yield. Willing me to yield, and my laughter faded with her performance.

Whenever I'm near you,
You make me so mad.
I don't even like you, so why am I sad
The moment that you leave?
You get under my skin.
You mess with my head,
You won't leave me alone,
But it's gotta be said,
I don't want to love you,
But I do. I do. I do.

The girl had spirit, I had to give her that. And damn, could she sing. The city was just beginning to stir, but she made everything inside me still. She sang the entire song, from tip to toe, and I didn't stop her or even look away.

"How was that, Benny?" she asked when the last notes fell like the leaves at our feet.

Oh, so now I was Benny. And she knew damn well exactly "how it was." It was brilliant. She was brilliant, and I wanted her to sing another.

I wasn't sure I would survive another. I might start agreeing to her every demand.

I stood and held out my arm. "You can sing, Esther Mine. No doubt about it. We might need to work on your subtlety, however."

"We?" she asked. The tinge of hope pushed me over the edge. Fine. I would write her a song, and I would help her get it in the rotation on the stations where I had some pull. That was all.

"Do you perform at Shimmy's tonight?" I asked.

"I do. I do. I do," she sang.

"All right. I'll be there. And afterward, I'll say hello to your band," I promised.

"And then what?" she pressed.

"Then we'll see," I said, careful not to commit further.

She studied me, and I shook my head. "That's the best you're going to get tonight. Let's go back to the hotel, and I'll call you a cab," I said.

"There's a 5:00 a.m. bus. The stop is on the next corner."

"Then I'll walk you to the corner."

"If you do, I won't be able to change out of these shoes."

I wasn't following.

"The shoes are power," she explained on a sigh. "And if they demand a little payment in exchange for that power, so be it."

"Change your shoes. I promise not to even look at your feet," I said. "And then, for God's sake. Go home. You're dangerous."

She pulled a pair of flats from her bag, and I looked away as promised. But when she straightened, it was impossible not to notice the difference. The top of her head was below my shoulder.

"You said that's the best deal I would get tonight. What about tomorrow?" she asked.

"How about you sleep on it, Baby Ruth?"

"I haven't slept in twenty-four hours, and most likely won't sleep more than an hour or two before I have to do it all again. But I know what I want. I want you to write me a dozen songs. And I want you to make the whole world sit up and listen and fall in love with me."

"I can't do that."

She sighed heavily. "What part? What part can't you do?"

"I can't make the world listen. Or love you. You'll have to do that part."

"I've never been able to make anyone love me," she said, throwing her words back over her shoulder as she walked away. "See you tonight, Benny Lament. Don't let me down. And stop calling me Baby Ruth."

The Barry Gray Show

WMCA Radio

Guest: Benny Lament

December 30, 1969

"So, Benny, your father took you to hear Esther Mine sing," Barry Gray says. "Do you remember the date?"

"November 5, 1960," Benny Lament answers.

"And was it love at first sight?"

Benny laughs. "I don't know if I'd call it love. But I was caught, no doubt about it."

"Caught . . . as in hooked?" Barry Gray asks, a grin in his voice.

"Yes, sir. Hooked. And I squirmed and fought just like a big fish who knows he's met his match."

"For my listeners out there, Mr. Lament is about six foot two, six foot three. Is that right, Benny?"

"That's right."

"You're a big man."

"I'm a big man. And Esther Mine is a little, tiny woman."
"You're not just big . . . you're white, Mr. Lament."
"I am."
"And Esther Mine is not."
"No."
"But you say you'd met your match?"
"I'd met my match."

3

Beware

Pop didn't stay in East Harlem when he stopped boxing professionally, but he didn't go very far. Just across the Harlem River. He and my mother bought a unit in a building in the Belmont neighborhood of the Bronx, a block from her parents. Her father, Salvatore Vitale Sr., had a fruit stand on Arthur Avenue that grew into a big store. He used the store as a cover for all the shady shit he—and Sal Jr.—did for the mob. He died in a hail of bullets, lying between rows of obliterated fruit, a month before I was born. My grandmother, now eighty, still lived in the same house. I think that was part of the reason Pop never bought us a big house or moved us out of the neighborhood into the suburbs with Sal and so many others. Nonna Vitale was Sal's mother, but Pop was the better son.

"It's what Giuliana would have wanted," I'd heard my father say a thousand times when Sal complained about needing him closer.

"I pay all Mama's bills, and she has live-in help," Uncle Sal said. "She doesn't need you there, Jack. I do." It was a point of contention between them, though I think it probably made Sal trust him more. Pop didn't seem to want any of the things most people wanted; he definitely didn't want the same things Sal wanted. Pop never got flashy. He wore the same hat for years, the same dark suits and white shirts that he ironed himself. He didn't buy expensive jewelry or wear a fancy watch. He was Sal Vitale's right hand, but he never let his power or his position go to his head. Maybe that kept him freer than most. I don't know. He still wasn't free.

He still came when Sal called, though he worked as a bodyguard more than anything else. He stood in the shadows, making sure no one approached, making sure Sal could eat and drink and laugh in peace. He drove him around in a big, black car, and everyone knew that Jack Lomento kept Sal safe. Pop didn't call attention to himself, but the whole neighborhood knew who he was, regardless. That meant they all knew who I was. I was Lament's kid. The musician. When Mrs. Costiera died and left me her piano, we'd had to bring it in through the balcony with a crane. Nobody ever complained about my playing, though the walls were thin, and I never stopped. Or maybe they were just too afraid of Pop to say anything.

"This is where I was happiest," my father always said. "Why would I want to leave?"

I left the Sheraton at two and drove to the old neighborhood and spent half an hour trying to find a place to park. Pop's car was next to the curb right in front of our building, in the same spot it always was when he wasn't working. Nobody ever took his spot or laid a hand on the car. When a visitor made the mistake of taking the space, he was quickly informed of his mistake and told to move immediately.

"That's where Lament parks," people would say. "You gotta move."

Once, someone made the mistake of ignoring the warning and returned to the spot to find their car gone. It had been moved two blocks over. I suspected Frankie used his tow truck to enforce the unofficial zone, but he never copped to it.

It was Sunday afternoon, and everyone was home. I finally parked at the church, sliding into a space a parishioner had just vacated, and walked home, noting how the people got older but nothing else changed. A few folks called out my name, and I waved and tipped my hat, but quickly walked the other way. I'd been roped into playing the organ for Mass every Sunday growing up. I had to wear an altar boy's cassock and it would tangle around my legs and obscure the pedals. I liked the big sound and the power of the organ but hated the monotony of the music and the endlessness of the service. Pop never went, but he made sure I did.

I climbed the stairs to my father's apartment, my eyes on the treads, and wondered how many times I'd made the trip. Up and down, a million times, nothing changing but the size of my feet and the length of my stride.

I thumped on the door—*ba dum dum*—the same rhythm I always used, and I listened for Pop's footfalls. It took him a little longer than usual.

I thumped again.

"Is that you, Benito?" I heard him ask.

"It's me, Pop," I said through the door.

A clatter of locks and the door swung wide. Pop knew full well all the evils in the world. He always locked the door.

"You're staying, right?" he asked, looking for my suitcase.

I didn't want to. But I would. I'd anticipated the argument and decided it wasn't worth it. My things were in the trunk of my car.

"Yes."

"Good. Smart." He clapped me on the shoulder and stepped aside, letting me enter. He kept his back straight, but the skin beneath his blue eyes was dark and thin, hanging in ripples that extended into the wrinkles on his pale cheeks. He'd never been pale before. Even the skin that was covered by his undershirt had always been caramel colored. It was sallow now. In the haze and the half light of the club and the darkness of the street the night before, I hadn't noticed.

"You're looking at me funny," he grunted.

"You don't look good, Pop," I said softly.

"Well, as you reminded me last night, you look just like me, so prepare yourself, son. Someday this will be you." He waved a hand back at himself, trying to be funny, but the words fell flat, jangling between us. My father knew I didn't want to be like him—he'd always known—and our resemblance was a fact we danced around.

"No, really. How you doin', Pop?"

"Not bad. Same old. Sit down, kid. I'll make you something to eat."

I'd also known he would insist on feeding me, and I didn't argue. It was what we did, and I was grateful for the ritual.

"It's freezing in here," I said. "Too cold to be sitting with that window open."

"Your mother used to open the windows and sing, and the whole block would kind of quiet down. She had big dreams of singing for thousands. I guess singing for this neighborhood was the closest she ever got. Sometimes she sang that song from *Carmen*. I told you the story of Carmen. Saddest story in the whole world."

I didn't think Carmen's story was as sad as my mother's, but I didn't argue. "I know about Carmen and Mom and the window, Pop," I said as gently as I could. I wasn't chiding him. I was letting him know I hadn't forgotten.

"I know you do. But I been thinking about her a lot. Maybe it's that girl . . . that Esther. Mom never made it. I want Esther to make it."

He didn't look at me when he said her name. He reached for the coffee and poured me a cup.

"Pop—" I started, but he continued with his story.

"I'd sit here"—he pointed his spatula at the table—"nice and quiet, and she'd push the window open and begin. Everyone knew Giuliana

Lomento." Pop always said her name like she was a famous soprano, singing in a real opera, and he never used her maiden name. He always claimed her.

"I can still see her, clear as day, singing right there." Pop pointed at the tiny fire escape and the drapes that fluttered on either side of the window. They weren't the same curtains that had been there when Mom was alive. When I was growing up, Pop had had a woman come in once a week and clean up after the two of us and stick a few meals in the icebox. She'd washed the drapes every couple of months. Ironed them too, until they were threadbare. Pop had finally taken them down, but they were folded in his bottom drawer.

I walked over to the window and pushed it shut. He didn't protest, but he hadn't lost the faraway look.

"She could do with her voice what you do with your hands. You got her love for music. It just comes out in a different way," he mused, his eyes on the steaks he was frying.

"I have your hands, Pop," I said, waggling my fingers to bring him back. He was scaring me a little.

"You do," he grunted. "They look just like mine. I don't know how in the hell you fit them on those little keys."

He set my plate down in front of me, dished up one for himself, and sank into the chair like he'd done a thousand times before. More than that. And I'd done the same for him. Maybe Mom had waited on us way back when, but I didn't remember it. It was this, me and Pop, breaking bread together in the same old chairs at the same scarred table. I always sat here. He always sat there.

"I met Esther Mine." I kept my voice measured like it didn't matter, but I was watching him. He'd brought her up again; the whole thing was a little bizarre.

Pop's eyes rose to mine, and his hands stilled. I was startled once more by the age in his face.

"You did?" he asked.

"Yeah. I met her. She's nothing like Mom, Pop. I don't know what the fixation is."

"You went back inside Shimmy's when I left?" he asked, his eyes narrowing.

"No. I walked a bit. Wanted to play. Ended up back at La Vita. When I got back to my hotel she was waiting for me. She'd been waiting a long time."

"Huh." He set down his fork and sat back in his chair.

"Pop, you don't look good," I said again.

"You come into my house and insult me like that?" he muttered, feigning anger. "I look fantastic." He flexed his arms and stuck out his chest, but I didn't laugh, and he waved me off like I was no fun at all.

"I'm getting old, Benito. You just haven't been here to see it. I feel good. I feel good," he said, thumping his chest. "No complaints. Now tell me about Esther."

"No, you tell me about her. I get the feeling you know a little more than you're saying."

"She . . . was waiting for you?" he asked, ignoring me. "At your hotel?" He frowned. "That ain't safe."

"In the lobby, Pop. Apparently, Ralph told her who I was and how to find me."

"Ralph, huh?" My dad scowled.

"Ralph and Pete or whoever was working the door."

"So you gonna tell me what happened or what?" he said, cutting into his steak.

"She wants me to help her."

"Write her a song?"

"Manage her."

He stopped carving. "What does that mean?"

"It means she wants me to handle her career. Find her work."

"Well. Whaddaya know. Did you like her?"

"Yeah. But . . . Pop, what in the hell is going on? Who is this girl? And don't tell me you don't know. 'Cause this all just feels a little crazy to me."

"Did I ever tell you how I met your mother?" Pop asked.

I sighed and shoved a piece of meat in my mouth. I hadn't ever known my father to lie to me, but he would do what he damn well pleased until he was good and ready, and he had a meandering way of getting ready.

"Yeah. You did. You met Mom when you started working for Sal," I said.

"Yeah. But she already knew who I was."

"Because she saw you fight." I answered the way I knew he expected me to.

"That's right. She saw me fight. On the street. We used to stage our own bouts, right out in the open. People would throw down their bets, we'd whale on each other until the cops came, and then split the winnings. She saw me lose in spectacular fashion."

I frowned. This part was new.

"I thought you only lost to Bo Johnson."

"I did. But he beat me on the street before he beat me in the ring. I beat him sometimes too in the early days. He was quicker than I was, but I knew how to take a punch and keep going. I wasn't afraid of him. He wasn't afraid of me. We tried killing each other before we figured out we could work the crowds together. Make some good money. Hone our skills."

"I didn't know that. I thought you met after the war. After you were already the champ."

"No. No. I knew Bo Johnson long before that. We were both born and raised in Harlem. We kind of looked out for each other. Oh, he had his gang, and I had mine. The Irish, the Jews, the Italians, the Negros. Different neighborhoods run by different groups. Not much has changed, I guess. But some streets run together, neighborhoods overlap, and that's what happened to us. You meet in the middle. Or you kill each other. We got along, me and Bo. Not sure why. But we did. He was my friend. And I loved him."

I stared at him, my fork hovering over my plate. I wasn't surprised by his sentiment; I was surprised he was sharing it. Pop loved hard, but he loved selectively. And he loved quietly. He was a man of action, not of expression.

"The war started," Pop continued, ignoring my stare. "I went to France. He went to Texas. Didn't see him again for a long time. He signed on with a promoter, and I managed to stay alive and come back home. We met up again in Harlem when he took my title. You know the rest." Pop sighed, slow and heavy, and pushed his plate away. He'd only eaten a few bites.

"I really don't know the rest, Pop. We haven't talked about Bo Johnson since Mom died."

"But you still remember?"

"I do. How could I forget?"

He sighed again and rubbed the bump on his nose. I had a bump just like it, and I rubbed at it just the same.

"You know . . . it's funny," I said. "Bo Johnson's been on my mind since last night. And here we are . . . talking about him for the first time in twenty years."

"Nobody ever talks about Bo Johnson anymore," Pop muttered. "They should. He was the best."

"What ever happened to him, Pop? Why did he come here that night? He told me not to talk . . . and I never did. I never, ever did. There were stories about him. About Sal. About a woman. But I didn't understand most of it. I just knew I'd made a promise to not tell, and I kept it. I forgot all about him. When I listened to Esther sing . . . all that low, rumbly power. I thought of him. He had a voice like God."

"Yeah. He did." My father laughed like he was hearing that voice in his head. "He had a voice like God, and an ego to match. Bo got involved with a woman he shoulda left alone. Her name was Maude Alexander."

I kept eating, hoping he'd go on. After a minute he did, though I could tell he was giving me the bare bones and leaving off the meat.

"You ever heard of Maude Alexander?" he asked.

I shook my head.

"Her grandfather, Thaddeus Morley—her mother's father—was one of this country's first millionaires. He made his money building bridges and railroads. He built his fortune right alongside Cornelius Vanderbilt. He even built his mansion next door, on Fifth Avenue. That was a long time ago. The mansion is gone now . . . most of the Morleys are gone too. Maude's father, Rudolf Alexander, was a bootlegger. He took the Morley money and used their railroads to move his booze. He made a killing during Prohibition and even more money during the second war. If you control the movement of goods, you control the world. He got involved with the labor unions too. He has a law degree that he waves around, and he's smart enough to make the little man think he is on his side. He even ran for president a couple times as 'the voice of the common man.'" He laughed, mirthlessly. "He wasn't ever one of the little guys."

"So what happened to Maude?"

"She was what they call a socialite. Rich. Beautiful. One of the most beautiful women I've ever seen. Name always in the papers. But she didn't just go to parties and make the fashion pages. She was a trained opera singer. Giuliana loved her voice. We used to listen to her on the Sunday Night Showcase on WOR. We took you to hear her sing once. You mighta been too young to remember. We were going to leave you with Nonna, but your mother said she wanted you to hear. Giuliana was sick and going out was hard, but it was a concert in the park, a little more family friendly. So we brought you along. Sal and Aunt Theresa came too.

"You and your mother were transfixed. You hardly moved. You sat in her lap, and you wore the same expression. Pure happiness. Peace. It was beautiful. The woman had a voice. She was really something."

"I think I remember her name . . . now that you mention it."

"New York was obsessed with her. Sal was obsessed with her too."

"Sal?" I asked, taken aback.

"Sal," Pop answered, grave. I just shook my head.

"He has a way of making things go bad," I muttered.

"Don't say that, Benny."

I shook my head again, but let it go.

"Maude liked him too, for a while. He was handsome. Powerful. Persuasive. I think she was flattered. Women like Sal . . . and she liked that he was trouble. I don't know why women like trouble. Giuliana didn't like trouble."

"She married you, Pop," I reminded him, my voice wry.

Pop frowned at me, like the irony was just occurring to him.

"Keep going. The Alexander woman liked Sal. Sal liked her . . . then what?"

"She didn't like that Sal had a wife. She didn't want to sneak around. If she was going to be a mobster's girlfriend, she wanted to be on his arm, on the front page, not tucked away in his bed."

"She told Sal no?" Nobody told Sal no. Not even my father.

"Not in so many words. She flirted with him, but she had her eye on someone else."

"Bo Johnson?" I asked.

"Yeah. Bo Johnson. Poor son of a bitch. He shoulda run. Bo was a star in his own right. When he wasn't in the ring, he dressed in the best suits, tailored to show off his strength. He carried a cane and wore a bowler hat. He mixed with men and women that would have barred him from their soirees if he wasn't a celebrity. Bo loved to take what he wasn't supposed to even touch. He loved the white girls for no other reason than it made everyone nervous. And the white girls loved him.

Maude loved him. Maude Alexander's world was all about glitter, glamour. She didn't think the rules—unspoken and spoken alike—applied to her. And they didn't. Not for a while. You got enough money and fame, you can do what you want. The rags called her set the glitterati. But New York's upper crust didn't much like the mobsters or the movie stars, and they really didn't like Bo Johnson hanging around one of their own."

"What could possibly go wrong?" I said, sarcastic. I already had a pit in my stomach, and the tale had nothing to do with me. I pushed my empty plate away and sat back to hear the rest.

"Sal was jealous. Bo and Maude flaunted their relationship. They both liked the press, and they got lots of it, most of it bad. I tried to stay out of it. Bo was my friend before I ever met Sal, but Sal was my boss. Sal was family."

Sal was family. How many times had I heard that growing up?

"But there were bigger consequences than just Sal Vitale, if you can believe that," Pop said. "Some people don't like mixing the colors."

That was an understatement if I'd ever heard one.

"The Alexanders were embarrassed by it all," Pop said. "Bo and Maude left New York, and the next thing I heard, Bo was locked up for transporting a white woman across state lines for 'immoral purposes.' They call it the Mann Act." Pop waved his hands helplessly. "I didn't understand it. Something about kidnapping and white slavery. The authorities put the both of them through hell. Bo was in jail for a year even though Maude Alexander refused to testify against him. I didn't help him then. I had too much on my own plate. Your mom died while he was locked up, and I lost track of the mess until he showed up here that night. You remember?"

"Yeah. I remember."

"Maude had a baby while Bo was in the slammer. A little girl. She'd gone back to New York. Her family kept it out of the papers. No one saw her or the baby. I didn't know anything about it until Bo told me."

I was starting to see the pieces of Pop's disjointed retelling falling into place. I don't know why I was so surprised. I'd thought of Bo Johnson when I'd heard Esther sing, like my ears recognized what my eyes never would.

"Bo got released, came back to New York, and saw his daughter for the first time. He and Maude were making plans to go to Europe. They thought they could live there, and he could fight and she could sing. But three days later he arrived at Maude's house, all the arrangements made. He said the baby was asleep in her crib, but Maude was dead."

"What happened?" I asked, stunned.

"Some say she killed herself. But Bo wasn't convinced. He was afraid they'd pin it on him, and he would be back in jail forever. He brought the baby to me with instructions to take her to a woman named Gloria Mine in Harlem. I don't know how they knew each other, or if they were related, or what."

"So you did," I said, remembering the night, my father's absence, and the mewling sound.

"I did. I did what he asked and washed my hands of it."

"So Esther Mine isn't a Mine at all."

"Nope," my father said, his gaze heavy. "Mine is the name of the woman who raised her, but Esther is the daughter of the greatest fighter who ever lived and Maude Alexander, one of the best voices I've ever been privileged to hear, including your mama's. Esther should be treated like entertainment royalty. But instead, she gets whispered about and avoided, because nobody knows the truth for sure, and nobody wants to open old wounds or get on Sal's bad side."

"A woman like Maude Alexander, pregnant. She dies, and her baby is gone. How do you cover that up? People ask questions."

"None of the papers even mentioned a child."

"You just told me you washed your hands of it," I said. "This happened more than twenty years ago, but you're still keeping tabs on Bo Johnson's daughter."

"I've kept an eye on her. That's all." He sighed again and rubbed a hand over his tired face. "Bo didn't have nobody else. Neither did she."

"Does Sal know?" I had a million questions but settled on the one that surfaced first.

"What have I always told you, Benny?" my father said, wagging his finger at me.

"Sal knows everything," I answered, grim.

"Yep. You always assume Uncle Sal knows everything. Then you won't do nothin' stupid." We were face-to-face over the kitchen table, but his voice grew so soft I had to hold my breath to hear him. "If he knows I helped Bo Johnson that night, he never let on. He was wrecked over Maude's death, but if he'd asked me, I woulda told him. Just like I'm telling you."

My father had rules; he never hit me, and he never lied to me. He wouldn't volunteer information, but if I managed to stumble on the right question, he would tell me. I don't know why. A kid shouldn't know the things I knew. I had learned to stop asking about the things I didn't want to know.

When Albert Anastasia, a known mob boss, was gunned down in the Park Sheraton Hotel barbershop a couple of years ago, I asked my father what he knew about it. Albert Anastasia was a no good, rotten son of a bitch. I didn't know all his dirty deeds, but I knew that much. Sal hated him. When he wound up dead in spectacular fashion, swaddled in hot towels and riddled with bullets, not many people were upset.

"Who killed Anastasia, Pop?" I'd asked him.

He'd looked at me, the way he always did. And he said, "Is that something you really want to know, Benny? 'Cause once you know, you know."

I'd asked him if he pulled the trigger.

"I didn't."

"Do you know who did?"

"I know who did."

I'd left it at that, though I had no doubt Pop knew exactly what had gone down, and it would be a helluva story. Pop was right. I didn't want to know. Nobody did. It had been three years, and nobody had been charged with his murder, despite the coverage and the publicity. Maybe the authorities considered it "family business," and no one really wanted to get involved.

I considered leaving this story alone too. It also had "family business" written all over it. Which made the whole thing even more bizarre. Pop had his rules, but he'd never brought me into his dealings or involved me in his work.

"Why did you take me to Shimmy's last night?" I asked.

Pop was silent, his hands clasped in front of his mouth. For a minute I didn't think he'd even heard me, and when he finally started to speak again, the story he told was his own.

"I didn't have music like you do. I wasn't good at anything. I was big and strong . . . and mean. Just like my father. You look just like me. I looked just like him. Nothing we can do about that. I didn't like looking in a mirror 'cause all I saw was him. I hated him. He gave me every reason. But I loved him too. And that love never made any sense to me. I wanted to make him proud, yet I wanted to be nothing like him. Now I have a son who wants to be nothing like *me*. It's a funny world."

"Pop." I sighed, shaking my head. He patted my cheek, and his eyes were wet.

"No. It's okay, Benny. I'm not a good man, and maybe you can't be a bad man and a good father at the same time—I don't know. I know you saw too much. You knew too much. You know who I am and some of the things I've done. Not all. If you knew all . . . well, you'd hate me more than you already do."

"I don't hate you, Pop. I have never hated you." I'd been angry. Disappointed. Scared. But I had never hated him.

"Well . . . that's good." His hand was still on my face, and he patted my cheek again. "But I *did* hate my father. I didn't hate him because he hit me. I didn't hate him because he swore at me and made me miserable. I didn't even hate him because he drank what little money we had, and I was hungry and cold. I hated him because he hated me."

"Why did he hate you?"

"Because I looked just like him?" Pop shrugged and his hand fell away. "Because I needed him? I don't know. I think he probably just hated me because he had nothing but hate to give. When I won my first big bout, I bought him a case of the best wine I could afford, which was still pretty damn cheap. He drank it all. And he drowned in his own piss and vomit."

I hadn't ever heard this part. I was quiet, waiting for more, but he shrugged it off, leaving his father's memory to lie forever in his own waste.

"When you came along, I promised myself I would be different. I would take care of you," he said, his voice stronger.

"You have," I said.

"I swore you would never be hungry. I swore you wouldn't ever sleep on the floor because there were fewer bugs there than in your bed. You wouldn't ever see me drunk. You wouldn't ever wonder if I was coming home. You wouldn't ever feel my fists or get my boot."

"And I never did." He had kept every promise he had made to himself.

"In order to keep those promises, though, I had to provide. You know why money is the root of all evil?"

I shook my head. "Why?"

"Because if you don't have money, it affects everything else. It'll drive a man into the ground if he can't take care of his own. That's what men were put on earth to do. Protect. Provide. And I decided I could and would do anything to do that. I'm not smart. I'm not skilled. I can't build or create or repair. After Bo Johnson laid me flat in the ring . . . and damn near killed me, I realized I couldn't even fight."

He stood abruptly, as if suddenly it was all too much. He took my plate and scraped the bones into the trash before he repeated the action with his own. I stood as well, clearing what was left on the table. I didn't press him or ask for the rest of the story. He was stewing, gathering his thoughts. There was more. I didn't know how we'd jumped from Bo Johnson to lost bouts and a father's responsibilities, but I had no doubt it was all connected in Pop's mind.

"I don't expect you to understand. I don't even *want* you to understand. But you gotta know," my father said. "You gotta know."

"What do I gotta know?" I asked.

"You gotta know that I loved you. And I tried to do right by you."

"Pop? What is this all about?" I was so confused. Of course I knew he loved me, although neither of us had ever been good at saying the words.

He waved me away, waved his words away, like he could erase them from the air, erase the emotion from our throats. "Forget about it, kid. I'm getting old. I'm just glad you're here. Why don't you play me something? I don't get to hear you much anymore. Go on. I'll do that." He took my empty coffee cup from my hands and set it in the sink with the other dishes. "Go on. Play for me, Benny," he insisted.

I sat down at the old piano and ran my fingers up and down the keys, reacquainting myself with them. Every piano is different. The tension, the spring, the timbre. It always took a few numbers to feel at home on a new set of keys, but this piano and I were old friends. With my left hand, I played the opening bars of "Habanera" from *Carmen*, so distinct and low. *Dum da DUM dum, dum da DUM dum.*

My father smiled. "That's it. Play that one for your mother."

I riffed on the melody, not in the mood for the tempo and intensity of Bizet, and "Habanera" turned into something painfully slow and lonely. I didn't know French, but I knew the story, and it was damned depressing. Carmen ends up dead—stabbed—at the hands of a man she'd teased, taunted, loved, and then rejected. The whole opera could be summed up in the opening lines of "Habanera": "If you don't love me, then I love you. If I love you . . . beware."

I wrote a song, sitting there, and called it "Beware." Inspired by Carmen. Inspired by my mom. It needed a horn section to bring it to life, and I scribbled out an entire score in the margins of the Sunday crossword puzzle. I played for so long that when I finally looked up from the keys, hours had passed, and Pop had turned on the lamp beside me. The dishes were tidied, and he was asleep in his chair, his hands folded across his stomach. It was dark out. The winter months made the night come early. I needed to wash up and change and retrieve my car before I went to Shimmy's, but I thought I had time to close my eyes. I was suddenly exhausted, and the refrain of the last few hours clanged in my head. *Beware, beware, beware.*

I stood and walked to the couch, the same couch that had always been there, the couch where Bo Johnson sat the night he asked my father to help him. I stretched out on it, pulling a cushion under my head, and I closed my eyes, listening to my father breathe, listening to the sounds of the neighborhood beyond the window where my mother once sang. I dreamed of Carmen and Esther Mine.

The Barry Gray Show

WMCA Radio

Guest: Benny Lament

December 30, 1969

"You say you were hooked, Benny. You say you'd met your match. But when did it become love?" Barry Gray asks.

"I was hooked, but I wanted nothing to do with her. And it wasn't just her. It was attachment in general. I'd always been able to walk away from entanglements. A pretty face turned my head, but it didn't slow me down. And then Esther Mine entered stage left. I'd never been in love before. Or since, come to think of it. So it wasn't something I had a lot of experience with."

"But you'd written songs about love."

"Not really. I'd written songs about avoiding it. About being irritated by it. About being saddled with it. I wrote songs like 'Beware,' 'Can't Cut You Out,' 'The Wrong Woman,' and 'I Don't Want to Love You.' None of them were about commitment."

"And why was that?" Barry presses.

"I wasn't interested in settling down or tying the knot. Ever. My mother died when I was young, and my father never remarried. Maybe we Lomento men only love once." Benny Lament pauses. "All I know is that I fell in love very . . . reluctantly."

"That's not very romantic. All our female listeners are very disappointed in you right now," Barry Gray says.

"But it's true. And even as I felt myself slide, I knew it wasn't wise, but I couldn't help it. I was terrified it would end badly, and on the way to an ending, it would be hell. I'd spent my whole life treading carefully, purposefully, knowing that each time I put my foot down there existed the potential for detonation."

"It must have struck you funny then, that this woman who hooked you, so to speak, was Esther Mine, and she sang with a trio that called themselves Minefield."

"Ironic, isn't it?"

4

The Wrong Woman

When I woke, the night was gone. My father was no longer in his chair, my left shoulder ached from being pressed against the old couch springs, and daylight crept through my mother's window.

I had missed Esther's show.

I'd slept with the reassurance of a babe in its mother's arms. No fear, no future, no past. Just sleep and safety. It happened every time I slept beneath my father's roof, as though I took the weight of my life from my shoulders and hung it in the coat closet where the scent of my father would guard it until I shrugged it on again.

Sometime in the night he'd placed a blanket over me, and his bedroom door was closed. I used the bathroom, shaved with Pop's razor, and used a toothbrush that I was pretty sure was mine from the last time I'd stayed. Then I straightened my clothes and hair and left, needing to retrieve my car and the things in the trunk.

The cars parked along the streets had cleared with the Monday exodus to work and school. I bought a coffee and a bagel at the corner and downed both in less than a block. I wasn't in any hurry, and the morning was sunny but cold. No wind. No rain. Just brisk and bright, waking me up and unwrinkling my thoughts. I tried not to think about Esther Mine. I'd failed to do what I'd said I'd do, and my conscience was uneasy, despite the comfort of familiar surroundings.

I was distracted, and I realized suddenly that my feet had taken me down a well-trodden path, as if returning to my neighborhood catapulted me back to my old routines. I stood in front of Enzo's Gym. His red door and sign needed repainting. The cartoonish gloves were barely visible on the faded wood. A stranger to the neighborhood would pass it by without a second glance; the red door was boxed in between the butcher and a pawnshop. Those businesses had changed hands through the years, but the gym was still Enzo's, far as I knew.

I wondered if he was still hitting the bags and training hoodlums from the Bronx. I'd spent as much time in his gym as any kid in the neighborhood, and I'd never wanted to be there. Pop made me. I could still remember him coaxing me up the stairs.

I can't lay a hand on you, son. I can't do it. I promised myself when you were born that I would never lay a hand on you. And I never will. But you gotta learn how to use your hands for something besides playing the piano. I set you up with Enzo. He'll teach you.

Enzo had been excited that first day, thinking I was going to be like my dad. A fighter. I'd done everything he told me to do and kept my mouth shut, but when he put me in the ring to spar about a week after our lessons began, I'd refused to fight.

"You're stubborn. You know that? And you're wasting my time. Get outta my gym," Enzo had said.

I was embarrassed, and I'd cried when I got home. I also thought it was over, but Pop must have paid Enzo a visit, because I was back at it the following week. Pop marched me in, stuffed a wad of cash in

Enzo's hand and said, "He doesn't have to be a fighter, Enzo. But he's still gotta know how to fight."

Enzo put me right back in the ring. It was a game, he told me. Four of the other boys and me.

"Your job is to keep 'em off you. You're bigger than all of 'em. Stronger and quicker too. Keep 'em off."

They had circled me, their faces lit with curiosity. I recognized the expression. I'd felt the same emotion when I watched my fifth-grade teacher, Miss Morgan, walk slowly down the aisle while we were taking our tests, her hips swishing under her pink skirt, the smell of roses wafting around her.

"You as tough as your old man?" one yelled. That was always the question. You as tough as your old man?

I went cold inside. Not the kind of cold that feels mean. Not the kind of cold that feels empty. The kind of cold that comes from dread. I knew what I had to do, and I didn't want to do it.

"You gonna fight us, Benny?"

I wasn't going to fight them. I wasn't going to throw a single punch.

The smallest kid came at me first, darting in and swinging wildly. I braced, tucking my arms against my sides and shielding my face the way Enzo had taught me. But I didn't dodge and parry the way I did against the big bag. I let the boy land the blow. He whooped and the other kids swarmed. I stayed on my feet, even when the biggest kid kicked at my kneecap. I stayed on my feet and took their abuse, doing my best to protect my hands, my heart, and my head. A flurry of punches, both heavy and hesitant, rained down, and for a moment our grunts—theirs of effort, mine of pain—made violent music.

"He's soft!" one kid spat. "This isn't any fun."

"He's not soft. He's hard as a rock," another muttered.

"He's a big, dumb pansy. That's what he is. This ain't no fun."

Enzo cleared them all out of the ring and handed me his handkerchief. It was grimy, but I swiped at the blood from my nose, glad I couldn't stain it worse than it already was.

"If you don't fight back, those boys will never let you forget it. They'll never let you in," Enzo said.

"I don't want to be part of their goddamn group."

Enzo cuffed the back of my head. "Watch your mouth, kid."

The blood from my nose was now in my throat, and I spit into the bucket at Enzo's feet.

"I know you coulda taken most of those guys. Given at least as good as you got. So why didn't you?"

"If I fight back, and I'm good at it, they'll think I'm like my dad. You'll think I'm like him too."

"What's wrong with being like him?" Enzo asked.

"I don't want to do what he does."

"You'd rather have people think you're weak?"

"I don't care what they think. Sooner or later, they won't think about me at all," I said. That was my goal. I didn't want them to notice me at all. I wanted to be invisible in my father's world.

I tried the door to Enzo's, and it swung open without a sound.

"Well, what do you know?" I muttered. I contemplated just letting it swing closed again. My car was in the church parking lot right around the corner, and I had things to do. I didn't know why I was here. Maybe it was the conversation in the kitchen the night before, the trip down memory lane, but here I was.

You as tough as your old man?

The place echoed with those words. I stepped into the gloom, taking the stairs and trying to make out the patter and squeak of the speed bag, the whir of the jump ropes, and the stench of sweat and cigarettes. A wave of nostalgia knocked me back, and I halted at the top of the stairs, eyeing the space. Two elevated rings, bags along the perimeter, a mop bucket abandoned in the middle of the floor. The place was empty, but it was clearly still in use.

"Enzo?" I called out, not wanting to startle him. I walked a few steps, peering into the corners, and I called his name again. The framed images on the walls stared down at me, insolent and colorless, old ghosts in the shadowy room. I found the one of Pop, his arms raised and his shorts pulled so high he was all chest and legs. Enzo had a picture of Bo Johnson too, come to think of it. I walked along the row of photographs until I found it. Esther Mine was there in his eyes and the set of his jaw.

"Well, son of a bitch," I whispered.

"You still babying your hands, Benny Lomento?" Enzo rasped, ducking and weaving as he threw a hard right. I braced and tucked instinctively, but he pulled his punch and clasped me around the neck. I'd been afraid of startling Enzo, and he'd snuck up on me instead.

"Yep. Still babying my hands. You still beating on kids?" I answered.

"Every damn day," he chortled.

"That's good. That's good. Just glad it's not me anymore."

"I did beat on you pretty good. Made you strong, though." His hand was still at my neck, and he let it slide, squeezing my shoulder.

"Yeah. You and Pop. Made me strong." I patted his hand, and he released me.

"How is Jack? I don't see him much anymore. He used to come in here and help out every now and again. Sal keepin' him busy? Heard he was in Cuba for a while."

"Yeah. Well." I didn't ever talk about Sal. That was a hard, fast rule. "Pop's okay. We're all getting older."

He grunted his agreement, and we stood for a moment, our eyes lifted to the pictures on the wall, to the men who weren't young anymore either. Most of them weren't alive anymore.

Enzo pointed up at Bo Johnson. "You know who that is?"

"Yes."

"Hell of a fighter. He did a number on your pop."

"Yeah. I know."

"Oh ya do, do ya?" Enzo cackled. "I guess I'm not surprised. Most guys don't tell their sons about getting thumped. But that's Jack for ya. He's got nothin' to prove."

"He got beat by the best."

"That he did. That he did." Enzo sighed. "Some guy showed up here a while back, wanting to know if I knew where he was."

"Who, Pop?"

"Yeah. Your pop. And Bo Johnson too."

"You don't say?"

"He said he was a reporter."

"In this neighborhood? What did you tell him?"

"I told him I haven't seen Bo Johnson in more than twenty years."

"Why was he askin'?"

"He was doing a story, he said. For the papers. About the old boxing community. It surprised me. He seemed to know Lament and Johnson were old friends. I didn't think anyone remembered Bo. Now you're here, and we're talkin' about him again." He threw up his hands. "That's how life is. You don't think about something or someone for years, then all of a sudden, they're everywhere you look."

"I didn't remember this picture until I stood right here," I said.

"Sad story, that one. Guy has all the talent in the world. Throws it away."

"What do you mean?"

"You don't know that part of the story?" Enzo asked.

I shrugged, noncommittal. I wanted to hear his version of it.

"He fell in love with that Alexander woman." Enzo shakes his head. "Trouble. All the way around."

I said nothing, and Enzo continued, almost pleading, like he'd made the argument a dozen times before.

"It took him off course. He coulda been the best there ever was. I thought your pop was the best till I saw Johnson fight. He was at a whole other level. Big, strong, fast, focused. Hungry. He had fire." His voice faded away.

"So what happened to him?"

He shrugged. "Nobody knows."

"Somebody always knows," I muttered. *You always assume Uncle Sal knows everything. Then you won't do nothin' stupid.*

Enzo just looked at me, his lower lip jutting out, brows lowered. He wagged his finger at me. "Don't fall in love with the wrong woman, Benny. Best advice I can give ya. I can't make you strong enough to survive that. Every fighter I've ever known was either made or broken by the women in his life. You remember that."

"Guess it's a good thing I'm not a fighter," I said.

"We all have our battles, Benny Lomento," Enzo countered. Bo Johnson stared down at me, and I turned away, oddly unsettled by the conversation.

"You want to get a workout in? I got some boys comin' in that could beat on ya," Enzo offered, but I just wanted to go. I didn't know what had inspired me to climb those stairs again. I was fond of Enzo, but I hated this place. It reminded me of who I was and who I didn't want to be. I told Enzo it was good to see him again, gave the old man a hug, and headed for the stairs.

"You remember what I said, Benny," he called after me. "Don't be like old Bo. Choose the right girl."

~

I went to Shimmy's on Monday night, but the stage was dark. The bar was open, a few tables were filled, but the jukebox was the only music in the place. I'd told Esther Mine I would be there, and I hadn't been. I didn't want to be the kind of man who said one thing and did another.

"Is Ralph here?" I asked the man behind the bar.

"Nah. Mondays are his day off."

"What about the group? Minefield. When do they play again?"

"Not until Thursday." He looked at me as though he thought he should know me, but I left without another word. The place was almost as depressing as Enzo's.

Tuesday, Pop and I watched the election returns sitting side by side on the couch. The predictions varied from station to station, but the polls showed Kennedy with a slight lead in the popular vote going into election day. CBS announced a sure win for Nixon—odds were a hundred to one that Nixon would eke out a victory. I didn't care, but Pop was tense. At nine we went to La Vita, where an election-themed party was taking place. The walls and chairs were draped in flags, and the dancing girls wore Uncle Sam top hats and star-spangled pasties. Pop was on duty, and I ended up pinch-hitting on the piano when at dawn the race still hadn't been called, and the band was all played out. The place cleared when California was called for Kennedy, putting him over the electoral college edge. Fat Tony took Sal home, and Pop and I walked to Charley's for breakfast before heading home. He was gray in the face, and his hands shook when he picked up his coffee. I didn't comment, but I made a note to talk to Sal. Pop wouldn't listen to me. Sal probably wouldn't either. But Pop didn't look good.

"So Kennedy wins," I said instead.

"Yeah. He's young. Good-looking. Says the right things. He's got the machine in his pocket. Sal said he would win. Chicago won't be happy." By Chicago, I knew Pop didn't mean the city itself. From all indications, Chicago put Kennedy into the victor's seat. Pop meant the union. He meant the Chicago bosses. They'd thrown in with Nixon at the end. The New York bosses wanted Kennedy to win because they thought he would protect their interests in Cuba. Sal and Pop were in Cuba as much as they were in New York. Sal had opened another La Vita—Due Vite—in Havana. I'd headlined for a month in the winter of '57, pulling in different acts to sing some of my songs, but that was the last time I'd been in Havana. Pop didn't argue with me when I wouldn't go back.

Sal did. He told me I could have been as big as Sinatra in Cuba. Sinatra was a big draw in Havana in the fifties. Havana was the place where men went to do what they couldn't get away with at home. It made my skin crawl. There were no rules. If there are no rules, no order, then nothing flourishes. Not even the bad guys. They just end up killing each other. Anastasia had been throwing his weight around in Havana before he got himself whacked. Senator Kennedy had been there too, come to think of it. A whole congressional delegation pretending to work while they looked the other way and took advantage of the Cuban delights. I doubted Kennedy would go back now. The place was about to blow.

"You going back?" Pop asked, like he was reading my thoughts. Havana was another thing Pop and I didn't talk about.

"Where?" I frowned.

"To hear Esther again." Pop didn't look up from his plate. He sure didn't eat like he was sick. He shoveled his eggs in like he'd missed a few meals. His appetite reassured me slightly, and I was more forthcoming than I would have otherwise been.

"I told her I would. I'm going to write her—them—a song. Maybe two or three. I'm going to see what I can do about getting it in rotation on WMCA or WABC."

"You should go on Barry Gray's show. He'd get people talking," Pop said. "I could put a word in for you."

Barry Gray had a radio program weeknights from midnight to 3:00 a.m. on WMCA in New York. He also had a temper and wasn't afraid to mix it up, which made him unique when everyone else kissed ass and crooned about nothing.

Gray had gotten his big break on WOR, a 50,000-watt station that was heard deep into the Midwest, up in Boston, and all the way down in Florida, and later hit it big doing remote broadcasts all around NYC for WMCA, from the most exclusive lounges with the swankiest stars, and reading from *Variety* magazine live on air, adding his own real-life anecdotes to the gossip on the pages. He interviewed people live—singers, politicians, entertainers, even mobsters—and never even had to book a guest. They just showed up. Until they didn't. He'd allowed Josephine

Baker, the Negro entertainer, to air her grievances against powerful syndicated gossip columnist Walter Winchell on his broadcast and had become an outcast overnight. The stars who had once clamored for a minute behind his microphone didn't want to draw the ire of Winchell and hurt their own careers.

Somehow Gray had managed to weather the Winchell storm, though it battered him for years. He'd gained a reputation as a fighter and an all-around fair guy, and amazingly, WMCA kept him on, even with their lineup, which had gone to playing music from sunup to midnight. But from midnight to 3:00 a.m., it was Gray's world, and though he'd stopped doing remotes and on-site broadcasts, he hadn't stopped talking. Looking back, it might have been the fact that Gray was an outcast that made him a champion of the underdog. For all those who ran away, ten more became fans because he was just like them.

Gray dined at La Vita every now and again, especially when he knew the headliners. I was sure Pop had bragged to him about his musician son more than once, but bottom line, Pop liked Barry Gray. I liked him too, but I needed rotation on the music programs. Gray's program wouldn't cut it.

"Nah. Don't do that," I told Pop.

"I wouldn't be doing it for you. I'd be doing it for Esther," Pop said quickly. Pop knew how I felt. The biggest fight we'd ever had was when I found out my scholarship to the Manhattan School of Music was not a scholarship after all. Pop had spent a year in jail on a racketeering charge that I was convinced he wasn't guilty of. Pop hadn't ever run the numbers or had his own gigs. He didn't loan money or own front businesses. He'd never been a boss in Sal's organization. He was muscle, and he didn't get a tidy paycheck. Sal gave him cash, and Pop wasn't great about paying his taxes, so he was an easy target with his "unreported income," and he wouldn't roll on anyone else to make the racketeering charge go away.

The day after commencement, I visited him in jail. He was so proud of me and crushed that he'd missed it. He'd wanted to hear about every detail, but it had embarrassed me to visit him there, and I was angry that instead of him sitting in the audience at the ceremony, it had been my Uncle Sal and Aunt Theresa clapping beside Nonna.

"I didn't want him there."

"Uncle Sal is so proud of you."

"It's his fault you're here."

"Uncle Sal is family. You know this."

"He's family, blood, but you take care of him. He doesn't take care of you. Why is that, Pop? Family works both ways."

"He takes care of me by looking after you," he shot back. "Who do you think paid for that fancy school? For your room and board and books and things? Who do you think is paying the mortgage on my apartment while I'm here? That's all Sal."

"What?"

My father winced, and his shoulders fell.

"I got a scholarship," I cried, horrified.

"Benny . . ."

"I didn't get a scholarship?" I whispered.

"Yeah . . . you did. But Sal's a big donor. He made sure the board knew what he wanted in return."

I was going to be sick.

"Oh, Benny. They don't give scholarships to people like us. Don't matter how good you are, son. We're the kind of people who have to pay—pay extra—to get into places like that."

I covered my face with my hands.

"I shouldn't have told you. I just didn't want you thinkin' bad of Sal. I don't want you talkin' bad about him."

"How could you do that to me?" I asked, the words whispering between my fingers. I had loved school. I had worked my ass off. And I had excelled in every way. I'd made great connections, and I'd played with some of the

best musicians in the world. I'd composed. I'd toured. I'd even learned how to conduct and had led the orchestra my senior year. Now it was all ruined. Tainted. I didn't know what I'd earned and what had been purchased for me.

"I don't want no favors, Pop. I want to make my own way. I want to earn what I get."

"He may have got you in. But you earned the grades. You graduated. And I earned every dime of that endowment."

The idea that Pop had earned my tuition was even worse. Gino's bloody hand had risen like a specter from my childhood. I'd worked at La Vita from the time I was ten years old; I don't know why that hadn't ever struck me as profiting from my family name. Maybe it was because I hadn't made more than anyone else. I worked, I got paid. I washed dishes when I was ten, bussed tables when I was twelve, and by the time I was fifteen I was playing the piano during band breaks. I was big for my age, and people just assumed I was old enough. The folks who knew better didn't say a word. Plus, I stayed out of trouble and didn't mess with the junk. Pop and Sal made sure of that. I saw more tits and tail than a kid should see, but I didn't touch, and I sure as hell didn't take part. At least not at the club.

I quit at La Vita the day Pop was released from jail. I took my tainted diploma and all my considerable contacts and experience, and I played for everyone, everywhere. I lived out of a suitcase, plunked out songs, and knocked on doors. I didn't want to be a star. Maybe that was what won people over. I didn't have dreams of Hollywood or Broadway. I wasn't in love with my own voice or my reflection in the mirror. My dreams were of a humbler variety. I wanted to make music, not mayhem. I was happy on the bench and felt no need to be behind the microphone, and in an industry of pretenders and has-beens, of addicts and narcissists, I stood out for my rare mix of talent and dependability. And I never used Sal's name. For the last eight years, I'd just been Benny Lament. Not Pop's son. Not Sal Vitale's nephew. And I'd made a name based solely on what I could do. Those who knew my family connections didn't bring them up. If it gave me an edge, I didn't ask, and they didn't say. Somebody had clued in Berry Gordy at Motown, but it wasn't me.

"Why do you care so much about Esther, Pop?"

"I told you."

"Nah. You really didn't."

"Bo Johnson was my friend," he said. But he pushed his plate away like he couldn't take another bite. So much for his appetite.

"I saw Enzo yesterday," I said. "I walked by the gym. Went up, he was there. He still has a picture of you on the wall. A picture of Bo Johnson too. I could see her in him."

"You haven't seen these, I don't think." Pop pulled two pictures from the inside pocket of his suit coat and placed them on the table between us. One picture was of Bo Johnson and my father together, their arms slung around each other's shoulders while they pretended to slug it out with the other arm. The other picture was of Bo Johnson and a woman, a woman as dainty and pale as Bo was dark and powerful. She stood beside him dressed to the nines: gloves, glossy waves, glittering earrings, and a black evening gown.

"Damn," I whispered.

"Esther looks just like her. People don't see it right off because Maude was white and Esther ain't. But it's there for the whole damn world to see if they open their eyes."

"Don't fall for the wrong woman," I murmured.

"What?" Pop frowned.

"Nothing. Just something Enzo said." I shrugged it off. Looking at them made me sad. "Did she mean to kill herself?"

"I don't know. They say she did. But she knew a lot of people's secrets."

"Does anyone know hers?"

"What secret is that?"

"Does anyone know about Esther?"

"I never told anyone. Not until you. I think some people know." He shrugged. "But nobody says nothing. Not to me, anyway."

"The family didn't try to pin it on him?" I pointed at Bo Johnson.

"They insinuated it was his fault that she died—but indirectly. No charges were ever brought. Bo was right about the baby. Esther was inconvenient. I guess the Alexanders assumed he took her—they knew she was his daughter—or they were just glad they were both gone."

"Someone else had to know the truth about the baby."

"It was hushed up. People talked, but it was all just speculation. The final word was that Maude Alexander killed herself, Bo Johnson took off, and life went on without them. Bottom line . . . nobody really cared to challenge the story."

"Not even Bo Johnson?"

"Bo was scared. And powerless."

"Does Esther know who she is? I mean . . . she calls her bandmates her brothers."

"I don't know, Benny. Probably. Gloria Mine raised her. She *was* her mother. And I don't know what good it would do Esther to dwell on it. Bo's gone. Her mother's gone. It's done."

"Enzo said nobody knows what happened to him. Do you think Sal knows?"

Pop's eyes rose to mine. He rubbed his hands over his lips, like he was holding back the words, and then he shook his head.

"Nah. I don't know. I don't know. But it bothers me. It's always . . . bothered me."

"Why you carrying these around?" I asked, tapping the table beside the two pictures.

"I pulled 'em out yesterday morning when you left. You hold onto them." He pushed the pictures toward me. "I thought maybe you could give them to her."

"Me? You thought I could give them to Esther?" I asked, flabbergasted.

"Yeah."

"Pop!" I laughed, incredulous. "You just want me to hand 'em to her? Maybe say, 'Hey! Too bad about your parents. Life's the pits. But here's a song.'"

"No," Pop said, "of course not. Just . . . you know. Someday. When you know her better."

"I'm not gonna ever know her better. I'm gonna go to Shimmy's on Thursday and meet the band. I'm going to write them a song and try to get them some airtime. As a favor to you . . . as a favor to Bo Johnson. And that's it. Then I'm out."

Pop didn't like that answer. He rubbed his lips again. "You sound just like me. That's what I told Bo."

"So I'm assuaging your guilt? That's what this is?"

"You got all the big words, huh?" my father shot back. "No. It's not about guilt. I just wanted someone to know. I feel better knowing that someone knows the story. His story. Her story. That's all. And you're not doing me a favor, bucko. That girl can sing. You'll be lucky if you can work with her."

"I know lots of people who can sing." I wasn't lying, but I wasn't being truthful either. Esther was special, and Pop knew it.

"Not like her. She's going to make it big. She's gonna be a huge star. You watch. And you'll thank your old man for hooking you up." He wagged his finger in my face. "Everyone will know her name and her voice. Mark my words."

"All right. All right." I held up my hands in surrender.

"Sometimes the best way to hide is in the spotlight. If the whole world knows who you are, it's harder to snuff you out," he grumbled under his breath as he lifted his coffee cup to his lips.

"What? Geez, Pop! Who's trying to snuff her out?" I cried, slightly louder than I should. Pop jerked and coffee sloshed onto the table, narrowly missing the pictures. Nobody seemed to notice; the tables around us were still empty, though the barstools were full of early-morning risers or late-night lingerers, like us.

"Nobody. Damn it, Benny. Shut up. Nobody. Forget about it." He set his cup down and tossed his napkin over the spill. "Let's go."

I tucked the pictures into my breast pocket and threw some money on the table. Pop stood up, and I followed him out of the diner, shoving my hat on my head as I shrugged into my coat. We both needed to go to bed.

"So . . . Thursday? You're going back on Thursday?" he asked, talking around his cigar.

"Thursday." I sighed.

"Can I come with you?"

"Yeah, Pop. You can come with me."

The Barry Gray Show

WMCA Radio

Guest: Benny Lament

December 30, 1969

"Folks, if you're just joining us, you're listening to WMCA in New York and *The Barry Gray Show*. Tonight I'm talking to Benny Lament, singer, songwriter, producer, and entertainer. He's sitting at the piano, ready to play, and we've got him for the full three hours."

"What would you like to hear, Mr. Gray?" Benny asks.

"Well, that is the question! You've got quite a few I could choose from. How many songs have you written, Benny?"

"Hundreds. But most of those never made it on the radio."

"But so many have. How many hits do you have under your belt?"

"I don't keep track. If I don't pay attention to how much I've drawn from the well, then I won't worry about it going dry."

"Why don't you play us one of them, one from the early years."

"Well. There's this one. Do you know who sang this?" Benny plays a few bars and sings a line. His voice is guttural and distinct, like a barge signaling its arrival. "I don't want to love you, but I do. I do. I do."

"The McGuire Sisters," Barry Gray says. "I love that song."

"That's right." Benny immediately transitions into another tune and sings, "I tried to cut you out. Now I'm bleedin' to death."

"That's Izzy McQueen!" Barry Gray exclaims. "I didn't even know you wrote that one, and I've done my homework."

"Sounds better with Izzy on his horn, but yeah, it's mine. Your audience will probably remember this one too." Benny proceeds to play a medley of hits, singing a line here and there, and Barry guesses the titles and artists as he goes.

"All of those hits came before Minefield," Barry Gray says. "Let's talk about the hits that came after."

"All right."

"Minefield's song 'I Don't Need Any Man' hit the Top 40 in December 1960. Less than two months after you met. We played it first here on WMCA. Some called it race music. I called it a hit. Tell me about the song. How did it come about? I think everyone wants to know this story."

5

Any Man

When I was nineteen, I met a girl I could have loved. Her father, a guy named Mario Bondi, was a business associate of Sal's. He had interests in Cuba too, but I never saw him with a woman besides his wife, which made me think he might be a cut above some of the other guys that were in and out of La Vita. He imported Cuban cigars, the good ones, the kind Pop and Sal liked. I don't know what other businesses he had, but he had homes in Cuba and Miami and one not far from Sal's on Long Island. Sal threw a big Fourth of July barbecue and the Bondis came. Margaret and I hit it off. I saw her at several other family gatherings that summer. Over Labor Day, I asked her to a dance on Manhattan Beach. Sal let me take one of his cars, and though I don't think he liked me, Margaret's father let her go. I think he was afraid of offending my uncle, but her mother smiled at me like Margaret had landed Sinatra.

I kept her close when we danced and held her hand all night, but I brought her home early, knowing I wouldn't be seeing her again. When I walked her to the door, she smiled at me shyly, a pretty turn to her painted lips, and I said good night and walked back to Uncle Sal's car. I rejected her. Purposefully, painfully. I was cruel though I didn't mean to be. I knew she liked me. And I liked her. But she would want things from me. The kind of things a young girl wants. Someone to be sweet and doting. Someone who would take her to dinner and to the movies and buy her flowers. I could do those things. I would *enjoy* doing those things. I would be happy walking at her side and lying beside her when she'd made me wait long enough . . . and it wouldn't be very long. She could be my girl.

But I didn't want a girl.

A girl became a wife. A wife became a mother. A wife and a kid became a family. My pop would be a grandfather. He would love that. Uncle Sal would come to our wedding and pat my cheeks and kiss Margaret and give us some money. He would welcome us to the family.

I knew where it all led. I knew what family meant, and I wanted no part of it.

So I turned away, and later that night I visited Agnes Toal on Marion Avenue. She worked in the cloakroom at La Vita, and she was a lot older than I was. Her hips weren't as slim as Margaret's, her breasts weren't as high, and her skin wasn't as smooth. But she didn't want anything from me but some kind words and some kisses. I wrote her a song too, sitting in my underwear on her bed, my harmonica in my hands, singing a line between measures.

I spent the night with Agnes Toal.
She made me beg, she made me moan,
But when the sun slid 'cross my toes
She made me go, she made me go.

Agnes had laughed at my verse and asked me for a chorus, and I gave her one. When I was finished she made me go just like I'd said she would, and that was what I wanted. I would never love Agnes Toal, and she would never expect me to. She was almost old enough to be my mother, and neither of us had any aspirations for a relationship. But that night, and many nights after that, when I kissed Agnes Toal I thought of Margaret Bondi and her hopeful smile.

Walking into Shimmy's with my pop that Thursday night felt a little like walking Margaret Bondi to her door knowing I wasn't ever going back. Knowing I was going to disappoint her and probably disappoint my pop. He'd asked about Margaret all those years ago. He would ask about Esther too, I had no doubt.

She was on the stage, singing with all the vinegar and verve of her previous performance, and my nerves began to thrum with the timbre of her voice. I didn't want Pop to watch me watch her, and I kept my eyes averted though my ears were pricked like a dog's.

Ralph was back on duty, and we took two empty stools at the bar. Pop ordered a bottle of Coke, and I did the same.

"A Coke?" Ralph asked, his eyes wide. My father was the strangest gangster in the world.

"I don't drink with my boy," Pop said.

I was almost thirty years old, but I was still his boy, and Pop and I didn't drink together. Go get a slice? Yeah. Get a sandwich? Definitely. But never a beer. It was one of his rules. Pop had seen his father drink himself to death, and he had never once offered me alcohol. I drank. Sure. But not with Pop. He drank in front of the radio or television or while reading the paper. If he was out with Sal, he didn't drink at all. He was working then—fixing—and booze made fixing hard.

My father also never yelled. He didn't need to. He never wasted words, and he usually got what he wanted. Pop was a philosopher of sorts. A supremely rational and unemotional one, and he always did what he said he was going to do. I grew up knowing that if he said he would take care of something, he would take care of it, even if the way he "took care of it" was not to my liking.

"Don't give people too many options. Give 'em one or two. Either-or. Keep it simple and be okay with whichever they choose. Tell 'em what will happen, and make sure what you say will happen, does happen. Word will spread. People will know you aren't bluffing or playing, and they'll fall into line. It's a relief to them, most of the time, to know what to do."

Sometimes he didn't give people an option at all. He didn't give Ralph one.

"Tell us about the band, Ralph," my father demanded when Ralph uncapped the Coke and handed it to him.

"Okay . . . uh, what do you want to know?" Ralph stammered.

"Well, you told Esther about my son. So I want you to tell us about them." This was Pop's way of tweaking Ralph, letting Ralph know he didn't like me being the object of conversation. "Who are they? What are their names?"

"We got Lee Otis and Alvin. They're all brothers. Money is the oldest, I think, and he's the one you'll have to win over. The other three call him Meanie when he isn't around," Ralph said.

"Money? That's his name?" Pop interrupted.

"Hell if I know. That's what they all call him. Money Mine. He's the one on the guitar. I told him he needs to cool it. He looks like he's thinking about who to kill. Alvin is on bass. He's friendly. Easy. Lee Otis is on the drums. He's the youngest. And he's quiet. Smart . . . I guess. Smart or really slow. Sometimes it's hard to tell. He's good with facts and stats, but not so good at conversation."

"What's she like?" my father asked, tipping his bottle toward Esther.

"Who? Queen Esther?" Ralph smirked.

"Why do you call her that?" Pop asked.

"Because she's stuck up," Ralph snorted. "She may be little, but she is *all* business. Sharp. Shrewd. Suspicious. Do not cross her, and don't let that pretty face fool you."

"Huh," Pop grunted. I could see from his expression he'd just taken a dislike to Ralph.

"By the way, I confirmed who you were." Ralph pointed at me. "But I didn't volunteer the info. Esther noticed you. I told you, she doesn't miss anything."

I had to look at her. She was staring at me. When our eyes met, her shoulders stiffened and her chin lifted, but she ignored me for the rest of her set. I'd planned my visit for the end of the night so I could talk to the band when they were finished, but Esther wasn't the only one who had taken note of our interest. The owner of the club, a man named Ed Shimley, who my father greeted by name, sidled up to us when Esther launched into her final number.

My father commended him on the entertainment. I asked to be escorted backstage.

"Now wait just a minute. You can't just come in here and steal my talent. We've got a contract," Shimley huffed.

"Oh yeah? And what does that contract say?" I asked calmly.

"I've got them for two hour-long sets every Thursday, Friday, Saturday, and Sunday for two years."

"I'm not interested in shaking things up. I write songs. I want her to sing one. You got a problem with that?" I asked. "They put out a hit song, it'll draw people here. That's good for you."

Ed Shimley looked from my father to me, certain he was getting swindled but not sure how.

"They spend the time between sets in the back room there," he grunted, still suspicious, but curious too. "You can talk to them. But I'm going to expect Sal to make it up to me if you lure them away."

"What's Sal got to do with it?" My father's voice was so cold the hair rose on my arms. I wasn't the only one. Ed rubbed a hand over his neck.

"You work for him, Mr. Lomento," Ed said to my father. "I thought your interest was his interest."

"Sal's got nothing to do with it," I insisted. My father was perfectly still beside me. "I write songs. She's a helluva singer. That's all."

"Huh. Well . . . still. I've got a contract," Ed grumbled. "So you keep that in mind."

We waited for the end of the set, and when Esther and the band exited the dais and disappeared through an adjacent door, Pop and I followed them, but he held back and stood beside the door like he wanted to stay out of it. I preferred it that way.

The three men seemed surprised at my presence, but Esther folded her arms and cocked her hip when she saw me. She didn't look happy. I hadn't shown Sunday night, and she wasn't going to be gracious about it.

"Nobody said you could come back here, mister," she said. The skinny guitar player—Money—stepped around her like he was eager for a confrontation. I don't know why. I outweighed him by fifty pounds. Alvin smiled, and Lee Otis tugged at the bow tie around his neck. His shirt was soaked through from playing. He tossed his sticks down and fell into a chair. There was an old piano in the corner with a rickety stool in front of it. Perfect. I just hoped it wasn't too out of tune.

"I'm Benny Lament." I extended my hand to Money. "I told Esther I'd stop by."

I heard her irritated sigh, but I kept my eyes on his. Money took my hand, and I figured he probably already knew who I was.

"You told me you'd be here on Sunday. It is Thursday, if I'm not mistaken. No exchanges, no returns, no open invitations," Esther said.

Alvin was still smiling, and he stepped forward to shake my hand too.

"So you're Benny Lament? The piano man? The man who played with Izzy and Miles and Coltrane?" he asked. "I've heard about you." Esther might be mad, but they'd been talking about me.

"Yeah. And a few others."

"So why you want to play with us?" Money asked, his tone insolent.

"I don't," I said, shaking my head.

"You're here, aren't you?" Money snapped. "I think you do. I saw the way you perked up when Esther started singing 'Ain't Nothin'' last Saturday."

"It definitely ain't nothin'. That's for sure," Alvin crowed.

"That's getting old, Al. That joke is getting so old." Lee Otis sighed. He chugged a glass of water and wiped at his brow.

Alvin started to laugh, a rolling sound from his belly that erupted from his mouth.

"And there he goes, laughin' at it the way he always does." Lee Otis was not amused. He rubbed a hand down his face and shook his head. Weary. He looked about sixteen, if that, and I got the feeling he didn't love the job.

"I definitely perked up," I admitted. "Esther is very good. I liked it."

"Oh, you liked it, huh?" Money asked.

"Why are you angry, Mr. Mine?" I asked, keeping my voice mild. Ralph was right. Money was the gatekeeper.

"Because he's been waiting on you," Alvin said, still laughing. "Money likes money. And we need help. We need a keys man. You may be a little paler than we like, but you are definitely a keys man."

"And what do you say, Miss Mine? Do you need a keys man?" As soon as I said it, I realized how it sounded. I hadn't intended it that way. I wanted to know her opinion on the matter. It seemed to me they were doing just fine with a guitar, a bass, and some drums.

"I don't need any man," she said, her voice so cold it made my teeth ache. I walked over to the piano and sat down on the stool. If I didn't get too excited it would hold me.

"Huh. Now there's a line. Why don't you sing it? It could be good." I played a few chords. The piano didn't sound too bad. I'd played worse.

"Sing what?" Esther asked. She'd followed me to the piano. Money and Alvin had too.

"You said you don't need any man. I think we could make a song out of that line. Tell me, what else don't you need, Esther?" I asked, already hearing the chorus. I just needed a verse.

"I don't need you talking down to me, that's for sure." She folded her arms and stuck out her chin.

"I'm looking up at you, Baby Ruth. So how could I be talking down?" I grumbled. She struck me as one of those women who made you work for every smile. I didn't have any patience for that. But I didn't need her to smile for me. I just wanted to hear her sing.

"Stop calling me Baby Ruth."

"Baby Ruth, now that's funny!" Alvin said, picking up his bass and plucking out a *waa waa waa* response on his instrument.

I ignored him. I really wasn't messing around. I was writing a song if Esther would let me. "How about this?" I asked and sang a line. It was rough, and I tripped a little, finding the rhyme.

"I don't need another sweater, Mother. I don't need a fancy hat. I don't need a diamond ring on my finger, I've had enough of that." I raised my eyebrows at Esther Mine, an invitation to provide another line. "What's next?" I asked.

She frowned, and I played the same lines over again, singing them slowly, daring her to add something new.

"I don't need you to give me permission, when I know that I can," Esther supplied, half singing.

"That's it," I said, and I brought it home. "I don't need anything you are selling." I grinned. It was just too easy. "And I don't need any man."

Alvin was already trying to add the bass to my melody, and Money strapped on his guitar. He found the chord, but the words were coming fast now, and I kept going.

"I don't need another lecture, brother. My mind is all made up," I sang. "I don't need an arm to walk me down the aisle, I'll pass that bitter cup. I don't need you to give me permission, when I know that I can. You might as well just stop talking, 'Cause I don't need any man."

"Come on, Ess. You know you hear it," Lee Otis said, drumming on his thighs. He was still slouched in the chair, but his eyes had lost their weary glaze and his sticks were flying.

"Everybody sing 'She don't,'" I instructed, and the men obeyed.

"I don't," Esther came back, full voice. "No, I don't need any man."

"Yeah, she won't," I added, repeating the pattern.

"I won't," Esther belted. "Boy, do you understand?"

I nodded. That was good. "Now here's where the story changes," I said and stepped onto the bridge I was building in my head. I couldn't sing it the way Esther would be able to, but she would get the idea.

"I don't need you. But I want you. I know that you can tell." My left hand was thumping out a double-time rhythm with my words, and Alvin began walking the bass beneath me. "I didn't mean to, but I want to. I've been lyin' to myself."

"Oh hell, yeah!" Alvin yelled.

Esther was right there, ready to go with the next verse.

"I'm not just another sister, mister. You better treat me right. I don't need a man who'll kiss me, forget me, and move on to the next."

She paused, not ready with the next line, and I cut in, supplying the one she'd already provided. "I don't need you to give me permission, when I know that I can." I couldn't stop the smirk that curled my tone. I liked teasing her. "You might as well just stop talking, 'cause I'm going to be your man."

Esther Mine began to laugh, but I kept going. "You don't need me, but you want me. And you know that I can tell. You don't mean to, but you want to. You been lyin' to yourself."

"I don't," she sang, laughing.

"You do," I said.

"I don't need any man," she sang.

"She don't," her brothers shouted.

"I don't," Esther echoed. "Boy, do you understand?"

"Guitar riff," Money hollered, and I let him take it away, following his lead.

"Big finish," I yelled, thumping away. "I don't need another mother, brother—"

"—sister, mister," Esther added.

"—sweater, whatever," I sang, stomping.

"And I don't need any man," Esther finished.

Pop was clapping from the door, and we were all laughing. It was a damn good song, and Esther Mine would sing the hell out of it.

"Unbelievable, Benny Lament. That was unbelievable." Alvin thumped me on the back. "And Ess! Dang, girl. You were spittin' out lyrics left and right. I didn't know you had that in ya."

"It was his fault." Esther pointed at me, her face flushed with triumph. "He just makes me so mad," she said, and then we were all laughing again.

"I gotta find a piece of paper before I forget all those words," I said, pulling a pencil from my pocket. Esther was still smiling, and it was the most beautiful thing I'd ever seen.

"Damn it," I whispered. "Damn it all to hell."

I was in so much trouble.

~

I left two songs and more than three hours later. Pop had abandoned his post and grabbed a chair. He'd shoved a couple of bills at the night security, and they'd left us alone in the back room. Lee Otis was stretched out on the floor, asleep. He apparently had school in the morning, and according to Esther, he never missed.

"He likes school, but we need a drummer. And we can't afford to hire anyone else. Plus, he's good."

"Speaking of money . . . ," Money Mine cut in. "What do we owe Mr. Benny Lament for this . . . privilege?" He said every word like he expected me to disappoint him.

"I told Esther I would give you a song. I did. We didn't talk money."

"But you gave us three," Alvin exclaimed.

I'd shown them "Beware," the song I'd written instead of coming to Shimmy's on Sunday night, and when Esther sang it, I broke out in a cold sweat. We started it out way down low, and by the bridge she was wailing and I was half standing, unable to keep my seat. Pop was standing too, his hands on his heart like the Yanks had won the World Series.

We also collaborated on a song in a Buddy Holly style called "Itty Bitty." It wasn't as heart-stopping as "Beware" or as sassy as "I Don't Need Any Man," but it had a great bass line, a rockabilly rhythm, and a good hook, and Esther sold it. She sold them all.

"I asked Mr. Lament to manage me . . . to manage us," Esther said, looking at her bandmates.

"Oh, you did? And when were you going to ask my opinion on that?" Money said.

"I am asking your opinion now. I wasn't sure he'd show up . . . again." She shot me a glare that said I wasn't completely forgiven.

"I am the manager of Minefield," Money said, thumping his thin chest, and Alvin sighed. Lee Otis didn't even stir.

"That's good. Because I don't want to manage you," I said.

"Why not?" Alvin asked, ducking as Money swiped at him.

"I write songs. I produce. I'm not interested in babysitting."

"You think you're too good for us? You think we need you?" Money hissed.

I stared at him blankly.

"Shut up, Money. You know it ain't that." Alvin laughed. "Guy plays like that, he can call me baby anytime he wants."

"I don't have any desire to make people do what they don't want to do. You want to manage this crew, great," I said. "You'll get no argument from me. I'm not interested."

"What about these songs?" Money twirled his finger, indicating what we'd spent the last few hours on.

"We get some studio time. Get them recorded. A three-song sampler. I get them in rotation. All I want is my name down as songwriter and a slice of your royalties on these three. The songs do well, I do well. The songs don't do well, I don't do well."

"So no money out the door for the songwriting?" Money asked.

"No."

"But you don't want to manage us?" Alvin asked.

"No."

"What does studio time run?" Money asked. His voice dripped with suspicion.

"See . . . us cats don't have any money," Alvin said, refusing to be quiet. But Esther wasn't saying anything at all.

"Benny . . . I'll call Jerry," Pop said from the corner.

"Jerry?" Money questioned.

"Jerry Wexler. At Atlantic. He'll work you in," Pop said.

"Atlantic?" Alvin whistled. "Damn, Money. Atlantic?"

"And what's that going to cost? What's Jerry Wexler from Atlantic going to charge Money Mine from Harlem?" I could hear the hope beneath Money's belligerence, and I wished Pop had kept out of it. Keep expectations low. That's what I did. That's what Pop usually did.

"Forget about it," my father said, shrugging. "Just make the record. Atlantic might even want to sign you to their label. These songs . . . and Esther . . . you guys are good enough. You really are."

"Pop . . . ," I warned.

"Pop?" Alvin parroted. "That's your father, Lament?" He walked toward Pop, his hand outstretched in greeting. "I thought you were just security making sure we didn't rob the bar when Shim went home."

All eyes swung to my dad, who shook Alvin's hand.

"Nice to meet you, Mr. Lament," Alvin said. Money just frowned, Esther stared, and Lee Otis sat up and yawned.

"Lomento," my father corrected. "But you can call me Jack," he said, shaking Alvin's hand firmly.

"We've got to go. We've all got jobs. Lee Otis has school. The buses don't wait," Esther said, her back as ramrod straight as it'd been at the beginning of the night. I'd rejected her again.

"Benny can take you; he doesn't have nothing to do. Save you some time," my father volunteered. "We're in separate cars. So, I'll wish you all good night . . . or good morning. It was a pleasure listening to you. I'll give Wexler a call. Forget about it."

"Pop," I said again. I don't know what he thought he was doing. He scowled at me. "I'm not doing it for you, Benito," he muttered.

"We're all going different directions," Esther said quietly.

"But if he takes us home, Esther," Lee Otis spoke up, hopeful, "you and I will have time for breakfast and a nap."

"Wait just a minute. I want to know what the plan is," Money insisted. "Are you going to get us some recording time, Lament? What's next? I am not signing anything, just so you know."

"Just . . . let me see what I can do. Then we'll talk some more."

"I don't trust you, Lament. You told Ess you'd be here last Sunday, and you didn't show," Money said.

"Money, he doesn't owe us anything," Alvin shot back. "Give the man some space. He'll get back to us, won't you, Benny?"

"I'll see what I can do," I repeated. I was ready to leave. The high from the music we'd created was fading fast, and the same old dread was pooling in my gut. I did not want them depending on me. I would make some calls—Jerry Wexler would be hearing from Pop, I was sure—and follow up with Atlantic, and that was all. Then I was out.

Alvin and Money went one way, Alvin thanking me and Money threatening to hunt me down if I didn't deliver, but Lee Otis stayed on my heels, and Esther followed him reluctantly. I guess I was giving them a ride. Thanks, Pop.

It was early enough that the roads were clear and daylight was still a ways off. Pop slid into Sal's Town Car and pulled away without a word or a wave. I opened the passenger-side door for Esther, and Lee Otis climbed into the back and promptly fell asleep. It was cold and his shirt was thin, but the kid was exhausted. Esther had to be tired too, but she still wore her heels—pink ones this time—and she freshened her lipstick and patted her hair while I drove.

She gave me directions—turn here, next left, keep going—without prompting, but she didn't make small talk, and I turned on the radio. WMCA's overnight deejay was playing Sinatra's campaign song for Kennedy. *"This might be the last time you hear this one, folks. At least for four more years."* I flipped it off. Four more years was soon enough. The airwaves had been plastered with politics for months. I was tired of it.

When Esther pointed at a building on 138th and told me to pull over, I did. The building was a mustard yellow and part of the neighborhood called Striver's Row. Fifty years ago if you lived on the Row, you were big time. Now it was as run down as the rest of old Harlem, in need of restoration and renovation. Pop had pointed out the neighborhood to me once. He'd been born in a tenement in East Harlem, a tenement that had been razed in the renaissance of the thirties, but the Row had outlived everything around it. Maybe because it was built to last. Maybe because it was designed for the wealthy. Pop liked the Row, both the architecture and the history. It boasted alleyways between the structures, a luxury in Manhattan where the real estate didn't allow for wasted space. At one time, the alleyways had been used for stables and private service entrances. A few old signs still remained, warning tenants to walk their horses. Now the alleys were filled with cars and trash cans.

People were already stirring. A few turned to stare as I pulled up to the curb in front of Esther's building, and an elderly gentleman stopped reading his paper on the front steps nearest us and looked at us expectantly.

"Hello, Mr. Glover," Esther said through the glass, and he frowned before tapping his watch like her time was up.

She nodded and waved but made no move to disembark.

"What is it about people that they can't mind their own business?" She sighed.

"They think you *are* their business. My neighborhood is the same way."

"Yeah. Well. I'm not their business. I'm nobody's business, and Money isn't our manager. He just thinks he is because he's the oldest, and he's used to bossing the rest of us around. None of us have signed anything. Not with him, and not with Ed Shimley, though I'm sure he's told you different. Shimley wouldn't sign a contract with us. He's paid us what he said he would for every show, and he's been mostly on time. I've got no complaints there. But we all know he can get rid of us whenever he chooses. Money knows how to play guitar. He's good. But he doesn't know how to sell. I got us the gig at Shimmy's. It's not much, but it's something."

"Did you show up and refuse to get off the stage?" I asked, teasing her a little.

"Something like that," she said, and I saw a hint of a smile. "No one speaks for me. Not Money, not Mr. Shimley, not old Mr. Glover over there, nobody. We need a manager . . . and if you won't do it, I will. I'll do it myself. So if we're going to record your songs, you need to put something in writing and give it to me. If I like it, I'll take it to my brothers. But you deal with me. You got that?"

I nodded. "Yeah. I got that."

"I look forward to hearing from you then." She opened the car door and stepped onto the curb. "Come on, Lee Otis. We're home, baby."

Lee Otis groaned and climbed out, stumbling toward the stairs where Mr. Glover still sat, watching us, his paper hanging limp from his hands.

"You have a phone number?" I asked, leaning over the seat and peering up at her.

That slowed her down a bit. She frowned at me.

"I'm not coming back to Shimmy's every time I want to talk to you," I added.

"I'll call you."

"No. Not gonna work. I need a number."

She sighed heavily and dug in her purse. I'd ruined her exit, and Mr. Glover was taking notice of everything she did. She scribbled something on a candy wrapper, and I added Pop's address to a business card and handed it to her in exchange. She studied it for a second, then she tucked it into her purse.

"Don't let me down, Benny Lament," she said, just like she had the first time, and she followed Lee Otis inside without a backward glance.

The Barry Gray Show

WMCA Radio

Guest: Benny Lament

December 30, 1969

"I have to ask. In 1960, you were a handsome, young guy. Unbelievably talented. You could write. You had connections. But you weren't writing songs for yourself," Barry Gray says.

"The handsome part is arguable. But no. I wasn't singing my songs," Benny Lament answers.

"With your voice and your piano, you were like an Italian Ray Charles. You could have been a big name all by yourself."

"I've never been very proud of my name."

"You changed it."

"Yeah. A little."

"Your given name is Benito Lomento. Your uncle is Salvatore Vitale. Our audience may remember his name from the televised Kefauver Senate hearings on the mob and organized crime. Before those hearings, our own FBI didn't want to admit there was a problem with organized crime in this country."

"They didn't want to admit it after the hearings either. It was good television. That's all. Politicians are great talkers, but most of them don't do much more than that. Except if someone gets in their way."

"The hearings took place in fourteen different cities across the United States, including eight days here in New York. As many people watched those hearings as watched the 1950 World Series that year. Your uncle testified along with many others."

"My uncle pleaded the Fifth, along with many others. But he looked good doing it."

"It brought him some unwanted attention."

"Unwanted?" Benny Lament laughs. "It brought people into his club. We were booked solid for years after those hearings ended."

"He owns La Vita, a popular nightclub in Manhattan," Barry Gray explains to the audience.

"Yeah, he does. Among other things."

"And you were playing at La Vita when you were still just a boy."

"La Vita is where I got my start. I owe my uncle that. But he had interests to protect, and our interests didn't always align."

6

Where You Belong

I ended up driving to Sal's house on Long Island after I dropped Esther and Lee Otis off. The morning was still new, and I was jittery with music and growing misgivings. Trying to catch Sal at La Vita would be difficult. It would get back to Pop, guaranteed. Someone would comment on my return or mention I'd been holed up with Sal, and Pop would ask me about it. For the same reason, I didn't want to call my uncle. I didn't want to have a conversation on the phone that Pop might overhear, either from my end or Sal's. So I pulled into Sal's driveway at 6:00 a.m. on Friday, knowing it was the best time to catch him without a guard.

I knew Sal's schedule because I knew my father's. It hadn't changed much over the years. When I was young, Pop worked almost every day from nine at night until nine in the morning. Mrs. Costiera was down a floor if I needed someone. Pop gave her a little money to fix me breakfast in the mornings and get me off to school, but he was always there in the afternoons when I got home. We had dinner together, and he made sure I did my homework, went to boxing on Tuesdays and Thursdays, and was in bed asleep before he left again. Other than the two hours of Mass on Sunday mornings, I spent the weekends at La Vita. I'd moved on, but things hadn't changed much for Pop over the years; he'd spent his time watching me or watching Sal.

He wouldn't be watching him now.

Pop would have gone home after he left Shimmy's. Thursdays and Sundays were his nights off. The two Tonys—Fat Tony and Tony Sticks—took shifts driving and guarding Sal when Pop wasn't with him.

Fat Tony wasn't really fat. He was just big, and next to Sticks, everyone was heavy. Pop had brought the Tonys into Sal's organization when they were young—maybe eighteen or nineteen. He'd worked with both of them at Enzo's way back before I came along, and Pop was of the opinion that Fat Tony could have been a contender. I'd overheard him telling Sal once, "He's big and quick, and he doesn't feel a punch. He didn't want it, though. And if a guy don't want it, it doesn't matter how good he *could* be." I remembered it only because I thought he'd been talking about me. I hadn't ever wanted it either.

Sticks had wanted it, but he wasn't built for it. He was all sharp edges, hooded eyes, and stamina, but he had no natural ability and no meat on his bones. Sticks's thinness made him even more intimidating. His eyes were flat and dark, his face skeletal, and he didn't say much.

The Tonys had become a team at some point. Maybe it was their time at Enzo's or the fact that they worked well together. Maybe it was simply fate or the whims of their boss, but they were the Tonys, and they always would be.

Sal, if he'd been at the club the night before, would have gone home by now too, but unlike Pop, he probably wouldn't be crawling into bed. Sal slept in the afternoons when he slept at all. He ate breakfast by the pool in the summer and in his sunroom in the winter. After breakfast he golfed or went to the track or conducted meetings in his office at La Vita, but he would be at home now.

Sal's paper was on the front walk, and I snagged it before knocking on the front door. Theresa might not be up, but Sal would be, I was certain. I knocked again, a little louder, and waited.

The woman who answered was simultaneously strange and familiar. She wore a black dress, a white apron, and a frilly white cap over her dark hair. She was too sexy to pull off the demure maid act, even with the stupid hat, and I wondered if Theresa had insisted on the silly uniform to dull her appeal. It didn't work. She looked as though any minute she would break into a naughty cabaret.

And then I recognized her.

She'd been a showgirl at Due Vite in Havana. The last time I'd seen her, she'd been naked in my bed. Apparently, Sal had decided to bring her home. Poor Aunt Theresa.

"Hello, Carla," I said.

"*Hola*, Benny." She smiled like I'd bestowed a great compliment on her by remembering her name. Poor Carla. I didn't smile back. It was too early for Carla. I'd regretted the indiscretion the moment I'd made it and had hoped to never see her again.

"I need to speak to Mr. Vitale," I said as gently as I could.

"It's been so long, Benny. You look good."

"Let my nephew come in, Carla," Sal's voice rang out behind her.

She jumped as though we'd been caught doing something wrong. She immediately moved out of the way, and I stepped past her and walked into the house. Sal stood at the foot of the large staircase, his hands shoved into his pockets as though he'd been waiting for me to arrive. He looked rested and unruffled, his graying hair brushed straight back off his brow, not a strand out of place. He favored black shirts, black slacks with a crease as sharp as the blade of his nose, and a thick gold watch. Salvatore Vitale made the men around him look underdressed, even when they wore their best, even at six on a Friday morning. I still wore the suit I'd donned the night before, but I'd known enough to check my hair, shake the wrinkles from my suit coat, and tuck in my shirttails before I approached the house. I was more than presentable, but he still commented.

"You look tired, Benito," he said. "Give Carla your hat."

I took it off but shook my head when she reached for it. I didn't want to find her—and it—when I was ready to leave. I waited until she'd retreated to the kitchen, her eyes bouncing back to me several times, before I addressed my uncle.

"I'm worried about my father," I said.

"Where are your manners, nephew?" His words were soft, his tone too, but I heard the censure. "You don't even greet me?"

I stepped forward, handed him his morning paper, and kissed his cheeks. One, then the other. He smelled the same. Clean. Perfumed. The scent had not changed from my childhood, and it made my palms sweat. He'd stood too close once when I was performing, and my hands had slipped off the keys. I'd solved the problem by breathing through my mouth when he was around.

"I'm worried about my father," I repeated as I stepped back. "He doesn't look good. His color's bad. His hands shake. He's thinner than he was the last time I saw him."

Sal sighed, just a soft puff of air like I was a child babbling on and he found me tiresome and predictable. He turned toward his study, expecting me to follow.

"I'm having a drink. I've finished my breakfast, but I can ring for Carla if you're hungry."

"No, thank you."

"Ahh . . . there they are. Jack did teach you, then," he said over his shoulder.

I didn't want to go into Sal's study, but I did. He'd remodeled. The room still resembled an old English pub, complete with dim lighting and heavy wood paneling, but the desk was different. The chairs too.

The walls that weren't covered in oak had been painted an Irish green, the wood floor covered in plush gold carpeting. Better to muffle the sound, I supposed. The bloody rug was gone. But it had been gone for a long time. The heavy, red curtains had been replaced with drapes that matched the carpet; I wondered if they would still hide an eleven-year-old boy.

Sal drew them back, letting the gray November morning pour across his desk. The cushioned window seats had been reupholstered in a dark leather, and the curtains no longer pooled into them. Once, I'd stood on the seat just right of Sal's desk, my heels and my palms to the glass, like I was standing on a ledge, hugging the cliff face. The curtains had shielded me entirely then. It'd been the best hiding spot in the house.

Sal poured himself a glass of brandy, offered me one, and when I refused again, sat in his big chair and folded one leg over the other. The chair matched the upholstered window seats, and it probably cost double what Pop paid for last month's mortgage.

"Sit, Benito," he insisted.

I did, still holding my hat. My gaze caught on the pictures hung between the tall windows. Some of those were new too, but some of them had been there before. The picture of my mother was the same. Pop had one just like it at home.

Sal had pictures with everyone, a wall full of New York's finest. Businessmen. Entertainers. Athletes. Politicians. Mayor La Guardia and Mayor Wagner, Frank Sinatra, Dean Martin, Marilyn Monroe. He had a picture with Kennedy and one with Nixon too. Those were new. Sal didn't have a political side. He played all sides against the middle.

And there she was.

Maude Alexander, her hand on her hip, a slight smile on her lips. I wondered if the picture had been in this room all along, if I'd failed to notice it back then because I hadn't known who she was. She wasn't touching Sal, and instead of looking at the camera, he was looking down at her, his arms folded, one hand at his chin, the other folded across his chest. It was a pose I recognized well. It made him look like he was thinking deeply. It gave him the air of an art critic or a wine connoisseur. I'd seen him stand just that way before he stabbed a man to death in this very room.

We were playing hide-and-seek. We weren't supposed to be in the house at all, but there was nowhere to hide outside. All our hiding places had been used and reused. Aunt Theresa had forbidden us from hiding beneath the tables; one of the kids had upended a punch bowl the last time.

I thought I was so clever, hiding in that big bay window in Uncle Sal's study, until the weight of the curtains started to make me sweat. It was getting dark outside—soon it would be time for fireworks—but it was July, and the house was hot. If anyone had run past the window outside, they would have seen me standing against the glass. I turned around and pressed my face against the pane. The glass was cooler than my skin, and it felt so nice. It also afforded me a view of the side yard. I practiced the faces I could make if the other children spotted me. They would laugh and come in the house and find me. The study was reflected in the window as well, in the short distance between the left and right sides of the partially opened curtains. I would be able to see them coming.

Uncle Sal came instead. Uncle Sal, Pop, the two Tonys, and a guy I didn't know. They shut the door behind them, and I was trapped behind the curtain, watching their murky reflections in the glass.

"It's been too long, nephew. You are looking at my walls as though you've never seen them before," Sal said.

"The room has changed." I pulled my eyes from the pictures and the past and met his gaze.

"Yes. You have changed too. The boy is gone. When did that happen?"

"You look the same," I said, ignoring the question I could not answer. I had not been a boy for a very long time. "But my father doesn't. He looks sick."

"He wouldn't want you to be saying these things to me," Sal murmured. "Jack has his pride. Pride is a good thing in a man. In a woman too. It keeps us from letting ourselves go."

"Or it gets us killed," I said, my voice sharp. I wanted to go. The walls of this goddamn room were closing in.

"You think your father is dying?"

"He needs to go to the doctor, Uncle."

"You should be here more. You are his whole life. He misses you."

"He has his work . . . I have mine."

"Making your way in the world. That's good. Making a name for yourself." He paused and took a sip from his glass. "But you don't like your name, do you, Benito? You call yourself Benny Lament."

I didn't say anything. It was useless to protest. My father was Lomento. I was Lament, and I would be lying if I said I didn't prefer it.

"You know, everyone says you look just like your father. But I can see my sister in you too. Vitale blood runs in your veins, nephew. You should be proud," Sal said.

"I am very proud of my mother." It came out as more adversarial than I had intended, and Sal's eyes narrowed slightly.

"You conduct yourself well. You are very professional. Very sharp. No scandal. No trouble. But one day you will need your family, nephew. One day you will need me."

"I need you now. I need you to say something to my father."

"If I say this to him, it will hurt him. He will think he has let me down in some way. You would have me wound him like this?" Sal asked.

"I want him to go to a doctor."

"Then *you* should insist that he does," Sal said, his gaze level, his hands steepled. "I will not have him thinking I have lost faith in him."

"You've noticed it too," I pressed.

"He doesn't look good," Sal admitted. My heart began to pound and my stomach clenched. It was one thing to tell myself the truth. It was another thing to hear it from Sal.

A knock sounded on the study door, and Carla walked in without waiting for permission. She carried a tray filled with coffee and croissants and set it down on the corner of Sal's desk. She poured us each a cup and set them on saucers before us. Then she yawned prettily and smiled at me behind her hand like she was trying to send me a message.

"I'm tired, Sal. If you don't need me, I'm going to go to my room," she said, her words heavily accented, but her English much improved since my Havana days.

Sal waved her away, and she sashayed to the door. She turned to see if we were watching. We were, and she smiled in triumph as she closed the door behind her.

"I've been up all night too, yet I don't need to go to bed," Sal said. "She can't keep up with me. No one can keep up with me."

"Where's Aunt Theresa?" I asked.

"She's with Francesca. Francesca just had a baby. A daughter." Sal sipped at his coffee and winced. Carla's talents didn't include coffee making, apparently.

Sal had twin daughters—Francesca and Barbara—and no sons. They were nine years younger than me, and I didn't know them very well, but I liked them, which was curious, considering I didn't like my aunt or uncle very much. When they were younger, they'd looked like little ducklings waddling after their mother, who was as rounded and blonde as Sal was dark and sharp. Aunt Theresa had Marilyn Monroe hair and none of her style. She was always made up—nails done, makeup on—but she always looked garish and unnatural, like a zebra draped in hot-pink velvet or a baboon swathed in lace. I wrote a song about Aunt Theresa living in the zoo when I was twelve. It was funny but mean, and when I sang it for Pop, he wouldn't allow me to play my piano for a month. I'd never been able to get it out of my head, though. Some things are like that. Cruel and . . . accurate.

It didn't help that Theresa wasn't kind or brave or interesting. And she didn't like me. Or Pop. She pretended to, but I think she was jealous of Sal's affection for my dad. And I think she was afraid Sal would leave it all to me—his big, bloody empire—and her daughters, rightful heirs to his ill-gotten gain, would be dependent on her . . . or worse, their husbands. Theresa endured it all for them.

She was the daughter of Carlos Reina, a mob boss out of Chicago. Pop told me once that she was kept in a box her whole life and let out only long enough to move into another. It was a good match for Salvatore Vitale, but not so good for Theresa Reina. Sal strengthened his alliances and broadened his family. Theresa became the wife of a man just like her father, and a man completely uninterested in her.

"You be nice to her, Benito," my pop always said. "She's a sad woman. Lonely. Your mother always felt sorry for her. Theresa tried for about ten years to have those girls. They saved her life. Just like you and your mother saved mine."

Sal was careful about many things. He was careful about the men around him. The men he hired, the men he trusted, the words he said, and the deals he made. But he wasn't especially careful with Theresa, as evidenced by Carla's presence in the house.

"Carla's your new . . . maid?" I asked.

"Carla wants to be a star, but she's got a lot to learn. I have Terrence teaching her some songs. Maybe you could work with her too. Maybe write her a song. I know she likes you." Sal pinned me with his dark eyes as he handed me a cup of coffee. Black. I took it.

"Carla can't sing," I said.

"Neither can you, yet people still want your songs."

"They don't want me singing them."

"She doesn't have to be the best singer. Nobody at the club will be listening anyway. She can hold a tune and she can fill out a dress. She'll do fine."

"I'm sure she will." Sal would make sure of it. I wasn't sure what was in it for him, though, long term.

"It seems we've both taken some little birds under our wings," he added.

I was grateful I hadn't yet raised the cup to my lips. I would have dropped it. I stirred in a packet of sugar, feigning calm.

"Terrence said you went and heard Esther Mine. You and Jack," Sal murmured.

The fear for my father became fear of another sort. I simply held my uncle's gaze, saying nothing. I didn't know where to step, so I didn't step at all.

"And last night you went back again. You must see something you like."

I didn't ask him how he knew where we'd spent the evening. It would imply that we'd been hiding it from him.

"She can sing," I said. My voice was calm, pitched exactly like his.

"She is very good. I've heard her myself. I play cards at Shimmy's once in a while. It's a dump . . . but you learn a lot from people when you're playing poker."

"Pop mentioned that."

"And did he tell you her story?"

"He knew her father."

"Yes. And I knew her mother. A long time ago."

His eyes flicked to the picture on the wall. "Esther isn't as good as her mother was. Or as beautiful. But maybe it is simply my preference for one woman over another." He shrugged. "It ruins her for me. But I am not the musician you are. You haven't signed yet, I don't suppose?"

He said every word with his coffee in his hand, perfectly blasé about the whole conversation, but I did not miss his meaning or his intent.

He'd heard from his stream of spies that Esther Mine had asked me to manage her. He was now asking for me to admit it to him or remain silent on the subject, which would make him believe I was holding out on him—keeping things from him—and that was never a good idea.

"She doesn't have a manager yet. The oldest brother, Money Mine, considers himself the band's manager," I said.

"So you were not asked to manage the group?"

"I was. But I have signed nothing, promised nothing, pursued nothing." Yet.

"That's good. It would be a bad idea. You don't need the trouble. I may not be a musician, but I am a businessman. That group is not a good investment."

I sipped my coffee. It was too sweet, too hot, and the rim of the cup smelled like Carla's perfume, like she'd rubbed it between her breasts to remind me of old times. I set the cup down and stood, grabbing my hat.

"Do you understand me, Benito?"

"I understand you, Uncle."

"I will find a way to talk to Jack. I will make him listen."

I nodded.

"He will do what I tell him."

I nodded again. I had to get out of Sal's house. I had to get out of this room.

I'd been trapped in Sal's study before.

I'd watched Sal kill a man where I now stood.

I'd watched the man bleed on the rug, gurgling at Pop's feet.

Pop stepped over the man and walked toward the window while the two Tonys began rolling the man up in the rug, quick and efficient, the way Nonna made cannoli. Pop's reflection grew larger as he neared, and his eyes widened in surprise. Then he yanked the drapes completely closed and the room was hidden from my view.

Sal followed me from his study, his hands in his pockets, and he stood at the front door as I walked to my car. He even waved before he closed the door, and I waved back. But I didn't back out right away. I felt sick. Maybe it was the coffee on my empty stomach. Maybe it was Pop. Maybe it was just Sal. I closed my eyes and breathed deeply.

"It's done. Forget about it. You aren't the only kid who's seen something they shouldn't. Eventually, we all see things we wish we hadn't."

I'd stayed hidden behind the curtains in that bay window for another hour, staring out into the growing darkness. When the fireworks began cracking in the distance, Pop had come back. Everyone else had gone to the pier. He'd opened the drapes, pulled me from the ledge, and carried me out of the house to his car. I couldn't have been easy to carry. I was a big kid, my limbs were stiff with terror, and I'd desperately needed to pee.

I must have babbled something about wetting myself, because Pop stopped about a mile from Sal's and helped me out again. I can't remember exactly where we were, only that when I started to go, my relief was so great that I began to cry. Pop stood back, giving me space to do both. A car honked as it whizzed by, and the blare loosened my tongue.

"Did Uncle Sal kill him?" I asked.

"Shh, Benny. Finish up there. Come on. We'll talk in the car."

"I saw his eyes. They were open. He was looking out the window. But he didn't see me. He didn't see me because he was dead. But you saw me. You closed the curtains . . . and you saw me."

"Yeah. I saw you." My father tugged me back toward the car and folded me into the front seat once more, but we didn't talk. We didn't talk until I was home in bed, my father sitting at my feet, his back slumped, his hands clasped.

"Did that man owe Sal money too?" I whispered, and my tears came again.

"Too?" My pop frowned.

"Like Gino."

"Ah. Like Gino. You still remember Gino," Pop muttered.

"Yeah. Was that guy like Gino?"

"No. Not exactly. But he wasn't a good guy."

"You said nobody's good."

"Some people are really bad."

"Like you and Sal?"

My father's face crumpled like the man in Sal's study. I thought for a moment he was going to cry too, but he cleared his throat and ran a hand over his mouth, straightening out his expression. "Even worse than me and Sal."

"Does Uncle Sal know I was there?"

"Nah. He doesn't know."

"Are you going to tell him?"

"No. I'm not going to tell him. I'm not gonna say a word about it. And you're not gonna say a word about it. It's done. Forget about it. You aren't the only kid who's seen something they shouldn't. Eventually, we all see things we wish we hadn't."

"Are you mad at me, Pop?"

"No," he whispered. "But you gotta promise me you won't hide like that again, Benny. Don't ever hide in places you ain't supposed to be."

I shifted into reverse, checked my rearview, and wiped the sweat from my forehead. I didn't really want to look at myself. I was a coward.

Don't ever hide in places you ain't supposed to be.

It was good advice.

Pop always had good advice. He'd always wanted what was best for me. Yet he'd introduced me to Esther Mine.

Still . . . I'd been warned. Back then and again today. I was treading where I was not supposed to be, and I would be wise to listen to my uncle. I flipped on the radio to drown out my thoughts.

"Hey wake up! Get up! We can start your day with a great big smile. Turn your radio on and stay awhile. Five seventy on your dial, when it's morning in New York." The jingle from WMCA greeted me cheerily, and Joe O'Brien followed behind, celebrating the arrival of Friday and the number-one song on *Billboard*'s Hot 100 for two weeks in a row.

"This one's from the Drifters, folks. It's called 'Save the Last Dance for Me.'"

The Drifters were with Atlantic Records. Atlantic was at the top of its game. My stomach twisted again. Pop said he was going to call Jerry Wexler and put in a word for Minefield. I flipped the radio back off. I was going to have to convince Pop to leave it alone.

~

He was asleep in his chair when I walked through the door at seven thirty. His feet were up on the footrest, his hands folded over his belly. He'd taken off his shoes, and his right sock had a hole in the toe. I pulled it from his foot and tossed it in the trash. He opened his eyes and looked at me blearily.

"Hey, kid."

"Go get in bed, Pop. You'll be more comfortable."

"I'd be more comfortable if I had two socks."

I yanked on the other sock and tossed that one too. "There's a bunch of socks in your top drawer. In your room. Where your bed is."

He rose, his feet curling against the cold floor. He was back twenty seconds later, his feet shoved into his slippers, his suit coat gone, and his sleeves rolled.

"Sit. I'll make you breakfast. You must be starving."

I sat down at the piano and stared at the keys, mentally rehearsing the songs from the night before. I could still hear them. Feel them. And no matter what happened with Minefield, I didn't want to forget them. I played softly, singing along, and stood to grab a composition book and a pencil from my things.

"Esther and the kid make it home okay?"

"Uh-huh." I didn't want to talk about Esther. It was enough that I couldn't get her voice out of my head.

"Took you long enough."

"Yeah. Well. I didn't know you were watching the clock, wearing holes in your socks waiting for me."

"Last night was something, wasn't it?"

I looked up from the keys. Pop was shaking his head, a spatula in his hand. "I don't think I've ever had more fun in my whole life." He blinked, his eyes growing wet. "You've got such a gift. I'm so proud of you. It just pours out of you. That music! Not just the piano. I've seen that. But the words. Where in the hell did you learn to do that, Benny?"

I stared at him. I didn't know what to say. I shook my head, shrugging, but his tearful pride washed over me, stinging my nose and flooding my throat.

"How does that feel, knowing you're right where you belong, every time you sit on that bench?" he asked.

"Ah, Pop." I couldn't see the keys anymore, and I wanted to wipe my eyes but didn't want him to see me cry. I blinked hard and played a furious scale, letting my fingers run away because I couldn't.

"That's exactly where you're supposed to be." He turned away and used the spatula in his hand to flip the eggs in the pan in front of him.

Don't ever hide in places you ain't supposed to be.

"And last night? I tell you what. You and Esther? That was magic. Watching you two doing exactly what you were put on earth to do. I'm just glad I got to see it. I wish old Bo coulda seen it too."

I didn't have the heart to tell him it wouldn't happen again.

The Barry Gray Show

WMCA Radio

Guest: Benny Lament

December 30, 1969

"Out of all the songs you've written for Minefield, what was your favorite? What song could you sing over and over again?" Barry Gray asks.

"Well, that's a hard one. You know I can't really sing, Mr. Gray," Benny Lament reminds him. "I sound like a hound dog with a cold."

Barry Gray chuckles. "Benny Lament says he can't sing, folks, but he has a dozen Top 40 singles where he's doing just that."

"Well . . . it isn't always about having the best voice. It's about being an original. That's more important than being the best vocalist."

"When you sing, you want people to know it's you. Is that what you mean?"

"Yeah. That's a big part of it. It's all in the delivery of the song and the song itself. At least it was before I met Esther Mine. Then it became about the singer too."

"You were determined to make her a star."

"No. Not at first. My father knew she would be, but I just wanted to write her a song. I'd never heard a voice like that."

"So how did you end up singing with her? You'd been a songwriter up to that point. A very successful one. But nobody outside industry circles knew your name. You were a behind-the-scenes guy. A piano man. You meet Esther Mine, you agree to work with her, and suddenly you're there on every track, even if it's just a voice in the background. It has become your gimmick. Minefield's gimmick. Why?"

7

No Shoes

I almost left town. I even booked a flight to Vegas. Sal had a new club in Sin City—Tre Vite—and I'd agreed to check out the house band he'd hired and maybe even play on opening weekend.

I almost left. But I didn't. I called Ahmet Ertegun at Atlantic Records instead. I got his secretary for two days, but I kept calling. I called for three days straight. I called thirty times. Pop might know Jerry Wexler, but I knew Ahmet, and Ahmet Ertegun was the one Esther needed to see. Studio time wasn't going to be enough; Minefield needed the backing of a label. I could take them to Detroit. Berry Gordy had something. He was just getting started, but he had a system, and his artists had a sound. Plus, they were all the same color. Berry would give Minefield a listen, and I knew he would make me a deal. I could talk to Jules at La Vita. Terrence too, just like Berry wanted, and get some of his artists booked. Everyone would win.

But I didn't want to go to Motown. It would feel like I was taking charge of the band, like I was signing on for the long haul, and it would take too long. I said I would see what I could do. So I would see what I could do. Then I was out.

I called Ahmet. "Benny Lament for Ahmet, please."

"I've given him the message, Mr. Lament," his secretary said, irritated by my persistence. "I've given him all the messages."

"I haven't heard from him. I'm going to keep calling until I do."

She sighed. "Please hold, Mr. Lament."

Ahmet came on the line about five minutes later. He was Turkish by descent, had grown up in Europe and Washington, DC, but he exuded New York. He was personable and energetic, and I'd never met someone who had a better ear or better instincts. He'd been trying to sign me to his label since 1949, when Atlantic Records was just getting its start, and he'd seen me playing at La Vita. I'd given him a few songs instead and played for his house band when he needed piano, and we'd been doing business ever since. He was a decent songwriter himself, but he was an even better judge of talent.

"Benny, you're driving my girl crazy. What's going on? This isn't your style. I usually have to call you," he said. "You got a song for me? I need something for Etta, and I haven't had time to write a note."

"There's someone you need to meet, Ahmet." I was sure he'd heard that a hundred times, if not more.

"You managing people now?"

"No. I'm still writing songs. And I have a few for you. But not tomorrow. Tomorrow I need you to meet someone."

"Tomorrow? I can't do it, Benny. I have half an hour at five o'clock on Tuesday. That's it. I'm booked to the teeth right now. Lots of great stuff happening."

I hadn't seen or talked to Esther Mine for a week. She was going to think I'd split. I almost had.

"I'll take it, Ahmet."

"You've got my attention, Lament. I'll be here. Five o'clock, Tuesday, Benny Lament." He shouted the information out like he needed his secretary to write it down, and the phone line went dead.

~

When Esther walked out of the big brick house with the wide shutters and the glossy gold door knocker and saw me waiting for her, she stiffened. Then she adjusted the strap of her bag, squared her shoulders, and walked down the steps toward me. I didn't know if it was hope or trepidation I saw in her face, but it echoed the same emotion that surged in my chest every time I saw her.

It was dark, but the home and the street were well lit. It was a nice neighborhood. Like Sal's. The people here were wealthy, and strangers were noticed. I'd worried that someone would call the police if I parked right in front of the house where Esther worked.

"Can you walk?" I called out, parroting what I said the night when I found her waiting for me at the Park Sheraton. She didn't have on her power shoes. She wore a pair of flat, ugly lace-up shoes like the nurses wore. She looked at her feet, and I wished I hadn't tried to be cute.

"I can walk. Are you frozen solid?" she replied, cautiously polite. It was cold enough out that my breath plumed in the air like I was having a cigarette. I wasn't. Esther said she didn't smoke, so I wouldn't either, at least not around her.

"I still have feeling in two of my fingers. I could play a mean 'Chopsticks,'" I joked.

"Why didn't you wait in your car?"

"It seemed like I was staking out the neighborhood."

"Lying in wait."

"Yeah. Something like that. And I stood out here because I was afraid I'd miss you."

"How did you know where to find me?"

"I called that number you gave me. Talked to Lee Otis. He told me."

"Why here?"

"You said I should come to you. I didn't know who I'd be dealing with if I knocked on your door."

A Negro woman in matching garb and the same sensible shoes exited the house behind Esther. She looked weathered and weary, and she was carrying a laundry bag almost as big as she was. When she noticed me she halted and gaped like she knew who I was and didn't like me. At all.

"Go on now," she said, stepping between us and shooing me away like I was a vagrant or a stray dog lifting my leg on her front steps.

"Benny, this is my mama, Gloria Mine. Mama, this is Benny Lament. He's a music producer and songwriter."

Gloria Mine didn't look reassured. She looked downright hostile . . . and maybe a little scared too. I tipped my hat in greeting. "Ma'am."

"You're the piano man?" she asked. She sounded almost panicked.

"You heard the boys and me singing his song. Remember? You said it was gonna be a hit." Esther's tone was almost cajoling. I offered to take the laundry bag, but Gloria Mine clutched the strap and frowned at me. Her eyes swung from Esther to me and back again. It was cold outside, and she and Esther wore coats, but their legs were bare above their ugly shoes.

"I'll take you home. We can talk on the way." I pointed in the direction she already seemed to be heading.

"Lord," Gloria Mine breathed, like she was praying for courage . . . or patience . . . or deliverance; I couldn't be sure which. She was unsettled by me, to say the least. "Come on, Esther. We'll miss our bus," she said, juggling the bag so she could grasp Esther's arm. Esther, stunned, let her pull her along for several steps.

"I'll take you home. My car's right there," I offered again.

"No, no, no. We'll take the bus," the older woman insisted.

"Mama, I need to talk to Mr. Lament. You can go on ahead or he can take us both home," Esther protested.

"We are not getting in that man's car, Esther," she insisted softly, but not softly enough. Maybe it was a color thing. Everyone I'd ever known was suspicious of everyone else. I understood her mistrust, but her reaction to me didn't feel like a general lack of trust. It seemed specific. I didn't try to reassure her. How could I? I had no idea what she was afraid of. My size? My color? My interest in Esther? Maybe it was all three, but she stepped between us once more.

"Please just go on, Mr. Lament. I know who you are. I know who your daddy is too. I knew the moment I saw you. Just go on. We don't want any trouble."

"You know who I am?" I asked, flummoxed.

"You know his father?" Esther said, frowning.

"I know his k-kind," Gloria Mine stammered. She grabbed Esther's arm again and began pulling.

"Mama. Go on ahead. I'll see you at home," Esther said. Whatever her "mama's" problem was with me, Esther didn't share it. I had a feeling it had something to do with Bo Johnson and my father. But that was none of my business, and I sure as hell wasn't going to start asking questions or offering up explanations when I didn't have any.

"No." Gloria Mine shook her head. "I won't leave you alone with him."

"I've been alone with him before, and I survived just fine," Esther retorted. "What has gotten into you?"

"I'll walk you both to the bus," I offered. "No problem. I just need a minute. We'll walk and talk."

Gloria nodded, reluctant, but she started walking, looking over her shoulder to make sure we were following.

"Shall we?" I asked, offering my arm. Esther rolled her eyes but didn't take it, and we trailed after the woman, widening the space slightly so she wouldn't hear.

"Goodness' sake. You'd think I was five years old," Esther said under her breath.

"She thinks she knows me."

"She knows your type."

"And what type is that, Baby Ruth?" My question was sharp; I used the nickname to soften it.

"You don't get to call me that," she muttered.

"Then you don't get to tell me what type of man I am."

She looked up at me, eyes searching, and then nodded. "Fair enough."

"I have an appointment for you. Tomorrow. Five o'clock at Atlantic Records. Can you do it?"

"Me? Or the band?" she asked, hesitant.

"Not the band. Just you," I said. I didn't want to deal with Money. Not until I knew if Ahmet was interested. And if Ahmet was interested, I could turn Esther and Money and the rest all over to him and be done with it.

"No. They have to come too." She was already shaking her head.

"I'm not trying to cut them out, Esther. But I have a half hour—that's all—with the main man at Atlantic tomorrow afternoon. If he likes you, maybe we'll get more. This isn't recording time, though he'll need to hear you sing."

"Sing . . . without the band."

"I'll play for you. We'll do a stripped-down version of the songs we worked on at Shimmy's . . . just so he can hear you and know what we've got."

"We?"

"Minefield."

"Not you?"

"I'm a songwriter. Minefield needs a label if you're going to get airtime. Atlantic's the best. This is a big opportunity. Take it."

Esther stopped walking. I stopped too. Her mother kept trudging along, not realizing we weren't following anymore.

"I said I'd do anything," she muttered.

"Yeah. You did," I said, wry. "And this will be much easier than what you offered. I promise."

She closed her eyes, lifting her face to the dark November sky like she was praying for guidance. Her lips were free of paint and her corkscrew curls were covered with a scarf, most likely to preserve them and keep them clean. Yet she was so damn pretty I had to look away.

"I clean that house back there. And that one"—she pointed—"and two on the next row. Mama and I wash clothes and tend children and scrub floors. And then at night I sing so that in twenty years I won't be where she is now. At this rate, I don't have much hope. So I'm going to trust you, Lament, that you aren't going to make me choose between my family and my future."

"Esther?" Gloria Mine had noticed the halt in our progress. The bus was coming.

"I'll pick you up tomorrow, right here, at four fifteen," I said, turning back toward my car. "I'm not making any promises. But bring your power shoes and leave the attitude."

"Don't let me down, Benny Lament," she called after me. Always the same threat.

"And Esther?"

"Yeah?"

"Ask your mother why she doesn't like me. Maybe you'll decide, when you hear what she has to say, that you don't like me either."

"I already know I don't like you," she shot back, but there was a smile in her voice.

"I think you do," I called, still walking.

"I don't," she sang. "I don't need any man."

"You do," I sang back.

"I don't," she belted, and I heard the bus lumbering to a stop, brakes squealing, drowning me out. She got the last word in, but I liked her too, and she knew it.

~

Esther was waiting at the stop, just as I'd instructed, but she wore the same tired shoes and her legs were still bare to the cold beneath her gray uniform skirt. When I pulled up she jumped in the back seat instead of climbing in beside me.

"What are you doing?" I frowned, turning in my seat. I didn't want to be the chauffeur.

"My mama didn't want me to go. She said she wouldn't cover for me. So I don't know if I'll have a job tomorrow.

"I couldn't change at work. I had to lie to my employer and lie to mama just so I could leave early. If I told Mama, she would tell Money. Plus, she doesn't like you. It was easier to lie. So you keep your eyes forward, and I'll do my best to make myself presentable."

I did as I was told and pulled away from the curb. It was rush hour, and we had to get to Atlantic at Sixtieth and Broadway in forty-five minutes.

"I don't know what Ahmet will want to hear. But I think you should sing 'I Don't Need Any Man.' I'll play and do the echo on the chorus. It shows off your voice and your personality, and if he likes the song, it'll be an easier sell for the band."

Esther didn't answer. She was too busy fighting with her clothes, muttering and mumbling to herself, bemoaning the wrinkles and the run in her hose.

"Does that sound like a plan?" I pressed, raising my voice over her private conversation.

"What?"

"Singing 'I Don't Need Any Man.'"

"I have a huge run in these." She shook her wadded-up nylons like they'd betrayed her.

"Don't wear hose," I offered, turning my rearview mirror so it wouldn't inadvertently show me something I shouldn't see.

"I don't need fashion advice from you, mister," she snapped. She was nervous. Frazzled. I could hear it in her voice.

"Esther, you could wear that gray uniform and those ugly shoes, and it wouldn't matter. As soon as you open your mouth, it's over."

"I told you . . . people don't like me. It's usually over *before* I open my mouth." She tossed her uniform over the seat and it slid into my lap, discarded. I tossed it back.

"Red or yellow?" she asked. I didn't remind her that she'd just told me she didn't want my advice.

"Red."

"Yellow it is," she muttered. "It's less wrinkled too."

"What's not to like?" I said, sarcasm dripping from my words. I was teasing her, but she smacked the back of my head like I was Lee Otis falling asleep on the job.

"No, no, no, no," she began to chant. "Oh no."

"What?" I groaned. I was trying to drive and she was damn distracting.

"I forgot my shoes. I forgot my shoes!" she wailed.

I laid on my horn and the car to my left let me slide in front of him.

"We have to go back," she said. "I forgot my shoes."

"Back? Back where?" I grumbled, fixing my mirror so I could meet her gaze. She was wearing a pale pink slip and the saddest expression I'd ever seen.

"You have to take me home."

"Esther, I take you home, and this appointment doesn't happen."

"I forgot my shoes," she whispered. "I set them out . . . and forgot to put them in the bag."

"Shoes don't make the woman."

"That's easy for you to say. You're tall. And you aren't a woman. You aren't a Negro woman!"

"True. But I also can't sing like you. You're there to sing. And you can sing in ugly shoes."

"You want me to wear those shoes with this dress?" She held the yellow dress up to her chin, incredulous. "Have you lost your mind, Benny Lament?"

I laughed and barely missed getting hit as I sped through the intersection.

"Then wear the uniform. At least then the shoes will make sense."

"No." She shook her head and squared her shoulders. "No. I would rather go barefoot than audition for Atlantic Records in that damn uniform and those shoes."

"Barefoot it is," I said.

"I can't believe this is happening," she moaned, but she ducked back behind the seat again, and when she cursed with a string of words that would have sounded silly if they weren't said with such venom, I bit my cheek so I wouldn't laugh again.

"You talkin' to me?" I asked.

"You're not helping, Benny."

I circled the block and whooped when a car pulled away from the curb right in front of me. I slid into the space, threw the car into park, and checked my watch. We still had twenty minutes.

"Ready?" I asked.

"No! I'm not ready. Give me five minutes."

Esther's head shot up again, her yellow dress in place, her hair rumpled. She began digging in her bottomless bag and pulled out a lipstick and a compact. She repeated her string of curses when she saw her reflection. She was entertaining, no doubt about it, and now that I wasn't driving, I could watch her.

"Do you remember the words?" I asked. "I don't need another sweater, Mother. I don't need a fancy hat."

"Just sing them while I finish," she demanded. Licking her fingers, she smoothed one coil at a time, taming the frizzy flyaways and reshaping her shining cap of curls.

"You don't need a pair of high heels, Esther, you don't need a pair of hose," I sang.

"You're going to mess me up," she warned. She dabbed a little powder on her nose and slicked her lips in red. Then she snapped her compact closed and met my gaze.

"I'm ready." She didn't sound ready. She sounded terrified.

"No shoes?"

"No shoes."

"Wear them until we get inside. It's cold, and those sidewalks are filthy."

She nodded, but when I came around to open her door, she was contemplating her still bare toes. She had pretty feet.

"People are gonna laugh," she said.

"No, they won't. I'll hold your hand."

"How will that help?"

"It'll give people something else to look at."

She wrinkled her nose, doubtful, but she shoved her feet in the ugly black shoes, pulled her coat over the sunny dress, and slid her hand into mine.

"Let's go, Benny Lament."

~

When we walked into Atlantic Records, the girl at the desk greeted me and waved me through. "Mr. Ertegun said to go on back, Mr. Lament. He's getting ready for a recording session with Mr. Charles, but you know the way." She didn't even glance at Esther's feet. She was too busy taking note of our clasped hands. It was human nature. People focused on what they found most fascinating.

The studio was buzzing, and I spotted Ahmet in the control room, headphones around his neck, gesturing wildly about something. When he spotted me, he waved and took off the set, walking toward me with a big smile on his face and his hands outstretched.

"Benny. Good to see you." He patted my shoulders, but his eyes behind his round, black-rimmed glasses were on Esther. I didn't think Ahmet was forty yet, but he was completely bald on top; the fringe of dark hair around his ears and circling the dome was all he had left. He looked like a guy you'd find in a lab or maybe at NASA. He was all teeth and eyes and energy, but when he smiled at Esther, deep dimples softened his face.

"Ahmet Ertegun, this is Esther Mine. She sings with a group called Minefield."

"Okay. Okay. Hello, Esther. Can I call you Esther?"

Esther nodded. She'd abandoned the black shoes in the reception area, but she still clung to my hand.

"Where's the rest of the band?" Ahmet asked.

Esther frowned as though I'd just been caught in a whopper.

"You said you had a half an hour, Ahmet," I reminded him. "I didn't think we had time for a full audition. But Esther is the band . . . if you like her, the band is just gravy."

"Ray will be here soon, Benny. He's recording tonight, so you can help us get some levels on the piano. Esther can sing. We'll kill two birds with one stone."

"Ray?" Esther whispered.

"Ahmet works with Ray Charles," I said. "Maybe you'll get to meet him. He's amazing."

Esther swayed, and I tightened my hand. "I'm gonna be sick," Esther said, her lips barely moving, her jaw clenched.

"Come on in here," Ahmet insisted, motioning toward the huge Steinway that was already arranged front and center. The top was open, the bench facing the window so the sound man and the artist were facing each other. Pegboard dividers were being carried out to line the walls. The holes in the partitions helped to absorb the sound so it didn't ping off the solid surfaces.

"Benny. You know the drill. Piano's already mic'd," Ahmet said. "Esther, just stand right here." He walked to a standing microphone and adjusted the height downward, instructing a tech to run a cord. "That's Tom Dowd in the booth. Jerry Wexler too. You know Jerry, Benny. That's where I'll be too. Let's hear what you got."

"I've never recorded before," Esther moaned under her breath.

"Just sing, Esther. That's all you gotta do," I murmured. I let go of her hand and urged her toward the mic. She looked like she was being pushed toward the edge of a cliff, and I reassured her again. "You can sing. You know how to do that. That's all this is."

Ahmet was already in the booth, and he pulled his headset back over his ears and spoke into the mic.

"Whenever you're ready."

I walked to the piano and slid home.

"This one's just to get the sound right. They'll be listening to the piano more than anything. If Ray's coming, that's where their focus is," I reassured Esther.

I needed her to blow them away, but telling her that wouldn't help.

Esther pulled a crumpled sheet from her pocket and smoothed it out.

"What's that?"

"It's all the words to the new songs. I was afraid I'd forget. I've sung with you one time, Benny Lament. I haven't practiced," Esther snapped. She'd pulled on her anger like a cloak.

"Do you want to sing something else? We can do whatever you want," I said.

She shook her head. "We're trying to sell Minefield. I can't sell Minefield if I sing someone else's song," she said, her jaw tight. "I'll sing 'Any Man.'"

I let my fingers rove, watching Ahmet and Tom work the soundboard on the other side of the glass as I played. Esther stared down at the paper in her hands.

Ahmet's voice came through the speakers. "We're just trying to get levels. Just sing a verse so I can sort it out. I'll stop you if I need to."

I played the intro to "I Don't Need Any Man," and Esther started to sing. Ahmet stopped her at once. A tech moved in and turned the mic so the dead side was facing me and the piano.

"Now step a little closer to the mic, Esther, so Benny won't drown you out. And drop the paper. I can hear it rustling." Esther frowned at the men behind the glass, but she inched forward. She was so straight and wooden that it was a miracle she could release any sound at all. She looked like a little toy soldier, brightly painted but completely expressionless and stiff. Her only movement was the rattling of the paper in her hand. She opened her fingers and released it, letting it flutter to the ground.

I played through the first verse, but Esther didn't sing.

"Sounds good, Benny. Let's pull Esther in," Ahmet suggested, as if Esther's failure to sing was just a miscommunication.

Esther was rigid at the mic, a statue without a pose.

"From the top, Baby Ruth," I urged.

I played the intro again, but Esther didn't come in.

"Just sing a few lines, Esther. So we can make sure we got you," Ahmet said. He didn't sound impatient, but I knew our time—and his interest—was ebbing.

Esther didn't even nod. She just started to sing, and they weren't the right words. I followed her as she sang a jumbled version of the first verse, but I halted before the chorus.

"How's that sound, Ahmet?" I asked, trying to cover for her. "Loud enough?"

"Uh. Lean in a little, Esther," Ahmet said. She didn't move.

"What if I play it down once. Just the piano?" I offered.

"Uh, yeah. Yeah. Let's do that," Ahmet said. "Let's hear it from the top. Just piano. We'll lay down a track."

I played "I Don't Need Any Man" like a man pleading for parole. I played the hell out of that song, hearing Esther's voice in my head so I could keep the tempo where I knew she would need it. I hoped she was following along, practicing in her head, but when I was finished and it was time for Esther to add her voice, she sounded like she'd already given up. We sang it down once, and she got all the words right, but it wasn't Esther. It wasn't even particularly good.

"What's this one called, Benny?" Ahmet asked, trying to be polite. "I like it. It's got a little Jerry Lee Lewis and 'Come to Jesus' all rolled into one. Ray's gonna like that sound."

"It's called 'I Don't Need Any Man.' Let's put the frosting on, shall we, Baby Ruth? Sing it one more time from the top, and sing it like you mean it."

"Stop calling me Baby Ruth," Esther hissed, and her spit gave me an idea.

I eased around the mics and stood. "Give me a second," I told her. "I'll be right back."

Ahmet stepped out of the booth and followed me into the hallway.

"She's a beautiful girl, Benny," Ahmet began, before I could even speak. "And I can hear that there's a voice there, even beneath the nerves. But I hate her guts."

"What?"

Ahmet sighed. "I don't hate her guts. I don't know her. But my initial reaction to her is . . . no."

"Why?"

"She's gorgeous."

"You said that."

He sighed again. "She's prickly as hell. I don't . . . I don't *like* her. And she's not ready. It's that simple."

"That's part of her charm," I said.

Ahmet laughed. "To each his own, but I'm not buying what she's selling."

I sighed. "What do you think of the song?"

"I love the song, and I haven't even heard most of the words," he said, enthusiastic. "I want it."

"You can't have it. It's hers. And I'm gonna show you why. Let me try one more thing."

"Ray will be here any minute," he protested.

"I'm going to move her next to me on the piano."

"The sound won't be as good. We'll get bleed," he argued.

"This song needs a little blood," I said, and Ahmet laughed.

"All right." Ahmet shrugged. "But I don't think I'll change my mind."

I walked back into the room, picked up Esther's mic, and positioned it just right of center above the piano bench. I sat down and sang several bars, accompanying myself, until Tom gave me a thumbs-up. Esther watched, still standing where she'd been positioned forty-five minutes before. I could tell by her expression that she thought it was over. Her mic had been taken. I stood, walked to her side, took her by the hand, and slid back onto the bench, pulling her down beside me. I made myself comfortable next to her, purposely taking up all but the very edge of the bench. Her skirts billowed around my right leg, and she gave a little shove with her hips.

"You're crowding me, Benny," she whispered.

"Talk into the mic," I said. "Nice and loud."

"You're crowding me, Benny Lament," she said, right into the mic.

"You don't need all that space," I said, tucking my face next to hers, like we were singing together.

"Move over."

"We're going to sing this one more time, and then we're done. Sing it like you did on Thursday, when you were mad at me."

"I'm still mad at you."

"Good. This song needs some fire. But right now, you sound scared. That won't do."

"We're going to sing it like this?" she asked. "Sitting down?"

"I always sing sitting down," I said.

"At least give me room to breathe!"

"No."

"You two ready?" Ahmet asked. His eyes behind his big glasses were wide, and the black fringe around his ears was messy from pulling his headphones on and off. He was grinning.

"Ready," I said.

Esther jabbed her sharp little elbow into my side, but I didn't budge. I was so close my breath stirred her hair when I turned my head. I began to play, crowding her further.

She pinched my upper arm, hard.

"Ouch. Are you gonna sing?"

"I don't need another sweater, Mother," she snapped, her voice cutting and clear, no hesitation, no doubt. She sang the first verse like she'd had enough. Like she was through with me and all men. And she nailed it.

I bit my lip so I wouldn't laugh when she growled out the chorus. I even sang the echoes—"She don't! She don't!"—even though I knew they'd need to be recorded again. This wasn't about getting a perfect take. This was about introducing Ahmet to Esther Mine.

By the time she reached the end, Ahmet was all smiles and upraised fists.

"Holy cow! That was amazing. That was fire. Son of a gun," he said, his laughter echoing through the tinny speaker. "The back-and-forth was perfect. Your voice works with Esther's, Benny. Especially when you're fighting."

"We weren't fighting," I said into the mic.

"We were too," Esther piped up, and the men in the control room all laughed. Esther didn't laugh, but her tension was gone. She relaxed against me for a millisecond before elbowing me once more for good measure.

"Now, move over," she insisted.

"Well done, Baby Ruth," I said. Then I rose, giving her some space.

The Barry Gray Show

WMCA Radio

Guest: Benny Lament

December 30, 1969

"So you sang with Esther Mine in an effort to distract her from her nerves?" Barry Gray asks Benny Lament, incredulous.

"I knew what she was capable of, and I was scared to death she wasn't going to get another shot at Atlantic," Benny answers. "I really wasn't thinking about anything else, though Money, Esther's oldest brother, was sure it was a calculated takeover."

"We really should mention the members of the band. Money Mine was on guitar. Alvin Mine was your bassist, and Lee Otis Mine, percussion."

"That's right. Lee Otis was only sixteen when I met him. He was still in school, trying desperately to finish, and the gigs made it hard. The gigs were hard on all of them. They needed a break, and I was trying to get them one. But when they found out Esther and I recorded 'Any Man' without them, Money wanted to kill me."

"Meeting Ray Charles that night turned out to be a huge break for Minefield. For all of you. He invited you to do some dates with him. You were there in March of 1961 when he pulled out of a show in Augusta, Georgia, because it was a segregated venue."

"Most musicians just want to play. They don't want trouble. They aren't picky. They just want to work. And Ray Charles couldn't see his crowds. It didn't make any difference to him how the crowd was configured. But something happens when everyone starts making a stand. The more folks that do it, the easier it gets for others to follow. A wave was starting to build, and Ray Charles was part of that wave. We were going to open for him at that show and play for thirty minutes. But when Ray pulled out, he told the venue—who sued him for breach of contract—that we would still perform. We ended up playing for ninety minutes. White kids on the dance floor, black kids in the balcony—"

"—but the first black-and-white duo on a segregated stage," Barry Gray finishes. "It made national news."

"It did. And it wasn't the first time."

"We'll tackle that topic next, but first. You're going to love this, folks," Barry Gray says. "We have a copy of that very first track. This is Benny Lament and Esther Mine auditioning for Atlantic Records in November of 1960. Listen to this."

"At least give me room to breathe!"

"No."

"You two ready?"

"Ready."

"Ouch. Are you gonna sing?"

8

Baby Ruth

"I want to sign you both," Ahmet said without preamble. Esther was still sitting on the piano bench in the studio, her hands in her lap, her bare toes curling against the floor. Ahmet had wanted to talk to me alone, and I was braced for a soft letdown. I was already planning to cajole him into giving me a discount on some future studio time. The band could record the songs I'd written, and they'd have something to shop to other labels or local radio stations.

"What?" I gasped.

"I want to sign you both," Ahmet repeated, beaming. "I've never seen a duo like you two. It could work. Not only could it work . . . it could be huge. As soon as you started arguing, it was like a lightbulb went off in my head. You're right, Benny. She's got a helluva voice. But it's the contrast—big and small, black and white, male and female, hard and easy—"

"You callin' me easy, Ahmet?" I said, smiling, but there was ice in my veins.

"Nah. Easy's wrong, but you know what I mean. You're cajoling, she's cutting, she's hot, you're cold. Or maybe you're hot, and she's cold." He shrugged. "Physically you look great together, but it's more than that. It's the sizzle and the slap." He was getting excited just talking about it.

"She's the voice," I insisted.

"And you're the music, Benny. Trust me."

I was so stunned, I just stared at him.

"It's almost a variety show. Comedy. Flirtation. Music. It's good. It's really good. And you aren't even trying. In fact, I think that's why it's so good. You aren't faking. It's real."

"No. No, Ahmet. I'm not a front man. I can't sing."

"You can. I've been telling you that for years."

"I don't want to sing."

"You don't want to sing because you don't sound like Nat King Cole. You sound like Benny Lament. You have your own sound. But you two together . . . you've got something."

"I didn't even sing. I teased her," I protested.

"And it worked. That song is a hit. I could release it right now—as is—and it would be huge. The tension is dynamite. Benny and Esther. You'll be the next . . . the next . . ." He snapped his fingers, trying to come up with a duo. "Bogie and Bacall or Ricky and Lucy."

"She has a band."

He shrugged. "So? Are they any good?"

"Yes. She's the star. But yeah, they're good."

"So they can back you two up. We'll call them the Laments." Ahmet clapped like he was on to something. "Esther and the Laments."

Oh, no, no, no. I could just hear Money Mine now. He would yell, and Alvin would laugh, and I would be saddled with a job I didn't want and attention I didn't need.

"Ahmet, no," I said, shaking my head. "No. That's not why I'm here. That's not what any of us want."

"Look, Benny. I don't know if she can do it without you. She isn't ready. So it's both of you . . . or neither of you. I'll sign you both right now. Together. Together, you're a no-brainer."

"Let us come back and bring the band. We have three songs. I'll pay for the session," I pleaded. "This song is better with the band. And wait till you hear Esther sing 'Beware.'"

Ahmet sighed and threw up his hands. "You're crazy. I don't understand you at all. But okay. Okay. Book a day with the band. I'll give it a listen. But trust me on this, Lament. You're pushing the wrong cart."

We were still hashing it out when Ray Charles and his entourage entered the building, and we went back into the studio, our negotiations tabled in the frenzy of the big arrival. Ahmet introduced me, but I beckoned to Esther as I shook his hand.

"Mr. Charles, I want to introduce you to Esther Mine," I said. The crowd parted for her as I pulled her toward me, still clutching Mr. Charles's hand. "You're going to want to remember her name. Maybe you'll have some time tonight to hear her sing."

"Woo, now. I like that confidence." He dropped my hand and reached out, clearly expecting Esther to extend her hand and take his, the way I had done. When she did, both of his palms enclosed hers.

"Hello, Mr. Charles," she said. "I'm Esther Mine. It's a p-pleasure to m-meet you." She glared at me like it was my fault she was nervous.

Ray Charles cocked his head, bowing toward her voice, and he kept a hold on her tiny wrist. "Little bitty lady, great big voice," he murmured.

Esther beamed, he asked us to stick around, and we ended up against the wall in the sound booth for two hours, just listening to Ray do his thing. It was something to behold. Ahmet pulled us into the session between takes, and I played "Beware" for Esther, who sat beside me once more and sang the song with all the passion and power of a modern-day Carmen. When we were done, Ray told Ahmet if we weren't going to sing that song, he wanted to. Ahmet had pulled me aside again, and I'd resisted his offer, insisting that he give Minefield a shot.

He'd agreed to scheduling the band for an eight-hour session at the end of the week. When Esther and I left it was after nine, and I bought us hotdogs from a street vendor. We devoured them and went back for more. Esther ate as many as I did, and that was saying something. She no longer seemed to care about the black nurse's shoes that she'd redonned when we left Atlantic, and she no longer needed me to hold her hand or invade her space. We walked to my car, side by side, our hands in our pockets and our bellies bursting. When I opened the passenger door, she slid into the front seat with a weighty sigh.

I hadn't told her what Ahmet said. Not all of it. Not the part about wanting to sign us both. I simply told her he'd liked the song, he'd liked her voice, and we were going back with the band on Saturday. She'd been thrilled.

"We'll have from eight to four," I said. "It's hard to sing that early, especially after working all night, but we'll take what we can get. You make sure your brothers are there, and I'll take care of the bill . . . if there is one. If Ahmet decides to offer you a place on his label, the time will most likely be covered by the contract. I'll negotiate a percentage with him on the songs." I was making shit up. Ahmet had said nothing like that, but we'd cross that bridge when we came to it. If I had to, I'd foot the bill for the session. I'd been planning to all along. It would ease my guilt when I split.

"I can't believe I met Ray Charles—and sang for him—and I wasn't even wearing my shoes." She started to laugh.

"He can't see, Baby Ruth. He had no idea you weren't wearing any shoes."

That caught her up short, the truth of my words shaking her momentarily, and then she laughed harder. "I wanted to slap you so hard, Benny Lament."

"I know." I started to laugh too.

"I wanted to slap you and break Mr. Ahmet's glasses and throw that microphone at the wall. But mostly I just wanted to get out of there."

"But you sang instead."

"Yes. Yes, I did. And I got to meet Mr. Ray Charles in my bare feet." She sighed, the sound a happy moan, and she closed her eyes like she wanted to relive it.

"Thank you," she added softly. She didn't open her eyes, and I wondered if it was easier for her that way.

"For what?"

"You didn't have to do any of this. I really don't know why you *are* doing it. You don't need me. That's perfectly clear. You got your own thing going." She paused for a moment, like she was gearing up to jump. "You don't need me. But I need you. I need you. So thank you."

"You're welcome," I said, ignoring the little voice that wanted to argue with her, the part of me that wanted to warn her that I wasn't sticking around, that I was out just as soon as I got her squared away.

I started the car and pulled out onto streets that weren't nearly as busy as they'd been hours before. Esther wasn't frantic or angry anymore either. She wasn't even laughing. She was contemplative and quiet, and I didn't know how to be with this Esther.

She began to nod and slump about five minutes later, and I realized with a start that she'd fallen asleep. All her starch was gone. Her stiff spine and her haughty chin had collapsed beneath her fatigue. I was afraid she would rap her nodding head against the dashboard, and when we stopped at a red light, I hooked her legs with my right arm and turned her body toward me, so her head and her knees rested against the seat. She looked about twelve years old.

I remembered the way to get her home, and I let her sleep until we pulled up in front of her yellow building on Striver's Row.

When I said her name she didn't even stir. I turned off the car and walked around to the passenger side. I gathered her things from the back seat—the uniform, the torn hose, the rejected red dress—and put them in her bag, and still she slept.

"Esther?" I shook her gently. It took me several more tries to rouse her, and when she finally opened her eyes, it took her a moment to fully register where she was.

"You're home."

"Did I fall asleep?" she gasped. "I never do that."

"Come on." I held her arm as she wobbled from the car. "Here's your bag. I'll wait here to make sure you get inside all right."

"I never do that," she repeated, her hands going to her hair. The laces of her black shoes had come undone, and I crouched to tie them, afraid she would trip, especially in her current state.

"Do you have your keys?" I said, standing once more. She was staring at me like I was crazy. She looked down at her feet and back at me like no one had ever tied her shoes before.

"I'm not drunk, Benny. I'm just tired, and yes. I have my keys," she said, but there was no bite in her tone. She climbed the steps like they were Mount Everest, but she made it to the top and unlocked the door.

"Good night, Benny," she said.

"Good night, Esther."

She paused, her hand on the door, and looked back at me. "You can call me Baby Ruth if you want to."

~

Esther had her brothers waiting, instruments in hand, outside Atlantic Records on Saturday morning, and she was wearing high-heeled lime-green pumps and a matching lime-green dress. Her lips were red and her smile came readily when I walked toward them, and I found myself grinning back like a fool. Money was staring at me like his guitar case held a tommy gun, and I was about to be sprayed.

"Esther told us what you did," he accused. "I don't know what your game is, man."

"We're trying to get a label, Money. Atlantic is the best. That's the goal. I'm not playing any games," I said, but his suspicions brought me back to earth and wiped the smile from my face.

Ahmet was in and out, and the session was handled by the engineer, Tom Dowd, and Pop's friend Jerry Wexler, who greeted me warmly. He didn't mention talking to Pop, but I knew he had. We listened back to "Any Man" and ended up adding instrumentation to it instead of starting fresh with the whole band. Money complained incessantly about how we'd recorded it without them, but Lee Otis shook his head, awed.

"That's perfect, just the way it is," he whispered.

Alvin agreed with Lee Otis, and we ended up adding a simple snare-and-cymbal jazz rhythm, a bass accent, and Money's guitar echoing the hook on the chorus. Then we moved on to "Beware."

"Beware" was heavy on vocals, and Tom had recorded the live session we'd done for Ray Charles. It was powerful, stripped and soulful, and when we tried to make it better, we lost the magic. We cleaned up some sections, added some bass, and then left it alone too, much to Money's dismay.

"This isn't Minefield! That's Benny and Esther," he grumbled. We recorded "Itty Bitty" with full instrumentation and minimal piano, but it was missing some of the sparkle of the other two.

"It's missing Benny," Alvin said. "He doesn't shine on this one."

"This one is Minefield's song," Money grumbled. "This one is us."

"You've got thirty minutes. Where do you want to spend them?" Ahmet asked, rejoining us at the end of the session. "I know Benny always has something cooking."

I had other songs. But they were all earmarked for other projects and other artists. The only other song that might work was the variation of "The Bomb Johnson" I'd toyed with a few times, and as much as I wanted to hear Esther sing it, I wasn't sure how it would be received. I had no idea how she felt about her father . . . or if she even knew he *was* her father.

"You need a signature song. Something that tells a story," Ahmet suggested, his face screwed up in concentration. "Like Billie Holiday . . ."

"Like Billie Holiday and 'Strange Fruit,'" I finished for him.

Ahmet just nodded, his hands steepled. "Devastating."

"You ever heard her sing it?" Money asked me, his voice cold.

"Yeah. I have. People would go to the Café Society just to hear her sing that song. It's not the kind of song that makes you a star. It's definitely not radio friendly. Nobody will play it. But . . ." I looked for the words to explain.

"It might not be the kind of song that makes you a star. It's the kind of song that makes you a legend," Ahmet supplied. "It's the kind of song people won't ever forget."

I nodded. That was it, exactly.

"I don't know, man. We need radio friendly. That song . . . that song just hurts," Alvin whispered. "That ain't us."

"I agree. You gotta earn a song like that," Money said.

"Maybe you need something a little less artistic and a little more rock and roll," Ahmet said.

"You ever heard the song about Bo Johnson?" I asked, going for it. I played the basic melody, holding my breath, avoiding Esther's eyes. I had a feeling about this song, and it was now or never. If it didn't go over well, no matter. But if anyone should sing it, Esther should. Minefield should.

"Is it yours?" Ahmet asked.

"Nah. It's never been recorded. It's a folk song, I guess. The kind of song that is sung and gets repeated, and nobody really knows where it came from or who started it."

"Bo Johnson? Bo Johnson . . . the boxer?" Esther asked, her brow furrowing.

"Yes. That Bo Johnson."

"What? He's Esther's daddy!" Alvin said, smiling. "Bo Johnson, best heavyweight champion in the whole world. There's a song about him?"

They were all looking at me, waiting, but no one seemed alarmed. If anything, they looked pleased.

"Yeah. Well . . . I knew that. About Esther."

"You did?" she asked, astonished.

"Yeah. My pop knew him. Way back . . . because . . . he was a boxer too." I shrugged. "He taught me this one. A long time ago."

I played it down, singing the chorus, thumping it out on the keys.

"You want Esther to sing a song about a fighter?" Ahmet asked.

"Why have I never heard that before?" Esther gasped. "Sing it again," she demanded.

I sang the lyrics, calling out the progression, and Ahmet just listened. Esther was scribbling everything down onto a sheet of paper.

"We'd need to write some verses," I said. "It's too simple as is. Just a chorus. But the narrative songs are big right now. And the contrast—" I looked at Ahmet. He was all about contrast. "The contrast of having a female voice telling the story. Especially when it's your . . . father's story . . . it could be something."

When Money nodded and Esther smiled, I felt a load lift off my chest. It was as if I'd confessed and been pardoned completely, with nothing more than a thump of the gavel. I don't know why I'd been so worried.

~

Ahmet called me Monday morning. As soon as I heard his voice, I knew he was out.

"We've got a problem, Benny," he said, not beating around the bush.

"We do?"

"I can't sign your girl. Or her band."

"Why? I thought you were in." I didn't argue with him about Esther being "my girl." We both knew who he was talking about. Minefield was my project. That was all he meant by it.

"I was. They're good. She's unbelievable."

"So what happened?"

"There's trouble. And I have too many artists depending on me and this company to go anywhere near it."

"What kind of trouble?" Sal's face flashed through my mind.

"You know where I come from, right, Benny?" Ahmet asked.

"Uh, Turkey?" I said, puzzled.

"That's right. I came to the US when I was twelve years old. I love this country. I love this city. I borrowed ten grand from my dentist to start Atlantic. Did you know that? I love what I do and the people I do it with. And I want to keep on doing it."

"I don't understand, Ahmet," I said, but he continued without pausing, like he hadn't heard, like he wanted out of the conversation as quickly as possible.

"I see that in you, Benny. You're like me. It's the music that drives you. It isn't the women or the fame or the money."

"Ahmet . . ."

"My father was a politician. An ambassador. Politics is an ugly business. It's better here, in the US. But not much better. I don't want anything to do with it, Lament. I'd cross a gangster before I'd cross a politician. Any day."

"What are you talking about, Ahmet?" I was genuinely confused. I had no doubt Ahmet knew my story. He'd known it for a long time, but he'd never said a word about it. Everybody was connected to something crooked in one way or another, whether they participated or not. Especially in New York.

"I was told to leave it alone. I wasn't given an explanation. I don't want one. But I'm out, Benny. I'm sorry. I truly wish you the best."

"What about our tracks?" I said.

"They belong to Atlantic Records. I didn't charge you for the time."

"I'll pay for the time! I need those cuts."

"They were pretty insistent about that part. They don't want her on the radio."

"Who is they, Ahmet?" I pressed.

He paused, but he didn't answer my question.

"I'm scared for you, kid. And if I were you, I'd walk. You've made some big inroads in this business. And you've done it with your talent. People will keep coming to you for songs. Keep your head down, and let this other stuff go."

"What other stuff? Ahmet, I need those tracks," I said. If we didn't have those tracks, Minefield had nothing. I couldn't walk away and leave them with nothing.

"I'm sorry, Benny. I truly am. I've got to go now. Don't be a stranger."

"Ahmet, wait. What happened? What is this all about?"

The drone of the dial tone in my ear told me Ahmet was gone, but I was too stunned to hang up. I stood there, the receiver to my ear, listening to the pulsing note. It was an F. The dial tone was an F. *F for Famiglia.*

I didn't know what to do. I considered calling Esther and immediately dismissed the idea. She was at work. And what would I tell her? *You know how you told me the gangsters decide who works and who doesn't in this town? Well, you were right about that. They don't want you on the radio. And there's not a damn thing I can do about it.*

But that wasn't what Ahmet had said. *I'd cross a gangster before I'd cross a politician, any day.* What the hell was that supposed to mean?

Pop and Sal were in Vegas. They'd left the day I'd started calling Ahmet, the day I'd thought about leaving too. Vegas was an "open town," which meant open territory for organized crime. Fair game. No boundaries, no family control. Sal's club Tre Vite, on Fremont Street, was opening soon.

Tre vite means "three lives."

Bo Johnson, Maude Alexander, and now Esther Mine. Three lives, all connected, all snuffed out because of their proximity to Sal.

I hadn't told Pop about my visit with Sal. He hadn't been to a doctor either, as far as I knew. I hadn't told him about Esther's experience at Atlantic or Saturday's successful recording session. I hadn't told him any of it, and now there was nothing to tell. I was filled with a useless rage about all the things I didn't know and couldn't do and couldn't seem to change. I slammed the phone down, grabbed my hat and my keys, and stormed down the stairs, determined to get my tracks and an explanation from Ahmet.

The Barry Gray Show

WMCA Radio

Guest: Benny Lament

December 30, 1969

"Your success seems to have happened so fast. Overnight. But that's always how it appears from the outside looking in. There were some very real obstacles," Barry Gray says.

"I was making a good living for a guy with no responsibilities. I had contacts. I had talent. I was thirty years old and doing exactly what I'd always wanted to do," Benny Lament explains.

"You didn't need Minefield."

"I didn't even want Minefield. And I didn't have the kind of money you needed to finance a career or launch a record label. I knew where to get it . . . but I didn't want to be owned."

"You needed backing within the industry."

"Minefield needed backing. But people were nervous."

"Why? Was it racism?"

"The guys at Atlantic were signing Negro artists right and left. Ahmet Ertegun and Jerry Wexler brought rhythm and blues into

the mainstream. Pop knew Jerry from the old neighborhood. They were good guys. It wasn't about race. It wasn't that."

"Then what was it?"

"Ahmet had a business to run, and someone made it very clear to him that Minefield wasn't a good . . . investment."

"You proved him wrong."

"Ahmet was the first one to see our potential as a duo. It wasn't Ahmet we had to prove ourselves to."

"Then who?"

"The world is full of powerful people who have their own agendas."

"Powerful people that didn't want a Negro woman and a white man singing on stage together?" Barry Gray asks.

Benny Lament sighs. "Let's just say . . . there was more to Esther's story than either of us knew."

9

ITTY BITTY

By the time I walked in the door to Atlantic Records, I'd rehearsed everything I was going to say, I'd planned my attack, and I'd done a full mental accounting of every dime I had. I was going to need it to pay for the studio time, the mastering, and the production of the tracks I couldn't leave without.

"He's gone, Mr. Lament," the secretary said when I asked to see Ahmet.

"I talked to him an hour ago."

"He must have called you before he left. He's not here, Mr. Lament." I stared at her, trying to gauge whether she was telling the truth. I hadn't made a great impression with my incessant calling, and I didn't think she liked me too much, but she didn't waver beneath my glower.

"Let me see Jerry," I demanded.

"He's not here either. But Mr. Ertegun said you might come by. I have something for you." She leaned down, and when she straightened, she had a small white box in her hands.

There was an envelope with my name on the top. I opened it, still standing at the secretary's desk. A single sheet of paper was inside—no letterhead, no date.

> *Benny,*
> *These are yours, no strings attached. Tom mastered them for you and made you some reference lacquers. I didn't want to discuss it on the phone. All I ask in return is that you keep Atlantic out of it.*
> *Best of luck,*
> *A*

Inside the box was a stack of ten-inch lacquer discs. No labels, no explanations. In black pen, someone had written *MINEFIELD / Masters*, the names of the songs, and my name on the plain white cardboard sleeves.

The secretary was watching me. "You'll want to get copies pressed, and there's a card in the box for that too. Connor doesn't do big orders, but he's quick and reliable. If you need," she said quietly.

I nodded numbly and left.

I didn't give myself time to think. I followed the address on the card to the vinyl press. It was a warehouse in Brooklyn, not too far from the docks on the Upper Bay. I checked the address twice and decided I was in the right place. It took me another ten minutes to find Connor. There was simply a vinyl record stuck to the outside door, but it was open, and Connor was inside. He was a wiry man in a dirty white undershirt, a pair of gloves on his hands and a cigarette in his mouth, but he nodded when I told him what I wanted.

"You got a reference copy?"

I nodded.

"Let's hear what you got there. Just to make sure it's your stuff. You don't know how many times people jack that up," he said around his cigarette. He had a hint of a brogue on his Brooklyn tongue, a combination I'd heard a lot of growing up.

I walked to the record player, which was perfectly pristine, unlike its owner, and turned it on, settling the needle into the track of the first reference lacquer. We listened all the way through, to everything in the box. Connor didn't stop moving; he fed his machines and ran his press as I stood there, hands in my pockets, considering my options. There were recordings of "Beware" and "I Don't Need Any Man" containing both the piano version and the version we'd layered with the rest of the band. "Itty Bitty" sounded better than I remembered, and the simple run-through of "The Bomb Johnson" was on the final master. I marked the white sleeves with the ID numbers stamped into the masters and placed them back into the box.

"That's some good shit," Connor said. "Sounds like Tom's work."

I didn't say anything. I'd been told to keep Atlantic out of it.

"What about your label?" Connor asked. I frowned at him. He walked to his counter and pushed a sheet of white circles toward me. "For the 45s. How do you want them labeled? Write them out. I'll make it look good, but I gotta know how you want it."

I ended up writing *LAMENT RECORDS presents* on the top and *MINEFIELD* on the bottom, with the name of the song written below that. I was making stuff up as I went along, but Lament Records felt right and it looked more official. And part of me just wanted to be contrary. I was putting my name on my act of rebellion.

I paid for a hundred discs to be pressed and packaged, with the band version of "I Don't Need Any Man" on the A side and "Beware" on the B side. "Itty Bitty" wasn't quite as strong as the other two, and "The Bomb Johnson" wasn't finished. I decided to wait on those. I didn't want to get ahead of myself. I was already pissing in the wind.

~

Terrence called me Thursday afternoon and asked if I would fill in for him at La Vita. Half the house band was sick with the flu, including Terrence, and he knew I could handle a few sets on my own.

"Chuck will still be there. He'll take care of sound. But you would be doing me and the whole crew a favor. The night off will go a long way to getting everyone on the mend. And I know you aren't hurting for business, but Thursday's crowd tends to be locals. Scott Muni from WABC has a reservation for nine. Never hurts to impress a disc jockey."

I told Terrence I would be there. It occurred to me that it was a perfect opportunity for Minefield to perform, but I pushed the thought away. Minefield already had a gig on Thursday nights. Plus word would get back to Sal, Terrence would kill me, and I might never play at La Vita again.

I'd left a message with Lee Otis for Esther to give me a call, but I hadn't heard from her. Either I'd just missed her or she hadn't called. There wasn't much I could tell her, and I thought maybe I could get the vinyls back—something tangible—before I talked to the band.

It was after eight o'clock, and I was nearing the end of a long set when Carla sashayed up and sat down beside me on the piano bench, a wall of perfume and pressure all down my right side. I'd been enjoying myself; I was essentially background music in the club. People were eating and visiting and a few couples were dancing. It was just me on the piano, low key and liberating, and she'd come out of nowhere and plunked herself down beside me.

She'd bumped me and made me miss the pocket, and though few in the audience would have heard the hesitation, I heard it. In music, rhythm is everything.

"Hi, Benny," she purred. She sounded like a Cuban Marilyn Monroe. It was an affect many women attempted, breathy and sugar sweet, but instead of making them sexy, it made them dull. Instead of being memorable, they all started resembling each other.

I shifted my hips and widened my elbows to create some space between us, some space to play.

"Not now," I muttered. My floor mic had been swiveled to the side where I could grab it if I needed to talk to the crowd, but I wasn't singing, and luckily, no one would hear us. Carla laid her head on my shoulder, and the waterfall of notes I needed to play fell harder and slower beneath her weight. She turned her lips into my neck, and I ground my teeth.

"You remembered my name when you saw me," she purred. "I thought you wouldn't remember me." Her hand, the one not holding her wineglass, slid up my right thigh.

I felt bad for her. I couldn't help it. She had always been hungry for attention, and I had no doubt she was lonely in New York, especially with Sal in Las Vegas. I was surprised she hadn't gone with him.

"Scram, Carla," I hissed. I didn't want to hurt the woman. I just needed her to get the hell off my bench. I hadn't been clear enough about my lack of interest, I guess. Now she was back, and she was throwing off *my* timing with her lolling head and long fingernails.

"I don't like this song," Carla pouted. "Play 'The Twist.' I want to dance."

"I don't play dance music," I lied.

"That's not what I hear. You can play everything."

I *could* play anything. I could also make a song last forever. Playing solo was freeing. I didn't have to think about anything but the music. Usually I lost myself in it. But not now. Now I needed to get rid of Carla. I riffed for a few more bars, bringing the song to a rather abrupt close. It'd been a short set, but I would make it up to the audience just as soon as I dispensed with Carla.

"Did you miss me?" she whispered in my ear as the audience, disengaged though half of them were, offered a smattering of applause.

"No, Carla. I didn't."

"That's mean," she whined.

"Do you like being lied to? I don't. So I'm not going to pretend I missed you."

I stood up and pulled her up beside me. She wobbled and wrapped her arms around my waist, and it was then that I saw Esther. She, Money, Alvin, and Lee Otis were being ushered to a table near the kitchen entrance. It was a table no one ever wanted, as there was a constant flow of traffic and a poor view of the floor and the stage. She was dressed in white, her sleeves capped and her skirt full, a dress about ten years out of date, but she'd paired it with high, red heels, red lips, and a red flower tucked behind her ear, and she managed to make it all work together. Money, Alvin, and Lee Otis wore the black suits I'd seen them perform in twice, but they wore red ties and pocket squares to pull the group together.

I frowned and looked at my watch. They were dressed to perform, that was obvious, and it was after eight o'clock. They should be at Shimmy's.

"Have dinner with me, Benny," Carla said, her arms still wrapped around me. Tito was hurrying toward me from the direction of the coat check.

"Benny, you got people asking for you. I had Jake seat them because I knew you were playing. I didn't know if they were your friends . . . or just using your name. They ain't been in here before, I don't think. They don't hardly look old enough to drink. But I thought maybe they were performers."

"I'll take care of them, Tito." I peeled Carla from my side and pushed her gently toward him. "Tito, this is Carla. Carla, this is Tito. Have you two met?"

Tito shook his head. He may not have met her, but I was pretty sure the entire staff knew the score. "Carla is Sal's friend, Tito. Her drinks are on the house. Her dinner too. But I don't want her getting anywhere near the stage when I'm playing again. Okay? Tell the Tonys or whoever is bouncing tonight. Keep her away from me and the stage."

Tito's eyes grew wide, and Carla frowned at me. I was being rude, but I was also being clear.

When I approached the table where the Mine family was sitting, Esther's eyes weren't on me, but on Carla, who had been seated at a table near the floor, her wineglass refilled and a menu placed in front of her.

The fifth chair at their table was empty, and I pulled it out and sat down, my back to the rest of the room.

"We weren't sure they served Negros in here," Money grumbled. "We had to tell them we were your friends."

"I sure *hope* they don't serve Negro in here," Alvin quipped. "I'm not big on eating Negro. Come to think of it, I've never eaten White Guy either. I've heard it tastes like chicken, though."

Lee Otis snickered, but immediately turned to me. "Can I have a Coke, Benny?"

"Absolutely. Whatever you want. La Vita's known for the *sfinciuni*. We'll order some of that too." Copacabana, the club owned by mob boss Frank Costello, served Chinese food. La Vita decided to embrace her Sicilian roots and served *sfinciuni*, *pizza siciliana*, all day, every day. You could order steak, seafood, or pasta too, but *sfinciuni* was the main attraction. That and alcohol. Always plenty of booze. I snagged a waitress and made the order, but Money, Alvin, and Esther shook their heads when I asked them what they were drinking.

Lee Otis said, "I don't think we're gonna be eating. We just lost our gig."

Alvin's smile slipped, and Money and Esther stared at me, sullen. I waved the waitress away.

"What is he talking about?" I asked.

"We lost the gig at Shimmy's," Esther said.

"Ed Shimley fired us," Money added.

The dread in my gut raised its burly head.

"Why?" I asked.

"He said it was time for a change, though he doesn't have anything booked. Ralph says it'll be jukebox only for the time being," Money said.

"We haven't missed a show in a year. Not one. We sang last Thursday even though it was Thanksgiving," Esther said.

"So we came here, looking for you, hoping you had a little good news from Atlantic," Alvin explained. "What kind of time frame are we looking at on those singles we recorded?"

"Ahmet's out. Atlantic's a no go," I said, ripping off the bandage nice and quick. It stung like hell, and it was just going to get worse.

Alvin, Money, and Esther stared at me in horror. Lee Otis took a long pull from the Coke the waitress sat down in front of him. For a moment no one spoke.

"So now what?" Alvin broke the stunned silence. "You got any Benny Magic up your sleeve?"

"Any gangster magic?" Money asked.

"What did Ahmet say?" Esther asked softly, and the other questions fell away in the face of that one. They all stared at me, waiting.

I didn't want to lie, and I didn't want to tell the truth. I didn't *know* the truth, not for sure. I decided to shoulder the blame. It was easier that way.

"It's my fault. Turns out the gangster thing isn't always a plus."

"I knew it!" Money threw his napkin on the table. "You're more trouble than you're worth."

"Can't you scare 'em, Benny?" Alvin pleaded.

"Scare Ahmet?" I shook my head. "He let me have the songs we recorded. Ahmet's a good guy. I'm having some 45s pressed as we speak. Two songs, A and B side. I'm going to make a visit to every station in the city and send a disc to the radio deejays in the biggest markets—I know quite a few—and I'm going to get us some airtime."

"Us?" Money hissed.

I was suddenly very tired of Money. "Yeah, Money. Us. I'm here too."

"You're here, but you ain't here. We're out of work. You aren't."

"It's not his fault we're out of work, Money," Esther said, but she looked defeated. Her back was still straight, but her expression was grim, and I had no idea if it was my fault or not. Sal told me to walk. I hadn't walked. Yet.

"Why can't we sing here? At La Vita? This is your family's joint, right? You could make that happen if you really wanted to," Money pressed.

"Ain't nobody playing now," Alvin added, hopeful.

The place was half full. It was a Thursday night. Not the busiest night of the week, and not the slowest. Terrence wasn't here. Sal wasn't even in town. Chuck would do whatever I told him. He could have the stage amped and mic'd in ten minutes. The dinner crowd would fill up the seats in the next hour. They would drink less and maybe dance a little more, but by midnight the place would clear out. My dread grew horns and a suicide wish. What the hell. What could anyone do after it was already done?

"You want to play? No sound check, no rehearsal?" I asked. Money talked big, but I saw his throat bob, and Alvin laughed like it was all a joke.

"He's callin' your bluff, Money," Alvin said.

"You won't get paid," I warned. "This is a free performance."

"We're not getting paid anyway. Maybe we'll get noticed," Esther said.

Barry Gray from WMCA was sitting in the corner booth with Scott Muni, a deejay from WABC who'd just made the switch from WMCA, and another man. Barry Gray didn't play the hits. He interviewed people; but it wouldn't hurt to impress him too.

"Are you going up there with us, Benny?" Esther asked. "Those are your songs. We can't do them without you."

"You heard him. He's here too," Alvin insisted.

"He doesn't have a red tie," Money protested.

Alvin sighed. "Now you're just being stupid, Money."

"He doesn't match," Lee Otis said.

"You think anyone in here gonna be thinking about that?" Alvin asked, incredulous. "They'll be thinking about color, all right, but they won't notice his tie. They'll be wondering how the white guy hooked up with us."

"Do you have your instruments?" I asked Money and Alvin.

"Yeah. In the coat check. We couldn't leave them at Shimmy's. We aren't ever going back there," Alvin answered.

"Piano's already mic'd, and Lee Otis can use the drum set that's up there. Give me fifteen minutes. Maybe twenty. I'll tell Chuck. He knows what the levels need to be. He does this every night. I'll introduce you to the crowd. We'll do the three songs we know, and you can do your regular set after that. I just need a key, and I can follow you wherever you go."

"Well, shit," Money whispered.

"Don't let me down, Benny Lament," Esther said, but there was no censure in her tone, just challenge. And I smiled.

"Don't let me down, Esther Mine."

~

Fifteen minutes later, I stood at the main microphone, the lights dimmed, the spotlight wide, Esther and the boys waiting to walk on. Chuck had done his thing.

"Welcome to La Vita, ladies and gentlemen. I'm Benny Lament. I'm not often the man at the microphone. I like to play. But I also like making music with my friends, and I have some new friends to introduce you to tonight. Please welcome to the stage, Esther Mine and Minefield."

I walked to the piano as Money, Alvin, and Lee Otis strode onto the stage and picked up their instruments. Esther took her place at the microphone I'd just abandoned, her white dress luminous beneath the lights, and for a moment she was alone. Then Chuck lifted the lights and I was in the circle with her.

We hadn't planned anything beyond basic song order, and for a moment we froze in the awkward space between entrance and performance. *Say hello,* I urged mentally. *Come on, Esther. Smile and say hello. It isn't enough to just sing. You have to perform.*

"Good evening. I'm Esther Mine, this is Money on guitar, Alvin on bass, and Lee Otis on drums. After tonight, I hope we'll be on a first-name basis," she said, her voice low and easy, and I breathed a sigh of relief.

"That's my girl," I said, sliding my fingers into position.

My voice ricocheted around the room.

There was a quick influx of breath, my own, Esther's, or the crowd's, I wasn't sure. For a moment I sat motionless. I didn't look at the crowd. Or at Esther. My eyes were trained on the keys.

My mic was on.

Chuck had mic'd me, just like I'd told him to, and I'd forgotten all about it.

"Where?" Esther said, shading her eyes and peering out into the silent crowd. "Where's your girl, Benny Lament? I'd like to meet her."

The crowd laughed.

I breathed. And then I began the opening bars of "Itty Bitty," slowed way, way down. It wasn't what we'd planned, but the lyrics were perfect for the segue, and since I'd stepped in it, now I had to fix it.

"She's always bossing me around," I sang into the mic, and I heard Money curse. They were waiting for their cue. "She's always telling me what to do. She's always standing in my way. She's always treading on my shoes."

"Who? Your girl?" Esther said, and I laughed out loud.

"Yeah, my girl," I shot back, and I kicked it up to double time. "Let's sing it from the top, shall we?" I said, and the boys didn't miss a beat. They swooped in, and Esther broke into "Itty Bitty" exactly the way we'd done it in the studio. The crowd was clapping, Esther was wiggling, and on the bridge I told the audience all about my itty-bitty girl with a great big mouth.

"I don't have a big mouth!" Esther folded her arms and stomped her high-heeled foot.

"Who says I'm talking about you?" I teased, and the crowd howled.

Money sidled in beside Esther and leaned into the mic.

"Don't worry, little sister. He's definitely talking about you."

Perfect.

One song rolled into another, and Esther and I bickered our way through ten songs, most of them songs I'd never played before. I was an accent, an exclamation point, but I'd jammed with enough musicians to follow along, and the performance was as natural—and as fun—as anything I'd ever done. Esther kept engaging me, keeping the shtick going, and the crowd ate it up. We didn't flirt, we fought, and Esther never strayed from the mic.

The set was a little scattered; Lee Otis lost his stick and had to lunge for it, Alvin forgot the second bridge on "I Don't Need Any Man," and Money looked like he wanted to slam the piano lid down on my head. But Esther sounded like a million bucks, and when the crowd wasn't dancing, they were smiling.

The Barry Gray Show

WMCA Radio

Guest: Benny Lament

December 30, 1969

"I can't believe that was your first performance!" Barry Gray marvels.

"That was it. Like most everything else with us, it wasn't planned. But it worked," Benny Lament says, laughter in his voice.

"I must tell our audience that I saw that performance at La Vita. It was early December, 1960. Esther Mine was wearing white. She looked like a little doll on that stage. I remember feeling nervous for her, thinking who is this? Then she opened her mouth and this huge sound came out. Her voice filled the place. I was dining with friends—Stanley Tunis from WRKO and Scott Muni, who'd just moved from WMCA to WABC—and we were all blown away," Barry Gray says.

"You three were a big reason we went on stage. We hadn't rehearsed together beyond a writing session and that first recording session at Atlantic, but you have to take chances sometimes to get noticed."

"I saw your performance, and I made an executive decision," Barry Gray says.

"You gave me a card when we walked off the stage and asked us to come on your show the very next night. If I remember right, it was a show about duos, which was why you didn't want the band."

"That's right. It was the ribbing you two gave each other that made your performance at La Vita so unique. I had quite a few local acts that night. Comedians and sportscasters and some Broadway actors and actresses. I'd prerecorded their segments, but you two had to go live."

"You worked us into the lineup. We were only supposed to introduce ourselves and do one song."

"And I gave you two. And you were fabulous. That appearance got your single in rotation from the Good Guys, and WMCA beat WABC to the punch. We had a little bit of a competition going."

"Scott Muni got 'I Don't Need Any Man' to number one on WABC."

"True. But we played it first, and we also had the live recording of 'The Bomb Johnson,' weeks before the single dropped." Barry Gray chuckles. "WMCA was also the first station in New York to broadcast a recording by the Beatles, but no one's keeping score."

"Of course not," Benny Lament retorts, his tone wry. "Minefield and the Beatles will be forever grateful, I'm sure."

"I'm counting on it," Barry Gray says. "Here it is, folks, the appearance that Benny Lament and Esther Mine made on *The Barry Gray Show* nine years ago."

10

The Bomb

We were at WMCA studios, located at the Sheraton-Atlantic at Thirty-Fourth and Broadway. It was midnight, Barry Gray was doing his show, and we hadn't been given any prep time or much instruction. We walked in, were shown to the recording studio, given a quick sound check, and told by Barry Gray that we were on in five. He was talking between segments, rolling commercials, and reading ads, and Esther and I watched him through the glass, waiting for our cue.

Esther was terrified. It was exactly like that first time at Atlantic. I could see it in her stillness, her fisted hands, the thrust of her chin, and the size of her eyes.

"Do you want to sit by me at the piano like we did for Ray?" I asked. Screw the sound check. We could make it work.

"No, I don't," she said, tone icy. "Though I noticed that's something you like to do."

"What?"

"I saw that woman sitting beside you at the piano last night when we walked into La Vita. She was very beautiful. Very drunk. But very beautiful. She had her head on your shoulder and her hand on your leg."

"That was Carla. And I didn't invite her to sit there."

Esther shrugged like it didn't matter to her, though it clearly did. "I'm fine right here," she said, voice cold.

"Are you sure?"

"Very sure," she said. She folded her arms and tapped her toe. She was dressed like we were going to sing to a live audience, with her heels, lipstick, and perfect curls. I didn't think she was actually mad at me; I think she was scared out of her pretty mind.

"Can you look at me, please?" I asked. She rolled her eyes, but she met my gaze. Yep. Terrified.

"What do you want, Esther?"

"I told you what I wanted on the night we met," she said. "I want you to make me a star."

"You say that's what you want, but you don't act like it. You act like you're mad at the world. And that's not gonna work."

"I got plenty reason to be mad."

"Reason or not, people can feel that. You think they're going to pay to have you glare at them or listen to you complain?"

"I'm not complaining."

"You're being difficult. Nobody gives a damn, Esther. They haven't walked in your shoes, and they're never going to. They're *your* shoes."

"I don't know what you want me to do."

"You want to make them give a damn? Then make them care about you."

"I can't. I told you, I can't."

"Yes, you can! You made me care."

"Well, then you're the first. How do you make the world care, Benny?"

"You tell them your story."

"Mr. Lament, Miss Mine, you're on in twenty seconds. I'll read the ad, say hello, and you take it away," Barry Gray said. "You'll have four minutes. I'll count you down and cut you off if you run long."

"Yes, sir," I said. Esther nodded.

"You're listening to Barry Gray on WMCA, and it's a cold one out tonight, folks. Here in Manhattan, it's a chilly twenty-five degrees at seventeen minutes past the hour. We've been talking to a collection of lively duos, mostly names you know and some you'd probably like to forget, but our next duo is new on the scene, so new they hardly call themselves a duo, but they fight like an old married couple. Please welcome Benny Lament on piano and songstress Esther Mine of Minefield, making their radio debut right here on WMCA. Tell us about yourselves, kids."

I didn't wait for Esther to speak up.

"Well, Mr. Gray, Esther Mine is the tiniest little woman you've ever seen. She wears high heels and bold colors to make you think she's bigger than she is, but the moment you hear her sing, you'll think she's the size of the Empire State Building." I played as I talked, my eyes on hers, willing her to follow my lead. I knew if I teased her a little, she'd remember who she was and what she could do. "I call her Baby Ruth."

"And I call him Big Ben," Esther shot back.

"Since when, Baby Ruth?"

"Since you're always droning on when you're supposed to be playing."

"Oh, that's good," I said.

"I might be small, but at least I know when to pipe down."

"Well, don't pipe down now. The folks want to hear that big voice."

"Don't tell me what to do."

"Someone needs to. Now sing." I was sweating, hoping Esther had followed the intro. We had four minutes until the hard break, and the song was three and a half. Barry Gray was spinning his finger, telling us to go, go, go. Then Esther was there, biting out the first line of the song as if we'd rehearsed it a thousand times.

I was the only echo on the chorus, but Barry Gray was smiling when we were done. He flashed five seconds with his open palm. He wanted us to fill the time.

"What did I tell you, folks. Little tiny lady, great big sound," I said.

"And there you go, chiming in again," Esther complained. "Ding, dong, ding, dong."

Gray was ready with the laugh track, and he waited half a second to let it ebb before he cut in.

"You heard 'em here first, folks. That was Benny Lament and Esther Mine from the group Minefield, live with 'I Don't Need Any Man.' Stay right there. We'll be back with more after a word from our sponsors."

The red light went off, and Barry Gray stepped out from behind his microphone.

"That was great," he said. "You two got more? I can squeeze three and a half minutes on the other side of the break."

Esther's eyes went wide. We didn't have anything else planned.

"Sure, we got more," I said. Barry Gray gave me a thumbs-up and stepped out of the room, leaving us alone with a ticking clock.

"Whatever you want to sing, Esther. We can sing it. Name a song. I'll follow you wherever you want to go," I coaxed. We weren't going to get another opportunity like this anytime soon. She thought about it for two seconds.

"I want to sing 'The Bomb Johnson,'" she said.

It was my turn to stammer and gape. "Anything but that," I said. "There's only a chorus."

"Nah. There's more. I wrote a whole song," she argued.

"You did?"

"I did. And I want to sing it right now. I want to tell my story. Just like you said." She was beaming, warming to her idea.

"Esther . . . this isn't the time or place."

"You write hits. Let's make this a hit."

"I don't write hits in twenty seconds on live radio. Let's do 'Beware.' You sing the hell out of that song."

"But this is going to be our signature song. Remember? This one . . . this is my song. If I don't sing it, who will?"

"You guys ready?" Barry Gray's assistant was blinking at us, a clipboard in his hands. "Our phone lines are full. People love the banter. Keep it up. We're back on in thirty seconds. Mr. Gray will bring you in."

"Benny, please. Let me tell his story."

We didn't have time to argue, and I knew that look. Esther wasn't asking.

"Sing me a line," I said, grim. I needed the key and a feel for her stylization.

"He was born in Harlem, and he ruled the streets," she sang softly. "He was the meanest man that you'll ever meet."

"Basic blues progression in A?" I was trying to piece it all together in my head.

"I don't know," she said, grinning. "Just follow me."

"Damn it, Esther," I hissed.

"Don't let me down, Benny Lament."

"And we're live in ten, nine, eight, seven . . . ," Barry Gray said.

I couldn't breathe. We'd switched places so thoroughly in the space of two minutes my head was reeling. Esther winked at me.

Barry Gray was talking, introducing us again.

"Are you two still fighting?" he asked. "Because I want to hear another song."

"What about a story, Mr. Gray? What if we did a story and a song?" Esther purred.

"I think that sounds wonderful, Esther. But what happened to Benny?" Barry asked. I guess I looked as panicked as I felt.

"Benny doesn't like it when he's not in charge. He's sulking right now. But I can make him play."

"I'll just bet you can," Barry said.

Esther sang the first line without me, her eyes on mine and her hands on her hips. By the end of the second line I was there, playing in the space, and she said, "That's it, Benny. You know the story."

"Tell me," I said, surrendering. "Tell the world, Baby Ruth." And she did.

"He never lost a fight, a champ in the ring. Then he met a girl who knocked him to his knees."

"Man, I know just how he feels," I groaned, and let my fingers dance for two measures before Esther broke into the chorus. "They call him the Bomb 'cause you never know when he'll go off."

"They call him the Bomb 'cause his swing makes the shingles blow off," I croaked, dropping the last note into the basement.

"They call him the Bomb 'cause he's big and loud," Esther wailed.

"They call him the Bomb 'cause he can level a crowd," I added.

"He's Bo 'the Bomb' Johnson, and you better watch out," we sang together.

~

Esther's smile was so wide she had to turn sideways to exit the building into Herald Square. She twirled the moment we walked through the big double doors, her frayed, red coat bunching up around her small shoulders. Her hat tumbled from her head, and I stooped to pick it up. The streets were empty, the sidewalks bare. It was 2:00 a.m. on a Saturday morning, but I was gripped with the sudden fear we wouldn't make it to the dawn. Maybe it was the adrenaline crash. It'd been a helluva week, and I just wanted to see Esther safely home.

"That was amazing, Benny. I want to do it again. We need to record it. The whole thing. That's a hit," Esther crowed up at the sky.

I nodded, numb. It *was* a hit. It was echoing in my head and my hands even now. I wanted to play it again. I wanted to find a piano and perfect it. Compose a horn section. Write a bridge. Tell Esther to sing it from the top.

I also wanted to hurl my body over Esther's and brace myself for the spray of bullets.

"What's wrong, Benny?" she said, touching my arm.

"I don't know if that was smart," I whispered, looking down into her upturned face.

"If what was smart?"

"Singing that song."

"Why? Didn't you like it? You said the best songs tell a story. I wanted to tell that one. And *you* were brilliant. You blow me away, Benny Lament. Like Bo 'the Bomb' Johnson. You can level a crowd. *We* can level a crowd. We are good together. We are great together! It's magic. I can't believe this is happening." She was flying high, smiling at me like I'd managed to give her the moon, but I was afraid.

Snowflakes were starting to fall, soft and fat, lazy, like they knew as soon as they touched the ground the journey would end and life would be over.

"It's snowing!"

"You were born and raised here, Baby Ruth. Don't tell me that makes you happy." Winter was miserable in New York. It was pretty for about five seconds. Then it was just cold, wet, and filthy.

"It makes me happy right now," she said, smiling. "Right now, it's perfect." The bits of white clung to her hair and ruddy coat, and she put her hat back on her head to protect her curls.

"Come on. Let's go to the car," I urged gently.

"I don't want to go home. I want to celebrate. Let's go dancing," she said. "I haven't been dancing for so long. Not since we started at Shimmy's."

"Dancing? Where? It's 2:00 a.m."

"It's Friday night, Benny Lament. Don't tell me the piano man from La Vita doesn't know where to go dancing on a Friday night."

"Well, you don't know me very well." My tone was mild, but she studied me for a moment.

"I think I'm starting to," she countered quietly.

The truth was, I didn't want to go home either. Pop would probably be home. He and Sal had had a late flight, but unless they decided to go to La Vita when they landed, they would be home. I'd wanted to tell him about the Barry Gray invitation; Pop knew Barry. Barry had spent a couple years in Miami, broadcasting live from a nightclub Sal had a stake in, and he and Pop had always been friendly. Everyone was connected.

The thought made me nervous all over again.

I still had some records, the vinyl slick and gleaming, with my makeshift label affixed, sitting in the back of my car. Connor had come through. I'd picked them up that very afternoon, just in time, and I'd told him I wanted two hundred more. It wasn't enough, especially if we wanted to distribute them to the record stores, but that wasn't the goal. I had to get them to the disc jockeys. I had to create a buzz before I went all in.

I'd spent two hours sitting in my car at the post office, addressing them to every station in the biggest markets, just like I'd promised, and I mailed them out. I posted one to Berry Gordy at Motown too, just because I knew he'd listen, and I might end up crawling to him on my hands and knees. I'd given a small stack to Barry Gray to pass around at WMCA. I'd managed to drop another stack off at WABC with Scott Muni before he left for the day. He'd promised to get it on air. It was a good start. I would hit everyone else when I had another big batch.

Now that "The Bomb Johnson" was out in the world, I had to find a studio where we could record it, immediately. That would be hard. If Ahmet had succumbed to pressure, they all would. My stomach twisted again.

"I know where we can go," Esther said, pulling on my hand and bringing me back down to earth. Her fingers were so icy I swore.

"Where are your gloves?" I scolded.

"I don't have any gloves that match this coat. You keep saying you don't want to manage me, yet you are the biggest mother hen I've ever met. You tied my shoes the other night. Tied my shoes!" She shook her head in disbelief. "What kind of man does that?"

"The kind of man that doesn't want to see a woman trip over her tired feet?"

She did a little shimmy combined with a two-step. "They aren't tired now. Right now they want to dance."

I sighed, but I didn't say no.

"You scared?" she taunted.

"Of what?"

"Of me?"

"Yes," I said.

She laughed, that big belly laugh that had so struck me the night we met. "Are you scared of being the only white guy in the place?"

"The best musicians I know don't look like me. I've been the only white guy in the place a few times."

"Okay, then. Let's go." She linked her arm through mine, tucking her cold hands in the opposite sleeve, and we walked to my car feeling like the only two people in the world. It was nice. Peaceful. And I did my best to set my apprehension aside, if only for a few hours.

~

I followed her directions, but when we pulled into her neighborhood and she told me to park, I turned to her, brows raised.

"This isn't a club. You change your mind?"

"Did you think we were going to the Lenox Lounge or something?" She grinned.

"No. But I didn't expect a church." Gothic pinnacles edged the top of the building that sat just off the corner of West 138th and Seventh Avenue.

"Church upstairs, parties down. You can rent out the space. It has a record player and a dance floor. What more do you need? It's a birthday party."

"For who?"

"A few people. Don't worry. The happy birthday part will be over. The old folks and the kids will have gone home. The young people stay and dance all night. It's mostly a block party, but my brothers should be here. I hope they were listening to the radio. I told them to listen."

Alvin, Money, and a few others were gathered in front of the steps, smoking and talking, even though the snow was still falling. When Alvin saw us step out of my car, he ground out his butt and ran toward us.

"All hell is breakin' loose, little sister," he said, smiling like hell was a good thing. "We heard you on the radio." He shook his head. "We had it on loud and proud inside."

"Everybody heard it?" Esther asked.

"Everybody. Mama was fanning herself like she was gonna faint. I had to walk her home. But everybody is still talking about it. They were excited when you sang 'Any Man,' but they were dancing too, you know. Enjoying the song. When you started to sing 'The Bomb Johnson,' folks got quiet. I'm talkin' church quiet. Everybody was listening, not even breathing." He shook his head like it had been something to see. "Some of the old people were still hanging around, and you shoulda heard them clap when it was over. They all remember him, and next thing you know, everybody's swapping Bo Johnson stories."

"You say Mama went home?" Esther asked. There was a note of unease in her voice.

"Yeah. But she heard it. Everyone was hugging on her like she wrote the song herself. She got a little worked up." He took her arm. "Come on! Come inside. Everyone is going to want to talk to you."

Money hadn't said a word, and when Alvin pulled Esther forward, Money held me back, slinging his skinny arm around my shoulders.

"Some of the guys are devoted followers of Malcolm X. You know Malcolm X, Lament?" he said, nice and soft.

"I've heard of him."

"He's a big deal around here."

"Okay."

"Barry Gray interviewed Malcolm X last March, and we all tuned in. So everyone was impressed that Esther was on the same show. But when you go in . . . folks might be a little surprised that you're white."

"I can leave." I *wanted* to leave.

"I'm not telling you to go. I'm just telling you no bullshit. These guys aren't usually interested in what white guys have to say. The flirtation on the radio was fine, but they're going to see what you look like, and they'll stare and stay back until they know you're all right. And cool it around my sister. Okay? None of that Baby Ruth and Big Ben shit you were pulling on air."

"We were performing, Money."

"The thing is . . . people don't fight like you two do unless they're fighting feelings. You aren't fooling anyone but yourselves. You like her. She likes you. You want to keep on playing your games, that's fine. It sells. I realized tonight that you two are going to make me a lot of money if you don't cut us out . . . or get us all killed."

He squeezed my shoulders like we were the best of friends, and the next thing I knew we were being swallowed by the crowd inside.

He was right. Everyone stared and most everyone stopped dancing. Esther reached for my hand, pulling me beside her, and Money let me go. Alvin did all the talking, and Esther and I didn't have to say much.

When someone shouted out for her to sing, she shook her head. "I want to dance! Now will someone please turn the music back up and get me some punch?"

Paper cups were passed toward us, and, as requested, someone put a record on, and we were forgotten. We drank the tepid pink liquid, seemingly free of any booze, and watched the party resume. There was no live band, but the record player was surrounded, and the floor was thick with writhing bodies barely avoiding each other at every turn. Alvin was dancing with two girls at once, swinging one from his right hand, the other from his left, and doing a pretty decent job of making his footwork neutral between the two. He twirled them and waved at us before clasping their hands again and dancing away.

"He never stops smiling," I said, leaning down so Esther could hear me.

"He compensates for Money. Money doesn't ever smile. Between the two of them, you have a normal human being."

"Between the two of them, you have Lee Otis," I said. Lee Otis had a soda in each hand, instead of a girl, but his legs were bouncing with the music. Money had gone back outside to shoot craps. Esther said he'd either be broke or flush when the night was done, but for the time being, all was well. Amazingly enough, no one was watching me and Esther. No one seemed to care at all. I relaxed for the first time in weeks.

"Let's dance," Esther said.

I laughed. "You'll kill yourself trying to dance in those shoes."

She just quirked her brow and popped her hip. Then she took my hands, stepped into me, and raised her face imploringly. The shoes made her just tall enough to kiss if she lifted her chin a little higher and I bowed my head.

"My fingers can dance, but my body . . . that's another matter entirely," I murmured, trying not to look at her lips.

"Then . . . just do the Lament," she coaxed.

"What's the Lament?"

"It's that thing you do." She grinned.

"What thing?"

"That thing you do when you just let the music take you wherever it leads. It's the reason you're such a good songwriter. You have great instincts, and you trust them. Just do the Lament."

"I can't," I argued. "It doesn't work that way."

"How do you know?" she said, cocking her head and waiting for the next record to fall. She squealed and jumped when Chubby Checker made a call for action.

Everybody on the dance floor squealed and cheered too. Chubby Checker had created a dance craze. Maybe Minefield should sing a song about a minefield. Something where we hopped from one foot to the next, like we were trying not to trip wires. Something with a three-count rhythm and a great drum solo. Or maybe that was macabre.

"Come on, Benny, and do the Twist," Esther sang, already swiveling her hips and swishing her skirts. Damn, she was cute.

I decided it didn't matter if I was any good. I tossed my suit coat toward Lee Otis, who managed to catch it while still juggling his drinks, and I let Esther pull me onto the floor. She didn't let go of my hands, even though the Twist wasn't a couple's dance. She clasped them instead, doing a swiveling cha-cha, which I copied, letting her lead the way, my eyes on her hips to gauge what we were doing next.

Everything she did, I did, though I didn't shake and shimmy nearly as well. When it got too complicated, I just watched her, enjoying the show, and kept hold of her hands while my feet did whatever they were going to do.

She laughed at me, throwing her head back as I swung her around. "That's it, Benny. I knew you could dance."

Nat King Cole's "Stardust" gave her an excuse to slow down. I pulled her close, my hand open on her back, her hand resting in mine, and kept a simple two-step going, telling myself we were just catching our breath.

Someone was in the mood for romance, because Ray Charles's "A Fool for You" was followed by the Platters singing "Smoke Gets in Your Eyes," one of the best songs ever written. It was a song I wished I'd written, the kind of song that broke your heart and made you want to fall in love at the same time. I concentrated on the words, on the melody, on the instrumentation, anything to not think about the girl in my arms. When Ella Fitzgerald started singing "Someone to Watch Over Me," I whispered in Esther's ear, "You could sing this one," and immediately regretted it.

She did, her arms looped around my neck, singing for me alone. I tightened my arms and closed my eyes, and she pressed her face into my chest. I shouldn't have asked her to sing. I wasn't just slipping anymore, I was tumbling, head over feet, and when she sang, nothing else mattered to me. My head emptied, and I lost all reason.

"You aren't breathing," she murmured, turning her cheek so I could hear her. "But your heart is pounding. Either I wore you out or you've just realized you're the only white boy for miles."

"I want to kiss you. And I'm pretty sure that's a terrible idea," I said so softly that the words only sounded in my thoughts, but she heard me.

Esther's breath caught, and she pulled back enough to look at me. Her smirk was gone, and her eyes met mine for a weighty second before she looked away. She wanted me to kiss her too, but she was as afraid as I was. We had stopped moving in the middle of the dance floor, couples all around us.

"Lee Otis is dancing," she whispered. "He's abandoned his sodas. He's not too bad."

I didn't care about Lee Otis's partner or his sodas or his moves. I cared about Esther. I cared about the mouth that hovered near mine. I cared about the look in her eyes and the way my heart reacted when she was close to me.

"You're ugly beautiful. The prettiest ugly man I've ever seen." Her voice wasn't warm. But it wasn't cool. She wasn't flirting, but she wasn't insulting me either. She continued, almost like she was talking to herself. "You got a nose with a bump as big as my elbow in it. Lips like a woman and eyebrows like those fur stoles some women like to wear to church. Can't hardly see your eyes beneath them. But then I do, and they kind of knock the wind out of me. And your cheeks—they're always gray with beard, even when I can smell your aftershave. Ugly beautiful. That's what you are."

"You just rattled off a big list of ugly. What about the beautiful?"

"It all works together. Like our music. It shouldn't make sense. But it does."

"So my face makes sense. My big nose and furry eyebrows and scratchy face and girly mouth," I said. Ugly beautiful. I knew exactly what she meant, and I was pleased. I knew I wasn't pretty, but I'd take ugly beautiful any day. Ugly beautiful was a hell of a lot more intriguing.

She nodded. "That's what you are. Big, ugly . . . and beautiful."

"You aren't pretty either."

She stiffened, and I smirked, but I couldn't hold the twist in my lips or stand the flash of embarrassment in her eyes.

"Come on, Baby Ruth. Don't look at me like that. Pretty is too mild a word. You're gorgeous. And you know it. There's not one thing that isn't beautiful about you. Not one thing."

"My eyes are too big."

"That's why nothing gets past you."

"I have a sharp tongue."

"Sharp mind," I countered.

"Dark skin." There was challenge in her gaze.

"Dark heart," I said.

She grinned, though I could tell she didn't want to. "There is nothing beautiful about a dark heart," she argued.

"Dark heart, you try to fool me, dark heart, you always school me, dark heart, you think I don't know you," I sang, my fingers flexing against the ridges of her spine, finding the chords I would play.

"What's that?" she asked.

"I don't know. It just came to me."

She gave me the same baleful look. Then she picked up where I left off.

"White boy, you try to tease me, white boy, you'll never please me, white boy, you think I don't know you."

"I'll never please you?"

"No." She shook her head. "You won't. I'll probably pick a fight with you every single day."

"Promise?"

She closed her eyes, and her lips trembled. "There you go, knocking the wind out of me again."

I had stopped dancing. We were on a precipice, and I didn't want her to fall.

"You don't ever get scared," Esther said. It wasn't a question. It was more an accusation. "When you're on stage or performing, you don't get scared."

"I'm scared all the time," I said.

"Not on stage. Not on those keys."

"Music doesn't scare me. Love scares me. Family scares me. Commitment scares me. But music . . . being on stage or even behind a microphone, that's a game. An escape. Music doesn't hurt anyone. I've seen plenty to be afraid of, but music was just never one of those things."

"I'm afraid no one will ever love me," she confessed with a one-shoulder shrug. I used the same technique all the time. If you told the truth like it didn't matter, it hurt less.

"And I'm afraid someone will love me too much," I warned.

"We're afraid of different things. That's good," she whispered. "Maybe together, we won't be afraid of anything."

"Or we'll be afraid of everything."

The Barry Gray Show

WMCA Radio

Guest: Benny Lament

December 30, 1969

"That was the night, right here on *The Barry Gray Show*, that the world heard Benny Lament and Esther Mine together for the first time," Barry Gray says.

"Not the whole world. Just New York. But it was enough to get the ball rolling," Benny Lament says.

"Radio was safe, though. Nobody knew what you looked like."

"It didn't feel safe. But I know what you mean."

"It wasn't just the way you looked, though. You created a movement with the songs you were singing too. This last decade has been an era of civil rights. But almost nobody was singing about civil rights in their songs in the early sixties. It was bubbling under the surface but the music was mostly sunshine and harmonies. Especially in the groups. So your song 'Dark Heart' really stuck out."

"Esther and I wrote it together."

"It's a song written exclusively for piano. It has a Bill Evans vibe—"

"I love Bill Evans," Benny Lament interrupts.

"I do too. But 'Dark Heart' was just piano. No drums. No horns. No bass. Just you," Barry Gray adds.

"Me . . . and Esther. It wasn't supposed to be a hit. It wasn't commercial enough. But people loved it."

"It was different, no doubt about it. 'White boy, you don't know me. White boy, you don't own me,'" Barry Gray quotes, half singing the lyrics. "'Dark Heart' was a song that talked about things most songs didn't. It was socially conscious ahead of its time."

"Yeah. I guess it was. But we didn't think of it like that. 'Dark Heart' is a love story," Benny Lament says.

"How so?"

Lament's sigh is audible. "I need a smoke to talk about that song."

11

About Time

Money lost all his money shooting craps, Lee Otis fell asleep in the corner with my suit coat beneath his head, and Alvin stepped between Esther and me before I could kiss her. It was better that way, I knew it, but Esther and I were both on edge as we walked in the predawn back to my car. Esther had left her purse on the front seat, and Money wanted me to get a stack of records from the trunk for him to sell or distribute. Esther was talking too much, like she needed to fill the silence to avoid picking up where we'd left off.

"They built these homes for rich whites. Wouldn't let colored folks live here until the 1920s. They started calling it Striver's Row, laughing at the Negros for wanting to live here. It's not fancy anymore. And I don't know how many of us are really striving. We're all too tired. They're not homes anymore either. They're all divided up into little apartments. But I think it's the prettiest neighborhood in Harlem, though I don't know if that's saying much. My father bought that apartment for my mother. She only had Money and Alvin then. Alvin's just a year older than I am. I've lived here my whole life."

I hadn't ever heard Esther babble. She was as unnerved as I was. I unlocked the passenger door, but she didn't climb in. She reached for her purse instead and stepped back.

"I'll drop you. No use walking in the cold, even for a block. And I've got the records in the trunk."

She relented immediately, pulling the door shut behind her, and I cleared the snow from the windshield with the back of my hand. Bo Johnson had bought Gloria Mine an apartment. He'd taken care of his own. At least for a while.

"Is she his sister?" I asked as I started the car. The wipers cleared the last of the slush.

"What? Who?" Esther asked, watching our view clear.

"Gloria Mine. Is she Bo Johnson's sister?"

"Gloria Mine is my mother, Benny. You met her the other day."

I eased out onto the road and headed toward the yellow row houses. There was no traffic, and Esther's building was on the north side of the street. I flipped an illegal U-turn before I processed what she'd said.

"Your mother," I repeated.

"Yeah. That's why I call her Mama," Esther teased. She pointed at an open spot in front of her building, and I pulled into it. Money, Lee Otis, and Alvin were waiting for us on the front steps. They wanted to see the records.

"But . . . you wrote that verse about a girl who brought him to his knees." Esther was talking about Maude Alexander. Wasn't she?

Esther was staring at me, her nose wrinkled, a rueful smile on her lips. "My mother loved Bo Johnson. He didn't love her nearly as much. But I didn't think that would make a very good song."

I was so confused.

"Mama and Bo Johnson were childhood sweethearts, but my mother married someone else. Money and Alvin's father. He died just after Alvin was born—some accident on the docks—and Mama needed help. By that time, Bo Johnson had some money. He was a big man in Harlem. He stepped in, bought her the apartment, and got her back on her feet." She shrugged. "When I came along, he took off. My mother married Arky Mine when I was two years old. Lee Otis was born a few years later. There you go. The Mine family in a nutshell. Kinda messy, but that's life."

"You all use his name." It wasn't a question, more a struggle to catch up.

"Who, Arky? Yeah. It's easier that way. He's been a good father to all of us. He works hard, and he's nice to Mama. I've never seen him tie her shoes, though," she added quietly.

I turned off the car.

"Your . . . mother didn't tell you why she doesn't like me, did she?"

"She told me your father is a mobster. Your uncle too. But I knew that."

I almost groaned out loud.

It wasn't my place. It wasn't my place *at all.* If Esther thought Gloria Mine was her mother, it was none of my goddamn business, but Gloria Mine's discomfort around me suddenly made a lot more sense. She thought I knew. She thought I would tell.

It would be callous to blurt it out. And if I was honest, I was afraid. I was afraid Esther would lump me in with all the rest. That she would lump me in with Sal and my father, that she would blame me, and that she wouldn't want to see me again. That thought scared me too. I didn't want to like Esther. I didn't want to think about her. I didn't want to take responsibility for her, to hitch my career to hers, yet that was exactly what I was doing. With every engagement, every song, every moment that we spent together, we were becoming permanently linked.

Talk about a bomb.

The nerves of the night before began to pulse in my chest. The spell was broken. Esther and I weren't dancing, the snow wasn't pretty anymore, and the real world descended like a cold, wet blanket.

Money wrenched Esther's door open. "It's damn cold out here. What are you two yappin' about? I want to see those records."

Esther and I both disembarked, and I opened the trunk and handed Money half the records I had left.

"After last night, we need to record 'Bomb Johnson.' People are going to want that one. I could sell one to everybody in Harlem," he said, looking at my paltry offering.

"Yeah. I know. That's next."

"I always get the feeling you're going to skip town. Why is that?" he asked me. Alvin and Lee Otis had joined us at the curb to marvel over the vinyl.

"Because all of you scare the shit outta me," I said. I was being totally, completely honest, but it sounded like a joke.

Alvin laughed, Lee Otis too, but Money was glaring at me, his eyes narrowed.

"We scare *you*. Oh, that's rich," Money mocked, but Esther wasn't babbling anymore. She was watching me like she too was just waiting for me to bolt. Her back was stiff and her eyes were wary, and she desperately needed a new coat. I put it on my mental list. I could buy her a coat and some gloves after I figured out how to tell her about Maude Alexander and Sal and Pop and all the rest of it. If I told her. I had to tell her. It wasn't right not to tell her. It was too big to keep it hidden. *Damn it all to hell.*

"When you gonna commit, Benny Lament? We've been dating long enough," Alvin said, still laughing.

"I'm here, aren't I?" I said, repeating what I'd said the night at La Vita. I slammed the trunk and rounded the car.

"You're here . . . but you're also leaving," Lee Otis noted.

"I'll call."

"You better," Money said, pointing at me. "This thing is gonna blow. We need to be ready. You're in this now, Lament. You're in this."

I waited for her words—*Don't let me down, Benny Lament*—but they didn't come. Esther walked with her brothers into the apartment that her father had bought Gloria Mine, and I drove away, wondering for the umpteenth time since I'd met her how I was going to prevent the blast that was all but inevitable.

~

I put my key in the door, but the knob spun in my hand and the door opened without it.

"Pop?" I called. The light was on and his suitcase stood near the table. It wasn't like him to forget the locks, but he was obviously home. I shrugged out of my jacket, loosened my tie, and pulled my shirt from my slacks. I could smell her. I could smell Esther on my shirt, and for a moment I just stood, my eyes closed, enjoying the scent. Lemons. She smelled like lemons and starch and something warmer. Vanilla? Or maybe maple.

The curtains were open again. The window too. A sudden gust swept Esther's scent away, and I swore. "Damn it, Pop. It's December." I strode toward the billowing white swells, impatient. Pop was missing Mom again. He always opened the window when he missed her.

His hat was on the floor in front of the window, and I stooped to pick it up, puzzled. I heard shouting coming from the street below, and I ducked my head out the window to see Pop sitting on the small landing, still in his suit and tie, his legs spilling down the steps, his left hand clinging to the rail, a gun in his right.

"Pop?"

"There was someone out here when I got home, Benny," he said, his voice strained. "Waiting for me."

"What? Where?"

He used his gun to point weakly down at the street that ran perpendicular to the entrance. I tried to see the street, but the fire escape blocked my view from the window.

"I shot him, and he fell. The police are going to be coming. Someone musta tripped over him. Took long enough."

"Come inside, Pop," I urged.

"I don't think I can climb back in."

"Why?" I begged. I knew better than to ask. Pop had always told me I shouldn't ask questions that I didn't want to know the answers to.

"He shot me too, Benny. I can't feel my legs no more."

"Come on, Pop. I'll help you," I said. My voice sounded like it came from someone else. I leaned out and wrapped my arms around him, but he begged me to leave him be.

"This is a good place to die. I couldna picked better if I'd tried. I've just been sitting out here, hoping you'd get home in time. If I close my eyes, I can hear Giuliana singing."

"Please, Pop. You gotta let me get you inside." I couldn't sit out there with him. The platform wasn't big enough. I braced my feet and pulled, inching him up and through the window. He was listless weight in my arms, and his gun clattered to the floor at my feet. With a grunt and a heave, I eased him down to the peeling linoleum. He was covered in blood. The white drapes fluttered around us, caressing him like a lover, and I searched for his wound to stem the flow. His eyes were clear, and he didn't seem to be suffering, but he pushed my hands away.

"I heard you and Esther on Barry Gray's show. I heard you on the radio. Last night. You sang his song. You sang Bo Johnson's song."

The blood seemed to be pooling around his hips. I turned him onto his side and lifted his shirt and his jacket away from his skin. His lower back was a bloody crater. I yanked the curtains from the rod to make a bandage. Pop kept talking.

"Sal wasn't happy, but I was. I was so happy. I told him it was about damn time everybody knew the story."

"Did he do this, Pop?" I said, pressing my bandage into his wound. "Did Sal do this?"

"Nah. I did this. I screwed up, Benny. I didn't think this through. I was tryin' to make things right."

I bellowed at the inefficiency of my first aid, and my father wrapped his hand around my wrist.

"Benny. Please. It's okay. It's okay."

I looked at him helplessly.

"It's better like this. I'm dyin' anyway. I've got cancer in my stomach. I was going to tell you. But it doesn't matter now."

"Oh no. Pop, no," I moaned. He raised his palm to my face, trying to comfort me, but the effort was too much, and his hand fell back to his chest.

"The secret's out. Now all you gotta do is keep telling it. Don't stop singing that song. And remember where you belong." His voice was thready, and he rested between words.

I dove for the phone and found the number for the police department. The wait between digits was interminable, the spin of the rotary dial rattling away the seconds like an automatic weapon, until there were no rounds left.

"Benny . . . ," Pop sighed.

I dropped the phone and ran back to my father. He groaned against whatever was coming, warning it away. I kneeled at his side and took his hand. Behind me, the receiver swung from the curling cord, back and forth, tick-tock, tick-tock.

"I love you, Pop," I said. I hadn't said it near enough. If he heard me, I won't ever know. He didn't close his eyes. He didn't squeeze my hand. He simply grew cold.

And he was gone.

~

The medical examiner came. The police too. I told them what I saw, from the moment I walked in the door and found Pop's suitcase and the open window. They had a body on the street with a gun in his hand to back up my story, not to mention the body in the kitchen and the gun on the floor. Cops swarmed, and I sat at the kitchen table in my blood-soaked shirt and trousers, Pop's handprint on my cheek. Sal arrived and, like magic, the police cleared. I don't know who called him.

Then the medical examiner took Pop away, and Sal and I were alone.

"Tell me what happened." I knew he meant the truth, not the version I'd told the police, but there was no difference.

"I got home. Window was open. Pop was out on the fire escape with a bullet in him. He told me someone was waiting for him when he got here."

Sal steepled his hands and studied the black phone on the wall as if it would tell him what I could not. The receiver still dangled from the telephone, but it was perfectly still now, no swinging pendulum, no metronome keeping time. Time had stopped, and I was trapped between before and after. Grief lurked in the shadows of the empty living room. It hovered near the bathroom where I would take off my clothes and wash Pop's blood away. It would ambush me in the room where his clothes hung and the pillows bore his scent, and it would smother me in the new bed he'd purchased to lure me home. But it wouldn't take me until I was alone. For now, it just waited.

"Did you know Pop was sick when I came to see you?"

"Yes."

"And you didn't think you should tell me?"

"It wasn't my place."

I dug the palms of my hands into my eyes. We were all alike, tiptoeing around the things that needed to be said. Needed to be confessed. Needed to be dealt with.

"His illness made him foolish. He started thinking he had nothing to lose," Sal said.

I raised my head from my hands. Sal stared back at me, his eyes flat.

"Who was the guy in the street?" I asked.

"A nobody named Mickey Lido."

"But who *is* he?" I insisted.

"He's no one."

"No one doesn't wait on the fire escape with a gun for my father to come home."

"Maybe he was waiting for you, Benito."

I froze.

"You didn't listen to me," Sal whispered. "Now Jack is gone."

"Did you send someone to kill my father?"

"I loved your father."

"That's not what I asked!" I roared.

He slapped me with both hands, his palms bouncing off of my blood-smeared cheeks, and it was only our shared surprise that stayed my fists.

"Your father was the best man I ever knew. I know you don't think so. You're too good for us. You look down on your family," he said, his voice soft.

"I want to be my own man."

"There's no such thing, nephew. Everybody is owned in some way or another."

"Who owns you, Uncle?"

He shook his head like I was a child, and he closed his eyes. "Maybe I should have laid it all out. Maybe I should have explained."

"Maybe someone fucking should."

He rolled his shoulders and shot his cuffs like he wanted to slap me again, and I longed for it. The shock was wearing off, and horror was crawling up my throat. His anger was a distraction.

"Do you know who Rudolf Alexander is?" he asked, his voice hard, his words clipped.

I knew the name, but I shook my head.

"Rudolf Alexander is Maude Alexander's father. I assume you know the Maude Alexander I'm referring to."

I nodded.

"Rudolf Alexander is a very wealthy man. A very powerful man. He married into old money and turned it into an empire. He was a lawyer for the Teamsters Union before he was appointed to the federal bench. And he has the president-elect by the balls. Anything he wants, he will get. Word is . . . he wants to sit on the Supreme Court."

Politics is an ugly business. I'd cross a gangster before I'd cross a politician. Any day.

Ahmet's words reverberated in my head, but I was too dazed to dwell on my new understanding.

"He's never been asked about his daughter or his granddaughter. I think he would rather those things stay hidden, especially considering the racial . . . climate . . . in the country right now. Judges are appointed, and he's been on the federal bench for over twenty years. Actually he was selected right after Maude died. Before his appointment to the bench he was a vocal supporter of the Mann Act, the very law that put Bo Johnson in jail for crossing state lines with his daughter."

"It's been twenty years," I argued. I couldn't process any of it.

"It hasn't been nearly long enough." Sal shook his head. "Your father loved Bo Johnson. But this isn't about Bo Johnson. This is about Rudolf Alexander. Jack got careless. Now you're mixed up in it too. And he's dead." Sal threw up his hands, and for a moment the anguish that stalked the room rippled across his face. He stood abruptly, walked to the phone, and settled the receiver back in the cradle. He kept his back to me, and I wondered if he was weeping. He'd wept at my mother's wake. Pop had cried too. Pop had cried for days.

"Go clean up," he ordered softly, but there was no quaver in his voice. "Don't worry about this." He indicated the blood on the floor. "I'll leave Sticks to keep watch. He'll call a team."

"A team?" I asked dully.

"To clean up."

"I don't want them touching Pop's things." *Oh God, Pop's things.* The grief was now circling my chair and licking at my skin. I clawed at my blood-stiff shirt, popping the buttons in my impatience. One hit the wall and another scurried across the floor toward the congealed puddle where Pop had died.

"I'll take care of everything," Sal soothed, turning toward me. His trousers were still creased, and not a single speck marred the black of his jacket, but the grooves in his face collected shadows in the harsh morning light.

"Is Esther Mine safe?" I asked.

He shrugged, showing me his palms. "She is for now. He'll leave her alone. She's been left alone all this time. She just has to be quiet, and all of this will be forgiven. All of this will fade away. As for you, a message has been sent. They will wait to see if you have received it."

The secret's out. Now all you gotta do is keep telling it. Don't stop singing that song.

I rested my forehead on the table, succumbing to the exhaustion I could no longer combat.

"Go. Don't worry, Benito. I'll take care of everything."

~

I slept for six hours, sprawled across Pop's bed. It was the closest I could get to him, and I could still smell his blood in my nose. When I woke, the kitchen was scrubbed, and the curtains were gone. I pulled my mother's threadbare panels from Pop's drawer and hung them on the empty rod. The phone rang all day, incessant and shrill, but I ignored it. The police came back for another statement and asked if I had noticed anything missing. I hadn't. Nothing appeared to have been touched.

Pop kept his money in his mattress and his treasures in an old shoeshine box in his closet. Both were still there. I didn't count the money, but I pulled out the box. It still smelled like shoe polish and old rags, though he'd had it all my life. It had belonged to his grandfather, and Pop always said it reminded him that no work was beneath him. Whatever he had to do to provide, he would do, just like his grandfather had done with his shoeshine kit.

"It also makes me grateful I'm not shining another man's shoes," he would say.

Better another man's shoes than his ass, I'd always thought, but I had kept that sentiment to myself.

Pop had a few letters from Mom and his first pair of boxing gloves in the box. A dozen pictures—one of his pop and one of his mother, whom he couldn't remember. His father looked just like me. Just like

Pop, though maybe not as big. He had a mean twist to his mouth and a hard cast to his eyes, and just like Pop, I too hated looking at him.

There was a picture of me sitting at the piano, playing with the ease I'd always felt on that bench. I was a priest at the altar, a fisherman by the shore, a farmer in his field. Sure and confident. *How does it feel to know exactly where you belong?*

The only thing that was missing from the apartment was Pop. Pop and his gun. He had a record, and he wasn't supposed to have one. The cops took it, but there was nothing to be done about it now. He'd killed and been killed. Case closed. They filed it in their report and gave me a receipt for the weapon.

"It's evidence, and you won't get it back," one cop said.

I didn't want it back.

One officer asked if Pop was Jack Lomento, the fighter.

Another officer asked if I was Benny Lament, the guy who'd played on Barry Gray's show "last night." *Last night?* Had it only been last night? In a matter of hours, my whole life had been folded and pulled, stretched and twisted like taffy on Coney Island. Singing on Barry Gray, dancing with Esther, dying with Pop. It had all happened in the space of hours, but I had traveled to a different universe.

On Sunday morning, I picked up the phone to call Esther and then forgot what I was going to say the moment the phone was answered. I hung up, embarrassed, and realized two seconds later that it had been Money on the other end, and I could tell him what had happened. I called back and Money answered again, his tone so belligerent it woke me from my fog enough to tell him my father had died, and I would need some time to sort out his affairs.

"Will you tell Esther?" I said. I sounded like a wind-up doll, hollow and false, a voice in a plastic chest.

Money was so silent on the line, I lifted the receiver from my ear and looked at it, thinking we'd been disconnected.

"Money?"

"I'm sorry, Lament," Money said, gruff. "I'll tell the others." I hung up, relieved that I wouldn't have to think about what the hell I was going to do about Esther for a few days. At least until Pop was buried.

I couldn't concentrate long enough to form a plan, but a plan would have to be made. Pop's death wouldn't be the end, and I couldn't foresee the end. Or even the next step.

Sal said he would take care of everything, but I didn't know what that meant. Did it mean he would take care of the man who killed Pop? That man was dead, though he'd only been a hire. Nobody ever sent someone within their circle; nobody ever knew who ordered a hit. The layers between the boss and the crime were substantial. An order was passed down through the network, a few guys were given the job, and it was done. If politics was like the mob, and I was guessing it was, nobody would ever be able to prove anything.

On Monday, the medical examiner released the body to the funeral home that Sal had already booked. I picked out a casket and ordered a stone—a simple one that matched my mother's. They would lie side by side in Woodlawn next to Salvatore Vitale Sr. and a smattering of other Vitale relatives. I boxed his clothes and stowed the treasures I wanted to keep. I removed the stacks of cash from his mattress—there was more than fifty thousand dollars—and put it in a suitcase. I wanted it ready if I had to run.

Pop didn't have any bills. He had a few statements and a treatment plan from a cancer specialist in Brooklyn, but everything had been paid in full. He'd signed a release, opting out of chemotherapy and radiation, but he'd looked into medicine for his pain. That seemed to be all. I didn't know if the doctor would talk to me, but I made a note to call anyway.

On Wednesday we had the wake. I played every song I could think of, sitting there by his open casket as people trundled by, crossing themselves and saying words that didn't penetrate the wall of music I was creating. Sal had wanted to have the wake at his house on Long Island, but that wouldn't do. It needed to be in our neighborhood. If we did it at Sal's, no one from the neighborhood would come; no one but mobsters and associates and the immediate family. I wanted something else for Pop, and we had it at Nonna's where we'd had my mother's wake more than twenty years before.

Nonna hid upstairs in her bedroom and refused to come out, even when Sal pleaded at her door. Pop had looked after her, and she'd outlived him. Just as she'd outlived her other protectors. I understood the desire to hide; it was the reason I played. People patted me as they walked past the piano, and all I had to do was nod and keep playing. There wasn't anything to say anyway. I left that up to Theresa and her daughters, who had come home for the wake with their husbands and Francesca's new baby. Theresa's relatives came from Chicago; it had been years since I'd seen them. Theresa's brother Frank had risen through the ranks and ran his father's operation, and he and Sal were tucked away for much of the day, talking of things I didn't want to hear. The house overflowed with family, and I had never felt more alone.

We kept the doors of the house open, front and back, even though it was cold, and we brought the line through the foyer, past the casket in the living room, and out the kitchen. By the time it was all done, the counters were brimming with food.

It was all anyone could do; feed the living and mourn the dead. The two went hand in hand. There were envelopes filled with cash too. Lots of those. Weddings and funerals meant cash payments from the bosses. Costello, Genovese, Bonanno, Gambino, and Profaci. They didn't come but they all sent money, delivered by an underboss or a soldier with a mournful expression and clasped hands. I shoved them into my breast pocket and vowed to burn them.

It was a stupid thought. I wouldn't right wrongs or avenge deaths with a pile of ash. And who was I kidding? I would put the money in the suitcase with all the other cash. Sal said he would take care of everything, and I was going to let him, whatever that entailed. So what did that make me?

The resounding answer was I was an orphan. It didn't matter that I was a grown man, I was an orphan. It was my mother's wake all over again. The same people. The same smells, the same confusion. But at Mom's funeral, I had still had Pop.

I sat at the piano in a forest made up not of trees but of people dressed in black and wearing shining shoes instead of roots. Pop was close by. He was the biggest tree of all, and when I looked up at him—up up up—his eyes were red rimmed. He took a step and sat down on the bench beside me, his back bent, his shoulders hunched, and he watched my little fingers on the keys.

I played quietly, stroking the keys that were directly in front of my eyes. Seven notes—C, D, E, F, G, A, B—and then the sounds started all over. I didn't plunk or pound. I listened, feeling the bounce in the keys, though I touched them so softly I could hardly hear the sound beneath the murmur of voices and the occasional sob. Some people cried because they felt sad. Others cried because they thought they should. I didn't cry because then I wouldn't be able to play. And when I touched those long white keys, Pop listened, and he didn't feel so sad.

This time, the keys did not comfort me, and they didn't bring Pop to my side. But I still didn't cry. I still didn't want people to stare. I just nodded and played and waited for it all to be over. When Enzo stopped behind me, his hands on my shoulders, and spoke in my ear, I slowed but didn't stop. I didn't want to encourage him or anyone else.

"Benny, I'm sorry about your Pop, kid. But I gotta tell you somethin' important." Enzo kept his voice low and his hands on my shoulders, and my hands stilled on the keys.

"I saw the paper today. It had a picture of your father, a real nice write-up on Jack. His boxing days, all of it. But they had a picture of the other guy too."

"The other guy?" I asked, my eyes on my hands.

"The son of a bitch who got him," Enzo muttered in my ear.

Ah. The dead "nobody."

"I recognized him, Benny. He was the guy that came to the gym a while back, asking about Bo Johnson. The guy who said he was doing a story on him and your dad."

A few people had noticed the music had ceased and had turned toward me. I played a few bars, softly, slowly, and the eyes drifted away.

"Guess he was lyin'. But I knew that. He looked like a snitch to me. Or a cop. I don't know what the hell it all means. But I wanted you to know. Be careful, kid."

The Barry Gray Show

WMCA Radio

Guest: Benny Lament

December 30, 1969

"Our audience may not be aware, Benny, but your father was murdered," Barry Gray says.

"He was."

"The police records, which are public, say it was a home invasion gone wrong."

"That's what the police records say, yes."

"The man who killed him had a record," Barry Gray presses.

"Yeah. And so did my father. Two bad guys took each other out, as far as the cops were concerned. Nobody lost much sleep over it," Benny Lament says.

"Some say it was connected to organized crime. A mob hit."

"That's what some people say," Benny answers, tone neutral, and Barry Gray changes the subject.

"Everything was happening at once. Minefield gets a big break. Stations are playing 'Any Man,' and listeners are loving it, requesting it. It's a huge, overnight hit. At the same time, your father is murdered. What was going through your mind?"

"I only knew that suddenly things had gotten bad. I didn't know who to trust. The only person in the world I trusted was gone. And Esther didn't trust anyone. Not me. Not herself. But it was too late to do anything but stick together."

"What did you do?"

"I did the only thing I could think of. The one thing I never thought I'd do."

"And what was that?"

"I went to my family."

12

Friends Like Us

The hardest part of that first week was the slow drip of moments I could not fill. I walked. I slept—badly. I ate. I showered, and I sat, only to look at the clock to find I had hours left to fill before I could do it all again. The rooms were too quiet, and unlike with my mother's death, the piano did not comfort me and the keys did not call to me. I played, but the songs all revolved around Pop, around things he had said or done, ways he had disappointed me, ways he had loved me. Many of the lines that kept coming to my head were songs that had already been written, lines that someone else had put to paper, and behind each one a memory followed. Like the first time I'd played at La Vita. I'd been so desperate to impress that I'd riffed for a full five minutes on Debussy without realizing Terrence had been signaling for me to cease for just as long. Everyone had wanted to dance, and I'd put them all to sleep.

Pop had clapped loudly and yelled, "That's my son," and out of respect, everyone in the room had clapped too, though Terrence had relegated me to the after-hours crowd for a full year. I'd been so angry with Pop, thinking he'd coerced a response. Maybe he had. But his pride in me was not fake. His support of my passion had never faltered, and it was the thing that haunted me most.

I had not been proud of Pop. I had not sought his attention or approval. I had made it very clear that I wanted nothing to do with the family he'd chosen and the path he'd taken. Now I was sitting in the home he'd made for me, paralyzed by indecision and grief, with no clue how to proceed. The phone rang incessantly, and every day brought a new delivery—flowers, food, notes from people who knew him. Jerry Wexler called me Sunday morning and offered his condolences, along with those of everyone else at Atlantic.

"I've been trying to get ahold of you all week, Lament," Jerry said. "I didn't make it to the wake. I was out of town when it all went down, but I wanted you to know how sorry I was to hear about Jack. He was good to me."

"He liked you, Jerry," I said. Nobody knew what to say about Pop's death, least of all me, and I'd relied on a few stale lines to comfort those who were trying to comfort me. In Jerry's case, though, it was true.

"I liked him too," Jerry said, his voice sincere. "Listen. I know it didn't work out at Atlantic."

"No hard feelings, Jerry."

"Good. Good. That's good," he said. "But I was thinking . . ." The volume of his voice dropped, like he was trying to be discreet, and I pressed the phone to my ear, straining to hear.

"There's a big holiday showcase in Pittsburgh next week. The biggest labels and the biggest acts all at one event. Different headliners every night. Ray's scheduled for Tuesday. The Drifters were going to open for him, but we lost Ben E. King. He's gone solo, and everybody's mad. We had this scheduled before they split, and they're all refusing to perform together, so we're scrambling for a solid replacement. If you can swing it, Ray suggested you and Esther Mine take the slot."

"But . . . we're not with Atlantic," I gasped.

"I know. And we wouldn't claim or promote you. It's too late to do anything about the billing. The Drifters are listed on the billboards, all the press releases, and the programs. Tickets have already been printed and sold too, obviously. The change will be announced that night, right before you go on. People will be expecting the Drifters. You might have a disgruntled audience. But it's a huge venue and a big damn deal, and Ray wants you. If you want the gig . . . if Minefield wants the gig, it's yours. No strings. Half hour, tops. We'll lose our deposit because we promised the Drifters and aren't delivering. That means you won't get paid either. But that kind of gig is career gold, Benny."

I was stunned, and Jerry could tell.

"I've got to talk to the band, Jerry."

"I understand. And it's shit timing. But maybe working will be the best thing for you."

"Yeah. Maybe," I said. "Does Ahmet know?" It was hard to imagine, given his concern during our conversation.

"Don't worry about Ahmet. You just be in Pittsburgh on Tuesday morning."

"I've got to talk to the band," I repeated.

"I need to know soon. By the end of the day, if possible."

I promised him I'd let him know and hung up the phone. And then I stewed. I picked up the phone to call Esther probably a dozen times, and I always put the receiver down again, unable to make a decision. I had to tell her everything. I had to tell *them* everything. We couldn't run off to Pittsburgh without a much bigger conversation, a conversation I didn't even know how to have. Especially over the phone. I packed a suitcase and organized my cash so I would be ready to go, if that's what I decided to do. Mostly I paced, running through scenarios and weighing my options, until I couldn't stand my own company.

I turned on the television to escape my thoughts and reheated some leftovers from the wake, eating because I was hollowed out. I sat at the kitchen table, my chair facing Pop's chair, listening as the local NBC news reported on snowfall and counted down the shopping days until Christmas. I rose to turn it off, irritated by the reminder that time had not stopped, and found myself face-to-face with pictures of a warehouse fire near the Brooklyn docks. I stared at the set, jarred.

> *"Officials are investigating, but right now, the damage appears significant. There are several businesses that have been affected, but at least one is a total loss. Authorities believe the fire started in a small vinyl production plant."*

It was Connor's place. I'd put in an order for another thousand records and paid for them. I was guessing they were gone, along with my money. I swore and turned up the volume, but the broadcast had already cut away to another story. A soft knock sounded, and I ignored it, caught up in my stunned speculation. The knock came again, this time louder and more determined, and I set my plate down in the kitchen, wiped my face and hands, and turned off the set.

I considered ignoring it but knew if it was Sal or one of the Tonys, they would beat down the door if I didn't answer, especially since they knew I was home. Maybe they had news. Maybe they would tell me whoever had wanted my pop dead—or *me* dead—was dead too, and it was all over. It was what I wanted—what I needed—and I felt a gaping hole where my guilt should be.

Esther stood at my door, wearing her red coat and her cap of tidy curls, her heels high, her lipstick bright, and her hands clasped in front of her like she was waiting to receive Communion. The sight of her made my heart stutter, and I resisted the urge to run my hands over my hair like a nervous kid. I was thrilled to see her, and that wasn't good. What in the hell was I going to do?

"They keep playing our songs," she blurted in place of a greeting. "We've been keeping track. They played 'Any Man' five times between noon and midnight. That's once in every program. They played our live performance of 'The Bomb Johnson' twice, and one of the announcers said they'd been getting calls about it all day. On WABC they played 'Any Man' four times from ten to ten. Lee Otis is making charts and graphs."

I swore softly.

"We have to record it," Esther demanded. "I know you're hurting. I know you'd rather I leave you alone. But I can't do that. We need you. I need you."

I shook my head, trying to clear it. *What in the hell was I going to do?*

She misinterpreted my shaking head, and her expression hardened.

"I keep coming to you, Benny Lament. Throwing myself at your feet. And you just shake your head." She had the same determined look on her face and the same starchy posture she'd had when she approached me at the Park Sheraton.

"Throwing yourself at my feet?" I almost laughed, despite my muddled thoughts.

"Are you going to invite me in?" she asked. "Or do I have to stand here begging?"

I stepped back and turned my palm in welcome, and she swept past me.

"How did you know where I lived?" I asked, shutting the door behind her.

"You wrote it on the card you gave me."

I did? I did. I'd wanted her to know where to find me.

"Did Money tell you I called?"

"Yes."

I waited for the sympathetic words and the sad eyes. The platitudes. The patting. Always the patting. But Esther didn't do any of those things. She searched my face instead, like she was gathering her own evidence and drawing her own conclusions about my well-being and state of mind. After a thorough perusal, she spoke, but she surprised me again.

"Am I your friend, Benny?"

"I don't have many friends, Esther."

"I didn't ask you for a head count," she shot back.

"You sure don't act like any friend I've ever had. So no. We're not friends," I said, irritated. Damn, she got under my skin.

She tipped her head to the side, studying me. "Then what are we?"

"I'm your manager."

She laughed. "Since when?"

I felt like an idiot. I'd been fighting the title, and now I clung to it to avoid admitting we were something more.

"So now you're my manager. But we're not friends?"

"No."

"Is that what you tell yourself?"

I shrugged.

"We laugh together. We sing together. We squabble. I think we even make each other better. But we're not friends?"

I didn't answer. We both knew I was a fool.

"Well . . . if we're not friends . . . then I don't know what a friend is," she grumbled, but she let it go. She shrugged out of her coat and sat down on the piano bench like she intended to stay for a while. She stared at the keys and fingered the B above middle C, the key with the chip along the bottom.

"It's like a broken tooth," she said.

"That's exactly what Pop used to say. He said it gave my songs a lisp."

"Tell me about him."

I opened my mouth and shut it again. "I don't know what to say."

"I liked him. He was proud of you. And he seemed kind," Esther prodded.

"He was. Kind . . . and compassionate. And at the same time . . . the toughest son of a bitch you've ever met."

The pictures I'd been digging through were laid out on the piano in clusters, and she reached for the nearest one, the one from his boxing days. It was bigger than the rest, and it drew the eye.

"You look like him," she marveled.

"I look exactly like him. But I would never wear my shorts like that."

"I can't picture you in anything but a suit."

"I'm a stiff. What can I say?" I handed her the picture of my father with Bo Johnson. She gaped at it.

"You said they knew each other . . . but they look like . . . friends."

"They fought each other, but yeah . . . they were friends," I said.

"Kind of like us," she said, and raised her eyes briefly to mine. She had me there.

"I never knew my father," she continued. "My mama has a few pictures. But I've never seen this one before."

"Most of the time I didn't know mine either. Or maybe I just felt like he didn't know me." I cleared my throat and rubbed at my prickly face. The bristles against my hand distracted me from the emotion behind my words.

"What does that mean?" Esther asked. "He raised you, didn't he? He was a good father. So why didn't you know him?" She sounded so confrontational that I got defensive.

"He taught me how to part my hair and fasten a tie, how to throw a punch and when I needed to turn the other cheek. I knew his tread, his smell, his voice. I knew his love for boxing and Borgatti's noodles on 187th Street. He loved the Yankees. He loved to hear me play. But no, Esther. I didn't really know him." The words spilled out, and I shook my head. I sounded like a petulant child. I was angry that he was dead, angry with him, angry with myself, and I couldn't explain it in a few sentences. I didn't want to talk about Pop. Not yet.

"I kinda think that's like saying we aren't friends," Esther said, her tone pointed. "Just because it's complicated doesn't mean it isn't so."

"Why do you always have to argue with me?" I muttered, sitting down beside her on the bench. She didn't move away, even when I placed my hands beside hers on the keys like we were about to play a duet.

"I'm not arguing. I'm correcting."

I snorted.

"Your father deserves better than that."

"Than what?" I sighed.

"You're dismissing him when you say you didn't know him. Just like you're dismissing me." She played the lowest key on the piano—bong—putting a period on her statement.

"I'm not dismissing you," I said. How could I dismiss someone who had taken up permanent residence in my thoughts from the moment we met?

"All right then. Are we friends?" she asked, smirking, giving me another chance to give her the right answer.

"We're friends, Esther," I admitted.

"Yes, we are. We most definitely are. But you're also my manager. I'm not letting you take that back."

I laughed. Laughing felt strange, like starting a car on a cold morning. My chest protested and then turned over reluctantly. Esther may not be gentle, but she was genuine. I found her frankness a relief. No sad eyes and sympathy from Esther Mine, and I was suddenly glad.

"I thought you were here to make me feel better," I said, admitting nothing.

"I never said I was here to make you feel better. I said I needed you. I'm here for myself."

I chuckled again, and this time it was easier. "You really need to work on your compassion, Baby Ruth."

"Do you want me to sing? I seem to recall that working the last time you tried to get me to leave when I wanted to stay," she said, laughing with me, the sound so rich and warm I almost moaned with pleasure.

"Oh, you mean the time you offered to sleep with me if you had to?" I teased.

"I was just testing you," she said, but the color deepened in her cheeks, and she lifted her hair from her neck like she'd grown a little warm.

"Well, I definitely want you to sing," I said.

She rolled her eyes. "I can't just sing a song at the drop of a hat."

"Sure you can. You have. You did!"

"I was desperate. I'm not desperate anymore. Can you write a song on demand?" she huffed.

"Songwriting is easy," I said, shrugging.

She scoffed and rolled her eyes.

"Give me a word. I'll show you."

She screwed up her nose and pursed her glossy lips.

"Chicken."

I grimaced. "What kind of word is that?"

She snickered. "Sorry. I'm hungry." Her stomach growled, underlining her claim.

"All right," I said, cracking my knuckles. "Let's write a song about a chicken."

"I can't wait to hear this."

"Key of E maybe? E for 'Esther'? Or C for 'chicken'?"

"How about G . . . for 'good chicken,'" she said, laughing. "I want some *good* chicken."

"Nah. You're not gonna like this chicken. He's scared." I played a few chords and decided on a rhythm. "Here we go. I got it." I cleared my throat and started the way Ray Charles began "I Got a Woman," where the piano answered the lines.

"You strut all over town," I sang and then let my fingers strut across the keys in reply. "But girl, I know the truth." *Bum ba di dum.*

"You're afraid of me, it's plain to see. You're chicken."

Esther whooped, and I sent my fingers scurrying from black to white like a fox in the henhouse, feathers flying everywhere.

"Yeah, you're scared. You're lonely. And you're chicken," I growled, and Esther threw her head back, laughing.

"Get low. Get way down low and flap your chicken wings," I demanded, picking up the speed. "Get high, get way up high, and swing now, baby, swing. I know you won't admit it. You'd rather dance and sing. But you're afraid of me, it's plain to see. You're chicken."

I finished with a bluesy flourish, another *bum ba di dum*, and a small bow.

"Good Lord, Benny Lament," Esther said, shaking her head. "You did it. You just wrote a song about a chicken."

"Songwriting is easy," I said again. And suddenly the pain was back, pressing on my chest and sinking down into the pit of my stomach. That was the problem with forgetting, even for a moment, that Pop was gone. I always remembered again.

Esther's laughter was suddenly gone too, like she felt the moment Pop returned.

"Is that why you do it?" Esther asked.

I shrugged. "Why do any of us do what we do? I can't help myself. Never could."

She took a deep breath. "Are women easy for you too, Benny?"

"Now where did that come from?" I said, scowling at her. She stared back, dark eyes searching.

"Sometimes I think you feel something for me," she said slowly. "You are kind in a way that makes me think you care. But you . . . you can't wait to get rid of me half the time. I can't figure you out. You tease me. You even tease me about sleeping with you. But you've never even tried to kiss me."

"It's easy to get entangled. I never get entangled," I said.

"Why?"

"I don't dare. The minute you start relying on something to make you feel better—smokes, alcohol, junk—is the moment you lose your power. Everything feels like a trap. Even people. Especially people."

"So you avoid everything that makes you feel good?" she asked.

"Music makes me feel good. Writing makes me feel good. Working . . . that makes me feel good."

"I'm going to start calling you Benny the Saint. Saint Benedict," she muttered.

"When I was little, I learned that wanting was better than having," I said.

"You ever been hungry? You ever been cold? You ever been alone?" she argued, shaking her head. "Wanting is not better than having."

"That's not the kind of wanting I'm talking about."

"What kind are you talking about?" she whispered. Tension was thrumming between us, and for a moment I enjoyed the sweet ache.

"Having something to dream about. Having something to look forward to . . . having something to move toward. That's the kind of wanting I'm talking about. It's the kind of wanting that's good for you. The kind that keeps you getting up in the morning. Even if it's just wanting to keep the hunger and the cold and the wolves at bay." I breathed deeply and then whispered, "You should try it."

She glared at me, and I winked. She stood from the bench with a huff, and I chuckled and pulled her back down, but this time I pulled her into my lap. Her face was level with mine. Her eyes. Her lips. Her breath. And I stopped laughing. We just looked at each other, eye to eye. I could hear her heart . . . or maybe that was mine. Thrumming. Pounding. So fast. *Ba DUM. Ba DUM. Ba DUM.* There was a song there.

"Hear that?" she asked.

"I hear your heart," I said. "Or is it mine?"

"It's saying hello," she answered. "Maybe goodbye."

"Oh no, not that," I said. "Please don't go."

"Don't say goodbye. Let's say hello," she whispered.

We'd said every line in the same rhythm and rhymed the cadence, listening to our hearts. "Did we just write another song?" I asked.

She laughed, that rumbling sound that made my eyes roll back in delight, and I kissed her.

I couldn't hear her heart anymore. I felt her mouth, the fluttering of her sigh, and her hands on my cheeks. Her fingers curled against my face, and I wanted to devour her, every sweet bite in one mouthful.

But I didn't do that. I didn't bite at all. I simply sat, my hands around her waist, my lips pressed to hers, and asked for entrance. She brushed her lips back and forth, spreading her welcome across my mouth.

She was a balm, and for a moment I let her soothe me, let myself feel her mouth and her hands and the press of her body. I wanted to keep kissing her. I wanted to do more than that.

I stood, still holding her, and her mouth didn't leave mine. The sweet ache of want became the roar of need, and our kiss changed, becoming supercharged and desperate, like we'd run out of time and had only seconds before everything changed. Maybe we did. My hands were on her hips, hers were in my hair, and through the haze of lust and longing, I recognized that this was not Agnes Toal. I would not be able to beg and moan and let her go. This was not Agnes Toal or Margaret Bondi or any of the other women I'd avoided or set aside. This was Esther Mine.

And I was in love with Esther Mine.

The thought doused me in reality.

"Wait, Esther. Wait," I gasped, lifting my head. I could not love her, not her body, not her mouth, not for one minute more if I didn't tell her everything: who I was, who she was, and exactly how much trouble we might be in.

Her lipstick was gone, and we were both panting. She swallowed, her eyes pleading and her lips parted, and I almost kissed her again. Instead, I set her down and stepped away, running my hands over my eyes so I wouldn't look at her. She stepped toward me, and I knew if she touched me again, I would not be able to do what I had to do.

I walked to the piano and found the picture Pop had given me at Charley's, the picture he told me to give Esther when I *knew her better.*

Somehow the old man had known I would. Maybe he knew me better than I thought.

"There's something you need to see," I said. "Something you need to know. And there's no easy way to say it."

She raised her brows, expectant.

I handed her the picture of Bo Johnson beside the small woman with the same haughty lift to her chin as Esther. The same straight back. The same tidy figure. The same cheekbones, the same jawline.

"What's this?" She frowned. "Who . . . who are they?"

"You tell me," I insisted as gently as I could.

"That's my father," she said. "That's Bo Johnson. But I don't know the woman."

"Look at her, Esther. Look at her. Then tell me who she is."

Esther did as I asked, and her breathing became harsh and her hands started to shake. The resemblance was undeniable.

"The woman is your mother. Her name was Maude Alexander."

Esther shook her head, adamant. "No."

"Sit down, Baby Ruth," I urged gently, taking her arm. She swatted at me.

"We're not friends, remember? So you shouldn't be touching me like we are." She slammed the picture down and strode for the door, scooping up her red coat on the way.

"Son of a bitch," I snapped, losing my temper. We'd gone from kissing to clawing in sixty seconds flat. My self-control was in tatters, and I considered just letting her go. Fat Tony was watching the entrance. He had a team in the street and one roving my floor. She would be safe. I groaned. Who in the hell was I kidding?

"Are you going to run out of here, Esther?" I said. "Because I don't really want to chase you down the stairs. I'd have to find my shoes and put on a jacket, and by the time I did that, you'd be long gone, even in those heels. So if you wanna run out, just go. But eventually you're going to want to hear this, so it might as well be now."

She hesitated at the door, teetering in her power shoes, and I moved up behind her and wrapped my arms around her, careful. Careful. I rested my cheek on her curls. It was like holding on to a subway pole; the tension thrumming through her made her vibrate.

"Listen to me, Baby Ruth. We're in trouble. And I can't explain any of it unless you know the truth."

She didn't relax in my arms, but she didn't pull away. She was listening.

"The way Pop told it, your father loved your mother, and she loved him. He wasn't ever with Gloria Mine. He'd been in jail on some bogus charge, and when he got out, he returned to Maude. They wanted to be together. They were making plans. And then she died. How did she die? I don't know. But I know your father came here, and he brought you. You were a baby, and he laid you right there, on that couch. He asked Pop to take you to Gloria Mine. I heard him say it myself. I didn't understand then. I was just a kid, and he was . . . Bo Johnson. We were both scared, though. I remember that."

"You met my father?" Esther gasped.

"You look more like her than you do him. There's something there, though. Around the eyes. He was huge, but then again, I was only eight years old."

"He was . . . here?"

"He sat right there." I pointed at the couch, seeing him in my head as clear as if it were yesterday. "I woke up to his voice. I thought it was God. That's what he sounded like."

"Why?" she whispered.

"He had a quality to his voice—a resonance—that I haven't ever forgotten. I thought maybe it came from his size or the width of his chest, but you have the same quality to your sound, so it can't be that."

Esther pulled away from me and staggered to the couch. She sat down like her legs had been shot out from under her, her polka-dot skirt swooshing up like a parachute. I sat down beside her, leaving space between us. She was slack-jawed and shocked, and I waited for her to recover and tell me to continue.

"Why didn't she tell me?" Esther asked. Her voice was flat, like something heavy was sitting on her chest.

I didn't have to ask who "she" was. The only "she" who knew anything was Gloria Mine.

"She's afraid. I could see it plain as day when I met her. She knows too much not to be afraid. I'm guessing she thought you'd be better off if you never knew anything. She just wrapped you into what was already there, the family she could explain."

Again, a long, processing silence.

"Why are you telling me this, Benny?" she asked.

"I didn't want to."

"Then why are you?"

"Someone killed my father. It wasn't a robbery. And it wasn't random. I think it had something to do with you. With you, and your parents. And maybe our music too."

She raised her dark eyes to mine, finally. Her gaze was shuttered, her face closed, but she wasn't running.

"Tell me."

I told her everything I could think of, every drop of blood, every word from my father's lips, every moment of speculation and self-doubt from the moment I saw her at Shimmy's that first time. I told her about Sal. I told her about the Mann Act and the year her father spent in jail. I told her how I'd sung him his song and how he told me not to be afraid.

She started to shake when I recounted how he said his mama called him the Bomb because he ruined everything he touched. I thought she was going to cry then, but if anything the tremors just wound her even tighter. She asked a few questions, and I did my best to answer them. When I didn't know, I told her as much.

When I'd said all there was to say, she sat in silence for several minutes. Then she stood and retrieved the picture she'd slammed down an hour before.

"I need you to take me home, Benny," she said.

I pulled on my coat and my shoes, picked up the bags I'd packed, and we left Pop's apartment. I wasn't sure when—or if—I'd be back.

The Barry Gray Show

WMCA Radio

Guest: Benny Lament

December 30, 1969

"Your song 'The Bomb Johnson' is based on a real person. It stayed at the top of the charts for months. Tell us about Bo Johnson, Benny," Barry Gray insists.

"My father said Bo Johnson was the greatest fighter who ever lived," Benny Lament says.

"Bo Johnson was also Esther Mine's father."

"Yes, sir. She's the reason we sang that song. She wanted the world to know his story."

"Bo Johnson never lost a fight in his professional career, defeating every opponent by knockout. I remember when he defeated James Braddock in '38," Barry Gray adds.

"He even knocked out my father," Benny Lament says.

"He ended your father's career."

"He did, but Pop was never bitter about it. He and Bo Johnson were friends."

"Bo Johnson's career came to an abrupt end when he was incarcerated for violating the Mann Act—also known as the White Slave Traffic Act—in 1939," Barry Gray says.

"Bo Johnson was incarcerated for leaving the state with Esther's mother, a white woman that he intended to marry," Benny says, his voice tight.

"The woman Bo Johnson intended to marry was Maude Alexander, an opera singer and heiress to a considerable fortune. She was the granddaughter of Thaddeus Morley and the daughter of Rudolf Alexander. The Morleys and Alexanders have become synonymous with names like Rockefeller, Vanderbilt, and Carnegie in New York," Barry Gray informs the audience.

"Powerful people," Benny agrees.

"They didn't care for the song?"

"No, Mr. Gray, they didn't."

13

Devil on the Doorstep

Esther's apartment was the same size as Pop's but six people lived there. Money and Alvin weren't home, but Lee Otis had the radio on and papers spread out on the table when we arrived. He jumped to his feet and began showing me his data.

"They're playing us as much as they're playing any of the artists in the top ten. We've all been taking shifts, listening. I've got it all right here. It's not just in New York either. WABC has sister stations all around the country that pick up the Hot 100 countdown and rebroadcast *The Barry Gray Show* in the overnight hours in fifty markets. Uncle Ross said they played 'Any Man' in Philly. We got family in Boston too. They've heard it. Mama's got a sister in Montgomery. She said she heard it twice in the last week, and she wasn't even listening for it."

Gloria and Arky Mine were watching a small television while Gloria ironed. As soon as we walked through the door, he turned it off and Gloria set the iron aside. She wore slippers and an apron over a pale pink dress, but there were pearls at her neck and rouge on her cheeks like she'd been to church. She kept running her hands down her apron in agitation, but Esther was stone cold at my side, and however much I didn't want to participate, I couldn't leave.

"We'll talk about all that in a minute, Lee Otis," Esther said gently. "Benny and I need a word with Mama now."

Lee Otis looked sheepish. "I'm sorry about your father, Benny. He was nice."

"Thank you, Lee Otis."

Arky Mine told his son to get his coat. "Let's go to the café, Lee Otis," he said. "I need a piece of pie. You can bring a book."

"I have pie, Arky," Gloria protested, desperate. "You don't need to leave."

"Give it to Mr. Lament. He's our guest," Arky said softly. "We'll be back in an hour. Best to get it over with, Glory. It's time." He nodded at me, kissed his wife's cheek, and touched Esther's shoulder as he passed.

Lee Otis didn't argue, but as he followed his father out, he glanced at Esther worriedly.

"What's this all about, Esther?" Gloria Mine said, sinking down onto the couch. She still hadn't looked at me. Esther sat down beside her, prim and straight, like a stranger in her own home. I sat in the chair Lee Otis had vacated at the table, trying to keep my distance. I felt sorry for Gloria Mine and terrible for Esther. I should have left with Arky and Lee Otis.

"You know exactly what this is about, Mama. The question is, Who else knows? Arky obviously knows. Do my brothers know? Do they know they aren't really my brothers?"

"Don't say things like that," Gloria cried.

Esther showed her the picture, but when Gloria moved to take it, Esther pulled it back.

"I need you to tell me who she is."

Gloria wrapped her arms around herself, and right then and there she prayed for help. "Lord Jesus, I need you," she whispered.

"No, Mama. I need you. I need you to tell me who this is." Esther waved the picture in front of her mother again, and I was afraid Gloria Mine was going to snatch it and rip it in two. Her eyes darted and her hands twitched.

"Esther," I warned, my eyes on the picture.

"What did you tell her?" Gloria asked, turning on me.

"He told me this white woman is my mother. Look at her, Mama."

But Gloria Mine didn't look at the picture. She didn't need to. She already knew.

"My father was Jack Lomento. Did you know him?" I asked.

"You look just like him. I thought you *were* him when I saw you. And I knew you would bring nothing but trouble." Gloria Mine sank back into the cushions and covered her face.

"My father brought Esther to you," I said. "Why did he bring her to you?"

Gloria peeked out from behind her fingers and slowly drew them from her face. She had begun to cry, but her tears seemed more fearful than sad, and when she spoke, her voice was resentful, but resigned.

"Bo and I were old friends. He had helped me when I needed it. He got me this apartment. He didn't have anywhere else to turn, and I owed him."

Esther stood abruptly, like she wanted to bolt, and Gloria Mine reached for her hand, and clasped it in both of hers. Esther sank back down.

"Jack Lomento brought you to me in the middle of the night," Gloria said to Esther. "He said Bo was in trouble, and your mother was dead, and he gave me some money and handed you over. That money was enough to get us by for a year. My mama lived with me then. And we'd been struggling so hard. My husband was dead, I already had two little kids, and I didn't want another one. But the money was a godsend."

"Why didn't you tell me?" Esther moaned. "Why did you let me think you were my mother?"

"You were a baby. The boys called me Mama. It was just a natural thing."

"I wasn't always a baby. I haven't been a baby for a long time. You could have set me straight a long time ago."

"His daddy told me it was better not to." She pointed at me as though it was all my fault. "He checked on me a few times and twice he gave me money out of his own pocket. But he was always careful, and he never stayed. He told me it was better for me and for you to just forget about Bo. He said he would make sure I always had money, but he never brought it in person after that first year. He would just send it in a package. Those packages kept the wolves away."

Esther's back had begun to bow, and her knees were bouncing with distress.

"I thought that money was from my father. You told me it was," Esther said.

Gloria Mine shrugged, helpless. "I never heard from Bo again. Maybe the money *was* from him. But all I know is the money always came through his father." Again with the pointing. "He never told me his name, but I knew who he was. He grew up in Harlem too. Ran with a different crowd, of course. But he was a boxer, just like Bo. They were friendly, as friendly as a white man and a colored man can be. Bo liked white folks." She shook her head. "And they killed him."

"How do you know?" I asked.

"Because he never came back," Gloria Mine said, her eyes hard. The room fell silent.

"Tell me about my mother," Esther asked after several seconds.

"I'm your mother." Gloria thumped her chest. "I'm the one who raised you."

Esther pressed a hand to her lips, and for a moment I thought she was going to lose the battle she was waging with her emotions.

She nodded, conceding the point. "You're my mama. But I need to know who my mother was."

"I don't know anything about her."

"Mama . . . please. Please."

"All I know is her name and her reputation. Maude Alexander. Some fancy white lady. She was always in the papers. Loved attention. Lived on Fifth Avenue, and she was trouble." She glanced at me like I was guilty of the same thing. "That's all I know. But that's her . . . in the picture." She nodded toward the photo in Esther's hand. "She sure didn't do us any favors."

Gloria stood and left the room, but a moment later she was back with a little pink dress and a tiny pair of matching stockings. She set them in Esther's lap. "When the man brought you, you were wearing these. The blanket you were wrapped in was that white thing you slept with until it was worn to shreds."

"You cut it into rags," Esther whispered, clutching the pink clothes.

"You were ten years old, Esther. It was in tatters."

"Why didn't you tell me then?"

"Tell you what?" Gloria Mine asked, her tone plaintive. "What good would it have done? You're hurting now. You didn't need to hurt then."

"I would have understood why you treated me different."

Gloria looked taken aback, and her hand fluttered to her chest. "I didn't treat you different! I loved you," she said, adamant. "I love you."

Esther's jaw tightened and her eyes shone, but she shook her head.

"Loving me was harder for you. But now I understand. I just wish you'd told me sooner."

"I wasn't *ever* gonna tell you. I wish you didn't know. No good can come of it. And now that you've heard it, you need to put it out of your head."

Esther stared at her in amazement. "How am I supposed to do that?"

"The Alexanders don't want you, Esther. I know that's a hard thing to hear. But you can't go knocking at their door, telling them you're their long-lost baby girl. They knew you were lost . . . and they didn't care. The Alexanders were glad you were gone. They got rid of Bo too. They'll run you off, or they'll hurt you, even more than I'm hurting you now. None of this needed to be said. Ever. Forget about them. They've forgotten about you. They've forgotten about Bo."

"They haven't forgotten about Bo," I said.

Both women looked at me. Esther in devastation, Gloria in condemnation.

"And they haven't forgotten about you," I said to Esther. *Son of a bitch.* What a damn mess. "And if they did . . . they're remembering now."

"How do you know?" Esther whispered.

I reached over and turned up the volume on Lee Otis's radio. Esther's voice filled the room.

"He's a bomb . . . and it's gonna get loud . . . He's a bomb . . . and you can't keep him down."

"They're playing it on the radio," I said. "Remember?"

"What were you thinking, Esther?" Gloria groaned. "That song is going to bring the devil to our doorstep."

~

Seconds later, the door burst open and Lee Otis and Arky barreled into the apartment, Alvin and Money behind them. Lee Otis had blood on his forehead and the front cover of his book was dangling by a thread.

"What happened?" Gloria Mine cried, rushing to her husband's side.

Lee Otis showed her the book, his expression beseeching. "Do you think we can fix it?" he asked. "Maybe stitch it up or something?" He was far more concerned about the book than his injury.

Arky led him to the sink and began dabbing his face with a wet cloth.

"What happened?" Esther repeated, looking at Alvin and Money.

"They were shooting at us," Money hissed. "A car drove by and the next thing we know, there's a gangster sticking his gun out the rear window."

"A big white guy came running up the street, shooting at the car. Otherwise we'd have been toast," Alvin added.

I ran from the Mines' apartment, raced down the hall, ran down the stairs, and yanked open the main entrance door. The "big white guy" shooting back had to be Fat Tony. There just weren't that many big white guys on Striver's Row, and Tony had trailed me all the way from Arthur Avenue.

Esther shouted for me to wait, but the blood was pounding in my head as I flew down the concrete entrance steps, looking for Tony's black Cadillac. He was striding down the street toward me, gun in hand, cigarette hanging from his lips, his long overcoat flapping around his legs. His car was halfway up the street, right behind mine.

"Benny, get the hell off the street," he shouted, waving me back inside. "All of yous!" he yelled. Esther and Money were behind me, Alvin behind them, and I immediately turned and ushered them back up the stairs and into the building.

"Who is that?" Money demanded, his eyes wild.

"That guy was the one shooting!" Alvin wailed.

"He was at your building," Esther said. "He watched me go inside."

"That's Tony," I said. "He's okay."

"What's happening, Benny?" Esther insisted.

"Gangsters are shootin' up the neighborhood. That's what's happening!" Money bellowed.

"Go up to your apartment," I told Esther. "Gather your things. We're leaving. We're going to Pittsburgh."

"What the hell, Lament?" Money shouted.

Then Tony was there, pounding on the main door.

"Don't let him in!"

I let him in.

Money was beside himself. He and Alvin dragged Esther up the narrow flight of stairs to the second floor, entered their apartment, and slammed the door.

"Everybody okay?" Fat Tony asked, holstering his gun. He'd lost his cigarette between the street and the entryway, and sweat dripped from his brow.

"I think so. Scratches. What happened, Tony?"

"I'm parked halfway up the block, just watching. Settled in, 'cause I don't know how long you'll be inside. I can see the whole street from the corner to this door." He indicates the entrance behind us with his thumb. "I notice four guys in a black Olds. White guys. Not too many white guys on the block. They stand out, the way Sticks and me stand out, ya know what I mean? They circled a few times, and I'm jumpy. I'd seen the kid and the old man come out and watched them go into the deli. They'd been inside for about ten minutes and were just coming out with coffee when them two other boys—the mean one and the smiley one—were crossing the street, heading toward the deli. Old man and kid see them and stop, waiting for them. Car is circling again, and I jump out. Just had a feeling, you know? Next thing I know, the car pulls up tight, right in front of the joint. I see a gun come out the window, aimed right at the kid and the old man. I hollered and started firing. I thought they were goners, Benny. I put some lead in the trunk of that Olds, and they sped off. They got a round off, but they were already moving, and they missed."

"You didn't recognize any of them?" I asked.

"White guys. Hats low. Guns. Never got out of the car." Fat Tony shrugged. "I didn't get a great look, but I don't think I seen 'em before. I usually know who's who. These guys are new."

"Where's Sticks?" I knew he wouldn't be far.

"He was circling. He's coming. We've had a few guys here, keeping an eye on things. But we stand out like sore thumbs in this neighborhood. We can't stake a place out or blend in, if you know what I mean. Everything's been quiet too. Seemed like it was a waste of time. I pulled the guys off this morning. I got lucky today. I was out and shootin' before they squeezed one off, but I wouldna even been here if I wasn't trailing you."

"Maybe they were trailing me too," I muttered.

"Maybe. Maybe so. But they were shootin' at the kid and his old man."

A hard rapping at the door made us start, and Sticks called out. "Tony?"

Tony opened the door a few inches so Sticks could slide in. He joined us in the dirty entryway and took a quick note of the layout before he gave us his attention. The stairs leading up and down from the front entrance were empty, the rows of doors all closed, the inner hallways quiet, like the residents sensed trouble and were waiting for us to leave.

Sticks nodded to me and looked at Fat Tony expectantly. It was the way they operated. Fat Tony did most of the talking, and Sticks did the cleanup.

They were complete opposites, not just in looks but in demeanor. Fat Tony had sobbed at Pop's wake; Sticks had just watched in terrifying silence, making note of everyone who came through and collecting those white envelopes, which he then gave to me.

I knew the Tonys weren't good men. But I also knew they had loved my father. They were like uncles to me, part of the Vitale family, and as distasteful as I found the ties that bound us, I was grateful for them too.

"I don't know what Sal thinks. This is comin' from me, Benny. Okay?" Fat Tony said, his voice low. "That didn't look random to me. Maybe those guys just wanted to scare the shit out of them." He pointed up the stairs, indicating the Mine family. "Maybe they just want them to know they know where they live and that they're watching. But something's going down. Me and Sticks both think so."

I looked at Sticks for corroboration.

"Takin' Jack out don't make no sense to me," Sticks grunted. "This isn't family business, Benny, if you know what I'm sayin'. This feels like somethin' else. But you ain't safe, and that little girl ain't safe. Her family ain't safe either. If I was you, I'd get out of town for a while." It was the most I'd ever heard Sticks say, and Fat Tony and I stared at him in surprise.

Sticks gazed back, sober, silent, his piece said.

"Who's with Sal?" I asked, my mind racing.

"Nobody at the moment. We're short. Plus, it's Sunday, so Sal's at home," Fat Tony said. "The Reinas have been in town since the wake. Mike and his wife were stayin' with Sal and Theresa, but they headed home today. Security's been nutso."

"I need to talk to him," I said.

"I'll take you," Fat Tony offered.

"No. Stay here. Keep watch," I insisted.

"I'm supposed to stay with you, Benny. Sticks will stay here."

But Sticks wasn't paying attention. His gaze was focused at the top of the stairs leading to the second floor. Esther was standing there, coat on, purse slung across her shoulders, looking down at us.

"I'm coming too," she said.

"I'll be back, Esther," I promised.

"I'm going with you."

"No. You're not. I'll be back," I repeated, firm.

"I want to talk to him."

"Who?" I asked.

"Your uncle. That's where you're going. I want to go too. I want him to explain what's going on."

Fat Tony's eyes widened but Sticks looked at me, a challenging gleam in his eye.

"That isn't a good idea," I said, shaking my head.

"You said he . . . loved . . . my mother," Esther said.

"Love might not be the right word." Fat Tony snorted, and Esther shot him a look so scathing, he gulped and excused himself.

"I'll be outside, Benny. You let me know what you want to do." He opened the door and stepped out onto the steps. Sticks hesitated and then looked back at Esther.

"I heard her sing once. Your mother. She was something special. We all thought so." He shifted his flat gaze to me. "She wants to talk to Sal, you should let her talk to Sal. Ain't gonna hurt nothin'. Might even help. I'll keep an eye on things here. Don't worry."

Sticks followed Fat Tony from the entryway, and I was left to marvel for a second time.

"I don't understand any of this, Benny. But I want to know what happened to my father. I want to know what happened to my mother, and I want to know why people are shooting at my family." She was holding on to the rail at the top of the stairs. Still standing, still straight, but barely holding on. She'd been hit with some big news in the last few hours, and the truths were still beating down on both of us.

"You don't know who you're dealing with," I warned. "Salvatore Vitale can make you disappear."

"The way he made my father disappear? The way he made my mother disappear?"

"I don't know that he did."

"Yes, you do. And you can go straight to hell with the rest of them, Benny Lament. You think because you didn't pull the trigger you can wash your hands of the blood your family's spilled?" Her lips trembled and angry tears streamed down her cheeks.

"My father's gone too, Esther," I whispered. "I watched him die. You don't get to lecture me about blood right now."

She swallowed, and her shoulders sagged in penitence. She swiped at her cheeks and swore beneath her breath.

"I'm sorry, Benny." She said the words like they were being ripped from her chest. I wondered if she'd ever apologized before. Didn't seem likely.

"Stay here, Esther," I said, turning away. I was so damn tired.

"Benny . . . please. Wait." Her heels clicked against the stairs, and I paused, my back to her, angry and scared, but unwilling to make her chase me. When her hand slipped into mine, I stiffened in defiance, but my traitorous fingers tightened around hers.

"Did your father trust your uncle?" she asked softly.

"I don't know about trust," I whispered. "That wasn't the way my father looked at it. He was totally and completely committed to him, though. Pop was loyal, through and through. He would have taken a bullet for Sal, no questions asked. He considered it his duty."

"Do you trust him?"

"With you? No," I said.

"What about with you? Would he protect you?"

"It depends. There's a hierarchy in everything. If I started to be a strain on the operation. If I put people at risk. He would take me out. But family is a big deal to him. It was a big deal to my father. And we're family."

"What are you going to do?"

"I'm going to ask for his help. And then we're going to Pittsburgh."

The Barry Gray Show

WMCA Radio

Guest: Benny Lament

December 30, 1969

"If you're just joining us on WMCA, you're listening to *The Barry Gray Show*. I'm here with Benny Lament, and we're talking music, murder, and one of the biggest stories of the decade, for a number of reasons."

"Esther and I had the deck stacked against us, that's for sure," Benny Lament says.

"There are a lot of layers to your story, layers folks may not know about. It wasn't just the obvious challenges of love and color."

"The obvious is easier to deal with, because you can prepare. It's when you don't know who's a friend and who's a foe that things get complicated. When you don't know who's pulling for you and who's plotting against you."

"Were you ever scared?" Barry Gray asks.

"I was. Always," Benny Lament answers. "Not of the music. Not of the work. But I was afraid of the things I couldn't control."

"Why?"

"My father told me once that men are put on earth to protect and provide. If a man can't protect and provide it'll make him mean . . . or it'll drive him crazy. I thought that was just an excuse until I loved someone so much that I would do anything to protect them. I understand now."

"You were worried you couldn't protect or provide?"

"I'm big. And I'm ugly. But some battles are bigger than one man."

"Bigger than one man and one woman?"

"Way bigger. But Esther said something once that I've never forgotten."

"What's that?"

"She said if you want people to change, you have to show them what it looks like."

14

Pandora's Box

I relented and took Esther with me to Sal's, though I extracted promises as we pulled into the driveway.

"I have to speak to him alone, Esther. Do you understand?" I asked. "He won't talk to me if you're there. He may not talk to me at all, once he sees you. When I ask you to leave, you leave."

"Will you tell me what is said?" she countered.

"No."

She frowned, but she didn't argue.

"Will you ask him what happened to Maude Alexander and Bo Johnson?" she said as we pulled up in front of his house.

"If he knows, he won't tell me, Baby Ruth."

"Then why are we here?"

"Because I don't have any place else to go."

Fat Tony had followed us in his own car, and when we pulled into Sal's driveway, he parked and accompanied us up the well-lit walk.

He knocked and rang the doorbell, like a deliveryman in need of a signature.

Esther stood beside me, her lips red and her eyes steady, but it was Theresa who answered the door. Not Sal. And not Carla. I hoped for Theresa's sake, and even for my own sake, that Carla was gone.

I greeted my aunt with a kiss on her cheek and introduced Esther, who held out her hand. Theresa took it, barely touching Esther's fingertips, but she did not move aside for us to enter.

"I need to talk to Sal, Aunt Theresa," I pressed quietly.

"Salvatore isn't feeling well. He's gone to bed," she said. "Come back tomorrow, Benito. Or maybe . . . call first."

It was eight o'clock.

"Uh . . . you're going to want to wake him," Tony said. "It's important, Mrs. Vitale. Can we come inside?"

Theresa considered the request, her lip between her teeth, her eyes on Esther.

"Mrs. Vitale?" Tony said, his brow furrowed. Theresa opened the door a little wider and moved aside. Tony pushed past her and disappeared up the stairs.

Theresa led us to the small sitting room to the left of the entryway, where guests were entertained, instead of leading us deeper into the house, to the living room where family typically gathered. I had jumped on the settee where we now sat, and played the huge Steinway that no one ever touched but me, but I'd never been escorted into the room like a stranger.

Theresa perched on a chair to the left of the settee, her legs neatly folded, but she toyed with the diamonds at her ears, a pair more suited to a night at the opera than an evening at home. They were her favorite pair—I'd seen her wear them a dozen times. They weren't especially large but the black, diamond-encrusted balls glittered brightly and caught the light when she turned her head. Against the bottled blonde of her hair, they looked cartoonish, like the Acme bombs on a Looney Tunes episode. She caught herself fidgeting and folded her hands.

"Are you taking care of yourself, Benito?" she asked, her tone wooden.

"Yes."

"Good. Sleeping and eating enough? You look tired."

"It's been a rough week," I said and bit at my cheek so I wouldn't grind my teeth.

"Yes. Of course. We all miss Jack." She blinked at me slowly, as though her furry black lashes weighed ten pounds. I had often wondered what Theresa looked like beneath the layers of paint and bleach and bubble-gum pink. She'd dabbed at her eyes at the wake, but I'd seen no tears. Francesca and Barbara had cried until no makeup remained on their grief-stricken faces. They'd loved Uncle Jack. Everyone did. But Theresa's paint had remained in place. Every last inch of it.

"You should be resting, Benito. Resting and recovering. Not working." Theresa's eyes flickered to Esther and she fingered her earring again. We listened as Tony descended the stairs again, then heard him walk across the entry to Sal's study, where he rapped softly before entering.

Theresa stood abruptly. "You will wait here," she insisted, and left the room, the swish of her skirts and the squeak of her shoes fading as she climbed the stairs.

Esther looked at me, her eyes wide, and I considered fleeing while we still could.

"She's strange," Esther whispered.

"She's sedated," I corrected. "And you'll see why."

Minutes later Sal joined us, his clothes as crisp and sharp as always, every hair in place, his sleeves rolled to his elbows, revealing forearms dark from days on the Vegas golf course. If he'd been in bed, he'd been quick about his toilette. It was much more likely that he hadn't been in bed at all. Tony trailed him.

He walked to Esther, who rose without prodding. He took her hand as his eyes roved over her face.

"You look like your mother," Sal said. He sounded almost surprised.

"No, I don't. I look like my father."

"His left leg was bigger than you are," Sal said. "Maude was beautiful. It was a compliment."

"Thank you," Esther said, tone even. Sal released her hand and walked to the little bar in the corner of the room. He poured himself a drink, his back to us.

"We were all in love with her. Everyone but Jack. Jack loved Giuliana."

Esther glanced at me, not understanding.

"Giuliana was my mother. Sal's sister," I explained.

"I see," she said softly.

"You're a singer too. Like Maude," Sal said.

She nodded. "Yes."

"I've played cards at Shimmy's. I've heard you, but always from another room. You don't sound like her. She was classically trained."

Esther said nothing.

Sal swirled his drink and sipped at it once. His hand was shaking. "She was magnificent." He sipped again. "Scotch?"

Esther and I both shook our heads. Fat Tony helped himself and sat down near the big double doors with his glass.

"Maybe you could sing for me now?" Sal asked.

"What would you like to hear, Mr. Vitale?" Esther asked.

"Something . . . old. Something slow. Something Maude would sing."

"I never knew her," Esther said softly.

Sal nodded slowly, ceding her point, then he finished off his scotch. "I did," he said.

"Yes. I know," Esther said.

Sal assumed his philosopher's stance, chin cupped, one arm wrapped around himself.

"Let me think on it. Make yourself comfortable. Pour yourself a drink. Tony will be here. I need to speak to my nephew. When we come back . . . maybe I will know what I want you to sing."

Tony's legs were stretched out in front of him, and his arms were folded across his girth, his little glass in his hand. He raised it to me, as if saying, "Don't worry."

Esther made herself a club soda, and I followed Sal from the room. He strode toward his study, and when we entered I closed the door behind us.

"Tony told me what happened in Harlem today," Sal said, all the softness he'd shown Esther gone from his voice. "Is that why you're here?"

"In part."

"If they wanted to kill her, Benito, they would. It's just not that hard to do. They are telling you both to shut your goddamn mouths," he hissed.

"It's too late for that, Uncle."

He snorted. "Your whole life you've never said two words. Why can't you be quiet now?"

"It's too late," I said again. I was not being insolent. I was being honest. Fate seemed to have all the momentum.

"There are no secrets, Benito," Sal said, divining my thoughts. "Not in my world. Everyone knows who Esther is. Alexander knows who she is. He knows where she is. He's always known. And he left her alone because she was no threat."

"She didn't know."

He frowned, his brows rising as his mouth turned down. "And now she does?"

"Now she does. I told her everything I knew, which isn't a whole hell of a lot."

Sal sighed and poured himself another drink from the bottle on his desk. "Why did you bring her here, nephew?"

"She wanted to meet you."

"Why?" he muttered.

"She wants to know more."

"I know nothing that she'll want to hear."

I stared at him, waiting. He downed his drink.

"I don't understand Jack. He didn't owe Bo Johnson a damn thing. All these years, he's looked after that girl like she was his responsibility. Now you're doing the same thing." He pointed at me with his glass. "She's got you tied in knots. Her mother was like that. Bewitching."

"You were in love with her?"

"I would have left Theresa for her. It would have broken ties with the Reina family, and her father would have made life hell, but I would have done it. Theresa and I had no children, and a man should be able to leave his wife if she can't conceive." Sal shifted in his chair, sighing. "Theresa knew I was in love with Maude. I tried to be discreet in the beginning, but Maude didn't want to be inconspicuous. She enjoyed the attention. She let us all dangle, all but one. When she met Bo Johnson, she had no interest in anyone else."

"That's what Pop said."

"That's what he said, huh?"

I nodded. Pop didn't need my protection anymore, but my stomach twisted at the admission.

"I thought when Bo Johnson went to jail, she'd want me back. Did he tell you that?" Sal asked softly.

"No."

"She let me in her bed . . . once. That's when I realized she was already pregnant. She was quite possibly even more beautiful pregnant than she was before. I'd never made love to a pregnant woman. But I liked it. I even told Maude that I would take care of her and the baby if she married me. I think I surprised her. And until Bo came back, I think she was considering it. Considering me."

I wished I'd accepted the scotch. I had not expected his honesty, and meeting his gaze was painful.

"See?" Sal grunted. "I do not know anything Esther Mine will want to hear."

"Do you know where Bo Johnson is?"

"I hope he's dead."

"But you don't know?"

"I don't know. I don't care."

"You don't care, but you've made it hard for Esther to get work. You put the word out, and people listened."

"It was for her own good. That's what Jack didn't understand. That's what you don't seem to understand." He shrugged like he was surrounded by imbeciles. "I can't protect you if you don't listen to me."

"I don't want protection. Not for me."

"For the girl?"

I nodded. "For the girl. And if that means being a Vitale, then so be it."

His eyes widened in sudden understanding.

"I never thought I'd see the day," he marveled. He laughed suddenly, the sound grating. Mocking. "Son of a bitch. Benito Vitale Lomento wants to join the family."

"My whole life, I wanted nothing to do with this mess Pop called family," I said, keeping my voice even, but my blood raged. "I watched a man die. I watched the Tonys wrap his body in a rug. I watched my father wash blood from his hands and from his clothes more times than I can count. I saw him hurt people I liked. I watched him go to jail in the name of loyalty. And finally, I watched him die. I know you don't think this family owes me anything, and maybe it doesn't. I swore I'd never ask. But the mob takes care of its own. Wives and kids are off limits. I'm not going to do what my pop did, Uncle. I'd be no good at it anyway. But I'll give a percentage of my earnings every month to the boss. It'll be clean money—no drugs, no girls, no rackets. I'll earn it, and I'll turn a percentage over. That percentage will grow exponentially if I can keep my wife alive. You said you'd make me a star, like Sinatra. I don't need you to do that. I'll make myself a star. I'll make her a star. And you'll get your cut."

"Your wife?"

"I'm going to marry her."

Sal laughed, incredulous. "You've suffered a terrible loss, Benito. You're not thinking straight."

"I am."

"This is not a fight I want, Benito. I do business with these people."

"With Alexander?"

"With everyone."

Everybody's rotten.

"My father was gunned down by 'these people.' My father, who served you faithfully every day of his life. I don't want revenge. I don't want a war. I just want to keep Esther alive. That's what Pop would want too. If she's a Vitale, maybe Alexander will decide it's just not worth it."

Sal stared at his empty glass for several long seconds, his hands steepled and his gold watch winking at me from his brown wrist. He didn't raise his eyes when he finally spoke, and his voice was tired.

"Can you promise that you won't betray your family, that the things you hear and the violence that you may be called upon to participate in will never be repeated or divulged?" He sounded like he was reading me the oath already, but I knew that wasn't how it worked.

"I have never repeated or divulged anything I've seen or heard, Uncle. That part won't change."

He sighed heavily, and he lifted his black gaze to mine. "Chicago. New Year's Day. The commission will meet. Afterward . . . the new members will be sworn in. There's been a bit of a . . . recruitment drive. You'll take the oath. You'll be a made man. A soldier in my organization." He held up three fingers. "You got three weeks to change your mind. After that, Benito. It's done. There will be no going back."

"Where?"

"You won't know. You go to the Blackstone Hotel. There will be a car waiting. Once you're inside the car, you'll wear a blindfold. When it's done . . . you'll be brought back."

Chicago. New Year's Day. I nodded.

"Until then . . . keep your head down. Don't say anything on a call that you don't want the world to hear. You understand? Don't say where you're going or where you've been. Don't talk about your business. Or your women. Don't talk about Esther. Learn to say what needs to be said without saying it."

I nodded again.

"Don't call attention to yourself. Don't call attention to her. And stop singing."

"I'll see you in Chicago, Uncle."

"I am not the enemy, Benito. But you don't have any friends. Remember that."

~

Esther didn't end up singing for Sal. He stayed in his study when Fat Tony walked us out.

"I'm going to stay here. Be careful going home," Tony said. I nodded, relieved. He and Sticks wouldn't be able to go where we were going anyway. I had a long night ahead, but I just said good night and thanked him. He would worry when we were gone, but that was unavoidable.

Gloria Mine was still ironing and Lee Otis was fixing his book when Esther and I returned to the Mines' apartment that night. Arky sat in the corner, his hands folded, watching his family come unglued with a furrowed brow. Alvin wanted to know where the hell we'd been, and Money launched into all the reasons why everything was all my fault.

"You show up, and all of a sudden we're getting shot at," Money complained.

"It's the song. It's the song about Bo Johnson. You gone and stirred a hornet's nest," Gloria said, her voice quavering.

"And I'm going to keep singing it. I'm going to sing it until the day I die," Esther said, unbuttoning her coat. She moved to the coat closet near the door and yanked it open. Inside was a small stack of drawers and a row of shoes and dresses. She tugged a worn valise from the top shelf and started packing.

"Don't say that, Ess," Alvin warned. "Don't talk like that."

"You want to put me in the ground, Esther? You want to put your brothers in the ground too? What about Arky? What if we lose our jobs?" Gloria scolded, but Esther was stony eyed and unapologetic. She continued gathering her things.

Her brothers watched her—we all did—and no one knew what to say. Esther hadn't known the truth, so I was guessing her brothers hadn't known either. But they knew now. They knew all about Bo Johnson and Maude Alexander now. It was written all over their stricken faces. Their sister had been pushed from their family tree, made a stranger, and no one knew how to make it better.

"What are we gonna do, Benny?" Alvin asked, turning to me.

"I'm taking Esther to Pittsburgh," I said.

For a moment there was a collective stunned silence in the kitchen. But it didn't last long.

"You can't go alone. A white man and a colored girl? You're just asking for trouble," Gloria gasped.

"We've already got trouble," I said. "There's nothing I can do about that."

"It's like Pandora's box," Arky said.

Alvin frowned. "What are you talking about, Daddy?"

"It's a story in Lee Otis's book. The girl, Pandora, is told not to open the box. All manner of trouble and trials are in the box. But she's curious. She can't resist. So she tries to just take a peek. But once the box is opened, it's too late. She can't put the trouble back in the box."

"We've got a gig in Pittsburgh, opening for Ray Charles," I said.

"Ray Charles?" Lee Otis squeaked.

"You can't leave us. We're a band, remember?" Money said.

"We're family," Alvin inserted. "We're always going to be family."

Esther flinched, but Alvin patted her shoulder.

"We're coming too," Money said.

"You can't go!" Gloria cried. "You have work. Lee Otis has school. What about college? He's worked so hard."

"It's Pittsburgh. Not Timbuktu, Mama," Alvin soothed. "And Money and I got nothing to stay here for. It's a job. We can get another one . . . or we can make some real money right now, right, Benny?"

"Lee Otis can't go to school. He can't go anywhere. None of us can. Not with people trying to pick us off. We need to get out of town," Money grumbled.

"I've already done enough to graduate, Mama. Even if I never went back," Lee Otis reassured, but he looked scared. I was scared too. But Pop had said, "Make yourselves so big they can't snuff you out." We had a window and momentum, and I was going to take it.

"I'll call my cousin in Montgomery. You can all go there for a while," Gloria protested.

"They're playing our songs in Alabama too, Mama. Cousin Eileen heard 'Any Man' twice. Remember?" Lee Otis said.

"Can't put the trouble back in the box," Arky said again.

"The 45s I gave you . . . do you have any left?" I asked Money. If we were going to Pittsburgh, I needed to gather as many as I could.

"Just the few I kept for us."

"And the rest?"

"I got contacts too, Lament. Every joint in Harlem with a jukebox or a deejay got that record," Money bragged.

"And we told them it was mobster approved," Alvin added, grinning. "I made sure everybody knew it was a Benny Lament production. I might have mentioned Salvatore Vitale too. That name has some power."

Gloria Mine moaned again. "There won't be money coming in anymore, will there?" Gloria asked me. "He's gone."

I stared at her, not understanding.

"He sent money. Your father. Jack Lomento. But he's dead now . . . and there won't be any more money."

"He was still sending money?" Esther gasped, and Gloria bowed her head.

"I've been saving it," she said, embarrassed.

"Where is it?" Esther hissed.

"Esther, if you're leaving, we're gonna need that money," Gloria argued.

"Esther," I said, reluctant to step in. "Leave it. I've got money." I addressed Gloria. "Mrs. Mine, take the money you've saved. Go see your sister. Just until all this blows over. The rest of us will go to Pittsburgh. Pack one bag," I told the boys. "Just a change of clothes—maybe an extra shirt—and two suits to perform in. Keep it simple. Black. Gray. Add your touch. A hat. Some glasses. A bow tie. It's about the music, not the costume. And with a name like Minefield, we don't want to look cheerful."

"And then what? We can't come back here," Money insisted. "That's not much of a plan."

"I don't know. I'm going to make some calls. I've got a few ideas."

"I don't trust you, Lament."

"Yeah. So you've said. I don't trust you either, Money," I hissed, nerves shot. "And I sure as hell don't need you. So you can be quiet or you can stay here. Doesn't matter to me."

"You'd like that, huh? Having Esther all to yourself? Leaving us here with the mess you made?"

"Money, stop," Alvin chided. "Benny and Esther are the whole show. Nobody's coming to see us. Esther can sing . . . but she needs Benny. We all do."

Esther zipped her valise closed and pointed at Money. "You couldn't have done what Benny's done. We're on the radio, and we're opening for Ray Charles. He did that. He's the boss. So shut up."

"You choosing him, baby sister?" Money asked. "Or have you just decided you're not our sister after all?"

Esther flinched again, and my hands formed fists. Money Mine was an asshole. "You want in, or you want out, Money?" she asked, her voice low. "Decide now."

He stared at me, sullen. I stared back, and Gloria prayed, though I wasn't sure who she was praying for.

"When opportunity comes along you take it. You don't wait for the next bus," Esther warned. "This bus is pulling out."

"You aren't going to stop the train, Money. So you'd best get on board." Alvin added a metaphor of his own. He made a motion like he was tooting a horn. "That sounds like a song lyric, doesn't it, Benny?" He was smiling again, his good humor restored. Nothing seemed to get him down. But I felt like throwing up.

The Barry Gray Show

WMCA Radio

Guest: Benny Lament

December 30, 1969

"It's hard to describe to the audience what happened in a very short span of time," Barry Gray says. "People were talking about you two. Everyone was talking about you two. It wasn't just your music. It was you. Esther Mine and Benny Lament. It was your story, Bo Johnson's story, and Maude Alexander's story all colliding in spectacular fashion. You can't buy that kind of exposure. I like to think I had something to do with it, that WMCA radio had something to do with it, but the truth is, you two exploded onto the scene. And once you captured public attention, there was no stopping it."

"It was Pandora's box," Benny Lament says.

"Like your song?"

"The secret's out, everybody knows, people are watching wherever we go," Benny sings the popular lyrics. "We wrote that one in the car on the way to Pittsburgh, along with quite a few others."

"You wrote it in the car?" Barry Gray laughs.

"Esther and I were always writing. It was constant. It was how we communicated best. We were either writing or arguing. Sometimes both at the same time."

"So the tussle is real . . . it's not just part of the act?"

"We have always worked off each other in a way that was so natural that we didn't have to plan the give-and-take. In fact, that might have ruined it. The verbal wrestling kept us sharp, and it actually saved us both from breaking during what was a really stressful time. We always had a strong set, but the order was never set in stone. We both had the freedom and prerogative to change it up to make a show work. The band just learned to keep up."

15

Lines

We left New York before daybreak Monday morning, loaded in my car. Money, Lee Otis, and Alvin in the back seat, and Esther beside me. Lee Otis's drum kit and the other instruments were tied up top and we each had a bag in the trunk. I had the money from Pop's wake—it wasn't insignificant—and the money from his mattress, which would take care of the cost of cutting an album and mass distribution. I hadn't been able to withdraw any money from my account, but I could write a check if I needed to. I wasn't worried about money. Money—the brother and the bank—was always a pain, but it was the least of our problems.

Sal told me to lie low, but we weren't going to. After Pittsburgh, we would head to Detroit. I had to talk to Berry Gordy and convince him to let me buy studio time without using the Motown label. I didn't want to bring the devil down on his back. His was the only studio new enough, independent enough, and far enough away that I might be able to convince him to help me. And the fact that Esther and I weren't the same color wouldn't bother him at all.

Pop said not to trust anyone, and I didn't trust anyone. But I couldn't do what I needed to do all by myself. I just hoped if I kept moving, the thing that was chasing us wouldn't catch up. Or even better, that we'd be too big to take down.

Sometimes the best way to hide is in the spotlight. If the whole world knows who you are, it's harder to snuff you out.

It was 370 miles to Pittsburgh, and no one had gotten any rest the night before. I urged Esther to sleep like her brothers. They were propped against and sprawled over each other like they didn't mind the close quarters.

"They've slept that way all their lives. They never had much choice," she said.

"That's one thing I always had."

"What, space?"

"Yeah. It's an only-child thing, I guess."

She laughed, but the sound was mirthless. "It just occurred to me that I was an only child too." She shook her head like she couldn't get her mind around it.

"Sleep, Baby Ruth."

"Nah. I'll stay awake with you," she said. "My worries are too loud to sleep."

"You want to tell me?"

She sighed, stewing it over, and when she finally relented, her voice was small and plaintive, like the woman had dissolved into the darkness and left the child behind.

"How can I be sad about people I never knew?" she asked. "I never knew Bo Johnson or Maude Alexander. But I . . . miss them. I . . . ache . . . for them. And that doesn't make any sense."

"Sure it does."

"What were they thinking?" she whispered. "It never would have worked."

I was silent beside her, hands on the wheel, eyes on the road, but the ache she spoke of rose up in my own chest, and the image of Bo Johnson and Maude Alexander flickered in my head. Beautiful people, side by side, thumbing their noses at society. They took what they wanted . . . and paid the ultimate price.

"But I understand it," Esther continued. "Because sometimes I forget too."

"Forget what?"

"I forget . . . that you're white."

"Is that something you need to forget?" I asked.

"It's something I *want* to forget."

Of all the things she'd ever said, of all the thorny words and glances we'd shared. Of all the heat and the tumult we'd experienced in the time we'd spent together, those words bothered me the most. They echoed a history I could not change and a reality I could not fix.

"I can change my hair and wear a different suit. I can avoid garlic and stop smoking. There's all kinds of things I can do to be a better man. But I can't do a whole lot about that, Baby Ruth."

"It's not about being a better man."

"Then what is it?"

"I don't know if it's something you can understand. It's something you would have to experience, every day of your life. It's . . . easier . . . for you to look past it."

"Look past what?"

"Color."

"Do you think it should be hard?" I asked, incredulous. "Do you want me to look at you and see Esther or just the color of your skin?"

"I'm telling you, Benny, that looking past color is not so easy for me. All my life, I've had the lines drilled into me. The lines you do not cross. You stand here. You live there. You can be on stage, but you can't sit at the table. You can clean the house, but you can't buy it. And always, always, keep your distance from the white folks. I heard Mama say to Money once, 'Those people will kill you.' And she believed it. She'd seen it. And she made us believe it too. So when I forget that you are you, and I am me . . . it feels like a miracle. And I understand Bo Johnson. I understand why he thought loving my mother might work."

"But you haven't kept your distance," I said. "You sought me out. And you can't tell me you were ever afraid of me. Because you weren't." My chest still stung from her words.

"I know you won't believe it, seeing how forward I've been. But, besides asking Ralph who you were, I've never had a conversation with a white man before you. 'Yes, sir.' 'No, sir.' 'Thank you,' and 'You're welcome.' That's been the extent of my interactions. But I dreamed about you, before you ever came along."

My eyebrows shot up, and I looked over at her, away from the road for half a second, trying to determine whether she was pulling my leg.

"You can laugh, if you want to. I know it's silly. But it's true. I swear it on Lee Otis's life. I worried about it too. I worried because I couldn't understand it. Dreamin' about a big white man playing piano." She laughed softly. "I've dreamed about you for years, but I never told anyone. Who was I gonna tell? Mama? She'd have beat some sense into me. Then you showed up at Shimmy's, and I found out who you were. Benny Lament, the piano man. Big shot. Goin' places. There you were, in the flesh, listening to me sing. I don't put much stock in the Bible or in spiritual things. But I'm no fool either. When God holds up a sign that says 'Pay attention, Esther,' I'm gonna pay attention." Her voice wobbled but her back got straighter, even as tears started to stream down her cheeks. She folded her arms, defensive, but the tears kept coming, like vulnerability was harder than pain.

I didn't know what to say. The ache in my chest had shifted into something new. Something hopeful. Something sweet. I handed her a handkerchief. It was one of Pop's. I hadn't been able to part with his goddamn handkerchiefs, and I'd been carrying one in my pocket since the wake. She took it from my hand and pressed it to her face.

"That's twice now," she said, her voice ringing with aversion. "I don't cry. Ever. I don't cry, and I don't fall asleep in the presence of strange men, even in a car, even when I'm tired. I don't even know who I am anymore." The irony of the statement struck her as funny, and she laughed as she mopped at her cheeks. I didn't have to point out that for the first time in her life, she knew exactly who she was.

"You know, Benny. I went to your apartment yesterday to comfort you. I know I didn't succeed. I said some ridiculous thing about needing to record our songs, but that wasn't why I was there. I went to see if you were okay. To be your friend. But you're so much better at it than I am."

"At what?"

"Being a friend. Taking care of people." She waved Pop's handkerchief at me. "You do the mother hen thing really well."

"No, I don't."

"Yeah. You do."

I didn't argue further, but she was wrong. I took care of myself, and I always had. I looked out for Benny. For number one. I'd never been a good son, a good grandson, a good nephew, or a good friend. I was a good musician, and that was all.

When I didn't protest, Esther folded up the white handkerchief; she kept it clutched in her hand, as though she thought she might need it again, but she abandoned the subject.

"I always wondered why Mama wasn't the same with me. She never treated me bad. She wasn't harsh. But she didn't have the same affection for me as she did for my brothers. I thought it was all in my head. That I was sensitive. Needy. Now I feel like I've been the butt of a joke that everyone understood but me. I should have known. I see that now.

"Mama never said a bad word about my father. Never complained. The money helped, I'm sure," she added, her voice wry. "She told me he left her with a sack of cash and a letter." Esther shrugged like it didn't matter anymore, but I knew better. It would always matter.

"I always thought it was kind of odd, how much she liked him and how well she spoke of him, especially since he didn't stick around. It makes sense now, though. He didn't leave her. He just left me."

I wanted to defend Bo Johnson, but I didn't. Esther's voice was introspective, not self-pitying or accusatory, and I let her talk, uninterrupted.

"The money made her nervous, though. She never flashed it or called attention to the fact that we had enough to eat and the bills were paid. She took in ironing and alterations, but it wasn't high-paying work. She'd worry that the money would stop, and there were months when it wouldn't come. But the next month there would be more, and she'd breathe a sigh of relief and praise my father like she was saying grace. 'Thank you, Bo Johnson.'" Esther raised her hands and closed her eyes, mimicking Gloria Mine perfectly. "Lee Otis heard her once and started thanking Bo Johnson in his prayers too. Mama smacked him and told him not to say that name again. She was more careful after that, but even still, she never said a bad word about him."

For a long stretch we were silent, the topic exhausted. I thought Esther would give in and close her eyes, but she didn't.

"Why did she name him Lee Otis?" I asked finally, plucking out a wandering, random thought.

"She thought it sounded smart."

My eyebrows shot up.

"Don't give me that look, Benny. Lee Otis is smart."

"I never said he wasn't. But Lee Otis sounds like a baker . . . or a bread company. Lee Otis Breads."

"Ask him anything. He knows every song—who wrote it and in what year. Rockabilly, jazz, blues, even the classic stuff. He knows it. He's a walking encyclopedia. He loves information. He soaks it up like a big kitchen sponge. He should be a scientist. Or a doctor. But we make him play. Just like Mama made me sing."

"She made you sing?" The statement surprised me. "You didn't want to?"

"I didn't want to do it all the time. I didn't want it to be work. But I had a gift. Mama said, 'Having a gift and not using it is like having a garden and letting your family starve.' It was more responsibility than I wanted. I resented it."

"My piano teacher, Mrs. Costiera, used to say, 'Not everyone has a tree inside them.'"

"A tree?"

"Learning to play the piano was the most natural thing in the world for me. It felt like remembering, like it was something I'd done before. The more time I spent, the more the scales fell from my eyes and my mind, and the river of music that ran through my veins became this rushing current. Plucking melodies from the water was like plucking low-hanging fruit from a tree. When I told Mrs. Costiera how easy it was, she smacked me in the forehead with the palm of her hand." I adopted my thickest Italian accent, which always made me think of my old teacher.

"'You must still take care of your tree,'" I said, mimicking her. "'Give thanks for it. Water it. Prune it. Keep the birds away and the beasts away. If you don't care for your tree it will stop producing fruit. And there will be nothing to harvest.'"

"Use it or lose it," Esther summarized.

"Yeah. Basically. But Mrs. Costiera didn't really have to convince me. It was all I ever wanted to do."

"I wanted to write books," Esther murmured.

"What kind of books?"

"All kinds." She shrugged like it didn't matter, and I waited in silence for her to tell me more. My silence made her defensive. "I'm smart. I was reading before I was five. I taught myself. The way you taught yourself piano. I didn't want to dance or sing. I wanted to read. I wanted to learn. I wanted to write. But reading didn't pay. Learning didn't pay. And I could sing, so that's what I did. I got my first big gig when I was thirteen."

I whistled.

"When I was thirteen the money stopped for a whole year." She looked at me in the soft glow emanating from the dash. "For months we waited. We were desperate. Mama started taking me to auditions. But I didn't get any work. I had too much attitude."

"Even then?" I teased.

"Even then. I've been this way all my life. Better get used to it, Benny Lament."

"So what happened? Did Gloria give up?"

"Mama was even more stubborn than I am."

"So . . . no?"

"No." She chuckled, but her voice hitched as though the laughter surprised her. "I haven't ever laughed about that. What do you know?" she said. "She took me to El Morocco on Fifty-Fourth. They had the African theme—zebra stripes on the seats and the walls that looked like the inside of a genie's bottle. Rumor was they were putting together a new show. I was small, but I was pretty and I had lighter skin." Her voice trembled, and I didn't know if it was anger or sorrow or laughter that caused the quaver. "They liked it when the girls weren't too dark."

Ah, definitely not mirth.

"I didn't have to do anything complicated. Didn't have to dance at all. It was the opening number, and I sang a song about flying away."

"Let's hear it."

"Close your eyes, raise your feet, and we'll go flying, you and me," she sang quietly. She glanced over her shoulder at her sleeping brothers, like she was embarrassed. "They lifted me up on a 'flying carpet.' That's the reason I got the job. I sounded like a woman and I didn't weigh more than a child, so it was easier to swing me around. About six months into the job, I fell off during a live performance and broke my arm. They hired someone else, and I was relieved. Mama tried to get me back out there, but then the money started coming in again, after a year of nothing, and she stopped pushing."

"You were thirteen?" I asked.

She nodded, and I did some quick math. "That was the year Pop was in jail. That's why you didn't get any money."

"It started up again when he got out," she said, like it all suddenly made sense.

"Yeah. I'm guessing that's it."

"Why is this all happening now, Benny? Why did your father push you toward me now?"

I'd asked that same question a hundred times. I could think of only one reason. "He was dying. He was trying to make sure you would be okay when he was gone."

~

When the sun rose, Esther slept, as if the light reassured her. It reassured me too, and my eyes got heavy. I turned on the radio, needing sound and distraction, and caught the tail end of a top-of-the-hour update on a station out of Philly.

> *President-elect John F. Kennedy has chosen Rudolf Alexander to be his secretary of labor. Alexander has a long history of fighting for union rights and is thought to be on the short list for Supreme Court justice. If Felix Frankfurter, the aging justice, retires this year, this appointment to secretary of labor may be a temporary one.*
>
> *Rudolf Alexander was a highly effective lawyer for the labor unions and, no stranger to politics, made an unsuccessful bid for the presidency in 1932 but lost his party's nomination to Franklin Delano Roosevelt. The two men*

were bitter rivals, but it was Roosevelt who appointed Alexander to the federal bench in 1939.

He married Kathleen Mortimer, the heir to the Mortimer fortune, and has used that prominence and wealth to champion the rights of the working man. He's sixty-eight years old—no longer a man in his prime—but he's long been a trusted advisor of the young president-elect and a close friend of the Kennedy family.

I switched the radio off, suddenly wide awake, and spent the next hour in an addled haze. Nothing seemed real. I'd been operating in a state of shock since I met Esther. Then Pop died, and the shock became horror. Horror became disbelief. Disbelief quickly became disorientation. I was at a point now where nothing fazed me.

Halfway between New York and Pittsburgh, I pulled off the highway and filled up my tank, took a leak, and bought a cup of coffee for everyone in the car. They drank with grateful groans, stretched their legs, and used the facilities too, though we got a few curious stares. Maybe it was the instruments hog-tied to the top of a car without a rack, or maybe it was the oddity of a white man traveling with four Negros. We definitely weren't inconspicuous.

The realization made me jumpy, imagining a car with four gunmen trailing us all the way from Harlem. When we climbed back in the car, I begged for a distraction. I needed my piano but settled for the next best thing. Everyone was awake. We might as well work.

"We're going to write an album," I informed Esther and her brothers. "We've got 'Any Man,' 'Beware,' 'Itty Bitty,' and 'The Bomb Johnson.' We need ten songs, minimum. Five for each side." I reached across Esther and pulled a notebook and a pencil out of the glove compartment. I had them tucked everywhere, the result of being a workaholic.

"What about 'Chicken' and 'Dark Heart'?" Esther said, opening the pad. "And what about the heartbeat song?"

"'Chicken'? You wrote a song called 'Chicken'?" Lee Otis asked.

"No," I said.

"Yes," Esther argued. "He wrote it in about five seconds too. So if you think he can't come up with six songs in the next few hours, you'd be wrong."

"We need *good* songs," I added.

"Can you write without your piano?" Esther asked.

I shrugged. The music always started in my head, not my hands, though they definitely worked together.

"If Lee Otis can sit up there with you, I can fit my guitar back here. I can't write shit without it," Money said.

I pulled over again, and five minutes later, Esther was tucked between me and Lee Otis, who used the dashboard for a drum. Both Alvin and Money had managed to wedge their instruments in the back seat and began adjusting their strings.

"Let's hear that chicken song," Lee Otis insisted.

"How did it go, Benny?" Esther asked. "It was the key of G, right?"

"The key of G. For good chicken," I murmured. Esther grinned, and my nerves eased.

"Are you two messin' with us?" Money complained.

"You strut all over town, but boy, I know the truth. You're scared of me, it's plain to see, you're chicken," Esther sang, her pitch perfect, her delivery on point.

"Well, what do you know?" Alvin laughed. "I like it. But it's making me hungry."

We finished "Chicken" in twenty minutes, and Esther wrote the lyrics out in neat lines before we moved on to the next. The heartbeat song, as Esther had called it, became "Let's Say Hello."

"We need to give it a heartbeat rhythm. *Ba DUM. Ba DUM. Ba DUM,*" I said. Lee Otis did as I asked, keeping up the pulse with his sticks.

Esther and I sang it back and forth the way we'd done just before I kissed her. I didn't even dare look at her, but my chest got hot remembering.

I hear your heart, or is it mine?
It's saying hello, maybe goodbye.
Oh no, not that. Don't wanna go.
Don't say goodbye. Let's say hello.

We picked our way through another verse, but by the time we reached the chorus, it was obvious. It just needed some horns. "Don't say goodbye!" Esther wailed, making the phrase climb, and I answered as though we were rolling down the other side. "Don't say goodbye," I answered. "Don't say goodbye," she repeated, leveling up, and Money got the concept and came in with me on the rejoinder.

"Don't say goodbye. The heart don't lie. Let's say hello," Esther composed, her hand scribbling as she sang.

Esther forgot nothing. I felt naked without the piano, and the inspiration didn't come as readily, but she had an ear for melody and a memory that astounded me. When I was at a loss, trying to hear it in my head, she supplied a lyric, and Money and Alvin threw in their two cents every ten seconds.

Arky's insistence on Pandora's box had given me an idea for a song, and Money had a Chuck Berry soundalike called "Dancing Shoes" that showcased his skills. We tweaked the lyrics and improved the progression so it was a brand-new song. It made me think of Esther and her attachment to her heels. We changed the name of the song to "No Shoes," and the song oozed with attitude.

I had a number called "Cold" that I'd given to Roy Orbison, but he wasn't releasing it as a single, and I still owned rights. His version was guitar heavy, but I'd written it with a little less croon and a tad more bite, which suited Esther. By the time we reached Pittsburgh, we had nine songs plotted and put on paper.

"What was the other one you said? Something about a dark heart?" Alvin asked.

I wished Esther had kept that one to herself. It was too private. Too personal, and I didn't want Money reaching over the seat and strangling me.

"Let's leave that one alone," I protested, but Alvin wouldn't let it go.

"They can't all be up-tempo. We have 'Beware,' but that ain't a love song. We need a ballad. Something people can slow dance to. Something like the Platters would sing."

"Let's hear it," Money insisted.

"I don't remember how it goes," I said.

"Liar," Esther said softly.

"Baby Ruth," I warned.

"I want to hear it," Alvin insisted.

I refused, and Esther mercifully held her tongue, but when everyone else had nodded off again, she began to sing, and "Dark Heart" became more than just a few lines composed while we were dancing.

"You two are going to get us killed," Money grumbled from the back seat, surprising us both, but we had an album.

The Barry Gray Show

WMCA Radio

Guest: Benny Lament

December 30, 1969

"You opened for Ray Charles in Pittsburgh at the Syria Mosque. Surprised everyone. The Drifters were supposed to perform, but Minefield took the stage instead," Barry Gray says.

"Nobody knew who we were. 'Any Man' was getting some airtime but I think it's safe to say we weren't household names," Benny Lament replies.

"You were heckled and booed."

"At first, yeah. The crowd wanted the Drifters. But we won them over."

"A news article from the *Pittsburgh Post-Gazette* following your performance called you electric. Explosive. They also accused you of inciting the crowd."

"That wasn't our intention," Benny Lament says.

Barry Gray reads a quote from the article. "With a voice that belied her size, Esther Mine of the group Minefield worked the

crowd into a frenzy that spilled out into the streets and resulted in several arrests for looting and disorderly conduct last Tuesday evening. Esther Mine and Benny Lament, Minefield's manager, were arrested for inciting a riot upon leaving the stage but released after paying a fine and agreeing to leave the city."

"The whole thing was bizarre. The crowd was dancing and clapping. Esther and I were doing our thing—arguing and singing—and the audience was with us. We ended with 'The Bomb Johnson,' and the crowd was quiet when she told them the story behind the song."

Barry Gray adds an anecdote. "Elvis Presley was banned from the Mosque as well."

"I think they just banned his hips," Benny says, and Barry laughs, but he presses Benny for more details.

"Why were you arrested?"

"By the time the song was over, the crowd was on their feet. It was like we'd lit a fuse. People were screaming and shouting. Some were crying," Benny says.

"A white crowd?"

"Mostly. If I remember right, we had a Negro crowd on the mezzanine."

"Segregated in Pittsburgh?"

"Not officially. But it's like Esther says . . . sometimes the lines are just understood."

"So you shared the story about Bo Johnson, sang his song, and a riot broke out?" Barry summarizes.

"I actually think our arrest was what made it all turn ugly. It was like the very thing Esther was singing about—the story she'd just finished telling—was playing out in front of thousands of people."

16

Benny and the Laments

The Syria Mosque in the heart of Pittsburgh was a brown brick edifice guarded by an enormous sphinx on each side of the entrance and had a rich history of hosting every kind of musical act from Louis Armstrong to Rachmaninov. It was an aging powerhouse with seating for over three thousand people, and we were told it was sold out for both shows that night, one at eight and one at ten thirty. Portions of the weeklong musical variety show would be broadcast live on channel three as well and covered in live segments by the three networks—NBC, CBS, and ABC. I doubted we'd get a mention—Ray Charles was the draw—but it rattled me, nonetheless.

The Mosque had a reputation that brought the big names, and Minefield wasn't a big name. We weren't even a little name, but when we arrived at the Mosque on Tuesday morning, per Jerry Wexler's instructions, we were escorted to a dressing room not much bigger than a janitor's closet. *THE DRIFTERS* was written on a slate board next to the door. I made sure the attendant knew who we were, but they didn't fix it. I rubbed the words off with my handkerchief but didn't have a piece of chalk to replace them.

We tried to rehearse in the cramped dressing room, but the close quarters made us all even more irritable than we already were, and we waited in the stage wings for two hours, watching as the sound crew bustled and rearranged and moved around us, continually telling us it would be our turn soon.

At five o'clock the press started setting up for their remote broadcasts, and we still hadn't had a sound check. If I didn't do something, we weren't going to get one. Ray Charles would arrive, and Minefield would have to make do.

Money had retreated to his own corner, Lee Otis was twirling his sticks like he wanted to take flight, and Alvin had lost his smile. Esther was scowling, her jaw tight, her posture rigid, and I hadn't had more than a few hours' sleep in what felt like days. The lack of sleep hurt my voice more than anything else, and it wasn't doing the band any good either. I'd had enough.

We needed to rehearse on that stage, even if we didn't have sound, or we were going to fall flat, and I couldn't let that happen. The Steinway was in place for Ray, the lid opened toward the audience.

Ignoring the stagehands and the sound engineers, I sat down at the piano and without waiting for the others, pounded out the opening measures of Beethoven's Fifth to wake everyone up and get my blood surging. Beethoven's Fifth merged into "Beware," and Esther began to sing, standing at the lone microphone. It screeched and the speakers popped, but we ignored the protests of "We're not ready for you!" and kept going.

By the time we'd reached the end of the song, Lee Otis was sitting on the raised drum set, making the cymbals sizzle, and Alvin was playing a walking line on his bass, which miraculously had been connected to the amplifiers. We slid immediately into "Itty Bitty," as it allowed Money to join in.

Ten minutes into our "rehearsal," we were interrupted and told that Mr. Charles was ready to take the stage. When I insisted on doing at least one more song, the main engineer shook his head.

"I have all your levels noted. We're running behind schedule. Mr. Charles is here for his sound check."

"We waited for three hours, and we go on first," I argued. "We need a few minutes. You want the audience to complain? They aren't going to like that we're here instead of the Drifters. We don't give them a good show, it's not going to be us they come to for a refund." I still hadn't even been mic'd, though the piano sounded amazing, and just feeling the keys beneath my fingers had done wonders for my mood.

"You're not the Drifters?" a stagehand gasped, overhearing. The main engineer rolled his eyes and held up his hands in reassurance.

"We know who you are. Don't worry about a thing. Go. Rest. Get ready. It's all under control," he said.

"Yeah? Who are we?" Money asked, belligerent.

"Uhh." The engineer looked down at his clipboard frantically. "You are . . . Benny and the Laments." He smiled, triumphant. "I'm a huge fan of your music."

"What the hell?" Money growled. Lee Otis snickered and Alvin groaned, shaking his head.

"We're Minefield," I said, resisting the urge to laugh at the sheer ridiculousness of it all. Plus, Money's outrage was palpable, and goosing him was oh-so-satisfying. If I didn't get some distance from him soon, I was going to snap.

"Minefield," Esther repeated.

The engineer frowned at his papers. "Oh yeah. Right. Right. You're the manager? Benny Lament?" He pointed at me. "It says here 'Benny Lament.'"

"I'm the manager, yeah. Benny Lament," I said. It was the first time I'd owned it, outright, and Alvin clapped me on the back like he was welcoming me to the family.

"Don't worry, Mr. Lament. It's our job to make you sound good," the engineer reassured. We were ushered off the stage, promised that all would be well, and sent to the changing area until showtime. Money had smoke coming out his ears and murder on his breath.

I told them all I'd be back in an hour and a half and went to take a nap in my car.

I emerged an hour later and found a toilet and a sink a few doors down from the janitor's closet. I shaved my stubble and slicked my hair before donning my black suit and a red tie that Lee Otis had proudly presented to me. When I joined the others, they were ready and waiting and eating from a bag of sandwiches Alvin had poached from the staff lounge.

Esther wasn't eating. She was pacing, but when she saw me she smiled, relief flickering across her face. She was wearing the white dress she'd worn at La Vita.

"It worked for me last time," she said. "And we need all the luck we can get."

It was working for her this time too. I didn't know how she'd managed to ready herself without a wrinkle or a smudge, but she was perfect from head to toe. Shining curls, a flawless face, and power shoes.

A quick rap sounded on the door, and a stage manager I recognized from earlier stuck his head around the corner. "Twenty minutes to curtain call," he said. "We'd like you in the wings in ten."

We made a quick game plan, huddled in the room.

"We're not going to give them time to be disappointed," I said. "We walk out, the lights go up, and we play. No intro, no hello, just music. Esther can introduce the band after the first song."

"We should do 'Any Man' first," Esther said. "It's fast. It's mean, and it's hungry."

"Just like us," Alvin quipped. "Fast." He patted his chest. "Mean." He pointed at Money. "And hungry," he finished, indicating Lee Otis, whose cheeks were stuffed with bread.

"Agreed," I said, ignoring Alvin. "And it's the one some of them might have heard."

"We'll follow your lead," Money grumbled. "After all, we're Benny and the Laments."

I ignored him too.

"We gonna pray?" Lee Otis said, swallowing his last mouthful.

"I'll say it," Alvin offered. "Circle up."

I frowned, uncomfortable, but everyone closed in around me, and Esther's hand slipped into mine on one side, Alvin's on the other. Money grumbled, but he linked hands with his brothers, and they all bowed their heads. For a moment, Alvin hesitated, like he was finding his words. I didn't bow my head. I didn't close my eyes. Instead, I studied the earnest faces of the four people around me, and emotion rose in my throat and swelled in my chest.

"Lord God, lift us up," Alvin pleaded. "Give us courage and protection. Bless our voices and our hands. Take away our fear and give us faith. Comfort Benny. He is a grieving son who has lost his father. He needs you, Lord God, and we need him. We thank you for your goodness and mercy in bringing us together, and we pray over the journey ahead. In Jesus's name, amen."

"Amen," Lee Otis echoed loudly.

"Amen," Esther and Money agreed.

I couldn't speak. My mouth moved around an amen, but my heart was too full. In a few lines, Alvin had given me more family than I'd ever had in my life. He released my hand, but Esther didn't, and for a moment she just stood with me. Money, Alvin, and Lee Otis walked out of the room, and seconds later we followed, making our way to the stage together.

~

My microphone didn't work. We began just as we'd planned, launching into "Any Man" the moment the lights came up. The sound was big and full, the mix perfect, but the microphone I'd swung into position on the piano wasn't jacked, and when we all echoed Esther on the chorus, no one could hear me. Which meant, fortunately, that no one heard me when I let out a string of foul words that promised violent death to every member of the sound crew, particularly the ass-kissing engineer who called us Benny and the Laments. I'd give him something to lament about.

A murmur rippled through the crowd when people realized the Drifters weren't going to appear, and the audience wasn't immediately mollified, even with the relentless beat of "Any Man" and Esther's pipes. I heard a few demands for Ben E. King when we rolled into our second number, but most folks were listening intently and clapping along.

"You're being awfully quiet over there, Benny Lament," Esther crooned three songs in. She had to be freaking out, but she was hiding it well.

I shrugged, spreading my arms, exaggerating the motion to play up to the crowd. I tapped my microphone and shrugged again.

"Benny likes to boss me around," Esther pouted.

I wagged my finger at her, and the audience booed me in lighthearted commiseration with Esther.

"No microphone? Guess that means I'm in charge." She laughed, a husky, rolling chuckle that made my toes curl and my heart flip. It had the same effect on the audience.

"He says I have a big mouth. Can you believe that? 'Itty-bitty with a great big mouth,' he says. I'll show him."

It was an obvious cue, and we were off and running, playing "Itty Bitty" with more gusto than we'd ever played it before. Esther wiggled and the crowd bounced, but I was sweating.

Esther was doing great, the sound—besides my microphone—was dynamite, and I was clowning it up from the bench, but it wasn't the same. The sharp edge we'd had every time we'd performed together just wasn't there, and the back-and-forth that made our act unique was absent, and Esther knew it. As "Itty Bitty" ended, she picked up her mic and began dragging it toward me. The audience started to laugh. The microphone stand was bigger than she was.

I stood up and stalked toward her, afraid that the cord wouldn't stretch and we'd lose her mic too. I towered over her but kept my hands clasped behind my back like a gentleman out for a stroll. For a moment, I considered how we must look, side by side, big and small, white and black, man and woman, and I prayed Ahmet Ertegun was right, that the contrast would interest and intrigue our audience. I ducked my head and spoke into her microphone.

"Where ya going, Esther Mine?"

"Well, I was going to share my microphone," she said sweetly.

"Admit it. You missed me," I said to her, smiling.

"I'm just tired of singing all your parts, you lazy ox," she shot back, and the audience roared in laughter.

We bickered back and forth for a minute before I was shooed back to the bench, and we kicked off three more songs—"Chicken," which the audience loved, "No Shoes," and "Maybe," by the Ink Spots, just to give the audience another song they knew.

"We only have time for one more song," Esther said as the clapping faded.

The audience booed, and Esther nodded sadly.

"I know. I know. I'll miss you too. Even more than I missed poor Benny tonight." She turned and waved at me, and the crowd chuckled.

"And because you've been so kind, and I'll miss you so much, I'm going to leave something with you. A little piece of myself. I sing this song everywhere I go now. This is a song about my daddy and the woman he loved." The audience stilled. I stilled.

"Some people say I look like my mother. But I think she looked more like you. Or you." Esther pointed at a white girl to her right and another to her left.

"And my daddy looked like you," she said slowly. Clearly. She pointed to a big, dark-skinned man on the balcony. "That's right. You heard me. My mother was a white and my daddy was colored. And he was the best heavyweight boxing champion in all the world. They called him Bo 'the Bomb' Johnson. He was big and strong. But not strong enough, I guess. Not strong enough for this world. Not strong enough to love a white girl like Maude Alexander."

It was so quiet in the hall I could hear the hum of the sound system and Lee Otis shifting nervously on his stool.

"Now Bo Johnson is gone, and nobody knows where he is," Esther said, her voice ringing. "The woman he loved is dead. I think she died of a broken heart. But I'll never get to ask her."

Esther was an actress on a stage, selling the story and delivering the words in a voice that filled the farthest corners of the room and rose to the dripping chandeliers above us. And the audience hung on every word.

"But her song isn't gone, because I'm here." Esther spread her arms wide. "I'm here, and I'm standing up here telling you their story. I'm telling you my story too. Maybe my story will have a different ending."

She sang the first verse the way we'd done on Barry Gray's show, no accompaniment, no intro. But she was perfectly on pitch, and when she dropped into the chorus, we all came in on the downbeat, double time. Money sang my lines though he couldn't hit the lowest notes and had to improvise; it didn't matter. The song was a hit, and when Esther blew the crowd a kiss and we all bowed and waved, the whole place was on their feet.

An intermission was announced, the curtain went down, and the stage was readied for Ray Charles. At least I would have a microphone for the second show. Sloppy, rushed sound checks made for sloppy, rushed shows, but we'd made it. And Esther had risen to a whole new level. She'd opened herself up wide in front of her audience. She'd made them love her. She'd made them listen. And she'd done it all by herself.

News that the Drifters weren't going to perform had spread, but when the curtain rose for the ten thirty show, we were met with polite clapping and the curious craning of necks, but no surprise and no obvious disappointment. The audience was gawking. Word had spread about our closing song; word had spread about *us*.

We kicked it up immediately, moving from one number to the next without slowing. I had a microphone, and the crowd seemed to enjoy our tug-of-war, but it became clear almost immediately that they were waiting for something. The expectation in the audience was palpable. By the time we debuted the heartbeat song, which we hadn't played in the first show, the whole place had started to thrum. Lee Otis's drums parried with our musical conversation and the elevated pulse of the crowd.

"I hear your heart, or is it mine?"

Everyone was on their feet when we finished, and I knew it was time to give them what they'd been waiting for. They wanted to hear Esther's story.

"Hey, Esther," I said.

"Yes, Benny?" Esther said.

"Are you thinking what I'm thinking?"

"Well, Benny. I was thinking we were gonna sing some more."

The audience laughed, but it was a breathless sound, like they knew what was coming.

"I'm thinking you should tell this fine crowd who we are and why we're here."

Esther proceeded to do just that, introducing every member of the band and then introducing Bo Johnson and Maude Alexander. If anything, it was even better the second time. When the curtain closed, the audience was on their feet and some people were crying.

~

We watched Ray Charles perform from the side of the stage, relieved that our job was done and that it had all gone so well. Ray regaled the crowd for a full ninety minutes, backed up by an orchestra, a band, and a chorus of singers, but he could have done it all by himself. He sang everything from country to gospel to rock 'n' roll, and we got to watch it happen. Money, Alvin, and Lee Otis were struck dumb by the experience, and it was a pleasure to see Money at a loss for words. He wasn't impressed by much, but he was floored by Ray Charles.

We didn't get to say hello or thank him—the sheer number of people in his entourage and in his show made it impossible to get close—but I made a note to find Jerry Wexler and tell him what the whole thing meant to us.

We didn't know there was trouble until we headed down the corridor toward the little changing room where we'd left our things. Four policemen stood beside poor Jerry Wexler and a man I would later find out was the owner of the Mosque. Jerry looked like his head was about to explode.

"Benny Lament?" one of the officers asked, stepping forward.

"Yeah."

"Esther Mine?" He looked at Esther, walking slightly behind me, her brothers bringing up the rear.

I stepped in front of her, extending my arms to shield them all. The corridor was narrow and there was nowhere to go. Money and Alvin were weighed down by their instruments, but even if they could have run, it would have been a mistake. Money cursed and I felt Esther's hand on my back, clutching my suit coat.

"What's the problem?" I asked.

"Benny Lament and Esther Mine, we have a warrant for your arrest."

"I don't know what this shit is, Benny," Jerry exploded. "But I'm calling everyone I know."

"What the hell?" Money seethed.

"Jesus, don't leave us," Alvin whispered.

"Just us?" Esther asked, raising her voice above the din.

"Esther Mine and Benny Lament," the officer repeated. "The rest of you are free to go."

I started to dig for my keys and my wallet, and the officers cried out for me to put my hands in the air. I did, dropping my keys on the ground.

The officers stepped forward, two flanking me, two flanking Esther, separating us from Alvin, Money, and Lee Otis, who looked on in paralyzed horror.

"Take the keys to my car, Money," I said. "Get your brothers out of here."

I was calm. Cool. But when they clapped the cuffs on Esther, my vision blurred and an inferno bloomed in my chest. Time slowed and sound ceased, and our eyes met for a millisecond before we were propelled down the corridor and out the rear exit doors into the hazy darkness that wrapped the venue.

Between the first show at eight and midnight, when Ray Charles finished his second show, a crowd had formed outside the Syria Mosque. Demonstrators had gathered with signs and bullhorns. Some signs said *Justice for Bo Johnson* and *Where is Bo Johnson?* Another sign said *Remember Maude Alexander*. Like with most protests or big events where security is spread thin, some people took advantage. Apparently a few nearby businesses were looted and some windows smashed. Someone spray-painted *BO JOHNSON* on the men's room wall inside the Mosque.

I don't know if it was Esther's story or if it was just the temperature in that town, or if it was all just a fortunate pretext to reel us in, but someone with considerable pull made a call to the authorities, and warrants had been issued for disrupting the peace and inciting violence. As Esther and I were led away, I told Jerry Wexler to find us a lawyer.

"Don't worry about the money, Jerry. Just get someone down there, and do it quick," I shouted. "Take care of Esther first."

Flash bulbs exploded, a cry went up, and whatever attempts the police had made at avoiding the crowd or escaping notice were thwarted. Esther and I were led to separate cars. I shouted her name, but she didn't raise her head, and then I couldn't see her anymore. People pressed around the vehicles as the cars moved out, and the sirens employed to intimidate only seemed to ignite the bystanders. Whatever was happening, it wasn't going unnoticed, and that was the only thing that kept me from coming undone.

~

I wasn't given a phone call, though I demanded one at the top of my lungs for two hours before my voice gave out for good. Then I banged on the bars, clanking my cuffs repeatedly against the metal, trying to create enough of a din that I wouldn't continue to be ignored. Esther had been taken somewhere else. I hadn't seen her since they'd put her in the back of the second car. My cash and my checkbook were in my car, parked behind the Mosque. It occurred to me that Money might not know how to drive.

The police had taken the contents of my pockets when they booked me. I'd threatened them with Sal's name and hated myself for it. It didn't work anyway. If the men on duty had heard of Salvatore Vitale, they didn't seem to care. Pittsburgh was a long way from New York. I even threatened them with Carlos Reina, Aunt Theresa's father, and the only Chicago boss I knew, thinking maybe they'd know him better. I didn't know the outfits that ran Pittsburgh.

Reina's name had them exchanging looks, but it hadn't stopped them from sticking me in a holding cell and leaving me there all night.

Two other guys shared the same space, but both were too zoned out to mind my hollering or share my distress. They had each commandeered a bench, leaving me no place to sit, but I was grateful to just be left alone.

I fell asleep propped up in the corner, Alvin's prayer in my head. I awoke to hands patting me down and foul breath in my face. I came up swinging, knocking both of my cellmates on their asses. They howled and cried for help, and their bellyaching brought an officer running. They gave me my phone call then, and I called Sal, but it was Theresa who answered.

"Tell Sal I'm in jail . . . in Pittsburgh. I'm going to need him to send someone to post bail."

"Benito? What are you doing in Pittsburgh?" she asked blearily. "Are you with that colored girl? I don't think she's good for you, Benito. You need to come home."

"Theresa?" I interrupted. "Tell Sal."

"I'll try," she said, yawning, and she hung up the phone.

~

The lawyer's name was Bat Blumenthal, and he wore a little straw hat with a striped band and a light suit that belonged in a Southern courtroom or on stage with a barbershop quartet. He carried a briefcase that probably cost as much as a Stradivarius, but he was amiable and folksy, talking to the officers like they were all old friends at a family cookout. I had no idea how he'd fallen in with Sal, until one officer started dragging his feet and Bat Blumenthal leaned across the counter and quietly laid out, in a stream of legalese, exactly what was going to happen to him and the entire Pittsburgh PD when he was done with them.

"I don't know who issued those warrants, but I can promise you this, you're the ones getting all the bad press. You've already got reporters camped outside. Mr. Lomento and Miss Mine are on the front pages of every paper this morning . . . as are you, Officer."

I was released Wednesday at noon, after paying a five-hundred-dollar fine and signing something I didn't read. My possessions were returned to me, and an officer led me to a small room where Bat Blumenthal and I could confer.

"Where's Esther?" I demanded.

"Charges against you have been dropped if you agree to leave the city. But the Mosque might sue you for damages to their building. They had some windows broken and tires of concertgoers were slashed," Mr. Blumenthal replied easily.

"We didn't do any of those things."

He shrugged. "I know. They claim she incited the crowd and you, as her manager, were responsible. She's being charged with several counts."

"How do I get her out of there?"

"You can wait until her court date . . . or you can pay five thousand dollars and get the hell out of town today."

"Five thousand dollars for what?"

"Damages to the city. She signs a statement acknowledging responsibility, pays the fine, and charges will be dropped. Otherwise, we can go to court. This is bogus. But if we fight it, it'll mean she stays right where she is until she's arraigned, which they're slow-walking. It might be next week before I can get her out."

"Can I write a check?" I asked, grim.

"You got cash?" he countered.

"In my car. But I don't know where my car is."

"Miss Mine's brothers are here. Your car is too. Jerry made sure of that. If you pay with a check, they'll make her wait until it clears. Give them cash, get a receipt, sign their release, and go. Live to fight another day."

"Wait . . . Jerry sent you?"

"He did. But I trust you'll cover my bill?"

I nodded, dazed. "Of course. Of course I will."

I wondered if Sal had even received the message.

~

Alvin, Money, and Lee Otis were in my car in the police department parking lot when I walked from the building. Bat Blumenthal, the attorney, had exited minutes before me to hold an impromptu press conference on the other side of the building, drawing the reporters away.

Through the windshield, I could see Money sitting in the driver's seat, Alvin beside him. Money's eyes were closed, like exhaustion had gotten the best of him, but Alvin, sitting beside him, must have said something because he jerked, coming awake. Alvin was out of the car before I reached it, and he hugged me like I was Jesus, walking on water, and he was Peter sinking into the sea. Lee Otis was there a second later, embracing us both, his cheeks streaked with tears and his suit so rumpled he might as well have spent the night in jail with me.

"Esther's still in jail. They won't let her go until we pay a bunch of money," Lee Otis said. Apparently, Bat Blumenthal had filled them in.

"You got our things?" I asked.

"Yeah. It's all there. In the trunk," Alvin said.

Money held back, not as exuberant as his brothers, but he tossed me the keys, and I opened the trunk and pulled my suitcase full of Pop's cash from beneath the bags. Its weight reassured me like nothing else could, and I opened it just enough to scan the contents before snapping it shut again. Money liked money, but he hadn't touched any of it. I didn't touch it either. I dug into my shaving kit instead and took out the bills I'd stashed in the bottom. Never keep your money all in one bag. Too easy to steal, too easy to lose. I had money stashed all over the car and folded in the inner pocket of my coat. I kept a wad in my billfold and some tucked in the crown of my hat.

I retrieved Esther's coat and her purse and walked back inside the jail, promising the Mine brothers that I'd return, this time with Esther. I think they had begun to believe me.

The officer who led her into booking was young—maybe twenty-two, twenty-three, but he looked eighteen. He signed Esther out, took my money, returned Esther's possessions, and then handed me a sheet of paper and a black pen.

"Will you sign this for me?" he asked, his cheeks growing pink.

"What for?" I asked.

"I would really like your autograph."

I stared at him, stunned, wanting to break his pen in two. Esther took it from his hand.

"Do you want me to sign it too?" she asked softly.

"Yes, ma'am. Yes, I do. My wife's been singing 'Any Man' all week. She says it's the best song she ever heard. I took her to the eight o'clock show at the Mosque last night. It was fantastic. She'll die when she sees you've signed this. It's our anniversary."

Esther signed it with a flourish and handed the pen to me.

Handing over five grand was easier than signing that autograph. I understood extortion. Having no shame was something else.

"But if I was you, I'd head back home. You don't need to do this to sell records, do you?" the officer asked, lowering his voice like he was giving us the inside scoop. Helping us out.

"Do what?" Esther asked, her voice level.

"Tell that story. It just riles people up. Can't you just sing the song? Your music is amazing."

"Are we free to go?" Esther asked, her chin high.

"Yeah. Sure. All done here," he said, nodding. She walked away without a backward glance.

Esther's eyes were ringed with fatigue and her white dress was wrinkled and streaked, but before we stepped outside she applied her lipstick, pulled on her coat, and squared her shoulders, readying herself for whatever audience might await us.

The Barry Gray Show

WMCA Radio

Guest: Benny Lament

December 30, 1969

"You've been on the country charts, the R&B charts, and the pop charts all at the same time," Barry Gray says.

"Sometimes with the very same song," Benny Lament says. "Our music crossed genres, so it attracted a wide audience. We didn't just look different, we sounded different. When Minefield broke onto the scene, we had 'The Bomb Johnson,' which was a narrative song, 'Itty Bitty,' which was rockabilly, and 'Any Man,' which was rhythm and blues. 'Beware' sounded like a jazz standard."

"The charts were one thing. But performing on stage, in front of an audience, was a different ballgame. Last year, 1968, on the popular program *Star Trek*, a white man kissed a black woman on American television. And it was also last year that Petula Clark, the white, British singer, touched Harry Belafonte's arm on live television which made international news. There were stories in *Time* magazine and *Newsweek*."

"It sells," Benny says.

"What does?"

"Controversy. Trouble. People can be ugly, no doubt. But newspapers and television and magazines don't always expose the truth. I think the truth is that most people don't care that a white man kissed a black woman, or vice versa. But the magazines claim everyone is all upset about it. One person in a hundred or a thousand might be upset about it. The upset gets all the attention because it sells."

"All of that is true. But you dealt with your fair share of upset. You and Esther never touched on stage. You bantered. You argued. For the most part, you sat at the piano and she stood at the microphone."

"The event coordinators were always nervous, especially after we were arrested in Pittsburgh. It was understood that I would stay at the piano and Esther would keep her distance. We were constantly lectured not to incite the crowd."

"How do you avoid it when just your presence together sets some people off?"

"You can't. I think it was Rosa Parks who said every movement has a face. That's been the hardest thing for me. I never wanted that kind of attention, and I've never had a particularly pretty face," Benny says.

"Well . . . that's why some of us do radio," Barry Gray quips, self-deprecating.

"Or play piano." Benny laughs.

"If not the right face . . . are you the right voice for the movement?" Barry asks.

"There are a lot of great voices out there. A lot of powerful voices," Benny says. "A movement might unite behind a face, but it needs every voice."

"There weren't many people doing what you two did," Barry Gray argues. "I can't think of any. Not singing together. Not sharing the stage."

17

But I Do

Bat Blumenthal's plan to control the press had worked beautifully. Only Alvin, Money, and Lee Otis waited in the back lot.

Lee Otis ran into Esther's arms, and she embraced him quickly before releasing him and herding us all toward the car. We climbed in without speaking. I knew the fight that was taking place underneath her stony façade and her ramrod spine. She didn't want to break. I didn't want to break either. But the break was coming. Bubbling in my chest. I backed out of the dingy lot and put Pittsburgh in the rearview mirror. Money broke the silence when we reached the city limits.

"You two need to cool it," Money complained from the back seat. "It's one thing for us to be an act—God knows people aren't even ready for that—but you start being flirtatious . . . carrying on like you do . . . and you're just asking for trouble."

"You know how change happens, Money?" Esther said, not even turning her head. But her eyes were fierce.

"How does it happen, Esther?" He sighed.

"You show people what it looks like. We're showing people what it looks like for whites and coloreds to be together. Even if it's just together on stage."

"Is that what you are? Are you together? 'Cause if you two are together, where does that leave us? They ran us right out of town. We waited in this car all night, scared to death. You think that was bad? It's just gonna get worse. Someone is going to get hurt. Someone is going to get killed."

"I'm going to need you to shut up, Money," I said. I didn't yell. I didn't curse, but I would kill him if he said another word. And maybe he knew it, because silence settled over the car, and within minutes, the three in the back seat were piled up in their preferred sleeping position, the long night over, the danger past.

"Are you okay, Benny?" Esther asked so softly I almost didn't hear.

"I'm okay, Baby Ruth. Are you okay?"

"I'm okay."

"Did they hurt you?"

"Just my pride. Just my faith in humanity."

"They let us out." It was a stupid thing to say, but I hadn't been sure they would.

"They should never have put us in."

"No. They should never have put us in," I agreed.

The sun had almost set, and Esther turned her face toward it, toward me, watching it disappear above the trees that lined the road to my left. We were heading north, and the light was being swallowed by the west. When it was gone, she faced forward as if the time had come.

"I want you to go, Benny," she said.

"Go where?"

"I want you to leave."

I stared at her.

"I want you to go," she insisted.

"No, you don't."

"Don't tell me what I want!"

"You're afraid."

"And you aren't?" she shot back.

"I am. But I'm not going anywhere. Not without you."

"I don't want to be the reason something happens to you."

"Something has already happened to me." It had been happening since the moment we met.

"I don't like the way I feel," she said, dropping her chin to her chest.

"How do you feel?"

"Like there's a fire in my belly but my skin is ice cold. Like it's not worth it. I know I talk tough. But it's not worth it."

"What's not worth it?"

"Something happening to you, or to them." She shrugged a shoulder toward her brothers. "It's not worth it!"

I took her hand and she pulled it away. I took it again and brought it to my chest.

"The only thing I ever wanted in life was just to play. I wanted to make music. It was the only thing I let myself want. I didn't let myself love too hard or look too long at anything else. That isn't true for me anymore."

"It's not worth it."

"It is. You are. We are. They are." I indicated her sleeping brothers in the back seat. My words sounded like song lyrics. Silly, small. Overly romantic, and I swallowed against the need to take them back. But they were true, and I was too tired to compose a better line.

"I love you, Baby Ruth."

She closed her eyes, like she couldn't bear to hear it, but her hand tightened in mine. For a moment she just breathed, her eyes closed, and then she exhaled.

"I love you too, Benny Lament. And I just want to slap you for it. You made me love you. Why did you do that?"

"I didn't try."

"I know. And that made me love you more. I don't *want* to love you."

"I don't want to love you either," I confessed.

"Then we won't," she said, adamant.

"But I do," I said quietly, and my insistence made her lips tremble.

"This wasn't part of the plan," she moaned.

"There was a plan?" I asked.

"I just wanted more than Shimmy's. And there you were. Big and handsome and ugly."

"That doesn't make any sense."

"I explained ugly beautiful to you. It does too make sense," she huffed. "The plan was to get your attention."

"Well, you did that."

"The plan was to get you to manage me."

"You did that too."

"The plan did not include any of this."

"It didn't include jail?" I teased.

She just shook her head. "Do you think history repeats itself?"

"Yeah. I do. Because people are people. Life is messy and hard. And change is slow."

"It's not going to get easier, Benny," she whispered. "I'm telling you right now. Money is right. It's gonna get worse."

"I know. So I think you should marry me."

Her head spun toward me so fast, she swayed on the seat, and I almost rear-ended a truck. She gaped at me, and then she laughed. I laughed too. It was the laughter of relief, the laughter of disaster avoided, of life reaffirmed, but we laughed so hard we had tears rolling down our cheeks.

Maybe it was sitting in a jail cell, maybe it was the darkness ahead, the suspicion that our reputation would precede us and that the heckling and harassment would get worse, but Esther's laughter became sobs. She clung to me, her fingers intertwined with mine.

"Don't be scared," I whispered.

"I'm not scared," she said, her voice hitching with her tears.

"Then why are you crying?"

"I'm not crying. My eyes are watering. I smell like"—she sniffed at herself, still crying—"I smell like puke and pee, and you smell even worse. And Lee Otis is gassy. His stomach must be tied in knots."

I cracked a window. "You're crying. You also think I'm kidding. But I'm not. I want you to marry me."

"No, you don't, Benny Lament."

"Yes, I do."

"No, you don't."

"Are you going to argue about whether he's serious or not?" Alvin groaned from the back seat. "It's not a bad idea. You two being married might make some folks madder . . . but it gives you a license to act the way you do. Folks can't complain that you're indecent if you're married."

"They can't get married!" Money argued. "It isn't even legal in most states. That'll just make everything worse."

"Pull this car over," Esther snapped, pounding on the dash. "Do you hear me, Benny Lament? Pull over."

I turned on my blinker and did as I was told. It wasn't an ideal place to stop, but I didn't have much choice. As soon as the car was motionless, Esther opened her door and stepped out.

"Esther?"

I flipped on the hazards and followed her. She turned on me with a vengeance.

"You haven't even kissed me since we left New York. And even then it was only once. Once! And now you're asking me to marry you?" she asked, outraged.

We were caught in the beams from the headlights, and I strode back to the car, yanked open the door, and shut them off.

"You all right, Benny?" Alvin asked. He was laughing. They were all awake, laughing at me.

"Stay there!" I barked. "And close your eyes."

I strode back to Esther and wrapped my arms around her little frame, hoisting her up so her face was level with mine. If she smelled like the cell, I didn't notice. She just felt right. Warm. And I wondered how I'd resisted so long.

"I'm going to kiss you now. If you don't want that to happen, you better tell me," I said.

She stared at me, silent, waiting, motionless in my arms. And I grinned. It was the only time in my memory she hadn't argued with me.

She took my face in her hands and pulled my mouth to hers. For a moment we simply pressed our lips together, eyes open, bodies tense. Then she bit my lip.

"Ow!" I almost dropped her on her little ass.

"They're watching us," she hissed.

"I know," I sighed. "But aren't you used to everybody staring at us?"

"I guess I am."

"Then let me kiss you."

"Okay."

I turned, still holding her in my arms, so that my back was to the car, giving us all the privacy we were going to get. And then I kissed her. Our mouths fit the way our voices did, and I felt her lips curve in triumph, like she'd won the prize. She tasted like she sang, bold and bluesy, with a flavor all her own, and I forgot about everything else—the fear, the future, the idling car behind us, and the distance still ahead.

When she buried her face in my shoulder, panting for mercy, her arms wrapped around my neck, I didn't let her go.

"Imagine what it would be like without your brothers ten feet away," I said.

"What were you waiting for? I've been thinking about that for days."

"I knew once I started, I wouldn't be able to stop."

"Then maybe it's good they're ten feet away."

"Yeah. But I'm going to do that every chance I get."

"And I'm going to let you."

~

I needed to find a place to stop that wasn't on the side of the road. It was about three hundred miles to Detroit, we were exhausted and hungry, and the radio personality warned cheerily of snow. It was already raining. I didn't want to spend the night on the Pennsylvania Turnpike in a blizzard, even with Esther beside me.

We exited at Route 19, a place called Cranberry Township, and pulled into the Blue Ridge Restaurant. It shared a corner with a tiny gas station guarded by four pumps. I eased in behind a farm truck, and a bell clanged merrily. A boy of about eleven came running from the station, skipping puddles, and took the nozzle from the pump.

"Fill it up, mister?" he asked as I stepped out of the car.

"Yeah. Food any good?" I pointed toward the restaurant.

"It's all right," the kid answered honestly, wiping at his red nose. "If I were you, I'd get the pancakes. They're always good, and they serve 'em all day." He began filling up the car, staring in at Lee Otis, who stared back.

"What about hotels? Is there any place to stay around here?" I asked.

"For all of ya?" the kid asked. He took out a squeegee and began washing the windows, counting the faces inside the car.

"For all of us."

"Would two rooms do ya? My mom rents out rooms. There's nobody using them right now." He pointed at a big white house set back from the street on the opposite corner. A small grocery store partially blocked the view, but a lane ran back to it from the highway that snaked through the little town.

"Two would be fine. We're going to go in and eat." I handed him a few bills, enough to cover the gas and a little extra for his trouble. "Why don't you go ask your mother if the rooms are available. We only need a night, but we'd appreciate a hot shower too, if we can get it. I'll pay well."

"I got ten more minutes on my shift, if you can wait until then," the kid said.

I agreed, climbed back in the car, and slid into a parking spot in front of the Blue Ridge Restaurant.

"They ain't gonna rent us a room here. If we're lucky, they'll let us sleep in someone's barn, and it's too damn cold for that. Let's keep going. I'll drive," Money said when I urged everyone out.

"Please don't let Money drive, Benny," Lee Otis begged. "He about killed us when we had to get the car from the Mosque to the jail. Someone will definitely get hurt if you let him drive. He doesn't even have a license."

Money cursed and Alvin sighed, and I hoped it wouldn't come to that. I was running on empty, and so was everyone else.

"Let's eat. If the rooms across the street don't pan out, we'll find something else," I said. The Mine siblings followed me reluctantly.

We walked into the diner and seated ourselves, just like the sign said. Two men sat at the bar, one in a suit, one in coveralls. They nodded at us, and the farmer gawked, though his look wasn't insolent, just curious. I noticed both men had a stack of pancakes in front of them and figured the kid knew what he was talking about.

Esther and her brothers were uneasy, though, and it struck me that everywhere we went it was the same. They were always on edge in a new place. It was almost as if they expected mistreatment. Like they braced themselves for it. Even if most of the time it didn't come. Even if the majority of people were fine, courteous, kind even. It had clearly happened enough, for long enough, that they never relaxed.

"You never know if you'll be treated well," I said out loud, the truth slamming into me with sudden clarity. I had my own hang-ups and my fair share of stereotypical treatment. Most people did. But I had never thought twice about walking into a diner or a motel or a department store.

"Oh, now he gets it," Money muttered, avoiding eye contact with the men at the counter. Alvin and Lee Otis said nothing, but Esther left her coat on like she expected to be turned away. She left it on while a Lucille Ball look-alike took our order and filled our cups with coffee. She left it on until our plates were placed in front of us, the pancakes stacked high and the bacon fragrant, and didn't remove it until the waitress retreated with a cheery "Eat up!"

There was a collective sigh, an unacknowledged relief, and we ate with silent gusto, pausing only when the boy from the gas station knocked on the window near our table and motioned for me to come outside. Immediately the tension returned.

"I have mud on my boots, mister. Miss Dot would have yelled if she saw me walking in there," the kid explained when I joined him outside.

I told him I understood.

"Mom says you can have the rooms. Ten dollars per room, and she'll throw in breakfast for another five dollars. She'll do your laundry too, if you have it, but that'll be extra. But the bathrooms come with the rooms, so the showers are free."

My nose stung with an unexpected need to weep, and I patted the kid—I later learned his name was Roger Duncan—on his shoulder. I told him we'd take the rooms, and we would be over as soon as we finished our meal.

~

Carol Duncan was a blonde woman about my age with a pretty face and a mouthful of crooked teeth. She smiled with her lips closed, but she had an open gaze, and she showed us the two bedrooms with quiet hospitality.

"Whatever you want washed just leave in the hamper by the door. I'll spot clean your suits and press them and tack it onto your bill in the morning. There's a bathroom in each room, a double bed in one room, and two sets of bunkbeds in the other. I'll let you figure out what works best as far as sleeping arrangements. I can have breakfast ready at seven or as late as nine."

"Seven would be good. We're tired," I said. "But we need to be up and out early." I wanted to keep moving. Moving, moving, moving, so no one could stop us.

"Seven it is," she agreed, and I paid her, promising to settle up again in the morning when the laundry was done.

We found out her husband's family was among the original settlers of the town, which was named after the wild cranberries found in abundance along Brush Creek. "Now Roger's the only Duncan left. His father, my husband, died in Korea. Roger was born after he left, so he never got to meet his father. But he looks just like him."

"I look like my father too," I said, speaking in present tense, and the slip made me wince, but only Esther noticed.

"My late husband owned a smelter," Carol continued, "but that was a little more than I could handle on my own. I hired someone to run it and I run the house, and so far we're making it, but we don't get a lot of business. Keep us in mind anytime you're passing through."

The house was old, but the plumbing was fairly new, and everything was clean and comfortable. Mrs. Duncan left us to get settled, reminding us to set our laundry in the hallway. The brothers insisted on the room with the two sets of bunk beds—Esther called dibs on the bottom bunk beneath Lee Otis—which meant no one had to share a bed, but it also meant I got the big bed in the second bedroom all to myself.

"You're buying, you get the best bed," Alvin insisted, but I shared my bathroom because Esther disappeared into the one attached to their room and didn't come back out. The four of us were showered, shaved, and fast asleep before she was finished with her toilette.

An hour later she opened the door to my bedroom and closed it behind her. I'd left the lamp on and the door unlocked, hopeful that she would come see me before she went to bed, but I hadn't been able to stay awake. I smelled the bleach and the home-baked bread aroma on the pillowcases, a smell that made me think of Mrs. Costiera and my bed at home, and I was out.

"Benny?" Esther whispered, pulling me from a dream world where Pop was still alive and Mrs. Costiera was trying to rouse me for school. "Are you awake?"

"Yeah," I lied, scrubbing at my half-closed lids, trying to remember where I was.

Esther hovered by the door, uncertain and small in a white nightgown, and Pop and Mrs. Costiera dissolved as she scampered across the room like a kid on Christmas morning and bounded onto the bed. She flipped off the lamp and tucked herself in beside me, and I gathered her close, notching her head beneath my chin. Her hair was in pin curls, the sections twisted and pinned in neat whorls all over her head.

"Why'd you turn off the light?" I complained, wanting to look at her.

"I am not looking my best, but I'm feeling damn good. I am scrubbed, plucked, and perfumed. My skin smells like honey butter."

I turned my nose into her throat to see for myself and groaned in pleasure. When life gives you lemons . . . make honey butter.

"You want to kiss me again?" she said, and I could hear her smile.

"I want to kiss you again." My mouth found hers in the darkness, and for several long minutes, that's what I did, kissing her until my body begged for more and my hands started roaming and Esther started humming.

We were too loud, and we would only get louder, and it wasn't a song I wanted anyone else to hear.

"I am not making love to you with your brothers in the next room," I said, pulling my mouth from hers.

"Please?" she said sweetly, and I laughed, burying my face in her neck to muffle the sound. I filled my hands with her hips and my head with all the marvelous things I could do if we were truly alone, but beyond the single-word plea, Esther didn't entreat me further, and I remained still, getting my body under control. Esther stroked my hair for a moment, but when her movement ceased and her heartbeat slowed, I thought she'd fallen asleep. I eased my head from her chest and my limbs from around her to make her more comfortable.

My eyes had adjusted to the new darkness, and when I looked down at her, I realized she wasn't asleep at all. Her eyes were wide and wet, and a new ache rose in my heart. It wasn't lust or denial. It wasn't the need to touch her honey-butter skin and bury myself in her body.

"I'm not really okay, Benny," she whispered.

I touched her cheek in commiseration.

"I know, sweet girl," I whispered. "Neither am I."

"I'm so tired. But I've got so many things to say."

"They didn't hurt you?" I asked again. My idea of hurt and Esther's might be different. Visions of her mistreatment had haunted me all night.

"No. I was scared I wouldn't get out, though. They gave me my one call, and I called my apartment, wondering if maybe Mama or Arky would pick up. Arky answered. They didn't go to Montgomery. He said everything was fine there and not to worry. He wanted to hear about Pittsburgh and Ray Charles. He didn't know about the trouble, and I didn't tell him I was in jail. He couldn't have done anything anyway."

"They messed up. They arrested us in front of a crowd. In front of cameras and reporters and television crews. When the mob takes somebody out . . . it's quick, it's quiet, and it's over. Whoever issued that warrant and sent the cops to pick us up didn't think it through."

"Amateurs," Esther scoffed, her sass rising to the surface.

I grinned and kissed the top of her head and she laid it against me, snuggling down into the crook between my chest and my arm.

For a moment she was quiet, contemplative, but I waited her out, resisting the pull of sleep and the lure of her warmth against me.

"Do you like me, Benny?" she asked finally.

"I like you, Baby Ruth."

"You don't even call me by my real name half the time," she complained.

"That's because I'm a gangster, remember? We have a nickname for everyone. Just be glad I don't call you Fat Esther or Esther Sticks."

"Why do you like me?" She wasn't laughing. I wanted to hear her laugh.

"You're funny as hell. You're mean. You're tough. You always smell so good."

"I smell good?"

"You do. Like bacon and eggs."

"What?"

"Like a sizzling steak."

"Benny!" she said, pinching my arm.

My chest rumbled with laughter. I was getting slaphappy I was so tired, but the private time with Esther was too precious, and if we slept, it would be gone.

"I said I'd make you a lot of money," she said quietly.

I waited again, not sure what she needed from me.

"We haven't made any money. I've cost you a pretty penny, though," she said.

"The money will come."

"You'd be making more if you'd never met me."

"You're an investment."

She shook her head, refusing to be put off. "I'm trying to understand. Why are you doing this?"

"You're a *long-term* investment?"

"Damn you, Benny Lament. You talk in riddles," she wailed quietly, pressing her palms into her eyes, like I was making her crazy. The time for teasing was done.

"I used to think the same thing about my dad. He didn't lie, but the only straight answers he ever gave me were about things I didn't want to know." I sighed and tried again. "I don't know why I'm doing it, Esther. Maybe because Sal told me not to. Maybe because my pop was so adamant about you. I don't know. All I know is, the moment you opened your mouth, I couldn't stop thinking about you. You haven't been out of my head for one second since."

"But . . . do you like me?" she persisted, needing the words.

"I like every damn thing about you."

"Everything?" she asked, so doubtful I almost laughed.

"Everything. I like your sass. I like your temper. I like your clear eyes and your dark heart." She propped her head on her hand and stared down at me, her lips quivering on a smile.

"I like the way you look," I added.

"That's because I look damn good," she said, smirking, trying to lighten the weight of my words, but I kept going.

"I like the color of your skin and the curl in your hair and the curve of your waist and the tilt of your head and the shape of your ears and the length of your neck and the wiggle in your walk. I like the way you hold yourself. The way you push your shoulders back and keep your spine so straight, like you are daring the world to take you on. I like that you're small, but mighty. Little, but loud. And when you laugh I forget my own name."

"All that?" she asked, her voice faint, her lower lip tucked between her teeth. And I liked that too.

"All that, and a million more things. I like you, Baby Ruth."

She didn't lean in to kiss me. She just stared down at me with such naked devotion that I had to fill the silence or I would roll her beneath me, Money, Alvin, and Lee Otis be damned.

"I don't think I told you one other thing," I murmured.

"Told me what?"

"I was so proud of you. In Pittsburgh, standing up there on that stage and taking on the whole world. I was so proud of you."

"Why?" she whispered.

"You are just like him. Just like Bo Johnson. You're a fighter. You're one hell of a fighter."

"You're a fighter too, Benny Lament. It's our heritage."

"Yeah. I guess it is."

She leaned in and kissed me then, but she didn't tarry. She straightened almost immediately, one last thing—one big thing—left to say. She tucked her knees underneath her so she was sitting beside me, looking down at me. I crossed my arms beneath my head, waiting.

"I came in here to tell you I couldn't marry you," she said in a rush. She pressed her fingers to my lips when I started to protest. "Shh. Just listen. I told myself it was the right thing to do."

"The right thing for who?" I asked, arguing around her fingers, but she ignored the question.

"The thing is . . . when you're close to me, everything inside me goes still. My heart stops. My breath slows. And my mind opens up, like I'm pushing open the windows and breathing in spring. Everything is so quiet that it's . . . loud. So loud that it drowns out everything else. That's what you do to me. And I like it," she confessed.

Emotion was rising in my throat and tickling the backs of my eyes.

"So I'm not going to think about how hard this is going to be for you and how scared I am, and how people are going to try to take that stillness from us. We won't have any peace, Benny. You won't have any peace. And all that hurt you're carrying inside you, the hurt you don't talk about, I'm probably not gonna fix that. I can't give you that same stillness you give me. But I am going to marry you, because it's what I want. And for once in my life, I'm taking what I want, lines be damned."

Lines be damned.

"So don't let me down, Benny Lament," she said, shaking her finger in warning. Then she flopped down beside me like she hadn't just handed me her heart and soul and taken mine in return.

"That's another thing I like," I muttered.

"What's that?"

"You're smart."

"Because I said I'd marry you?" she teased.

"Yeah." I kissed the top of her head again.

"Can I sleep here?" she asked, yawning so wide she could have swallowed the bed whole.

"Do you snore?" I asked.

"Probably."

"Me too."

Her hand crept up to my cheek and the other joined it. She cradled my face like I was dear to her, even as she turned her head into my chest and became boneless against me.

I was going to tell her that she would have to wake up before her brothers, and go back to her own bed, but I was asleep before I got the words out.

The Barry Gray Show

WMCA Radio

Guest: Benny Lament

December 30, 1969

"You just showed up in Detroit, at Motown Records, and knocked on Berry Gordy's door?" Barry Gray asks Benny Lament.

"Yeah. Berry and I knew each other. He'd tried to hire me only a few months earlier. He thought having a mob guy"—Benny laughs at the description—"pushing his labels made all kinds of sense. He was determined to create a sound and a system that transcended race music, which was what people were still calling songs released by Negro artists. Berry Gordy wanted to be mainstream. Forget the chitlin circuit, he wanted to be everywhere. To play everywhere. No ropes, no lines, every radio station, every venue, and all audiences."

"Sounds like Minefield and Motown were a match made in heaven."

"Motown Records was just getting started. They were maybe two years into the process. Berry had a dream and a little studio on the main floor of his house. He didn't have a big name or industry backing. He had a system, though. And he had a big enough personality to think he could conquer the music world."

"In ten years, he's come a long way. The Motown story is another triumph of the decade," Barry Gray says.

"No doubt about it. But in December of 1960, when I introduced Esther and her brothers to Berry Gordy, Motown only had a few artists—the Miracles, Mary Wells, Singin' Sammy Ward. Maybe the Supremes too, though I don't think they'd even had a hit yet. We met Marvin Gaye that Christmas. He played drums in the studio band."

"Marvin Gaye. Imagine that."

"The talent that Motown attracted and produced was off the charts."

"So you show up, convince Berry Gordy to let you record at Hitsville U.S.A., and in two weeks, you had an album."

"We did. Berry Gordy made it happen."

"Yet Motown wasn't even on the label."

"No. In the end, we were a little too controversial for a company just getting its start. But just like Ahmet Ertegun and Jerry Wexler at Atlantic, Berry did what he could. I think that's one of the amazing things about our story. So many people really wanted us to succeed. They wanted us to be heard. Against all the odds."

18

Motown Sound

We left Cranberry Township with clean clothes and improved spirits; even Money seemed moderately optimistic, though it didn't last. We spent the first few hours on the road hashing out song order and rehearsing what little we could in our cramped quarters. Everyone wanted to know all about Berry Gordy and Motown Records and whether or not he would sign us to the label. I didn't mention that I hadn't talked to Berry, and he didn't know we were coming.

About a half hour out, Esther needed to stop, and I pulled off at an exit and found a service station with the restrooms outside, the doors visible so she wouldn't need an escort. I put a few dollars of gas in the car, and then climbed back in, keeping an eye on the restrooms. Everything made me jittery.

"Is everyone at Motown colored?" Lee Otis asked me when I slid back behind the wheel. "Are they gonna let you in, Benny?"

"Motown ain't like the mob, Lee Otis," Money said, meeting my gaze in the rearview mirror.

"What do you mean?" Lee Otis asked.

"The mob only lets Italians in, isn't that right, Lament?" Money pressed. "I heard you can't be a member if you're not one of them. Nobody but Italians. Can't trust anyone but blood. So we're out."

"I didn't know you wanted to be in," I said.

"You want to join the mob, Money?" Lee Otis asked.

"No. I'm just pointin' out that it's a little ridiculous for Benny to think marrying Esther will make all her troubles go away."

I didn't think Esther marrying me would make her troubles go away. I just hoped some of her troubles would think twice. The fact that Money had homed in on my strategy made me twitch. I was glad Esther wasn't in the car.

"You're always talking, Money," I said, wishing for the umpteenth time that he would just be quiet for once.

"I'm always thinking," he corrected, tapping his forehead before folding his arms, like the matter was done. "And you know I'm right."

"Trouble never goes away, Money," Alvin said, lifting his eyes from the newspaper I'd snagged for him from the little stand outside the station. "It didn't go away in Nashville when those students started doing sit-ins at the lunch counters last spring." He tapped a headline at the top of the page. "Says here six businesses in downtown Nashville are now serving Negros at their lunch counters. The sit-ins are happening all through the South. Disciplined nonviolence, they're calling it."

"What does that have to do with Benny marrying Esther?" Money said.

"I'm just saying you can't hide from trouble. You can't fight against it, not with fists and weapons. That just makes more trouble. You can't even run. You just have to stand still. You have to hold your ground and let it come." Alvin was warming to his topic like a preacher, and he tapped the news article again.

"And when they revile you and persecute you, you turn the cheek, but you don't turn away. In Luke it says blessed are you when people hate you and exclude you—"

"Even when they exclude you from the mob," Lee Otis chimed in.

"Especially when they exclude you from the mob," I said under my breath.

"'For the sake of Christ, then, I am content with weaknesses, insults, hardships, persecutions, and calamities. For when I am weak, then I am strong,'" Alvin quoted.

"That's bullshit, Alvin," Money said, waving his hand in his brother's face. "We've been weak for too long. I'm damn tired of it. And that's not Luke, it's Corinthians."

"I didn't say it was," Alvin responded, trying not to lose his temper. "I was talking about two different verses, Money."

"I'm going to exclude you now, Alvin," Money said, plugging his ears and closing his eyes. Thank God. I was done with this conversation.

Money wore me out, but he was no fool. He was too perceptive and too persistent, and I didn't have any answers for him. Nonviolent protest might work at a lunch counter, but it wasn't going to do a whole hell of a lot if a man like Rudolf Alexander wanted us dead.

"So that's the plan, then? We're not going to ask for trouble, but we're not running from it either?" Lee Otis said, scooting forward so his long arms hung over the front seat.

It was as good a plan as any, although technically I'd asked for trouble the moment I'd asked Sal for help.

"Are they gonna throw you in jail every time we perform, Benny?" Lee Otis asked me, his eyes solemn, his voice low.

"I'm going to do everything I can so that doesn't happen," I promised him. I looked at my watch. Esther had been in the bathroom for ten minutes.

"What is taking her so long?" I muttered.

"It's Esther. She's particular. Or haven't you noticed?" Money said, coming out of his temporary exclusion, but he opened his door to get out.

"I'll go check on her," he said. At that moment, she hurried from the door marked **WOMEN**, almost running, her purse bouncing at her side. My stomach plunged, and I started the car, ready to go as soon as she opened the door.

"I heard 'Any Man,'" she gasped, falling into the passenger side and slamming the car door behind her.

"Damn it, Esther," Money hissed. "You scared me."

"They have music piped into the bathrooms. Nice bathrooms too. Good soap. Clean." She waved that away, returning to the point. "I was just checking my lipstick when the deejay said, 'Coming in at number forty this week, a brand-new song from a brand-new band. This is "Any Man," by Minefield.'"

"Number forty?" Alvin breathed, closing his newspaper with a snap. "We're in the Top 40?"

"We're in the Top 40," Esther yelled, laughing and drumming her feet against the floor. I was already driving, my heart and my head out of rhythm with each other.

"Now the guys at Motown gotta let Benny in," Lee Otis chortled. "Who needs the mob when you're in the Top 40 Club?"

The Top 40 didn't have machine guns and politicians in their pockets, but I didn't say anything.

"All I want to know is when do we get paid?" Money said, but he was smiling too.

~

The Motown studios were in the garage of a two-story white house on West Grand Boulevard in Detroit. The kitchen, right next to the garage, had been converted into a control room, and Berry Gordy Jr.'s family lived above it. I wondered how they ever got any rest or peace. The studio was rocking around the clock, spitting out music in assembly-line fashion. I'd been there a few times in the two years since Berry had opened his doors in January of 1959, but I'd never shown up unannounced, and I'd never felt so unprepared.

We pulled up in front of the house a little after noon on Thursday, December 15, and muted vibrations were already emanating from the walls. **Hitsville U.S.A** was written in curling script above two doors separated by a big glass window. Snow lined the long walk in lumpy piles, along with the remnants of a snowman. His arms and nose were missing, and he wore a pebbled grimace and a permanent wink. He looked exactly like I felt.

I thought about asking Alvin for one of his prayers.

"Money?" I said instead.

"Yeah?" he answered.

"Take the car around the block a few times."

"Why?" Immediate suspicion.

"I want to see if Berry's available before we all traipse in there," I said, running my palms over my hair to make sure the strands were in place. My hair was smooth, but my stomach was in knots.

"I'm coming with you," Lee Otis said, scrambling to climb out over Alvin.

"Me too. I'll gladly wait outside. Maybe take a walk," Alvin said, stepping out.

Esther was slicking on her lipstick and patting her hair, and she wasn't having it either. She pushed her little feet into her big heels and opened her door.

"You all are a bunch of babies. I'm a good driver," Money said. "But I'm coming too, Lament."

I closed my eyes and said the line from Alvin's prayer that had been in my head since he uttered it. I liked it better than the Rosary.

"Give me faith instead of fear."

A car pulled up behind us and stopped at the curb, and I disembarked behind the others.

"Benny Lament," a voice called out. "Is that you, man?"

Smokey Robinson was lanky and lean, with sharp cheekbones and pale eyes made all the more striking against his tawny skin and dark, well-coifed hair. And he was young. We'd hit it off immediately, though I had him by a decade. Maybe it was a shared, relentless need to make music or the single-mindedness of knowing exactly what we wanted to do, but we understood each other.

I introduced Smokey to Alvin, Money, Lee Otis, and Esther. Smokey's eyes widened and his cheeks dimpled when he shook Esther's hand, and he shot me a look that said, "Oh, I see."

"Every Friday morning we have a meeting, but some of us are heading to Grand Rapids for a show tomorrow, so we're meeting today," Smokey explained. "Right now, matter of fact. Berry will be glad to see you. Come on. Come inside. I'm a little late. Now I got an excuse." He grinned.

As we followed him up the walk to the concrete porch that jutted out beneath the double doors, he turned and looked at me.

"We saw you on the news. What the hell went down in Pittsburgh? People are talking about you, Lament."

I just shook my head and reached for Esther's hand. I would have to explain soon enough, and I would prefer to only do it once.

Berry Gordy was an upbeat man with a can-do personality and a big smile that made even Alvin up his game. "You can tell anybody anything, as long as you smile when you do it," he liked to joke, but Berry Gordy was no fool. He was sitting at the head of a conference table, but he stood, exclaiming in surprise and welcome, when we entered behind Smokey.

"Look who I found outside," Smokey said. "Everybody . . . this is Benny Lament. And just in case you don't know Benny, he's played with everybody and written songs for *everybody*. Including for a few of ours."

The table would seat at least a dozen, though only seven chairs were filled and a few empty seats were pushed against the wall. I recognized Berry's father, Berry Gordy Sr., who Berry called Pop, something we had in common. I'd also met Berry's older sister, whose name was Esther too, though I called her Mrs. Edwards. The rest of the faces, besides Smokey's, were unfamiliar to me. I knew some of the studio musicians, but I'd never been in on a board meeting before. From the introductions, most everyone around the table was family. There was a shared resemblance among them that made the relationship evident—big smiles, round noses, warm eyes, nice teeth. They were good-looking people. Smart, ambitious, and industrious too, and I hesitated, all too aware of the position I might be putting them in.

I introduced Esther and her brothers to the rest of the room, apologizing for the interruption, but Berry urged us to sit, shooting questions at us as we opted for the chairs along the wall instead of the chairs at the table. This wasn't quite how I had wanted this whole thing to go down. I needed Berry alone, but that apparently wasn't going to happen.

"I got your disc in the mail a week ago, Lament," Berry said, clasping my hand. "I listened to it, and I told Smokey, 'I want this song and this band.' And he tells me it's already on the radio." He threw up his arms. "Why you bother sending it, Benny, if I can't have it? Or them?" A record player sat along the wall to Berry's left, and he stood up and snagged the 45 I'd mailed the day Esther and I performed live on WMCA.

"This says 'Lament Records,'" Berry said. "You producing now?"

"You don't even have a label?" said the man Berry had introduced as his brother, George. "How did you get that kind of play? I heard 'Any Man' yesterday on the radio."

"I told you . . . Benny knows people," Smokey said.

"And they know him," Money inserted himself into the conversation. I didn't think it was a compliment, but Smokey nodded, agreeing with him.

"I think I saw you two on the news. Something about Pittsburgh and Ray Charles," Mrs. Edwards said, looking between Esther and me. I had walked into the room holding her hand.

"We sang in Pittsburgh Tuesday night," I said. "We opened for Ray Charles at the Syria Mosque."

"And they spent Wednesday in jail," Alvin said proudly.

"What? Why?" Mrs. Edwards gasped.

"'Cause they like each other a little too much," Money griped. "Makes people uncomfortable."

"It doesn't make me uncomfortable," Alvin said. "Disciplined nonviolence. That's what it was," he said, quoting from the newspaper article he'd shared with us in the car.

"Benny wants Esther to marry him," Lee Otis said, and everyone got quiet for the space it took to form a slew of new questions.

Good hell, what a train wreck. I rubbed the side of my jaw and tried to figure out how to get Berry alone.

"How old are you, Lee Otis?" Smokey asked, interested in the only one around the table younger than he was.

"Seventeen," Lee Otis said.

"He's sixteen," Esther corrected.

"I'm seventeen," Lee Otis insisted. "Today's my birthday."

The room erupted in congratulations, and Esther rose and wrapped her arms around Lee Otis's handsome head, pressing her cheek to his hair.

"Oh, Lee Otis. I'm so sorry, baby. I forgot."

"What for? This is the best birthday of my whole life. I'm at Hitsville U.S.A."

Berry's smile grew two sizes, and that was saying something. Lee Otis had just scored major points.

"Let's hear it," Berry Sr. said, pointing at the record player. Berry loaded it up and sat back down, his arms folded. By the time "Any Man" was done playing, he was standing up again, with a hand in the air.

"Let's take a vote," Berry said.

"What are we votin' on?" someone said, confused.

"Is that a hell of a song or what?" Berry said, his hand still raised. Everyone around the table raised their hands as well, but a few didn't look too happy about it. We'd barged in and become the center of attention, and there were clearly other items on the agenda.

"If it's playing on the radio right now, why do you need us?" Mrs. Edwards asked, her brow furrowed.

"We need to record a whole album," I said, going for broke. "I've got ten songs, ten days, and ten thousand dollars to spend if we can do it here. That's what I need from you."

Mrs. Edwards's eyebrows shot up and her expression cleared. She was a businesswoman, and she liked the bottom line. "Keep talking."

"What else you got? You said you had ten songs," Smokey interrupted. Of course Smokey wanted to hear the songs.

"Let them hear 'Itty Bitty,'" Money insisted, setting the reference lacquer on the table.

I did. Then I showed them "Beware" and the unfinished version of "The Bomb Johnson."

"The Bomb Johnson," Berry said, rubbing his chin. "I know that name. We got a picture of him down at Brewster rec, where I box sometimes. He was the best. What ever happened to him?"

Esther and I shared a look and Alvin cleared his throat.

"That's just a piece of it. There's a whole song," I said. "We sang it live on WMCA radio in New York last week. That got the ball rolling."

"There's a whole song and a whole story," Esther added.

"The story songs have done pretty well. Like Johnny Horton's 'Battle of New Orleans' and 'Sink the Bismarck.' It's not my style, but people love a good story. I want to hear it," Berry said. He looked at his watch. "The studio should be clear. They were just playing with some tracks. Let's go."

We got the instruments from the car, and within ten minutes, Alvin, Lee Otis, Money, Esther, and I were being ogled through the glass like fish in a bowl, with Berry, Smokey, the engineers, and several members of the Gordy family listening in.

"We're not recording, Benny. We just want to hear your songs," Berry said. "We'll talk about recording when we've heard a little more. Start with Bo Johnson."

"You good, Baby Ruth?" I asked from my seat at the piano.

"I'm good, Benny," she said, and the folks on the other side of the glass got quiet. Esther hadn't said much, and she hadn't warmed up or sung anything down, but she began like she'd done at the Mosque, talking to her audience.

"This is a story about my daddy, the best heavyweight boxing champion in all the world, and the woman he loved," she said into the mic. "They called him the Bomb."

She snapped four times and sang, acapella, right on key.

"He was born in Harlem, and he ruled the streets. He was the meanest man that you'll ever meet . . ."

And we were off and running.

We sang everything they hadn't already heard—"Chicken," "Pandora's Box," "No Shoes," "Cold," and "Let's Say Hello"—but when we sang "Dark Heart," and Alvin, Money, and Lee Otis sat silent, listening to me and Esther, her voice caught, and I thought she was going to break. I should have known better. The emotion in her voice didn't detract. If anything it made the song better, though the whole thing was so personal I couldn't look up from my keys. I let my hands do what they needed to do, sang my part, and professed my love, pretending it was only Esther who could hear me, who could hear us.

Of course it wasn't. The figures on the other side of the glass waited until the last note faded, and then Berry spoke into the microphone.

"You got more?" he asked, his voice gravelly.

"I think we're done," I said, clearing my throat in commiseration.

"Well, we've heard enough," Berry said. "We've heard more than enough. We just didn't want it to end."

~

We took a break, and I gave the secretary, a young woman named Mary, some money to order sandwiches for the whole place as well as a cake for Lee Otis's birthday. Berry and his sister herded me and Esther into Berry's office and closed the door, shutting everyone else out. I didn't look back to see how anyone felt about it. Berry sat back in his chair, his hands clasped loosely in his lap, his feet wide, his eyes distant. Mrs. Edwards sat too, and Esther took a chair beside her. I couldn't sit. I leaned against the wall instead and shoved my hands into my pockets.

"You know we got to be better than everybody else, don't you, Lament?" Berry said softly. "Everybody gives me a bad time . . . says I'm trying to make my artists look like happy Negros, all shined up and sweet, no trouble at all."

I didn't comment, and he kept going.

"But people don't want to hear trouble in their music. Everybody's got their own troubles. They want to hear hope. They want to feel good. They want to dance. I can't help anyone—not my artists, not my family, not this company—if I don't push hard and demand a certain standard. We gotta be better than everyone else," he said again. "I'm creating a movement here. And people can laugh and mock and tell me I'm just a crowd-pleaser. Hell yes, I am. That's what good music does. It pleases. The eyes. The ears. The soul. And people come back for more of what pleases them."

"I don't know how pleasing we are," Esther said softly, and I moved to stand behind her chair, putting my hands on her shoulders. Berry and his sister watched the interaction, and Berry blew out a pent-up breath.

"Well, you're trouble. No doubt about it. You two together in there . . . this whole place about went up in flames. I can see why they put you in jail. It's a public safety issue," he said, but he'd started to laugh.

"I can't believe they put you in jail," Mrs. Edwards whispered, shaking her head. She wasn't laughing. Her jaw was tight and her eyes were hard.

"Sammy Davis Jr. is married to a white lady," Berry said. "Pearl Bailey married Louie Bellson—best white drummer I've ever seen. You won't be the first interracial couple in showbiz."

"But you can't get married here," Mrs. Edwards said. "If that's what you were wanting to do."

"Are there laws against it?" I asked. In some states there were. In many states there were. Money was right about that.

"Not color laws. But at least one of you has to be a resident of the county. You aren't. In Chicago, you just need some identification that says you're older than eighteen and you have to apply, in person, at the county clerk's office. Fill out the application. They'll give you the license while you wait. But you can't marry until the next day."

"Mrs. Esther Gordy Edwards knows her stuff," Berry said. "She went to Howard. She's married to a politician too; you know that, right? And this year she went to the Democratic National Convention, first elected Negro woman delegate ever." He rattled off her résumé like he was proud but teasing her too, and she rolled her eyes at him the way Esther rolled her eyes at her brothers. It made something loosen in my chest, seeing them. Hearing them. Putting myself in their hands.

"What Berry's trying to say is we've got high standards," Mrs. Edwards said. "We have to do what we think is best for this company, long term, if we're going to make it go. But we need money. And we need attention. And you can give us both right now."

"It's Christmastime. Everything slows down—and speeds up—at Christmas. We got plenty of shows scheduled, but not as much studio time booked," Berry began. "So nine, ten days of studio time can be arranged."

"That's all we need," I said, trying not to let my relief show.

"That's not all I need," Berry said, his gaze frank. "I want in. I'll move everything else to make it work. You can record all night for the next two weeks, if you have to. But I want Motown on that label."

"No, you don't, Gordy. I'll pay you top dollar for the time. But you don't want this," I said. Esther's shoulders stiffened beneath my hands, and I squeezed softly, apologizing silently.

"I've always known you were the real deal. I would pay you to push Motown records. Hell, I've tried to get you to work for me. I know your background."

"This isn't just about color. This is crime and politics and sex and everything else that's wrong with the world," I said.

"You think I don't know what's wrong with the world, Lament?" Berry huffed. "I want Motown on that label."

"I hired an independent guy, a vinyl cutter, to press some singles for me. His shop was burned to the ground."

"We don't press the copies here." Gordy waved, as if that was no problem. He was purposely missing my point. "I just signed a contract with Southern Plastics in Tennessee. They're gonna press all Motown records. Nobody's gonna be burning Southern down. And if they do, the whole world will know about it, and it won't be pretty. You can burn down the little guys and nobody looks twice."

"They could burn down your studio," I said.

"No one's gonna burn us down," Mrs. Edwards shot back. "But I think you better tell us the whole story. From the beginning."

I did, with Esther adding commentary here and there. I didn't elaborate or talk about my uncle or my family, beyond Pop's friendship with Bo Johnson. Their eyes got big when we mentioned Rudolf Alexander, but when it was all said and done, they were more intrigued than intimidated.

"So why the hell are *you* doin' this, Lament?" Berry asked me, marveling, and Esther stiffened again. She was scarily quiet, letting me do most of the talking, but the conversation had become painfully personal.

"You ever loved somebody, Berry?" I said, frank.

"Yeah. I love a lot of people."

"I don't." I shook my head. "I don't."

He studied me, waiting for me to continue.

"I loved my pop. Now he's gone. And I love Esther Mine. That's it. I don't give a shit about anyone else."

"Kind of a cold son of a gun, aren't you?" Berry said, but he smiled as he said it. The smile faded with his next words. "I'm sorry about your pop, Lament."

I could only nod, and Berry's sister saved me from further response.

"You don't have to sing to be together. You could keep your heads down. Have a life together off the stage," she inserted gently.

"I've thought about that. But I can't do it. I can't stop playing, and Esther can't be quiet, not anymore. Once you know something you can't ever unknow it."

"So this Alexander . . . you think he's the one that scared Atlantic from working with you?" Berry asked.

"Not him directly, but yeah, someone in his employ."

"So now Esther's name is all over the radio, which wouldn't be a bad thing, since nobody has to know who she is. But then she sings a song telling the story of her father and Maude Alexander and makes it a runaway hit that the whole country is talking about. Add in the fact that you're a white guy, and—"

"And you got a shit show," I finished.

"Or a hit show," Mrs. Edwards said, wry.

"Did you write those songs with him?" Berry asked Esther.

"Some of them," she answered.

"Most of them," I corrected. "She wrote everything but the chorus and the bridge in 'The Bomb Johnson' too, without me. We work well together."

"You two have synergy. That's what I call it," Berry said. "You could just write together."

"That's not enough," Esther said, her voice firm.

"Let it out that the song is true," Mrs. Edwards said, nodding. "Don't shrug it off like it's just a song. When you stand up on the stage, tell the story. Tell it every time you perform, everywhere. Tell the story until there's no secret to keep hidden."

"That's what we've done," Esther said.

"That's what we plan to keep on doing," I said.

"You two are gonna be huge," Berry marveled. "I can't buy this kind of attention. We have a showcase—something we set up that we're calling the Motortown Revue—the day after Christmas at the Fox Theatre. We haven't sold enough tickets to cover the cost of the venue, but if word gets out about you two . . . we'll pack the place. We're going to Chicago after that. December thirtieth at the Regal. We're hitting the East Coast the first of the year. Uptown Theater in Philly, swinging down to DC, then Baltimore, then Richmond before we head to the Apollo in Harlem, bringing you right back home. All our artists will be on the tour, plus a few new faces I'm looking at. You do all those with us, and you'll help me put Hitsville U.S.A. on the map."

"If you put our names up on the marquee, there might be trouble," I warned.

"The kind of trouble you had in Pittsburgh?" Berry asked.

I nodded.

"I'm counting on it," Berry exclaimed. "That made the news here. That never happens. Trouble means free press. We'll up the security, and we'll sneak you in and out. There's a movie theater at the Fox too. We'll bring you in that way if we need to. Behind the screen." His wheels were already turning.

"We'll introduce you as our special guests. Motortown Revue presents Minefield at the Fox Theatre. You'll pack the seats, and our artists will get seen," Mrs. Edwards said.

"What about the police?" I asked. *What about Rudolf Alexander?*

For a moment Berry was quiet, thinking. It was his sister who spoke from a place of authority.

"You let us worry about that," she said. "We've got a long history with the police here. In '43 we had riots over the housing situation. Detroit was hopping with the war effort. Lots of jobs in the factories, and a bunch of Negros and whites both moved up from the South, bringing their sour feelings with them, and there was no place for the flood of new people, especially when the new people didn't want to live side by side or work side by side, if you know what I'm saying."

"The South wasn't a good place for colored people," Berry said.

"It still isn't," Esther said.

"Our parents came from Georgia when I was two. Detroit grew overnight. There was only one housing development that would rent to colored people. And we paid more for less," Mrs. Edwards explained.

"Still do," Berry added.

"I was twenty-two years old in '43, and I saw it all, firsthand," Mrs. Edwards continued. "People started pointing fingers, making charges to roil up their respective sides, and next thing you know we had police stepping in and President Roosevelt sending in the army—at wartime, mind you—to keep the peace. There hasn't been a whole lot of peace since . . . and it's been seventeen years. This place is a powder keg. Now we got car factories closing, and anytime people are out of work, old troubles and divisions start being stirred. You won't be showing us anything we haven't already seen."

"And you still want to put us on the stage?" I asked.

"You let me worry about the police," Mrs. Edwards repeated, her tone firm.

"That reminds me," I said, rubbing my hands over my bristly cheeks. The shave that morning at the house in Cranberry Township seemed like a decade ago. "We need a hotel. Someplace that won't stick me in one building and everyone else in another. I don't want to be on separate floors or separate wings. I don't want anyone looking at us funny either."

"Well, that's not going to happen," Mrs. Edwards said, but she gave me a small smile.

"Nobody knows you're here?" Berry said, chewing on his lip.

"Sal knows everything," I muttered. Berry and his older sister just stared at me, puzzled.

"I haven't told anyone," I said. "But that doesn't mean nobody knows."

"Lee Otis told Mama this morning. He called her," Esther said. "She and Arky know we're in Detroit. But no one else does."

"It'd be best if we could find you someplace to stay right around here," Berry mused.

"There's a house, fully furnished, three doors down. I know the owner," Mrs. Edwards said, rising and walking to the phone. "It's under contract, but it won't close until January and the renters moved out last week. It's clean, empty, and the utilities are still on. I'll see if you can stay there. I'll say it's for family and offer them two hundred dollars for two weeks. Will that work for you?"

I nodded, eager, and she looked up a number in the Rolodex beside the phone and started dialing.

"My sister will take such good care of you, you'll never want to leave," Berry said in a conspiratorial whisper. "Or you'll want to leave first thing tomorrow. Depends. She can be a little scary."

"I heard that, Junior," she muttered, still dialing.

Berry laughed, but he shook Esther's hand and then he shook mine, though I still wasn't sure what we'd agreed on.

"Let's make an album. Let's do the show. I'll talk to everyone else and get a vote on the rest, but for the next ten days, the studio is yours. After that, we'll see," he said. "For now? Welcome to Motown, Esther Mine and Benny Lament."

The Barry Gray Show

WMCA Radio

Guest: Benny Lament

December 30, 1969

"Now, I have it on good authority that you can play anything. Not just the piano," Barry Gray says to Benny Lament.

"Not anything. Drums. Harp. Most horns. Guitar. The violin. But just enough to fake it. Anything you want to master you have to fully commit to, you got to marry, and I'm a one-woman kind of guy."

"Why the piano? If you have an affinity for so many instruments . . . why did you stick with the piano?"

"I love the chords." Benny Lament plays a progression, connecting one chord to another. "Chords are like families. The notes go together, and there's a million combinations."

"You said Motown was like family."

"They were. And they let us be a part of that for a while. They would have taken us into the fold, but we had our own family matters to attend to."

Benny plays another progression, urging a segue, and Barry yields.

"Will you play us another song, Benny?"

"How about this one?" Benny plays the opening measures of "Lament." "This whole song is built around my favorite chord."

"You like dissonance," Barry Gray says.

"You gotta have dissonance to appreciate the resolution," Benny says.

19

Worth Saving

The house Mrs. Edwards found was truly just a few doors down on West Grand Boulevard. I was even able to park my car in the garage. An old woman and her daughter lived on the main level, but they were somewhere else for the holidays, and the house was blessedly quiet and convenient, albeit empty and small. Mrs. Edwards had gotten hold of a key and escorted us up a flight of steps to the flat that we would be staying in.

"A lot of these homes around here have been divided up to allow renters or two owners. I told you housing has been a problem for years. The woman who lives downstairs is getting old and her daughter just got married. I'm going to try to buy the lower half, and eventually this part too. Berry wants to buy the whole street and create an assembly line for his artists. Grooming, manners, style, the whole gamut. Each house would have a different function. But for now, this place is yours.

"There's no phone. Nothing really but the beds and the kitchen table. Looks like you have a few dishes and the fridge and stove."

"There's a couch and a chair," Lee Otis said. "And a radio."

"You can use the fireplace, but make sure the flue is open."

One room had a double bed, the second a pair of twins. The mattresses appeared to be in decent condition, but they would need to be made. Mrs. Edwards found some bedding and a few lumpy pillows in a linen closet.

I would be sleeping on the couch. I stretched out on it to see if I would fit.

"Will it do?" Mrs. Edwards said, watching me.

"I don't need much."

She nodded. "Good. Because there isn't much here, but we'll see about getting you whatever else you need. Maybe a few more pillows and some towels. Make me a list. I'll send Mary to the store." She checked her watch. "Berry said he'd be ready in an hour. He's got some ideas for a few of the songs. Something about horns and some harmonies." She smiled. "You know Berry. He always has ideas. You're going to be singing all night."

No one complained about the schedule. Well, Money complained, but not about the work. He complained about me and picked on Esther and grumbled about gangsters and white people in general, but when we were in the studio, he shut his mouth and played his ass off, and I was grateful for that. Recording—especially with Esther—was my idea of heaven. I wasn't lying when I said I didn't need much. I needed a piano, I needed a song, and I desperately needed Esther too. With those three things, the days passed in a blur of lyrics and laying down tracks, arguing with Berry when he wanted to add too much, and agreeing with Esther when she said it was all just right. We wrote two more songs in the middle of the chaos, just waiting around for Berry's engineers to do their thing, and Berry got to see just how good Esther was at writing songs.

"Girl can sing, but you've got yourself a writing partner, Lament. That was fun to watch."

"They're good together, aren't they?" Alvin said, nodding proudly, and Money grunted.

It took us eight twelve-hour days to knock it out. We typically worked from eight at night until eight in the morning and slept during the day. We finished the morning of Christmas Eve a little after 7:00 a.m.

"I think that's a wrap," Berry said, clapping, and the whole crew clapped with him. "We'll make a master today, and I'll get it sent to Southern Plastics before the post office closes on Monday. Tomorrow's Sunday—and Christmas—but be thinking about what you want on the sleeve. If you're going to call this album 'The Bomb Johnson' you need something that goes with it. Something that makes that statement. You got a picture of him? Maybe put it on one side, and a picture of the five of you on the other, you and Esther in the middle."

"What about the picture of your parents, Ess . . . the one Benny gave you?" Lee Otis asked softly. "Maybe we could take a picture like it . . . with the two of you."

"You got it here?" Berry asked.

"Yes. At the house. In my things," Esther said. I could tell she liked the idea. Her pulse was thrumming at her throat.

"Come back tonight for the party and bring the photograph. No presents. Just music and food and maybe some dancing and some drinks. We all get dressed up and fancy. It's Christmas Eve, and we're celebrating, not working, but George will be taking lots of pictures. Maybe we can squeeze in a little work." He laughed. "Now go and get some rest."

But Esther had other ideas.

"Do you think we could go to a department store, Benny?" Esther asked. "I have a little Christmas shopping to do."

We freshened up and drove to the diner on Twelfth Street where we'd eaten almost every meal since arriving in town. The clientele was mostly working-class Negros and a sprinkling of blue-collar whites. Esther got a few looks, but when you look like Esther that's to be expected. The rest of us didn't draw a second glance.

We drove downtown to Hudson's department store on Woodward Avenue, not far from the Fox Theatre where we would perform on Monday. Alvin pointed it out as we drove past. **Motortown Revue** was written in big red letters on the marquee, with a list of artists below it. Along the bottom our names had been added. **With Special Guest: MINEFIELD**.

In the white light of day, the big theater looked a little worn and tired, competing against the Christmas decorations that plastered the stores and businesses nearby. The effect was nonthreatening, even sleepy, and the worry that had been my constant companion took a temporary walk.

I'd been to Hudson's department store before, but never at Christmastime. It was packed with shoppers and dripping with tinsel and holly on every floor. And there were so many floors. A children's floor, a women's floor, and a men's floor. A floor for toys and a floor for homes and a floor for resting and dining. No floor seemed closed off to one color or the other, and the mix of people both white and black reassured me further. Santa and his elves were taking last-minute requests from children in the main lobby, and Esther turned to me and her brothers the moment we entered the store and told us to scram.

"I have things to buy and I don't want you seeing," she said.

"You can't go alone," I protested.

"I won't be. Look around you, Benny Lament."

I did, and immediately wanted to leave.

"We'll meet back here in three hours," she said. "That's one o'clock."

"Three hours?" I gasped.

"I've got things to do," Esther explained. "Go have your shoes shined. You could also use a trim," she said, eyeing my hair beneath my hat. I kept it slicked back with plenty of Murray's, but she wasn't wrong.

"Gangsters don't like people touching their hair," Esther explained to her brothers, a smile hovering around her lips.

"How would you know?" I frowned. I'd never complained about it.

"When I performed at Shimmy's, sometimes I would flirt with the mob guys in the audience. Touch their shoulders. Their chest, their cheeks. But never their hair. They're worse than the ladies. You can tug on their ties and steal their hats, but don't touch their hair."

"Well, that's not gonna happen anymore," I said.

"Oh no?" Esther asked, challenging me with a quirked eyebrow.

"No. You'll stay on the stage, behind that microphone. I'll stay at the piano, and any flirtation will happen between us. That's all. No more touching and flirting. It's foolish and dangerous."

Money was smirking, and Alvin was trying to cover his mirth.

"You jealous, Benny?" he asked.

"No. I just don't like our lead singer putting herself in a position where she could be hurt or disrespected," I said.

"She's just messing with you, Benny," Alvin said, hooting and slapping his leg. "Do you really think Esther would touch anyone's hair or flirt with them, or let them flirt with her? When Ralph tried to hit on her, she shut him down before he could even get three words out. She hardly even smiles. She can sing, but she isn't much of a performer."

"Hey!" Esther objected. "I can perform when I want to. Now go get your hair cut, Benny Lament, and quit bossing me around. I'll see you all at one."

She winked at me and handed Lee Otis a ten-dollar bill. I gave him another—Money and Alvin seemed to have a little money of their own—and everyone scattered, seemingly glad to have some time to themselves after weeks of nonstop companionship.

I bought Esther a coat. It was more than I should have spent, considering the way I'd been plowing through Pop's mattress money. But it would fit, she needed it, and no one else had ever worn it before. It had fur cuffs and a fur collar, and I bought a matching fur hat because Esther would wear it so well. On an impulse I bought her a pair of high black heels and a black dress with a bit of shimmer in the fabric. I'd seen her size when she changed in my car and had been up close and personal with her pretty feet. I bought Money, Alvin, and Lee Otis new white shirts and ties with the same black sheen as Esther's new dress, and then relented and bought them new suits too. If we were going to do a string of shows with Motown, the clothes we had weren't going to cut it.

I bought myself a new suit as well and a hat to match. Then I had my shoes shined, got my hair cut and my face shaved at the barbershop on the men's floor, and still had more than an hour to kill when I was finished.

The store was a wonder, with level after level of everything and anything you could want, but I wanted fresh air and silence, and I dropped my packages off to be wrapped at guest services and ended up wandering back up Woodward Avenue, toward the Fox Theatre on the corner of Woodward and Montcalm, which we'd passed on the way. Berry said they'd added another show and both had sold out.

"Five thousand people, each show. And so far, nobody's said anything about Minefield being a problem. Not the owner, not the event coordinator. Not the police. My sister said she'd handle it, and she's handling it."

The air was cold and the snow piled here and there was gray from the dirty streets, but the sky was blue, and I walked, my stride long, my topcoat unbuttoned, looking at the city around me. Up to the Fox and back to Hudson's only took me fifteen minutes, so when bells began to toll—bong, bong, bong, twelve of them in all—I followed the sound past the department store and down another block, in no hurry to go back inside.

The bells came from a clock tower that sat atop a building wrapped in yellowed arches and columns. Rows of rippling steps pooled at its base. The clanging clock and French architecture were at odds with the jutting skyscrapers on every side, like an aging Marie Antoinette on a golden throne in a room of concrete soldiers. From the looks of it, poor Marie was going to be guillotined again.

A sign proclaimed the structure as Old City Hall, and another warned of plans for demolishment. Some carolers sang on the steps, though they'd stopped to let the clock do its business. Wreaths hung on the pillars and a Salvation Army Santa rang his bell to my right. I dropped a dollar in his bucket and pointed at the sign.

"They want to tear it down?" I asked.

The Santa nodded, but there were people behind me, ready to contribute, and I stepped away, my eyes lifted to the clock tower that impaled the wintry blue sky. It had stopped clanging, but I checked my watch against its time. A sudden gust of wind had me reaching for my hat, and I pulled my topcoat closed. The sun was bright but the cold kept people hurrying around me, impervious to the old lady's last days.

One man stopped beside me, as though he'd heard my question. One gloved hand kept his hat on his head, but his arm obscured his face. He handed me a flyer with a drawing of the hall and the year it was built stamped on the front, and I read it with interest. **Save Old City Hall** was written across the top, followed by a plea for funds to stop the destruction and an address where donations were being accepted to save it.

"They're votin' whether to tear it down after the first of the year," he said, his voice just a rumble against the backdrop of the carolers and the persistent Salvation Santa. "You should come back on New Year's Eve. Couples from all around come here to kiss when the clock strikes midnight. They been doing that since 1871. This year will be the last, unless somebody saves it."

"That's too bad," I said, studying the structure with new eyes.

"You got a gal?" he asked kindly.

I nodded. "Yes. I do." I had a helluva girl.

"That's nice," he said, and he sounded like he meant it. "Then you should come back. Bring her. For old times' sake. You may never get the chance again."

"That's too bad," I repeated.

"Yeah. Some things are worth saving. Some things aren't."

I didn't see him walk away. The sun was blinding, and my mind was on all the things worth saving in my own life, and when I lowered my eyes and repositioned my hat, he was already a good distance away.

He wore a gray topcoat and red scarf with a bowler hat from a different era. He crossed Woodward without looking back and headed in the direction I'd just come from. The light turned green, filling the street between us with moving vehicles, and I looked back down at the flyer in my hand.

"Some things are worth saving. Some things aren't," I muttered. It sounded like a song. I folded the flyer to make it fit in my pocket and noticed some writing on the back. The words were hastily scrawled in black ink, but I had no trouble reading them.

Lament. Monday at the Fox. Bo Johnson.

I frowned at it, not understanding, and then I began to run, chasing down the man I'd failed to recognize, though his voice alone should have given him away. By the time I was able to cross the street he was long gone, and I couldn't find him. I returned to Hudson's department store limp with dejection and red-faced with exertion.

I retrieved my packages, now brightly wrapped and beribboned, and met the others, who were similarly burdened, in the lobby at the appointed time. Esther was all smiles and shining eyes, and I didn't know how to tell her. She commented on my hair and the flush of cold on my cheeks, but I kept the baffling encounter to myself. I didn't want to get Esther's hopes up, and I was too shaken to share anything at the moment.

The valet pulled our car around, and our parcels almost filled the trunk, but we stopped at the grocer on Twelfth Street and bought some wine to bring to Berry's party and enough food for a Christmas Day feast. The grocer even sold us a miniature tree, already lit and decorated from his front window display.

"I'm closing soon anyway. Won't reopen until Monday, and Christmas will be over. You might as well enjoy it."

The stocking selection was sparse, so I bought three pairs of cheap Christmas socks and enough candy to fill them, along with a pile of logs an old man was selling from the back of his Studebaker so we could use the fireplace that had sat cold since we'd arrived. My back seat was so full, we all crammed into the front seat, Esther and Lee Otis sitting on laps, and drove home with our bumper dragging.

It was fun, and Esther and her brothers were happy. But I could hardly breathe.

~

I made Esther open the present with the dress and heels inside in case she wanted to wear them to Berry's party. Then I caved and gave Alvin, Money, and Lee Otis their new suits too, with the excuse that if we were taking pictures we might as well look like a band.

I'd guessed well. The fit was good on all of them, though Esther insisted on hemming Alvin's trousers. His legs weren't quite as long as Money's, though he said he "more than made up for it in the butt." He more than made up for it in most areas, but I didn't point that out.

Esther's dress fit like I'd had it custom made, and she marveled that I knew her size. I didn't remind her that she'd changed her clothes in my back seat, that I'd gathered up her dresses and laced up her shoes, and that I'd spent a good deal of time thinking about her figure.

"You are always paying attention, Benny Lament," she said, like she was used to being ignored, and I promised myself that when I got the chance I'd show her what a good student I really was.

Lee Otis brought Esther his present as well. "I think you'll want to wear these too," he said. "They'll look just right with that dress."

Inside was a pair of earrings, black pearls that dangled from little silver loops.

"When I saw them at the jewelry counter today, they kind of reminded me of the ones your mother wore in the photograph," he said. "They aren't real . . . hers were probably real . . . but they're pretty."

Esther clipped them on and wiggled her head so they danced against her silky skin. The sheen of the pearls was the same as the gloss of her carefully arranged curls.

"I love them, Lee Otis," she said, kissing his forehead and leaving her lipstick behind. "That reminds me, I've got to bring that picture." She stuck her feet into her new shoes, grabbed up her old coat with a grimace, and went to the room she shared with Lee Otis to retrieve the photograph.

We all stood waiting for her, Money holding the wine and Alvin holding the door. But Esther didn't reappear.

"Esther," Money called. "Come on, woman."

"Benny?" she said. "Can you come here for a minute?" Her voice sounded strange and her brothers sighed in tandem.

"Go on," I insisted. "We'll be right behind you."

Esther was staring at the picture of her parents, a frown on her face.

"What?" I asked.

"Look at her earrings." She handed me the photograph. Maude Alexander wore little black baubles, smaller in circumference than a dime, but the pale column of her throat made a striking backdrop for their shine. They were pretty. I shrugged and handed the picture back to Esther.

"They do look a little like those." I inclined my head to the earrings Lee Otis had given her.

"She was wearing them." Esther's face was blank, but her voice was hard.

"Who?"

"That woman. Your uncle's wife. She was wearing them when we went to their house. She was wearing my mother's earrings," Esther insisted.

"Theresa's had those earrings for years," I said. "She wears them all the time."

"He must have given them to her," Esther said.

"Who?"

"Salvatore Vitale! He killed my mother . . . and he gave them to her."

"No." I dismissed her theory without hesitation. "Sal wouldn't do that."

"He wouldn't kill her?" Esther asked, incredulous. "Sal wouldn't kill Maude?" She laughed softly, like I was a bigger fool than she thought. "He wanted her and she refused him. You said so yourself."

"No . . . he might . . . kill her," I admitted softly. "But he wouldn't have given her earrings to Theresa."

"Why?"

"He would have kept them or thrown them in the bay. But he wouldn't have given them to Theresa. He hardly even notices her."

Esther shook her head, like she wasn't convinced, but she didn't know Sal. She didn't know Theresa. Not like I did.

"I promise you . . . it isn't what you're thinking, Baby Ruth. It isn't."

She released her suspicions on a heavy sigh and picked up the photo, and we left the apartment, but I caught her fingering her earrings throughout the evening, her face pensive, the gift ruined.

~

Berry said the photograph of Bo Johnson and Maude Alexander was perfect for the album, and we ended up posing for pictures of our own for the first half hour of the party.

"Don't smile," George insisted from behind his camera. "It looks all wrong. And you all need your hats. Lament needs a cigarette . . . or maybe a cigar. He only has one look."

"What look is that?" I asked, taking the cigar someone handed me and putting it between my lips.

"Gangster," Money supplied, and George nodded in agreement. "If ya can't beat 'em . . ."

I ended up sitting in the center, Esther to my right, Money on my left, Lee Otis and Alvin behind me. Everybody was angry or uncomfortable, and George said it was gold.

"We'll put it in black-and-white and give it an aged look, like the other one," Berry said, a drink in his hand and a smile on his face. "Classic."

I asked Berry if I could make a call, and he waved me toward his office. I left a buck on his calendar to cover the cost. I dialed Sal's house. No one picked up. I stewed for ten seconds and then called La Vita.

Sticks answered, the muted sounds of merriment behind him.

"It's Benny," I heard him say, and a minute later Fat Tony came on the line and the noise quieted.

"Benny. Merry Christmas, kid. You okay?"

"I'm good, Tony. I need to talk to my uncle."

"You just missed him. He and Theresa are having dinner with the girls."

"Without you and Sticks?"

"We got Nicky filling in for your pop. Driving. He's good, Nicky. Not as good as your dad. But good. We all miss him, Benny. Especially Sal. How you holdin' up?"

"I'm all right," I lied. I wasn't even sure what I would say to Sal or why I had called. I wanted to know if he'd heard anything from Alexander, whether he knew about Pittsburgh, and what I should expect in Chicago. He'd told me to stay put and I'd done the opposite; he wouldn't be happy to hear from me.

"Hey, uh, Benny," Tony said, his voice deepening like he'd dropped his chin. "They . . . uh . . . they found Carla's body. Washed up on the banks not too far from Sands Point. Sad deal." He cleared his throat. "They think maybe she had a little too much to drink and walked out on the pier. Fell in or somethin'."

I must have been silent too long.

"Benny, you there?" Tony asked.

"When?" I asked.

"They found her a few days ago. But they're saying she was in the water for a while."

"Why are you tellin' me this, Tony?"

"Well . . . the cops are askin' questions, you know. Nothin' to worry about. But someone mentioned your name. Said they saw her with you at La Vita."

"Saw *me* with her?" I gasped.

"Yeah. Here at La Vita. Hey. No worries. When you get back in town, they might want to ask you some questions, is all. Just thought I'd say, heads up."

The room was spinning, and I closed my eyes.

"I'll have Sal call you. He know where to reach you? Or maybe you can just talk to him in Chicago."

"You and Sticks gonna be in Chicago, Tony?"

"We'll be there, kid. And for the record, I think you're doing the right thing."

Everything was a riddle. Pop used to be that way over the phone, like he was convinced someone was listening. It was all coded words and inferred meanings. I didn't know what Tony knew or what he thought I knew, and I sure didn't know what he meant by "the right thing." I hung up the phone feeling far worse than when I'd called.

Carla shouldn't have been on the pier. Or in Sal's house. Or even in New York. And now she was dead, and I doubted her family in Cuba, whatever family there was, would ever know what happened to her.

The Barry Gray Show

WMCA Radio

Guest: Benny Lament

December 30, 1969

"Do you know who Albert Anastasia was, Mr. Gray?" Benny asks, almost taking the role of the interviewer.

"Albert Anastasia was a mob boss who was shot several times while he sat in a barber chair at the Park Sheraton Hotel in '57. Front page news around here. Gory pictures and all. But nobody was ever prosecuted for his murder," Gray responds.

"That's right. Funny how nobody ever knows anything," Benny says. "But before that, long before that, Anastasia was the leader of a bunch of contract killers who called themselves Murder Incorporated."

"Murder Inc. did the dirty work of the mob and all their criminal associates," Gray says. "Very notorious in the thirties, from what I understand."

"Yep. But in 1940, one of their own, a hitman by the name of 'Kid Twist' Reles got in trouble with the police, and to save his skin, he started ratting everyone out. He was all set to testify against Albert Anastasia, the big man himself, and was in police custody under 'constant guard' at the Half Moon Hotel on Coney Island when he was tossed out a window."

"Some say he was trying to escape," Barry Gray interjects.

"From what?" Benny says.

"From police custody."

"He was talking to the police so they would protect him."

"Bottom line, he fell from the window and he died," Barry says, his tone wry.

"Yes, he did. He was a bad guy. So nobody really cared, and no one was ever charged. But Reles was set to testify against Anastasia the same day. Anastasia walked, the five policemen who didn't protect Reles were demoted, though rumor was my uncle, Salvatore Vitale, gave them each twenty grand. And everyone else involved in Murder Inc. got the message: you snitch, you die."

"This was a long time ago," Barry says.

"Yep. A long time ago. I was just a kid, maybe ten years old, and this is all part of the public record. I'm not telling your audience anything that's not already out there. But it made a big impression on me. Mostly, I remember how upset my pop was about the whole thing."

"The papers called Reles the canary who could talk but couldn't fly," Barry Gray says.

"They also said Murder Inc. was responsible for as many as a thousand contract killings, though nobody ever knew for sure, and that just sold more papers."

"So what makes you bring them up now?" Barry asks.

"Because that was the world I grew up in."

20

The Oddest Things

I woke Christmas morning thinking about Pop, which wasn't unusual. Every morning since Pop had died, I'd come awake with him in my head, Esther in my heart, and Sal in my belly. My muscle and bone held it all together, but they were running my life.

In almost thirty years, but especially in the last ten, I'd walked through my life thinking about myself and my songs. I would go days without thinking about Pop, and then he would flit through my thoughts with his regular tread, and I would barely give him a nod before I forgot him again. Maybe that was how it was supposed to be. A child leaves the womb and lets go of the hand. He learns to walk instead of being carried, to eat without being fed, and to act without being instructed. That wasn't wrong. It was necessary. And I had plenty of reasons to want to be far away from Pop's world.

But Pop lived in my head these days. He looked back at me in the mirror. His hands played my keys, and his words fell from my tongue.

He was inside of me all the time, like he'd left his body and melded into mine, and there was no space for him . . . no space *from* him. I didn't know if what I was experiencing was just a new stage of development, a new phase of the parent-child relationship—infant, toddler, teen, adult, and finally orphaned son—but the growing pains were excruciating.

Sometimes in my dreams I walked with Pop, and he stepped out of my skin so I could breathe again, released from the burden of carrying his memory. We would walk along the beach at Sands Point, not far from Sal's house on Long Island. I don't know why my dreams took me there. I had never liked being at Sal's, though the North Shore of Long Island was beautiful. How could I? Sal's house looked like heaven, but it hid all sorts of hell. There were bodies in the rugs and dead girlfriends on the beaches.

"Merry Christmas, Pop," I whispered, pushing Carla out of my thoughts. There was no space for her.

Esther was already awake, though when I looked at my watch, I realized it was past noon. The long hours, stressful days, and late nights had taken their toll. I could hear Esther in the kitchen, pots and pans clanging. She'd been unable to shrug off her suspicions about Sal taking Maude's earrings, and I didn't blame her. I hadn't been able to shrug anything off for a long time, and I sure as hell didn't have any answers. We'd come home from the Christmas Eve party well after midnight, and we'd all retreated to our corners, everyone nursing their homesick hearts and private fears, and so tired it didn't do any good to dwell on them or talk them out.

Christmas was a giant pain in the ass. Everyone was a child at Christmas, a whiny, sad child with unmet expectations and a longing for past Christmases and people that we'd failed to appreciate at the time.

Pop had always made sure I had presents, though I hadn't been especially interested in toys or trucks or even books. He bought me records and instruments and even a record-cutting machine of my own, so I could record my own compositions. The thing hadn't been cheap, and I'd loved it, and spent hours tinkering with it. I hadn't acknowledged his efforts most of the time, and that realization left me hollow now.

I pulled a sweater over my undershirt and pulled on a pair of socks before starting the fire, though I wasn't particularly good at it. We didn't have a fireplace in the apartment on Arthur Avenue. By the time I got it going, my hands were soot streaked and the smells coming from the kitchen—bacon, fried potatoes, and pancakes—were gnawing at my belly.

I washed in the kitchen—Lee Otis had ducked into the bathroom before me—while Esther hovered over the stove. Nat King Cole was singing "The Christmas Song," and she was all in, flipping pancakes and singing along, wearing a baby-blue housedress and barefoot. I brushed my teeth and watched her move, enjoying the show.

"Where are your shoes, Baby Ruth?"

"You can't wear high heels with a housedress. And I'm comfortable."

"The floor is too cold. You should put on those nurse shoes."

"I couldn't do it. They're just too ugly."

I wrapped my arms around her, her back to my front, and placed her feet on mine.

"There. That's better," she said, laughing as I waddled around like a father penguin with her perched on my feet, protecting her from the floor.

"Merry Christmas, Baby Ruth," I whispered, kissing her cheek.

"Merry Christmas, Benny."

I nuzzled the side of her neck and the lobe of her ear before Money interrupted us with a groan.

"Merry Christmas, Money," Esther said, ignoring his displeasure, but I didn't let her go. I just scooped her up and dropped her in a chair.

"I'll get this," I said. "You sit. My pop and I always took turns. You cooked. I'll dish it up."

Money helped me, and Alvin and Lee Otis joined us minutes later, crowding around the food with enthusiasm. I brought the candy-filled socks from beneath our tree. I had an extra sock from the three pairs I'd purchased, and I dumped out my candy and used that sock and the spare on Esther's feet, crouching in front of her to pull them on. They weren't a match, but she looked damn cute.

"Way better than those ugly shoes," she declared, holding her feet up for inspection, but when I went to rise she leaned over and dropped a kiss on my mouth, right in front of her brothers, knocking me back on my ass. Her eyes were bright, like I'd done a whole lot more than put a cheap pair of mismatched socks on her icy feet.

Esther was moved by the oddest things, and I wished we were alone so I could ask her why. In my dead father's constant presence, I had fallen in love with a complicated woman, and in very strained circumstances we were revealing our scars.

Alvin offered up one of his prayers, something long and heartfelt that had Money pinching his arm because the food was getting cold. We ate breakfast in comfortable conversation, nowhere to go and nothing to run from. Afterward, we cleaned up breakfast and leisurely exchanged our presents in front of my paltry fire.

Lee Otis had already given Esther her earrings, but he gave me and his brothers each some playing cards and a cigarette lighter with our initials on them. I'd already given my gifts too—except Esther's coat and her fur hat, which she modeled for us, prancing around the little sitting room, the hat at a rakish angle, her chin held high, hands on her hips.

She shoved a box containing a buttery soft, navy-blue sweater onto my lap, but she couldn't even look at me while I opened it. I understood her distress. Presents with an audience was hard, and Christmas really was a huge pain in the ass. I modeled it, like she had done with her coat, my hands in my trouser pockets, spinning like I was on the runway, and my silliness took away some of the discomfort in her smile.

She had bought Money a pouch filled with fancy dice and a pair of cuff links in the shape of dollar signs.

"Oh, look. They say my name," Money quipped, but he seemed pleased.

She gave Alvin a pair of sunglasses like Ray Charles had worn in Pittsburgh; Alvin had admired them repeatedly. Lee Otis received a puzzle with ten zillion pieces, which he promptly opened, spreading it out on the bare wood floor in front of the fireplace, not even waiting for the final presents to be exchanged.

"I want to finish it before we have to leave," he explained.

"Where we going?" Alvin asked, sitting back and smiling, his new glasses in place.

"Tomorrow is the show, and we'll be at the theater all day. After that, Chicago, right Benny?" Lee Otis asked.

"Right." We were going to join the Motortown Revue on all their stops back to Harlem. I couldn't have planned it better myself. We had a reason to go to Chicago now, just in time for the meeting of the commission.

"What day are you getting married? We're doing that in Chicago too, right?" Lee Otis pressed. Unlike his brothers, he'd brought up the marriage several times and seemed insistent that it happen sooner rather than later.

"Don't remind him, Lee Otis," Money said. "He'll take off and we won't see him again."

"He won't run away from Esther, Money," Alvin said, scolding him. "But he might run away from you."

"License Wednesday, wedding Thursday?" I asked Esther. Of all the things that kept my stomach churning lately, marrying Esther wasn't one of them. It should have been, especially since I'd never planned on marrying anyone. I'd actually decided against it. And here I was, putting it on the schedule without a question or a qualm.

She nodded once, just a jerk of her head, and swatted at Money, asking him to pass out his presents.

Money and Alvin had visited a record store at Hudson's, and they'd made the find of the century. A 1930s collection of great performances from the Metropolitan Opera. Maude Alexander was listed among the singers and soloed on two tracks.

"It didn't even cost much," Alvin said, beaming. "We also found a bunch of records with Benny's name on them. We got you an Izzy McQueen single, Benny. 'Can't Cut You Out.' I haven't heard that one. They had books there too. We got you a new book, Lee Otis. Like the one that got the cover ripped off. But this one's got gold edges and a thicker binding." Alvin babbled as everyone opened their gifts, unable to control his excited commentary.

Esther stared at her mother's name, dumbfounded.

It had never even occurred to me to go looking for her mother's recordings.

Esther pressed her hand to her lips to keep them from trembling, and everyone got quiet, even Alvin, whose enthusiasm turned to sniffles.

"Can we listen to it right now?" he asked.

"Where?" Esther whispered. "We don't have a record player. And everything is closed."

"We could walk down to the studio," Lee Otis said. "I want to call Mama and Daddy too and wish them a Merry Christmas."

I didn't want to disturb Berry Gordy or his family. They deserved one day of peace and quiet, but we didn't have many other options.

"I'll bet the bar across from the diner on Twelfth is open," Money suggested. "They'll have a pay phone, and probably a record player too. And I could really use a beer."

We piled into the car and drove to the bar—Gene's—on Twelfth. Money was right. It was open, and at three o'clock in the afternoon on Christmas Day it was empty but for the mustached, bifocaled bartender (and the owner, apparently), who greeted us with "Merry Christmas" and seemed glad for the company. Lee Otis, Alvin, and Money fed nickels and dimes into the pay phone that stood at the end of a hallway between the washrooms, and Esther and I sat at the bar and ordered everyone a drink from Gene. When Gene set Esther's cherry Coke on the counter in front of her, she asked him if he had access to a record player. A jukebox sat against the back wall, but it was silent for the time being.

"Uh . . . yeah. Got one in the back in my office, along with a radio. I like the real old stuff—I get tired of the jukebox. Same set of songs, over and over. Sometimes I pipe in the tunes on the loudspeaker when the place is slow or we're closing up. You got a request?"

She handed him the record with a nervous smile and told him which track. He raised his chin so he could peer at the record through the lower part of his bifocals.

"Not what I usually listen to, but not a bad choice for Christmas." He finished pouring the rest of the drinks and set them on the counter beside us. A few minutes later, the pop and crackle of a needle in a groove sputtered through the speaker above the bar. The sound system was more like a gymnasium public address system, but we could hear it well enough.

The music had the flavor and quality of recordings from the thirties. The tempo was rushed and the singers all tended to sound the same, hollow and shrill. I wasn't a fan of opera music in general, but I had a few favorites. On the record, Maude Alexander sang "Musetta's Waltz" from Puccini's *La Bohème* but she also sang "Ave Maria," the last song on the collection. That was the one I had suggested she listen to.

We listened in silence, our hands wrapped around our cold glasses as Maude Alexander, in both Latin and English, asked us to "hear a maiden pleading, to see a maiden's sorrow, and hear a suppliant child."

"I *do* sound like her," Esther whispered. "Your uncle is wrong. Our voices are different. But they're the same too."

I'd always thought Esther had inherited Bo Johnson's pipes, but, like Pop said, Esther was royalty. She'd gotten it from both sides. Maude was very trained, that was obvious, but her sound was effortless, clear and cutting, and Esther had the same innate, full-throated wail.

Gene listened with us, his handlebar mustache quivering and his round glasses hiding his thoughts. When it finished, he retreated, and seconds later, "Ave Maria" started again. Alvin, Lee Otis, and Money joined us, climbing up on their stools and sipping at the foam that clung to the sides of their glasses. Lee Otis drank his Coke and asked for another before Maude Alexander had finished. The place sounded like Mass, the Latin prayer ricocheting off the benches and booths and rattling the bottles, but Gene let it play. I wasn't sure Gene's bar—or Gene—would ever be the same.

"You wanna listen one more time?" Gene asked, getting Lee Otis another Coke.

Esther nodded. "Please," she begged, and Gene rushed to do her bidding. He probably lost a few customers. More than one guy walked in and walked right back out, and Gene reluctantly handed Esther the record after the fourth time through. We finished our drinks in quiet contemplation, wished Gene a good night, and drove back to the house with Maude Alexander's voice echoing in our heads.

~

Money was moody and short tempered when we got home. The two beers at Gene's hadn't been enough to mellow him out, and the call home had put him on edge. He snarled at Lee Otis when Lee Otis asked him to help with his puzzle and bristled when Esther asked him to gather up his things from the couch where I would sleep. Alvin pulled him aside for thirty minutes, and they argued quietly behind the door of the bedroom they shared.

It was already dark; winter in Detroit was like winter in New York. Cold, dark, and long. I stoked the fire and Lee Otis resumed work on his puzzle, which he was certain he wouldn't finish. When Money and Alvin reemerged, their faces stormy, Money insisted on walking back to Gene's.

"I'm a grown man, and it's five o'clock. I am not going to do a damn puzzle by the fire like I'm eighty-five years old. I'll be back in a while."

I understood his impatience. We'd all been cooped up together, breathing each other's air and getting on each other's nerves for too long, and though I tried, and maybe Money did too, he and I didn't like each other very much. I'd stepped into the shoes he was used to filling and gained the affection of his brothers and the love of his sister, but I hadn't gained his trust. Money was convinced I was going to let them all down, and his certainty grated on us both.

"We have a show tomorrow," I reminded him. "Berry wants us at the theater for sound check at 10:00 a.m." I didn't voice my real concern; I didn't like him out there alone.

"I know, Lament. You ain't my daddy or my boss or my keeper. I can manage myself."

"I'll go too, Benny," Alvin reassured, grabbing his hat and his coat. "He just needs to blow off some steam."

Money was already stomping down the outside stairs, and Alvin hurried to catch up with his older brother.

They didn't come back for hours. Esther and I helped Lee Otis with the puzzle, though I begged off after an hour.

"Big men can't sit on the floor," I whined. "If I stay down here, you won't get me up."

By nine o'clock, Lee Otis was asleep, sprawled out with a couch cushion under his head, his puzzle littered around him, and Esther was curled in my lap on the couch. We had the radio on and tuned to a channel that played ten Christmas songs on an unending loop, and

Esther presented me with another gift. It wasn't wrapped and she presented it without fanfare, sliding it on my thick ring finger to see if it would fit. It fit just fine, and I wiggled my fingers, testing it. It would take some getting used to, but I didn't pull it off.

"There was a sale on a matching set. They were cheap. And we're going to need them if . . ."

"When. We're going to need them when," I corrected her.

"We're going to need them when we get married," she agreed.

I kissed her to seal the deal, but I made myself stop. Without lipstick, her lips were the color of flower petals and honeyed flesh, the color deepening as it disappeared into the crevice of her mouth. I groaned. We were as alone as we were going to get, but not alone at all.

"Will they stay out all night?" I asked.

"Maybe."

"Should I worry?"

She sighed. "They are grown men, Benny. But it doesn't stop me from worrying. Nothing to be done about it, though."

"Nothing to be done," I muttered, dropping a kiss on her mouth.

I was certain the moment I began kissing her in earnest, Alvin and Money would walk through the door. It seemed like a good plan, and Esther was willing to try it. The problem was Lee Otis lying at my feet. I rose with her in my arms and walked her into the only room in the house that had a lock. The bathroom was cramped, I couldn't explore her the way I wanted to, and the counter was pitifully low. I sat and she stood between my legs, the only position that worked for serious kissing, though I didn't think it would work for anything else.

"Big men can't sit on the floor or make love in bathrooms," I grumbled against her lips, and she laughed, letting me slip my tongue into the heat of her mouth. I quickly forgot about all the things I couldn't do and enjoyed the things I could.

She'd changed into the yellow dress she'd worn to sing for Atlantic, and she looked warm and sunny and ripe. I wanted to sink my teeth into her. I wanted to peel the yellow layers back and taste what was underneath. Before long, easy kissing in a quiet corner became something serious. Thorough and patient became frantic and rushed. Teeth and hands, touching and tugging. I tried to slow down, to be careful, to be romantic, but the urgency of the moment—the urgency of all our days combined—had me pulling at her zipper and opening her dress.

"This isn't the way I want to do this," I whispered, though I couldn't seem to stop.

"But this might be all we get," she said.

"Don't say that," I argued, but our hearts were pounding and our hands insistent. In another minute, my shirt was on the floor and her clothes were pooled at her feet.

Esther reached up to the string that hung from the single bulb above our heads, making her breasts rise beneath my mouth, and she yanked it down, washing us in darkness. I turned it back on, desperate to see her. She was lean and little but rounded and soft too, and my need to peel and taste became a need to look and please.

Her clothes were gone but she still wore her heels.

"Take off your shoes," I whispered.

"No," she whispered back, contrary.

She caught my lip with her teeth, and I lifted her astride me, her knees pressing against the counter, her hands on the mirror behind my head. The heels of her shoes bit into my legs, and I pulled them from her feet and dropped them to the floor.

"You have all the power already, Baby Ruth. You don't need those shoes."

She rose up and then sank back down, slick and small and so sweet that my eyes closed as her body opened around me. Her pace became frenzied, and I ran my hands from her hips to her feet, slowing her down.

"Easy," I begged.

"You're too gentle," she moaned.

"I'm always going to be gentle," I said, wrapping my arms around her, keeping her still, but I was losing the battle with my body. I was losing the battle with her.

"This wasn't how I wanted to do this," I ground out, half apologetic, half angry with her.

"If you're too gentle, it won't feel real," she insisted, gripping my face in her hands. Her eyes were dark and her lips were bruised, and I didn't understand her at all.

"You are so goddamn beautiful, Baby Ruth. I just want to make it last."

"Don't tell me I'm beautiful. That's not what I want. Not right now." She shook her head, adamant.

"Why?" I asked, incredulous. She tried so hard to be pretty all the time, and her words stunned me.

"Because it . . . isn't real. I want real. I want sickness and health. I want good and bad. I want . . . real."

"You want . . . ugly beautiful," I said slowly.

"Yes," she breathed, sounding almost relieved. "Bo Johnson and Maude Alexander never got that. I keep thinking about how they were all dressed up and posed for their picture. Like it was a play . . . or a performance. I'm not saying it was . . . but . . . I think that's how people saw them. And maybe it's how they saw each other. I just want us—Benny and Esther—to be real. Not a spectacle. Not a novelty. Not just people on a stage."

"Christmas-socks-and-cold-feet real?" I thought I finally understood why the little things always bowled her over.

"Christmas socks, holding-my-hand-so-people-won't-look-at-my-ugly-shoes, tying-my-laces, letting-me-touch-your-gangster-hair real," she said, and she was suddenly blinking back tears.

She was sitting naked in my lap, I was buried to the hilt inside her, and we were talking about socks. But I understood her completely.

"My left breast is a little bigger than my right," she said, insisting that I look for myself. "And I have a birthmark shaped like a goldfish on the inside of my thigh."

"I'll look at that in a minute," I teased.

"My bottom teeth are slightly crooked. This ear sticks out farther than the other." She pressed her curls flat to her head so I could judge for myself, but I was still looking at her breasts.

"And you have a weird addiction to high heels."

She grinned, sticking out her tongue between her perfect lips, but she pressed her forehead against mine, almost pleading, and stroked her thumbs over my bristled face.

"For better, for worse, for richer or poorer, that's so much better than what they got. And that's what I want. Can you give me that, Benny?"

"I'll do my best," I promised, shuddering with the weight of those words.

When she began to move again, a little frantic and a little wild, I wasn't near as gentle. And when she reached up to turn off the light, I didn't stop her, suddenly needing the darkness as much as she did.

The Barry Gray Show

WMCA Radio

Guest: Benny Lament

December 30, 1969

"I heard an interview you gave once where you said, 'Sometimes the world is out to get you. If we knew how bad the world really is, how ugly, how unfair, and how dark, we wouldn't be able to go on,'" Barry Gray reads.

"It was something my father said to me. I learned early that it was better not to know everything."

"Remnants of that world you grew up in?"

"And the world he grew up in. Everybody was dirty. Everybody was owned. Everybody was rotten. He said only the good die young because you have to be a little rotten to survive."

"Do you believe that? That you have to be rotten to survive?"

"Rotten or lucky."

"Have you been lucky?"

"That's just another way of asking if I've been rotten." Benny laughs. "I've spent my whole life trying to be different, just to find

out that I'm not different at all. I'm exactly like my father. I was so hard on my pop. I hated my family. Who I am. I hated the way I looked because I looked exactly like him. I even hated my name."

"And now? Have you given up on being different?"

"Different is the wrong word. Now I just try to be better. I'm not a good man, but I do my best."

"Maybe that's the definition of a good man. Doing your best."

"Maybe it is."

"Have you forgiven the world, Mr. Lament?" Barry Gray asks softly. "It seems to me you have a lot to forgive."

"None of us can help who we are. We are born into the world we are born into. The family. The skin. Nobody gets to choose those things. You can't be mad at a man for who he is. Only what he is . . . and the choices he makes."

"What choice did you make?"

21

Twisted

It was after two o'clock in the morning when Alvin and Money returned. Esther had gone to bed. Lee Otis too, but I paced like an anxious mother, teetering between driving to Gene's and marching them out of there or letting them take care of themselves like they'd been doing long before I'd come along. I argued with myself that before I'd come along, no one had been shooting at them or playing their music. But before I'd come along, they'd still been young Negro men.

They didn't need me to tell them the world was dangerous.

When I heard the scrape of a key in the door, I wilted in relief, flipped off the lamp, and lay down on the couch, determined to appear as though I were fast asleep and had been for hours. The light above the sink in the kitchen was on, and it illuminated the space well enough that I could see them through the slits of my eyes as they passed through to their room.

They had their arms around each other like they'd had way too much to drink and needed support. Alvin sounded like he was weeping. Alarm shot through me, and I spoke up from the couch.

"What's wrong?" I barked.

Money jumped and Alvin staggered.

"Shit, Lament," Money snapped.

"Nothing's wrong, Benny. I'm just so happy," Alvin sobbed.

"He's drunk. He gets like this. His joy overfloweth," Money said. Money didn't sound drunk at all.

I said nothing more, and they continued through the sitting room and into the bathroom where Alvin peed for five minutes; the amount of liquid he released was impressive. I heard the flush of the toilet and the sounds of the sink before he exited and Money ushered him into bed, talking softly to him all the while. The light in the hallway was turned off and a door gently closed, and I thought at last I would be able to sleep.

"We got to talk, Lament," Money said, padding into the sitting room. He turned on the lamp and sank into the chair at a right angle to my bed.

He'd removed his hat and his suit coat and rolled up his sleeves. His face and forearms were damp, and small water droplets clung to his hair like he'd washed to revive himself and gotten a little wetter than he intended.

"Esther still awake?" he asked.

"She's been in bed for hours. But I wouldn't think she's been sleeping well. It's hard to sleep when you're worried."

"Is that why you're still awake? You worried, Lament?" he mocked.

"I told her I'd wait for you. You made me wait a long time."

"And that pissed you off? You aren't used to worrying about anyone else, are you? You don't have anyone you have to look out for. Nobody but Benny Lament, right?"

"You said we needed to talk. So talk, Money. And then go to bed before I smack you in the mouth."

Money shook his head like I was a big damn joke, but he got to the point.

"My mother told me something when we called home today," he said, his voice low, his gaze hard.

"Okay."

"She said Bo Johnson called."

Of all the things I thought he would say, that wasn't one of them.

"When?" I gasped.

He shrugged, like the when wasn't the important part. It wasn't.

"After we left Pittsburgh, I guess. I don't know. She didn't say. She said Bo Johnson called. Wanted to know about you. Wanted to know about Esther. He heard his song on the radio. On Barry Gray."

"Holy shit. He heard it?"

"That's what Mama said."

"What else did she say?"

"She told him we were here. Singing. I guess Esther told Arky where we were headed when she called home from jail."

"He knows we're here." It was a statement, not a question. That was one thing I already knew.

"He knows. I thought the dude was dead. He just gonna show up, now that his daughter has a little fame? Now that she's saying his name on the radio?" Money was angry, and it was not the reaction I expected. I thought Bo Johnson was beloved.

"If I tell her he called, she's going to be looking over her shoulder, searching every crowd, wondering when he's going to show up. She doesn't need that. None of us do. We got enough to deal with."

"You didn't tell Alvin?"

"Nah. We all took turns on the phone. Mama told me. That's all. Esther was listening to Maude Alexander. She didn't even talk to

Mama," he grumbled. "She should be ashamed of herself. I haven't told anyone but you."

I rose and retrieved my coat. I took the folded flyer from the pocket, unfolded it, and handed it to Money. Then I told Money about the encounter at Old City Hall on Saturday.

"I didn't even look at him. I was looking at the building and everything going on around me," I explained.

"I don't like this."

"I don't like it either."

"Why didn't he just talk to you right then? Make himself known?"

"I don't know."

"Maybe it ain't really him."

"It was."

"How do you know?"

"I know his voice."

I told Money about the eight-year-old kid I'd been, and about Bo Johnson's late-night visit to my father. So much of the story had been shared. Esther's brothers knew the broad details and the individual players. Maude Alexander, Bo Johnson, Jack Lament, and even to some extent, Sal Vitale. But I'd never shared my childhood encounter with Bo Johnson with anyone but Esther. Looking back, I wasn't sure even Pop knew. I hadn't talked. Not then. And it hadn't seemed especially relevant until now.

"Son of a bitch." Money whistled softly. "So what you gonna do?"

"I'm going to see what happens tomorrow."

"You aren't going to tell Esther?" he asked.

"Are you?"

He sighed, rubbing his hands over his hair. Then he shook his head, adamant. "No. I'm not going to spin her out like that. Not until I know he's for real. And even then . . . who the hell does he think he is? Showing up like he has a claim. He walked away."

"I don't know if it's that simple," I said. It was easy to judge what you didn't understand.

"He isn't family," Money said, his voice growing strident.

"Shh. Quiet, Money."

He dropped his voice, but he leaned toward me so I would be sure to hear. "And you aren't family either, Lament. You don't become family when it feels good or when it's convenient. Me, Alvin, Lee Otis, and Esther are family. My mama and Arky are family. Not Maude Alexander and her 'Ave Marias,' not Bo 'the Bomb' Johnson. And not you."

He was hostile again, just like that, and I was weary. Of him. Of the couch beneath me. Of the indecision and doubt that dogged my every move.

"I'm not family. Okay. Fine," I said. "Who gives a shit? What does 'family' even mean? Does it mean you'll kill for each other? Bleed for each other? Lie, steal, and maim for each other? Does 'family' mean everyone looks alike? That we're all persecuted the same way? Is that what 'family' means, Money? Because I've had lots of experience with that kind of family, and I'm not interested. Maybe family is just the people you choose."

"And you choose us?" he asked, scoffing. "Oh, thank you, Benny Lament, for choosing us," he said, sarcasm dripping from every word. "Esther's a damn fine-looking woman. And she can sing. Whoa, baby, can she sing. Great choice. But if you marry Esther, you aren't just marrying her voice and her pretty face; you get that, right? You're marrying all of it. Her history. Her brothers. Gloria and Arky. You're marrying her problems. You're marrying her temper. You're marrying her world. And I don't think you can handle it."

"What do you want from me, Money? What the hell have I ever done to you?"

"It's not what you've done. It's what you're going to do."

"Oh yeah? What am I going to do?"

"It's gonna get hard, and you're going to walk."

"It's already hard, Money. And you make it so much harder."

"I don't trust you. You say you love her? Great. Wonderful. That's just beautiful. But family ain't about love. It's about commitment."

"You sound just like my pop," I said.

That shut him up. He frowned at me, and I glowered at him.

"I think you've got it twisted, Lament. The people you choose? Screw that. Family isn't the people you choose. It's the people you're stuck with."

That almost made me laugh. It was so goddamn true. Money saw the quivering of my lips in the face of his accusations, and it took the fight out of him. When I didn't argue, he rose from the chair, tossing up his hands like he'd had enough. He walked to the kitchen sink and downed a big glass of water like he was dying of thirst, like I'd dried him out completely. Then he walked to his bedroom and shut the door. I don't think he heard my reply.

"I do, Money. I've got it twisted. I've *always* had it twisted."

~

Alvin was dragging the next morning, but he wore his new glasses and swallowed a gallon of water followed by a steady stream of coffee and was his optimistic self by rehearsal time. Money was watchful, Lee Otis resigned, and Esther had the look of a woman in love. I had to keep my eyes averted just to keep my head. We didn't touch and we hardly talked, but we were never far apart.

We didn't get much time on the stage—the roster was crowded with five other acts—but the time we did get was well spent and productive. Berry had changed his mind about the order of appearance several times, finally deciding that Minefield would lead out on the first show and end the second. I think part of him was afraid of a repeat of Pittsburgh, and that we'd be dragged off at some point. Having us lead off the night upped his odds of having us perform before all hell broke loose, and putting us at the end of the second show meant the least amount of chaos if we couldn't go on; the show would be over before the audience realized we weren't performing.

Berry had managed to have a thousand vinyl singles pressed in the ten days since we'd recorded "The Bomb Johnson." We'd recorded it first, just to get it out, and Berry's local contacts had delivered. We put "The Bomb Johnson" on the A side and "Any Man" on the B side, since we knew it was what people would want to get their hands on. We had nothing left from the original New York batch of "Any Man" singles, and the rest of the album would take a while. We spent the downtime before the first show labeling envelopes containing singles to every deejay Berry and I knew. He had a table set up for sales in the main lobby of the Fox Theatre, along with a team to staff it.

"I'll take a cut, but only enough to pay the help. You'll make a little green tonight," he said. "We'll get everything else out tomorrow. If the singles sell like I think they will, we may need to cut some more for Chicago and the eastern tour, but I'm on it."

He *was* on it. They all were. The security in the building was thick, the sound dialed in, and the performers ready to go. The Gordys ran a smooth operation. If it weren't for what awaited me in Chicago, I would have been looking forward to everything that came next, to watching Berry and his artists work, and to tagging along at their heels. But Chicago was a pulsing red light in my head. How could I feel anticipation when every step forward seemed to trip a wire?

Sal, Theresa, Carla, and Bo Johnson bumped around in my head, jostling for my attention, and I pushed them all from my thoughts. There wasn't room in my head for all my worries.

Money was jittery too; we hadn't discussed Esther's father again. There was nothing to say and nothing to do until the shows were over, and even then, I had no idea how Bo Johnson would make contact.

We began with "Any Man" like we'd done in Pittsburgh, and the crowd knew the song. From one number to the next, they were with us, screaming like I was Elvis when I dropped a low note, hanging on every word when I argued with Esther, and laughing when Esther argued back. The crowd was young and they wanted to dance, and for most of the show they were on their feet. Alvin had come up with a series of dance moves for the chorus on "Chicken," and the audience lapped it up, copying his movements by the final chorus.

We rounded into our final number and the lights dropped, pinning Esther in a white circle as she related the story of Bo Johnson to a silent crowd. She started softly, building the story before breaking into the song, whipping the crowd up as she threw it down. When it was all over and the final note sung, she stepped back from the microphone and took a bow as the lights came up and the crowd screamed.

That was when I saw him.

It was just a glimpse as I rose from the piano, a bowler hat bobbing just beyond the sea of waving arms, but it was him. The curtain closed and we exited to the right where the Miracles were waiting to take our place. I didn't know my way around the building, and I couldn't go out into the crowd, but there was a set of stairs that led to a rear exit and an employee lot where we'd parked that morning.

I made an excuse about needing the washroom and ducked down the long hall, avoiding this person and that, taking the stairs at a jog, afraid that Bo Johnson would slip away, or worse . . . surprise us when I wasn't prepared.

It was quiet on the street. The crowds were inside, enjoying the ongoing performance, and I walked around the theater without being stopped or stared at, although a man having a cigarette near the front entrance seemed to recognize me. He did a double take but looked away again. Then he dropped his cigarette and shoved away from the wall, walking in the opposite direction.

Woodward Avenue was prettier by night, draped in Christmas lights and strung with illuminated candy canes and oversized red and green bulbs. The Fox looked better at night too, the glowing marquee drawing the eye from the tired exterior. The street was busy with cars, but the sidewalks were relatively clear. I circled the perimeter twice, letting myself be seen, hoping he'd approach. Yet when he stepped out from the doorway of the jewelry store to the right of the theater, his hands in his coat pockets, his face shaded by his hat, I was still surprised. I'd left my own hat inside, my topcoat too, and I was suddenly cold standing there on the street, my heart pounding, my head bare, my hands loose at my sides.

"You look just like your dad," Bo Johnson said. The empty-barrel sound of his voice, rich and resonant, had not changed, and this became apparent now that I was listening. "When I saw you on Saturday, I thought it was him. My old friend, Lament. Then I realized it couldn't be Jack. He'd be old. Like me. And Jack is gone now, isn't he?"

"Yeah. He's gone." The truth of it thrummed in my chest like the bell in the condemned clock tower, and Bo Johnson bowed his head as though he felt the vibrations. He didn't look old. Maybe it was just the forgiving cast of the streetlights; the hair not covered by his bowler hat was a dappled gray, but his face was unlined. He was thinner than I remembered, smaller, or maybe it was that I was a whole helluva lot bigger than when I'd seen him last.

"You're little Benny Lomento. The kid who likes songs," he said. "Do you remember me?" he asked.

"I remember you," I said.

"I want to see my daughter."

"How did you know we were here?"

He pointed up at the marquee. "Minefield."

"You just happened to be strolling by? You just happened to know the name of the band?"

"Ha! You even sound like your dad. Smart-ass."

"How did you know he was gone?"

"Gloria told me. I called her. She told me all of you were here. In Detroit. Singing."

"You called her," I repeated. "Just like that. Out of the blue. After more than twenty years."

"I work nights driving freight. I heard you on the radio program. Barry Gray. Both of you . . . singing 'The Bomb Johnson.'"

"I told her it was a mistake."

"Yeah. You probably shouldna done that. It wasn't smart," he whispered. "But it was beautiful."

"Why wasn't it smart?" I knew my reasons for thinking so. I wanted to hear his.

"Because now . . . all the chickens are coming home to roost."

"Where have you been?" I asked, trying to control the accusation in my tone.

"Canada. I came across the bridge." He pointed in the general direction of the Ambassador Bridge that connected Detroit to Ontario. "I'd been watching the Fox, thinking maybe you'd show up here beforehand for rehearsal or something. I've got a room right across the street." He inclined his head to the other side of Woodward. "I was having a smoke when I saw Jack—I saw you—walk by."

"You could have just talked to me then. At the old hall. Why didn't you?"

"I wanted to give you a chance to . . . prepare . . . and maybe prepare her."

I was silent, considering.

"You didn't tell her?" he asked, and I knew he meant Esther. I knew he was talking about his cryptic note on the flyer.

"I didn't tell her."

"Why?"

"I didn't want to get her hopes up. I needed to see you for myself. Really see you."

"You trying to protect her from me?"

"Yes. I am."

"Good. That's good. Your dad was like that." He exhaled and his shoulders fell, and for a moment we just stood, not certain how to proceed. He offered me a cigarette and we stood smoking in silence.

"At least I got to see her sing. She took my breath away."

"She takes my breath away too," I admitted, surprising us both.

"Her mother was like that. God, that woman." He shook his head. "I couldn't stay away. You have that same look in your eye, Lament. But people will make it hard for you. Just like they did us. We didn't make it."

"Why do people care?" I asked. "That's one thing I can't figure out. Why in the hell do people care? Why did they care about you and Maude Alexander . . . and why do they care about us?"

"Everybody's scared. Nobody wants to be alone. So they group up. That ain't new. People been tribal since time began. I don't see that changin'. We all team up. Gang up. Group up. Even your father chose his side. He recognized he couldn't get by on his own. So he mobbed up." He shrugged. "It's survival."

"It's family."

"Did you mob up, kid?"

"Not yet," I whispered. But Chicago would change that.

"Not yet?" He didn't sound like he was convinced.

"Not yet."

"I always liked fighting alone. Course . . . I stopped fighting a long time ago."

"What do you want, Bo Johnson?" I asked. More than anything, I needed to know that.

"I don't want nothing. Not one thing. I just want to see her. And then I'll be on my way."

"Why now? You could have come back anytime."

He shook his head. "No. I couldn't. You're talkin' about things you don't understand. It was better this way."

"My pop said he didn't know where you were."

"It was better for him too . . . not knowing. No use making him choose sides. He helped me. I helped him by staying away. I helped her by staying away too. But I'd like to see her. Even if it's just once."

"What if that isn't enough for her?"

"Then we'll figure that out."

I nodded. It sounded like something I said when I didn't want to be pinned down.

"By the way, no one calls me Bo Johnson anymore," he said.

"What do they call you?"

He took a blue Canadian passport from the pocket inside his coat. "Don't even have to prove you're a citizen to apply. Just have to say you were born there, and you get one of these. See?" He opened the booklet up to the first page. A picture of him was on the right, his description on the left. I glanced at the name and froze.

"Jack Lament?" I asked.

"That's right. Everybody just calls me Lament." He grinned, sheepish, and then laughed, the rumble reminding me of his daughter, who didn't even know he was here. Who didn't know I was here.

"Son of a bitch," I breathed, scrubbing at my face. I needed to get back. "Meet us beneath the clock tower. After the show. It'll be about midnight before we can get there . . . but it's close enough to walk."

"I'll be there," he said. He took a deep drag before he began to walk away.

"Don't let me down, Benny Lament," he said softly, and I choked on the smoke I'd just drawn into my chest. In the last two months, those words had become the refrain of my life.

I watched to see where he would go, and I was careless.

I didn't see the car that slowed in front of the theater or the men who stepped out, twenty feet from where I stood. I puffed away on a borrowed cigarette, distracted and disturbed, staring after Bo Johnson with my back to the danger behind me. By the time I realized I was in trouble, pain was roaring in my skull, and the pavement rose up to slap me.

The Barry Gray Show

WMCA Radio

Guest: Benny Lament

December 30, 1969

"He's become a bit of a folk legend, hasn't he?" Barry Gray asks Benny Lament.

"Who, Bo Johnson?"

"Yes. Nobody ever knew what happened to him."

"Nobody ever knew for sure," Benny agrees.

"Do you know, Mr. Lament?"

A long silence.

"There have been sightings," Barry Gray says, trying to fill it. "Rumor has it Bo Johnson was there the night you were attacked in Detroit."

"He's Bo 'the Bomb' Johnson . . . and you better watch out," Benny sings, but he doesn't answer the question.

22

I Wish I Knew

The pain pulsed like a drum in my head, and I told Lee Otis to ease up on the tempo. My mouth didn't work. The request came out a garbled mess. I sounded even worse than usual. I hummed, deep in my throat, wondering if I was sick. I couldn't be sick. We had a show in Chicago. We had a whole string of shows. And I had to get married. Maybe Bo Johnson would come.

My lips were puffy and my tongue was huge. My nose was even bigger than my tongue. I could feel it, a thrumming, pulpy beak rising up from between my eyes and spreading over my cheeks. It all hurt, my entire head, and I couldn't distinguish one agony from the next. I tried to lift it, but my muscles didn't respond. Maybe my head was all I had left. Or maybe that's what it felt like to die. Painful, disembodied half consciousness.

As soon as the thought entered my swollen brain, I felt the pain in my left hand. I had a head . . . and I had a hand. I flexed my fingers. I think they moved. And the movement didn't hurt. Not exactly. The pain was more a searing burn than a sudden break, more skin than bones, and I concentrated on my right hand. Oh. There it was. No pain there. I continued on, blearily taking stock of my body and all its floating parts.

The pain from my hand scared me the most. I flexed my fingers again, both hands. That was easier than it had been. My head and my limbs were communicating. I managed to raise my right arm in front of my face. I couldn't see anything except for a narrow slit directly overhead. My right hand appeared to be fine. One, two, three, four, five fingers. I placed it back against the bed. I was in a bed.

I raised my left hand. It was bandaged and taped, like I was going to enter the ring. Someone had made me a glove out of gauze. I couldn't see what was wrong with it. My wrist didn't hurt. My hand was fine too. The pain was coming from my fingers. From just one finger. With my right hand I began to work on the gauze, unwinding it until I could see what was hidden beneath. I freed everything but my ring finger, and I was growing tired. I had to hold my arms above my face to see what I was doing, and even then, it was like staring through an elongated peephole. I kept peeling until all the gauze and tape was gone, and then I stared, horrified, moving my hand back and forth to center it in my line of sight.

My ring finger was a bloody stump, cut off below the middle knuckle. It was black and blue, twice its normal size, and less than half its length. Neat black stitches marched across the top, closing what would have been a gaping wound. I flexed my fingers again, and oddly, my horror faded. The stitched-up stump reminded me of a fat, purple-skinned monster with stringy black hair. But I had nine other fingers, and I could still play. I would have to adjust the chords, and maybe skip a few notes until I got the feel of it. But I could still play.

"Benny?"

"Esther?"

I tried to turn my head so I could see her, but she was there, looming above me.

"Oh, Benny," she said, and she sounded like she was crying. Or maybe that was me. The salt made my eyes sting, and I stopped trying to see.

"Are you okay?" I asked. The words came out a garbled grunt, but she understood.

"I'm okay. We're all okay."

"Someone took my ring, Baby Ruth."

"I know." She kissed my good hand, and I ran my thumb over her petal lips.

"But we're still getting married. And I can still play."

~

"Mr. Lament?" Two plainclothes detectives stood next to my hospital bed. They had their badges out, held near my face so I could see them, and I did my best to focus. The pain in my head wasn't much better, but the fur on my tongue demanded a drink.

"I need some water," I croaked. A nurse was suddenly there, adjusting my pillows and cranking my bed into a more upright position. She put a straw to my lips, and I drank until the water was gone, though she urged me to go slow.

You're so beautiful, Baby Ruth. I just want to make it last.

"Where's Esther?" I said.

"Are you referring to Esther Mine, Mr. Lament?" one of the detectives asked.

"Yes. I am."

"Negro patients are kept in another wing of the hospital, Mr. Lament," the nurse said with an apologetic smile.

"She's a patient?" I gasped.

"No . . . no. She's just . . . we're only . . . ," she stuttered. "We only allow one visitor at a time. We only let family come back when a patient is . . . recovering. She's in the waiting room with the others."

"You let both of them come back." I pointed at the two cops. The nurse blushed and shot the detectives a look.

"Yes . . . well. I didn't have much choice in the matter."

"I want to see her," I demanded.

"I'll go tell her you're awake," she promised, and left me with the two detectives. It was dark beyond the small window in my hospital room.

"What day is it?" I asked.

"Tuesday. December twenty-seventh," the thinner detective answered. I couldn't remember their names. He looked at his watch. "Just after six o'clock."

"We know you aren't one hundred percent, Mr. Lament. But we've got four dead bodies in the morgue, and we need a statement," the heavyset detective said.

Four dead bodies.

"Four dead bodies?" I asked, flabbergasted. "Who?"

"Maybe you can help us with that."

Help them with what?

"Who?" I insisted again, more urgent.

"Can you tell us what happened last night?" the detective pressed.

"I don't know what happened. Who died?"

"Do you remember being attacked, Mr. Lament?"

"No."

"We need you to tell us everything you remember."

"We played a show at the Fox."

"Yes. Do you remember anything after that?"

I remembered Bo Johnson, but I wasn't going to tell them that.

"I went outside for a smoke. We had another show at nine. I guess I missed that one." We missed the meeting with Bo Johnson too.

Midnight at the old clock tower. I hadn't told Esther. But someone had died. *Four bodies.*

"Is Esther okay?" Maybe I'd just dreamed her. "I need to make sure she and her brothers are okay. Then I'll talk to you," I said.

"We need to talk to you now, Mr. Lament. Can you tell us what happened when you went out for a smoke?"

I needed my clothes, and I needed to get the hell out of there. They must have given me some morphine. It was wearing off, and I felt terrible, but I could deal with the pain if I could just see if Esther and her brothers were okay. I needed to get out of here.

"Mr. Lament?"

"I walked a little. Just to unwind. Someone hit me on the back of the head. I'm missing my goddamn finger, and my girlfriend is in the Negro wing of the hospital. What the hell is the Negro wing?" I recognized that I was being belligerent.

But I was scared. I remembered talking to Bo Johnson. I remembered watching him walk away and choking on the smoke in my lungs. Now I was here. And I wasn't going to get out until they were done with their questions.

"Where am I?" I asked, trying to slow my heart.

"Detroit Receiving Hospital," the thin detective said. They reminded me a little of Fat Tony and Sticks, each playing off the other, opposites lumped together and made to do the job.

"Esther Mine is your girlfriend?" Fat Tony's twin asked.

"Yes. My fiancée."

"Is this yours?" He held up a little plastic bag with my ring inside. The ring that I'd been wearing since Esther had slid it on my finger.

"It might be. I can't exactly try it on. Did I mention my finger is gone?"

"You were wearing one like it when you were attacked?" Fat Tony Two asked. The Sticks officer stood silently by, fulfilling his role.

"Yes. I was."

"Most men don't wear a wedding ring before they're married."

"Well, I did."

"Do you know Money Mine, Mr. Lament?"

"Yes. He's a member of the band I play with. He's Esther's brother."

"Was he with you when you went outside to smoke?"

"No." My heart was racing, clearing the fog from my aching head. "He stayed inside. With the rest of the band." I looked from one officer to the other. "Is Money okay?"

"He found you . . . after you had been attacked. He's fine."

I reached for the water cup, but it was empty.

"Do you know who attacked you, Mr. Lament?"

"No."

"No idea?"

"No."

"Can you tell us everything you remember?"

"I needed a smoke. I walked outside. I got hit over the head. I woke up here. And my goddamn finger is gone," I said again. "But I'll take my ring."

"Were you aware that you are wanted for questioning by the NYPD?"

I stared at them. "I'm going to throw up," I warned. Painkillers always made me sick, and I drank the water too fast.

Don't be gentle.

I leaned over the side of the bed, and all the water came back up, hitting the floor with a wet splat. The detectives took several steps back. One swore. But they didn't leave.

"Mr. Lament? The NYPD? Were you aware?"

"I was not aware." Tony said they might want to talk to me. I didn't know it was official. I lied with ease, closing my eyes so my stomach would settle.

"Did you know a Miss Carla Perez?"

"Yes."

"Were you aware that she is deceased?"

"Yes."

The detectives were quiet, like I'd surprised them, but I didn't dare open my eyes to see. I was going to be sick again.

"Can you tell us what you know about her?" Cop Fat Tony said, resuming his stream of questions.

"She's a Cuban dancer. Worked in my uncle's club in Havana. I had a fling with her. A one-night stand more than two years ago in Cuba."

"How did you know she was dead?"

"I called a family friend on Christmas—Tony Diangelo who works at La Vita, my uncle's club—and he told me her body had been found on the banks near Sands Point. He said the police were talking to everybody, but he seemed to think it was an accident."

"When was the last time you saw Miss Perez?"

"I saw her at La Vita at the end of November."

"Did you resume your relationship?"

"No. I haven't had any kind of relationship with Carla Perez for years. I talked to her briefly when I exited the stage at La Vita last month. I haven't seen or talked to her again."

"Why was she in the US?"

"Cuba's a shit show right now."

They waited.

"I don't know anything about Carla Perez," I said. I took an experimental breath. Deep and slow. Better. I still didn't open my eyes.

"Your father was killed a month ago."

"Yes."

"You were arrested in Pittsburgh two weeks ago, approximately."

"Yes."

"You were attacked here, in Detroit."

I nodded. Oops. Nodding was out. My stomach dropped.

"You've had a bad month, Mr. Lament."

"Yeah," I whispered. I looked at them through my swollen eyes. "It's been a doozy."

"Now a woman you were involved with is dead." The fat officer shook his head like it was all a little hard to believe.

"Can you think of any way these things might be connected?" the Sticks copper said, looking up from his pad.

I stared at the officers, baleful. "I sure wish I knew."

~

The detectives asked me questions for another hour, but it was Money who the nurse returned with after they were gone. I was surprisingly relieved to see him.

He sat near my bed, his hands folded in his lap, his eyes on mine, while the unfortunate nurse cleaned up the mess I'd made and filled up my water. I sipped at it obediently this time. She smiled at me and left the room.

"They know who you are," Money grumbled.

"What?"

"All the nurses. They know who you are. You and Esther. You have a fan club."

"Is there really a Negro wing, Money?"

"Hell yes, there is. And it's more like a Negro hallway. A Negro chicken neck instead of a Negro wing. It's like that everywhere. Don't you know anything, Lament?"

"I'm beginning to think I don't know a goddamn thing." I sighed. "But I'm hoping you're going to tell me."

He swallowed, scooting his chair closer to the bed and resting his elbows on the side.

"Those cops said you found me."

"I found you. Yeah. I found you . . . and I saw the whole damn thing." His voice was so low I had to strain to hear, but I didn't ask him to speak up. There were things to be said that shouldn't be overheard.

"I knew you had to be looking for him. For Bo Johnson. It made me jumpy."

"I saw him at the end of our set."

"I came around from the left side of the building, east of the entrance. I was probably fifty yards away when I saw you. It just looked like you were having a smoke. All by yourself. I almost turned around and left you alone.

"Then I saw a black car pull up. It was just like the car in Harlem, the gangsters that took a shot at Lee Otis and Arky. Two of 'em got out and started walking toward you. Your back was to them. Next thing I know, one's swinging a pipe at your head and you went down. Face down. I'm guessing that's what broke your nose. They scooped you up under the arms like they were going to stuff you in the back seat of that car. It's a good thing you're big as hell, because they struggled. They dropped you and one of them grabbed your hand. I wasn't close enough to see what he was doing. But that's when I shouted. I'd just been standing there . . . frozen."

He looked at me, apology written all over his face. "It took me too long to react, Lament. All I could think was 'Don't get involved or they'll blame it on you.'"

"It's okay, Money," I said. And I meant it. "What happened then?"

"I started shouting, and that's when someone started shooting."

"At me?"

"At them," Money said. "At the bastards in the black car. As soon as the gun went off, I hit the ground. Those guys didn't know where it was coming from. But I did."

"Bo Johnson."

Money nodded, a single, sharp jerk of his head, and his eyes were blank like he was seeing it all again. "When he started shooting, the two guys left you and scrambled for the car, and I thought they would get away." Money paused, and his voice got even lower. "He shot out the back tire. It skidded, jumped the curb, and plowed into the jewelry store. An alarm started blaring. The guy on the passenger side opened his door and kind of fell out.

"Bo Johnson shot that guy first, from about fifteen feet away. The guy flopped like a fish, and nobody else got out." Money raised his eyes to mine. "When Johnson reached the car, he fired into it six times." Money raised his finger in the shape of a gun. "Boom, boom." Money changed his position, like he was pointing at someone new. "Boom, boom." Money shifted again. "Boom, boom."

"Two shots for each guy."

"Yeah. Then he just kept on walking. I got up and ran to you then. And I didn't watch him go."

We were silent for a moment, listening as someone in squeaky shoes walked by, pushing a clattering gurney.

"The cops were there quick. Maybe they expected trouble at the theater. Maybe they were just circling. But about a minute after the last shots were fired, they were swarming."

"What happened to your face?" He had a scrape across his forehead and one on his right cheek.

"Don't get involved or they'll blame it on you," he warned, waving his finger at me, his voice singsong. "I kept my hands up, and I told them I was with you, but there were bodies everywhere, and I'm a colored boy. Known for my violence." His bitterness was back. "They pushed me down, put cuffs on me. You were bleeding like a pig, Lament. I got it all over the front of my Christmas suit."

"You didn't tell them they had the wrong man?"

"The wrong Negro?" Money said, chuckling softly at the irony. Then he shook his head. "I told them I didn't see the shooter. Not his size or his color. I was covering my head and praying for my life. It was mostly true."

"I think I remember waking up then," I mused. "I saw you. Lying there not too far from me."

"You did. You started to get up," Money nodded. "You said, 'He's with me,' and you tossed me your goddamn keys."

"I don't remember that."

"You went down again, face first. Probably didn't help your nose any. But they believed you. The ambulance came. And I told the police what I saw. Everything. Except for Bo Johnson. Bo Johnson saved your life, those bastards deserved to die, and I ain't saying nothing about him."

"Neither am I," I whispered. I wasn't saying anything about a lot of things.

"Esther wants to see you. So I'm going to go now." He rose awkwardly, pushing back his chair. "I'll take care of things until you're better."

"I'm ready to get out of here, Money."

"I don't know if that's a good idea. Your face is a mess. Your finger is gone. I don't know how you ain't dead. Maybe it's all that grease you put in your hair. That pipe knocked you down, but it didn't split you open."

"We've got a show to do in Chicago," I said. "And I want to get married."

"You're crazy," he said, shaking his head.

"Do you think you could drive?" I said.

The Barry Gray Show

WMCA Radio

Guest: Benny Lament

December 30, 1969

"For all my listeners out there, Benny Lament is missing the ring finger on his left hand," Barry Gray describes. "But watching him play, you'd never know. Does it ever slow you down, Benny?"

"It did at first. I only played about three out of every four notes, but I didn't hit any wrong ones," Benny Lament says.

"It slowed you down but it hasn't stopped you."

"No. We adapt when we really want to."

"Can we talk about how it happened?"

"Sure."

"You were attacked in front of the Fox Theatre in Detroit."

"That's right. Guy took off my finger with a bolt cutter. Snipped it right off," Benny says, matter-of-fact.

"Who was it?"

"I don't know. But it wasn't Bo Johnson, to answer your earlier question."

"Why would someone do that?" Barry Gray asks, aghast.

"Someone wanted to stop me from playing."

"They didn't think a white man should be singing with a Negro band?"

"It's hard to know why people do the things they do. But someone definitely wanted to shut me . . . to shut us . . . up."

23

That's All

Money was a terrible driver, but I was a worse passenger. I had to sit in the front or I got carsick, and we fought worse than Esther and me on our worst days. Esther finally climbed up between us, like a teacher separating a fight on the playground.

The truth was, we were all afraid, and none of us were handling it particularly well. Berry Gordy had told me not to "worry about Chicago."

"Just heal up. Skip it. You can meet us in Philly," he said when we gathered our things from the house by the studio and returned the keys to Mrs. Edwards.

But I *was* worried about Chicago. Chicago was all I'd thought about since we'd left New York, and I told Berry we would be there if we were still welcome. He'd just looked at my bruised face and my wrapped hand and told us he'd see us Friday morning at the Regal.

The fear in the car wasn't just Money's lurching white-knuckle driving. In the five hours it took us to get from Detroit to Chicago, nobody slept and nobody sang. I knew I wasn't well enough to drive, though I could have probably still done a better job than Money. When we stopped for gas, it was my face that made people stare and not the company I kept.

"How you gonna go out on stage like that, Benny?" Lee Otis asked, after I made Money pull over on Highway 12 for the second time so I could throw up. "And how you gonna play with your hand so sore?"

"I'll be fine. I just can't take the painkillers they gave me. They make me sick," I explained. "I'm okay."

"You're not okay, Benny," Lee Otis insisted.

"This ain't fun anymore," Alvin said. "I think we need to go back home."

"People were shootin' at us at home, Alvin," Money said.

"I'm afraid," Lee Otis said, putting it out there in plain language, making us all address it. And no one could.

"Why are we really going to Chicago, Benny?" Alvin asked. "You can get married in New York."

"We don't have a gig in New York," I said.

"Maybe we should stop singing. Stop performing," Alvin said. "Just for a while." This was not the Alvin I knew.

"No. We can't do that," I said. "We stop . . . and it's over."

We grew quiet again, staring out our windows and not seeing anything but our own worries.

"When's it going to end?" Esther asked softly. I don't think she expected an answer, but Money gave her one.

"It isn't *ever* going to end. I've been saying it, but nobody wants to listen to Money," he complained.

"I don't understand. We stop . . . and it's over? Don't we want it to be over?" Lee Otis pressed.

"Why are you pushing so hard, Benny?" Esther asked, joining the chorus. "At least . . . wait until you're healed."

"Because the bigger we make ourselves . . . the bigger I make you . . . the safer you are," I said. I'd said it so many times it had become a mantra, but I didn't believe it anymore, and neither did they.

"I don't think this is about us, Lament," Money said. "This is about you."

I couldn't take it anymore. I couldn't breathe. I couldn't see. And I suddenly couldn't control my emotions.

"I need you to pull over again, Money," I demanded, hoarse.

"You gonna be sick again?" Money said, flabbergasted.

"Benny?" Esther said, touching my leg. I pulled away and she drew back like I'd slapped her. I was cracking, the water starting to stream out my swollen eyes and drip out my bandaged nose. I didn't want to shatter all over her.

"Please just pull over. Let me out."

Money chugged to a stop, stalling the car with a giant lurch. I climbed out and staggered for the trees that lined the road. They all waited at first, letting me go, convinced I just needed to expel the bile in my stomach like I'd done before. But I kept going, weaving in and out of the trees that shivered in the cold air, reminding me that there was no cover to be found. No cover. No end. No good choices.

"Benny?" Esther was running behind me, Alvin, Lee Otis, and Money trailing behind her, their blurred figures dancing between the trees, blotches of color in a white-and-black landscape. My car was just a dark, misshapen smudge behind them.

I collapsed onto a fallen tree, my heavy head bowed, and dug in my pocket for Pop's handkerchief. I mopped at my wet face, but it hurt, even though the handkerchief was soft with wear and time. It was my favorite one because Pop had had it the longest. If it still smelled like him, I couldn't tell. My nose was too swollen and my senses too dulled.

"Benny?" Esther called.

I couldn't answer.

She hovered for a moment, her brothers behind her, and then they joined me on the log, the five of us sitting in a long row facing a forest of endless trees. And I cried. For a long time, I cried. I had no keys to comfort me and no music to numb my pain. Maybe that's why I couldn't stop. I cried for my father and for myself. I cried for poor Carla Perez and Maude Alexander and my Baby Ruth who sat beside me with her hands in her lap, afraid to touch me as I came undone. I was all she had, and I was not up to the task.

"Should we pray?" Alvin asked gently.

Nobody said anything.

"I'll pray," he insisted.

Alvin prayed almost as long as I cried, but he prayed aloud, and he prayed for me. He prayed for Bo Johnson too and thanked God for him. It was then that Esther looped her hand through my arm and hung on, and I knew then that Money had shared the story of Bo's appearance and involvement in my rescue, shouldering that burden for me. I was relieved that I would not have to tell them.

"Violence is not the answer. We know that, Lord. But we are grateful for our lives and the life of our brother Benny," Alvin said.

When he ended, my tears had slowed, and I added my voice to the amen.

"What is the answer, Alvin?" I asked, my voice raw and wet.

"What do you mean?"

"You said violence is not the answer. I don't know the answer. I just wondered if you did."

He didn't have an immediate response, and no one else did either.

"Have you ever watched someone die, Alvin?" I said.

"No."

"I have. Twice. Bad men . . . both of them."

"Who?"

"One was my pop." The grief swelled again, overwhelming, and I gasped at its power. Again, Esther and her brothers waited for me. They didn't argue that Pop wasn't a bad man. They also didn't push me to continue, but after a few minutes I was able, and the words spilled out of me almost as quickly as the tears had. But I wasn't praying; I was purging.

"The other was a man named Patrick Sweeney. I didn't know who he was when he died. I found out later. He was a prosecutor on the take. He looked out for my uncle, made sure evidence went away, charges were dropped, witnesses changed their minds. Patrick Sweeney wanted someone killed—he wanted his brother killed—and he went to Uncle Sal. Uncle Sal went to Albert Anastasia, a mobster who ran a group called Murder Inc."

"Albert Anastasia? The mob guy who got hit a few years ago in the barbershop?" Money said, interrupting me midstream.

"Yeah. That's him. But this thing with the prosecutor was a long time ago. Almost twenty years. 1941. I was just a kid and heard the rumblings from Pop and the two Tonys. You met the Tonys."

"Murder Incorporated?" Esther asked.

"Murder Inc. was a group of contract killers for the Jewish mob, the Italians, the Sicilians, you name it. All organized crime organizations. They didn't discriminate."

"So the prosecutor, Sweeney, wanted to kill his brother and he hired this group," Money summarized.

I nodded. "Murder Inc. carried out the hit on Sweeney's brother, as directed. Sweeney wanted his brother to die—and he paid for the hit—but once his brother was gone, he made a martyr of him and used the death to make a name for himself."

"How?" Esther asked.

"Sweeney used his government job and access to track down the members of Murder Inc. One of the guys who carried out the hit on

Sweeney's brother was a guy named Reles. Sweeney had him arrested and then put the squeeze on him."

"Why didn't Reles just tell them Sweeney ordered the hit?" Money asked.

"The individual members didn't know who ordered the hit. It doesn't work like that."

"But you saw Sweeney die?" Alvin was stuck on my first admission.

"Reles got scared that he was going down alone, and he started turning on everyone else in Murder Inc. Big names like Buggsy Goldstein and Lepke Buchalter. The Jewish mob, the Italian mob. All big mob guys. Reles squealed on everyone to save himself. The guys he named were prosecuted, and some of them executed."

"But they were bad guys . . . right?" Lee Otis said, troubled. And there was the rub. A bad guy prosecuting bad guys.

"Where do you come in?" Alvin asked.

"My Uncle Sal was pissed because this prosecutor, Sweeney, was his associate, his contact. My Uncle Sal brokered the deal. The prosecutor got the hit he wanted, and then made all hell break loose in the organization he'd taken advantage of."

"I'd be pissed too," Money said.

"So Sal killed him," I finished.

Shocked silence reigned for a full five seconds.

"And you . . . saw him do it?" Esther asked.

"I was eleven years old, hiding behind the curtain in my uncle's study. I didn't know the guy. But I saw the light leave Patrick Sweeney's eyes, and the life leave his body."

Silence again, and I felt a new kind of grief wash over me. I didn't want Lee Otis Mine to know about all the ugly things in the world. Pop said everyone sees something they shouldn't eventually, but I didn't want to be the one to show him.

"Why are you telling us this, Benny?" Alvin asked, his voice low. I'd shocked him too.

"Because you asked me why we can't go home, and why I'm pushing so hard, and why we can't just skip Chicago," I said. "This is the world we're living in. This is the world I know." I thumped my uninjured hand against my chest. "In my world, everyone is dirty. The good guys aren't good, and the bad guys aren't all bad. Justice is taken care of in a different way, and family means . . . protection."

"It's the world Bo Johnson knows too," Money said. "And Rudolf Alexander and John Kennedy and Salvatore Vitale."

"So it ain't about color?" Lee Otis said.

I shrugged, helpless. "Some of it. Maybe. But not all of it. I don't know who and what we're dealing with. Not entirely. All I know . . . is that I can't fight that world all by myself. I can't protect you all by myself."

"I still don't understand."

"He's going to Chicago to mob up. Join the family," Money said, his tone final. "So Uncle Sal can kill the prosecutor . . . whoever the hell that is now."

Money was too smart for his own good. But it was a relief to have it spelled out in simple terms.

Esther's arm had grown slack around mine.

"There's a commission. A process. You don't just spit in your hand and say, 'I'm in,'" I said. "Sal told me to meet him in Chicago. That's what I'm going to do."

"So you were going to make me part of the family too," Esther said, her tone flat. I had to look at her. I tipped my head so I could see her face.

"That's why you want to marry me?" she said.

"You told me not to be gentle," I said. "This is as real as it gets, Baby Ruth."

She nodded slowly, her eyes solemn.

"Do you love me, Benny Lament?"

"I love you, Esther Mine. I love you enough to do whatever I have to do. Do you understand now?"

"Well, I understand now," Money said. But Esther said nothing.

"You think Alexander sent them? The guys that shot at us? The guys Bo Johnson killed?" Alvin asked.

"I don't know."

"They looked like gangsters," Money said.

"If it's mob related, it wasn't Sal. Sal would kill me before he'd cut off my fingers. He loved my mother. He loved my father. He would take me out if he felt it couldn't be avoided, but he wouldn't torture me. It would be quick, and it would be done."

"They tried to kill you," Money protested. "I saw it."

"Why cut off my finger?"

"So you couldn't play," Esther whispered.

"I couldn't play if I was dead, Baby Ruth. It doesn't make sense. They wanted to make a statement. Or make it look like a statement. They cut off my ring finger. My wedding ring. That gets out . . . it looks personal. Racial. It feeds into the frenzy. It tells a certain story. 'White piano man and Negro singer attacked. Wedding band cut off man's finger.'"

"It makes it look like something it's not?" Alvin asked.

"Maybe it's like Murder Inc.," Lee Otis said. "Maybe someone just hired them."

"Well . . . they're dead now," Money said, satisfied.

~

We stayed at the Blackstone Hotel in Chicago. I got two rooms, nice ones, and made no bones about who was rooming with me. The Blackstone, on the corner of Michigan Avenue and Balbo Drive, was a big, red, high-rise hotel where politicians, gangsters, and entertainers liked to stay. It was known as the "Hotel of Presidents," the place where big deals happened in smoke-filled rooms. John Kennedy was a frequent guest. Rudolf Alexander too. Uncle Sal and Theresa stayed there whenever they visited her family, and her father, Carlos Reina, got his hair cut in the Blackstone barbershop once a month. He was even known to have meetings with his bosses while the barber snipped away.

Pop and Uncle Sal avoided barbershops after Anastasia was taken down. They had a barber visit La Vita every so often instead.

I thought about hiding out in a dive at the edge of town, and then decided against it. I didn't want to stay in a dump. I was pretty sure there wasn't anywhere to hide, and our name was on the marquee at the Regal Theatre in the Bronzeville district. Everyone who wanted to do us harm would know exactly where we were and when.

But I was marrying Esther in front of a judge with a messed-up face and a target on my back. No party. No fanfare. No pretty white dress. And she deserved all those things. The least I could do was get us a nice room. And this was where Sal told me to be. I took heart in that.

The place was crawling with gangsters. Oddly, I took heart in that too.

Sal called me Thursday night, ringing through from the front desk.

Esther was coloring her nails. It was a long process, painting and fanning, painting and fanning, and she'd been at it for a while. She said she might be getting married at the courthouse, but she was going to look good doing it. One leg was drawn up in front of her as she applied a final coat of red to her toes. When the phone rang, she looked up at me where I was lounging on the bed, my eyes half closed, watching her go through her ritual with more pleasure and peace than I'd felt in a while.

"You know that call's not for me, Benny," she said quietly. I reached for the receiver with my good hand and brought it to my ear.

"Yeah," I said.

"Benito," Sal greeted me.

"Uncle."

Esther screwed the lid on her little bottle and fanned her toes, but her shoulders had stiffened.

"I heard about Detroit. I thought maybe you wouldn't come," Sal said. "Plans haven't changed?" He was guarded, talking in generalities the way he always did over the phone.

"No . . . Plans haven't changed," I answered. Esther's eyes were heavy on my bruised skin.

"Are you all right?" Sal asked.

"I'll heal."

"Can you . . . still play?"

"Maybe not as well as I used to. But still better than anyone else."

He grunted once, a suggestion of a laugh. "Jack would have liked that answer."

"It's the truth."

"Esther's with you?" he asked.

I hesitated. I didn't like the question. *Sal knows everything.*

"Yes."

Sal took the phone from his mouth, talking to someone in the room with him. Tony? The sound was too muffled to make out specifics. It sounded like he was at the bar. Clinks and laughter and faint music found their way through the line.

"I want you to come downstairs. You and Esther. We're in the lounge. Everyone's here. I'll introduce you. You can sing a couple of songs for us. Let everyone see you. Let everyone see her. The two of you, together. I'll give you my blessing, right out in the open, so no one can misunderstand. Maybe we can put an end to this."

"You'll give us your blessing?" I gasped.

"A line was crossed, Benito. Whoever did this didn't just insult you, they insulted me."

"How so?"

He was silent so long, I thought we'd been disconnected, but when he finally answered, his fury singed the hair in my ear, and he spoke as plainly as I'd ever heard him speak.

"They didn't just try to kill you. They purposely maimed you. They knew who you were, and they tried to take it. They wanted to take away your ability to make a living, to make a name. You don't do that to a man. Kill him, fine. But don't take away his ability to be a man."

He sounded like my father. *If a man can't protect and provide it'll make him mean . . . or it'll drive him crazy.*

"You sound like my pop," I repeated out loud. And just like that, a wave of grief rose up and knocked me over, and I tumbled in the surf of Sal's fury and my own devastation. I tried to recover by shrugging it off, using levity to find my balance. "But they didn't take my manhood, Uncle. I still have my dick."

"Yeah. And I still have mine. This ends tonight, Benito. But I need you to come downstairs."

"You want all your friends and associates to see me with my face bashed in?"

"Yeah. I do. Show them you can't be intimidated. Show them you're one of us."

Show them you're one of us.

I was silent, and Sal sighed. His voice dropped, like he didn't want anyone around him to hear.

"Everything I do is a statement. You think I don't know my own business? I own three clubs, Benito. I know how to put on a show."

"So what's the statement tonight?"

"You don't kill or spook very easily. You do what you want, with any woman you choose, and you do it with the whole world watching."

It was essentially my own plan, read back to me, but now Sal was on board. And if Sal was on board, he would make himself captain of the whole ship. He would call the shots. I was so goddamn tired.

I wanted to hang up the phone and cover my aching head. But that wouldn't solve anything.

"Benito?" Sal was getting impatient.

"All right, Uncle. We'll be down in . . ." I looked at Esther, trying to gauge how much time she would need. She was already taking out her pin curls and waving her toes in the air to help the polish dry.

"I can be ready in five," she said. "My toes will be ready in ten."

"Give us fifteen minutes," I told Sal. "We won't stay long. I don't know if my hands will cooperate, but Esther can sing."

"Esther can sing, you can play, and the stage will be set," Sal said. "We'll be at the show tomorrow too, Benito. No one will get near you."

"We?"

"Me and Theresa. The Reinas. The Tonys."

"All right."

"Fifteen minutes."

I hung up the phone and rose from the bed, swearing when my head swam and my stomach lurched.

"We're performing?" Esther asked.

"Yeah . . . singing for our supper," I grunted. Singing for our lives.

"Can you do it, baby?" she whispered.

It was the first time she'd ever called me "baby." The first time she'd ever used an endearment at all. I was Benny Lament, even when she was kissing me.

It'd been a while since she'd kissed me.

Actually, she'd hardly touched me since leaving Detroit. She was afraid to hurt me, I knew that. Afraid that her touch would cause pain.

I wrapped my arms around her, careful not to tread on her newly painted toes.

"I can do it if you're with me," I said.

"I'm with you, Benny. I'm with you."

"For better or worse?" I asked.

"Better or worse. Richer or poorer. In sickness and in health."

"Till death us do part," I finished. We'd applied for a marriage license that morning but had to wait the mandatory twenty-four hours before we could use it. In all this mess, it was the only thing I wasn't unsure of, the only choice I didn't doubt.

"Don't say that. Don't ever say that," she reproached.

"What?"

"I hate that line. We aren't going to talk about death. Or dying. We aren't going to think about it. We aren't going to invite it to our wedding. I want to live with you, Benny. Live. Not part. So I won't be saying that gloomy garbage when I marry you tomorrow."

"No? Then what will you say?"

"I'm going to say 'I do.'"

"Okay."

"I do, I will, and I promise. And that's all."

"I do, I will, I promise, and that's all," I repeated, the words sounding like a mantra . . . or a song lyric.

"Are you going to start singing, baby?" she whispered, smiling, reading my mind. Damn, I liked the way that word sounded on her lips.

"It sounds like a lyric."

"It does." She lifted her face to mine, and I brushed my sore mouth over hers.

"I do. I will. I promise . . . to never let you go. I do, I will, I promise. And that's all," she said, half singing it.

"That's all?" I sang back, my voice raspy.

"That's all," she answered.

The Barry Gray Show

WMCA Radio

Guest: Benny Lament

December 30, 1969

"You're listening to *The Barry Gray Show*, the last show of the year, the last show of the sixties, and I'm chatting with Benny Lament, renowned singer and songwriter. Some might even call you an activist," Barry Gray says.

"It's an honor to be here," Benny Lament replies, not acknowledging any of the labels Mr. Gray has just used to describe him.

"Let's switch gears, shall we? We can't talk about Esther Mine and Benny Lament without discussing civil rights in America."

"It's always the elephant in the living room," Benny Lament says.

"In 1958, a Gallup poll showed that ninety-four percent of Americans thought interracial marriage was a bad idea," Barry Gray says, his voice taking on a new seriousness as he begins to rattle off the stats. "Now, a little more than a decade later, those numbers have started to change. Miscegenation laws have been struck down in every state. In 1967, in the *Loving v. Virginia* case, the Supreme Court ruled that the choice to marry whomever one wishes, regardless of religion or race, is a constitutional right. But you married Esther in 1960, years before the Supreme Court weighed in. In many northern states, there were no laws prohibiting marriage between the races," Barry Gray summarizes.

"There weren't laws, but that didn't mean very many people were doing it. The problem was community. A white woman marries a Negro man, or vice versa—where do they live? Even in the places like Chicago or Detroit, where there were no laws against it, there were lines. Where do you go, how do you make a home, when the unspoken rule is whites live here, coloreds live there?" Benny Lament says. "What do you do?"

24

Ave Maria

I lost my nerve in the elevator. I saw my reflection in the mirror, my pummeled face sitting above my crisp collar and knotted tie. Blue, bloodshot eyes peering out from puffy, blackened skin. I saw Esther standing beside me in her red dress, her hands clasped and her lips painted, and I knew, with overwhelming certainty, that I was making a mistake. We were descending into the bowels of hell, and when the elevator pinged and the attendant said, "Your floor," I hesitated.

"Take us back up," I demanded. The attendant frowned but pressed a button to prevent the door from opening.

"Sir?" he asked.

"Benny?" Esther pressed.

I didn't have a gun. I didn't have a plan B. I didn't even have backup. We'd decided not to tell Money, Alvin, and Lee Otis where we were going. Better to keep them out of it. All I had was my Uncle Sal waiting for me with his den of thieves and a tiny, red songbird who would be caged or crushed if things went badly. I was selling my soul to the devil.

"Take us back up," I repeated.

"Did you forget something, Mr. Lament?" The Negro attendant didn't quite meet my eyes. He fidgeted, making me even more nervous.

"You know who I am?" I asked.

"Yes, sir. You're Benny Lament." He looked at Esther with a quick twist of his lips and a funny little bow, adding, "And you're Esther Mine. I'm Elroy Grady. I love your song. We're all singing it."

"What song is that?" Esther asked.

"'Any Man.'" He grinned and began to sing under his breath. "I don't need another mother, brother—sister, mister, sweater, whatever—and I don't need any man." He shook his head, marveling. "It's catchy."

"We're going to sing a few numbers in the lounge, Elroy. Maybe we'll do that one . . . just for you," Esther said.

"No. We're not going to be singing in the lounge. Take us back up," I insisted.

Elroy looked from me to Esther, but he didn't open the door and he didn't push the button to return us to our floor.

"My cousin buses tables in the Blackbird Room. That's probably where you're singing . . . right?" Elroy asked.

"What's his name?" Esther said, ignoring me.

"Percy Brown. Percy's gonna lose his mind when he sees you."

"We'll say hello if we see him, Elroy," she promised.

"He's colored . . . like us," he said, still keeping the doors closed, his eyes on Esther's. "He's the only colored fella on duty tonight. You'll see him." He turned to me. "He plays the piano too . . . like you, Mr. Lament. This is going to be a real treat."

"We'll try not to let him down," Esther said, her voice kind.

"The only way you'll let him down is not to sing at all. You'd be lettin' us all down then."

You'd be lettin' us all down then.

I closed my eyes and prayed for guidance. This was about so much more than me. It was about so much more than Salvatore Vitale or Rudolf Alexander.

"Are you two really together?" Elroy whispered, like he was afraid someone would overhear, even though we were the only ones in the elevator.

"We really are," Esther said.

"I knew it. That's nice. That's good. Percy said he wasn't sure. He said it might just be a gimmick . . . something to draw attention. But that's not it, is it?"

"That's not it," I said.

"Someone didn't like you two singing together . . . is that why you're all beat up?" he asked quietly.

There was no easy answer, so I shook my head.

"You two are making history. How does that feel?" Elroy asked, amazement underscoring his question.

I didn't answer again, and he frowned sympathetically.

"It doesn't feel too good right now, does it?" he said. Then he grinned and winked.

I grinned too, and the action reopened my split lip. I dabbed at the blood with my handkerchief, and then I laughed. It started out a chuckle, but it grew until I was wheezing, the mirth as much a release as my tears had been on the roadside between Detroit and Chicago. Elroy and Esther laughed with me, though not as hard, and I could tell by Esther's bemused smile that she wasn't certain I hadn't lost my marbles.

"There's always gotta be a first time, right?" Elroy said finally, still smiling. "There's always gotta be someone who shows the world how it's done."

"You wanna change the world, you gotta show 'em what it looks like," Esther agreed, and she tucked her arm through mine.

"I like that," Elroy whispered, nodding.

"We aren't the first, Elroy," she said.

"First I've seen. Hopefully you won't be the last," he replied. He hesitated, his eyes swinging between us. "You still want to go back up, Mr. Lament?"

I did. I wanted to get the hell out of Chicago. But I shook my head. "No. You can let us out, Elroy."

"Good luck, then." He let the doors slide open and we stepped out, as ready as we would ever be.

~

Sal had said everyone was there. It wasn't an exaggeration. Everyone was there. The room was densely packed with about sixty people who could make or break you. I recognized two actors, a politician, and three mob bosses and their consiglieres. There were plenty of wives too . . . or girlfriends. A sports broadcaster sat with the owner of the White Sox and his new pitcher.

At the corner table, his back to the wall, eyes to the room, was someone else I recognized. He was tall and thin, impeccably groomed, and sharp eyed. He was bald on top and didn't try to cover it. Instead, he'd shaved his pate smooth. The little round glasses and his hairlessness should have aged him. It didn't. It made him look more intimidating. I knew him from the papers, from occasional coverage on the evening news; he'd been in the news a lot more lately. I knew him from the wall of pictures in Uncle Sal's study. Two men sat at his table with him, drinking with the ease of the privileged set who knew the world couldn't—or wouldn't—touch them. My heart dropped, and the urge to get the hell out of Dodge welled in my chest all over again.

Rudolf Alexander was in the room.

Sal moved toward us, and the crowd parted, eyes pinging between us and back to my uncle, who had his arms held wide and high, like I was the prodigal son come home. The room grew quiet without Sal saying a word. Still, someone clanged a spoon against glass, signaling the boss had something to say. Fat Tony, most likely, though I couldn't see him in the crush. Esther's hand tightened on my arm, but she didn't let go.

"Nephew!" Sal greeted loudly. He took my face in his hands and kissed my cheeks enthusiastically, first one then the other, and I tried not to grimace in pain. Anger flickered across his features.

"You look like shit," he hissed.

I didn't answer. I knew he didn't expect me to. And I said nothing about Alexander. Sal was well aware of Alexander's presence, and Esther didn't need to be.

Sal turned to her, saying her name just as loudly, and he kissed her too, his lips barely brushing her skin, his hands patting her shoulders. It was his signal to the gathering that he approved. There were murmurs and gasps, but I was guessing it was more my appearance than Sal's greeting.

"Esther and Benny just got married," Sal announced, throwing his arms wide, voice booming, demanding everyone listen.

We didn't correct him.

"And I hope you will all help me welcome her to the family."

"Toast," someone yelled. Definitely Fat Tony.

"Toast," someone repeated, jovial.

A waiter rushed forward with a tray of champagne. Sal handed us each a glass, and Esther let go of me reluctantly so I could hold the stem with my good hand.

"To Benito and Esther. May you make beautiful music and a beautiful life together. I know Jack would be proud. My sweet sister, Giuliana, too. May they rest in peace."

"To Benny and Esther," Fat Tony shouted.

Glasses were raised, and goodwill rang out. I downed my glass, and Esther sipped at hers before setting it aside like she didn't trust the contents.

"Now you all know my nephew is a piano man. But you might not know that his lady is a singer. And tonight . . . Benito and his bride have agreed to perform for us," Sal said, urging us forward toward the piano that sat in the corner of the room, the lid lifted, the bench pulled out, the keys waiting. There were no microphones—it wasn't an official gig—but we didn't need them. The room was hushed, the curiosity tangible, and I slid onto the bench while Esther took her place beside the piano, facing the gathering. I left my injured hand in my lap. One hand would have to do tonight; Esther's voice would have to carry us. I looked up at her and winked. She smiled a ghost of a smile and squared her shoulders.

"As you can see . . . Benny Lament's got a broken wing," she said, projecting her voice over the silent crowd. "But you can still fly, can't you, Benny?"

"I'd rather not. Let's stroll, shall we, Esther? Nice and slow." It wasn't difficult to sound pained.

Our crowd chuckled.

"Nice and slow? Well, that's no fun," she pouted.

"Go easy on us, Esther."

More laughter, but I was dead serious.

"Something slow . . . easy." She cocked her head. "How about this?"

I waited, knowing she was playing to the crowd, but not knowing where she was taking us.

"Listen," she urged.

She began to drum out a heartbeat rhythm on her hips. *Ba DUM. Ba DUM. Ba DUM.*

"Can you hear that?" she asked the audience.

"I can hear it," I said, thumping her rhythm on my thigh.

"Help us out," she insisted, and the audience obeyed, the heartbeat becoming an entire percussion line. Then Esther added her voice.

"I hear your heart . . . or is it mine?" she sang, pitch perfect, her voice inviting and clear, drawing everyone in. She didn't wait for me to answer her back the way I usually did. She made the song a solo with no accompaniment on the first verse except for the beat she'd engineered from the audience.

"Oh, please not that. Oh, please don't go. Let's say hello," she crooned. I added the piano, my right hand comfortable on the keys, my chords a counter to the beat.

"Are you with me, Benny?" Esther asked.

"I'm with you," I said, making sure everyone could hear me.

"Then let's do that again."

We sang it from the top, the way we usually sang it, tag teaming and teasing each other, acting like we didn't have a care in the world. It was simple and sweet, nothing too hard or too impressive, and the audience clapped when we were done, but we hadn't bowled anyone over. I couldn't see Alexander from the bench, and I had no idea whether Esther had spotted him or, for that matter, whether she even knew what he looked like.

Sal sidled up beside Esther when the clapping faded, his hand on her shoulder, his gold-colored liquor sloshing in his glass.

"I knew Esther's mother a long time ago. Maude Alexander. She too was a marvelous singer."

The room bristled in discomfort.

"What a voice. What a woman." He raised his glass. "To Maude Alexander, may she too rest in peace."

A few people joined in the toast, their voices stilted and awkward.

"We have a special guest in the room with us tonight," Sal continued. "Maude Alexander's father and Esther's grandfather. Mr. Rudolf Alexander. A man who loves his country and will serve our new president well. We are so lucky to celebrate this happy occasion with him. Mr. Alexander. We are honored by your presence." Sal raised his glass again, and the whole room rushed to join in. I swiveled, unable to help myself, but couldn't find Rudolf Alexander through the raised arms.

Esther was stone beside Sal, and I could only gaze up at her, heart pounding, my hand throbbing. *I wanted to kill him.* Esther didn't even look at me.

"Sing us something else, won't you, Esther?" Sal purred. "You promised me not too long ago I could make a request."

"All right," she said.

"Something for your mother . . . and your . . . grandfather. Something that will remind us of her."

"Sal," I protested quietly, but my complaint seemed to wake Esther up.

"I know just the song," Esther said, clear and hard. "Something sweet. Something for Christmas. A blessing on the new year. A song for a . . . suppliant . . . child."

Sal's eyebrows shot up at her word choice, but he inclined his chin, the benevolent dictator, giving her his permission to proceed. He settled himself into an empty chair, right in front, and crossed his legs.

Holy shit, Baby Ruth. I knew exactly the song she was referring to. I could do it, even with one hand. The accompaniment was rolling, even simple, and I could make it simpler. But I didn't know if *she* could do it.

She looked at me then, her gaze flat and her nostrils flared like she smelled my doubt.

"Ave Maria," she sang, drawing out the word so I could find my place . . . and follow. Her voice was slow. Low. And bold. She didn't sing it in Latin, and she didn't sing in the same key her mother did. She didn't sing it like a trained soprano at all. She sang it like Esther. Like a woman throwing herself from a cliff because she damn well knew she could fly.

I came in quietly, playing beneath her, though she didn't need me at all.

Ave Maria! Maiden mild.
O listen to a maiden's prayer.
For thou canst hear though from the wild

Tis thou canst save amid despair.
Safe may we sleep beneath thy care,
Though banished, outcast, and reviled;
O maiden, see a maiden's sorrow
O mother, hear a suppliant child.
Ave Maria!

She delivered the song slowly, intently. She sang it with all the pain of the banished, outcast, and reviled . . . and all the triumph too. But Esther was no suppliant child. She was no maiden mild. She was a woman who needed no permission and no allowances. She didn't beg, she bled. She didn't whimper, she warned.

I'd never heard Schubert sung like that. Esther moaned and wept the words without shedding a tear, and I followed her, awestruck. When she ceased, the room was like a tomb.

"I don't sing it like my mother did. I'm really nothing like her. Actually . . . I think I probably take after my father," Esther said to her mesmerized audience, her voice mild but her eyes blazing. "Do you have another request, Mr. Vitale?"

~

When I stood from the piano a few songs later, Rudolf Alexander no longer sat at the table in the corner. Positioned as I was, I hadn't seen him go. Maybe he'd left the room after Esther's "Ave Maria." Or maybe he left when Esther's mockery on "Pandora's Box"—"The secret's out, everybody knows, people are watching wherever we go"—was still ringing around the room. My good hand was cramping, my injured hand screaming, but more than anything else, I was desperate to get Esther alone and seal us both off from the relentless tension. But Sal was there, standing between us, his arms around our shoulders.

"That was magnificent, Esther. Magnificent," he murmured as he urged us forward to meet his friends. He escorted us around the room, introducing us here and there. One face blended into another. I wasn't well, but I was past being able to differentiate between pain and stress, and I let myself be herded about until the room started to thin, people stopped staring, and Sal pointed at an empty table.

"Sit down, Benito. Have a drink. You look like you're going to be sick."

"I think we are going to go now," I said, afraid that if I sat, we would be stuck there for hours more. Esther was clearly of the same mind and remained standing as well. She wore the mask I'd come to recognize. Beautiful. Hard. Terrified. Angry. There would be a reckoning when she took it off. The sooner the better.

"Not yet. Sit. Have a drink."

I took Esther's arm. "Good night, Sal. Thank you for . . . the evening."

"Esther. Benito. Sit," he insisted. We remained standing.

Sal's face tightened and his eyes skipped around the room. He lifted his hand and signaled to Fat Tony.

"Fine. Go. I'm through with you, and I don't want you to be sick and ruin all my hard work." He almost sounded petulant.

"Did you know he was here?" I asked.

"Who?" Sal said, voice mild.

"Alexander."

Sal smiled, a brief baring of his teeth. "Of course. I invited him. We had business. All done before you even arrived." He waved his hand in the air, dismissing his words like it was nothing. "It will be better now," Sal said. "You'll see. Alexander and I have come to an understanding." He unbuttoned his pristine dinner jacket and immediately buttoned it again, as though he liked being bound.

"It's finished. Now go. You're swaying," he said, waving us off again.

"What is finished?" Esther asked, voice low. Flat. Emotionless.

"It's like your song," Sal said. "The song about Pandora. I liked that one. How did you say it? It's all out in the open now. He knows that I know. Everybody knows. You're mine. Both of you. I've claimed you. So it's finished."

I shook my head. It wasn't finished. It was just beginning. My missing finger pulsed, and Esther's hand tightened on my arm.

"Go." Sal shooed us away. "I'll see you tomorrow. At the show."

The two Tonys escorted us upstairs. Elroy was no longer in the elevator. A new attendant was on duty, and he kept his eyes averted from all of us. Sticks had blood on his right cuff. When I pointed it out, he shrugged and folded his hands, one over the other, so the blood was hidden. He lifted his eyes to the ceiling and we rode to our floor in silence.

"You're with us now, Benny. It'll be fine. You'll see," Fat Tony said as the door slid closed behind the four of us and the elevator whirred away. The long hall stretching out on either side was empty, hushed. But I felt no peace or comfort in the quiet.

"Everybody knows you're Sal's," Fat Tony reassured again. Judging by his constant reassurance, he felt no comfort either.

"Everybody knew who I was before. I'm still missing a finger," I said.

That silenced him.

"You want us to wait out here for a bit?" Fat Tony asked as they walked us to our door.

"Do we need that, Tony?" I asked quietly.

"Nah. You don't need it," Fat Tony soothed, but he didn't leave. He and Sticks leaned up against the wall, waiting for Esther to fish out our key.

She unlocked the door and pushed it wide.

"Good night, Esther," Sticks said softly.

"Good night," she answered, and fled inside.

"You're scaring her," I hissed.

"Go on, kid," Fat Tony urged, apologetic. "We'll just wait until you're inside. Humor us. It's been a strange coupla weeks."

I followed Esther inside and shut the door. She was perched on the edge of the bed, her back a ramrod, but she had kicked off her heels. Her glass mask was still firmly in place, and I walked into the bathroom, needing a moment. My reflection greeted me, and I immediately looked away. I turned on the faucet and reached for the glass I'd left beside the sink, holding it beneath the stream.

A severed finger—a tidy nail, pale skin, and a jagged ending just below the uppermost knuckle—bobbed to the surface.

I dropped it, the glass shattering at my feet.

"Son of a bitch!" I bellowed.

I stared at the gruesome display, and for a moment considered that someone was returning my finger. It curled amid the shards, beckoning to me.

"Benny?" Esther's voice was sharp. Close. I was flooded with dizzy relief that I'd closed the door.

"Benny? Are you all right?"

"I'm fine, Baby Ruth. I dropped a glass. Don't come in. I don't want you to cut your feet."

It was a white man's finger, large and freckled with age. A severed ring finger. Just like mine. But it sure as hell wasn't mine.

I grabbed a washcloth and fished it from the pieces of glass and dropped it into the toilet. I closed the lid and flushed it down, then tossed the washcloth and the remains of the glass into the trash.

There was no blood in the bathroom, no gory mess in the tub. No more surprises. Not in here. I yanked open the bathroom door, scaring Esther, and warned her away.

"Don't go in there. I'm not done. I might have missed a piece," I barked.

I flung open the main door, but the two Tonys were gone, and the hallway was as serene as it had been moments ago.

"Benny?" Esther was behind me.

I rapped on the door across the hall.

"I just want to say good night," I said.

"It's 2:00 a.m.," she protested. I was the one who was scaring her now. I was scaring her . . . and I was scared. Terrified. My heart and my lungs were battling in my chest.

Money answered, his skin creased from sleep, his eyes wary.

"What's wrong?" he said.

My lungs surrendered, the air whooshing between my lips.

"Are you all inside?" I asked, my tone remarkably calm. I was a fraud.

"Yeah. We're here. And we were sleeping. Peacefully. Where you two been?" He eyed Esther's red dress and my suit jacket before turning accusing eyes on me.

"Family business," I answered. "But it's done. I didn't realize how late it was. Sorry to wake you."

"Which family? 'Cause we're all in here, last time I checked."

"Good." I nodded. "All right. Good night." I turned away.

"What's wrong, Lament?" he insisted, his voice rising.

"Nothing. I just needed to see you."

"Well . . . here I am."

"Good night, Money," I pressed, hoping he would just let it go. I wasn't going to tell him—or anyone—what I'd found.

"Somebody need prayers?" Alvin called from deeper in the room.

"Nobody needs prayers," Money grumbled. "Go back to sleep."

"You drunk, Lament?" Money asked, suspicious.

"Nah. Just . . . just . . ." My voice faded away.

"You're scared."

"It's been a weird coupla weeks," I said, parroting Fat Tony.

Money's mouth twisted like he was searching for the right response. Then he nodded, acknowledging the truth of my statement.

"We're okay," he said, all rancor gone. "Good night, Benny."

"Good night," I said, backing away. I waited until he shut the door. Esther had already disappeared into our room. When she cursed, I panicked all over again.

She was standing in the bathroom, the door wide, balancing on one leg while digging a sliver of glass from the pad of her foot. Blood welled and fled to the crease beneath her toes.

"What are you doing? I told you not to go in there. I told you there was glass!" I yelled.

I swept her up into my arms. Angry. Furious. Tears pricking my eyes. I tossed her on the bed and grabbed her foot in both my hands.

"It was just a tiny piece," she spat. "I got it! Let go." She slapped at me, embarrassed by my manhandling. I pinned her legs and searched every square inch of her small foot, dabbing at the blood that had already stopped flowing with my handkerchief. I couldn't even see a slice.

She lay beneath me, heaving, her mask gone, her brown eyes huge in her face.

"It's gone," I whispered.

"You need to rest, Benny." She thought I was breaking, like I'd done on the side of the road between Detroit and Chicago.

I nodded, but my eyes roved the room. I wanted a new room. We couldn't stay in this room. I imagined waking to someone there, someone watching, or something worse.

I lifted myself off her and made a cursory check of every surface. The table. The closet. Under the bed.

"What are you doing?" she asked feebly.

"I just need . . . I just need to make sure . . . to make sure." I didn't have the words, and she watched me in silence.

I went back to the bathroom and got down on my hands and knees, running my good hand over the tiles to check for glass.

"Benny?" Esther put her hand on my back, but I couldn't touch her. I needed to wash. My skin crawled and my limbs shook.

I pulled at my bandage and turned on the water, trying to clean myself with one hand, but the soap slipped through my fingers and the water sprayed over my sleeves. Then Esther was there, pulling my jacket from my shoulders and loosening my tie. She made short work of my buttons and unthreaded my belt from the loops. Silently, she washed my face and my chest with a warm cloth and lathered my hands, all the way up to my elbows, before rinsing and drying me off.

"I'm going to rewrap your hand," she said. "Nice and tight to help with that swelling. Then you need to rest."

"What would I do without you?" I whispered.

"You wouldn't be here," she muttered back. "None of this would be happening. None of it. And the thing of it is . . . I told you to go." She looked up at me, her eyes so wet and dark I reached for the light behind us, flipping it off so I wouldn't have to see her concern. But the light from the entry spilled in through the open door, and I could not escape it.

"I told you to go . . . remember, Benny Lament? I told you to go in Pittsburgh when we got out of jail. You wouldn't listen. I told you to go. Why don't you ever do what I say?" Esther sounded like a mother scolding a disobedient child, like I was hopeless. Useless.

"You don't have to do any of this, Esther."

She folded her arms and shook her head, vibrating with disapproval. But her posture was ruined by the tears that were coursing down her cheeks. I pressed my bruised mouth to her chin and tasted her salt. She wrapped her hands around my neck.

"I keep telling myself that," she moaned.

"You do?"

"I keep telling myself I can go back home and take my brothers, and that I can end it. I'll clean houses with my mama and maybe find another lousy gig so I can show off my pipes every now and again."

"Someplace where you can sing 'Ave Maria.' The Vatican. St. Peter's Basilica. You would bring the angels to shame." Oh God, she'd been magnificent tonight, and it had been wasted on a roomful of mobsters and moguls, wasted on me.

Her small hands smoothed the skin at my neck though she was flaying me with her silent tears.

"I'll take you home," I promised. "I'll take you wherever you want to go. Or I'll leave you. I'll do that too, if it's what you want. I'll do whatever you want me to do."

She kissed my chest, pressing her mouth to the swell of muscle and bone that caged my heart. She kissed me and she cried.

"What about Percy . . . and Elroy?" she murmured, her breath warming my skin.

"Who?"

"The attendant in the elevator. And his cousin. Remember? What about my brothers? What about all the little Esthers? What about Bo Johnson and Maude Alexander?"

"I don't understand," I said.

"I can't quit. I can't stop. I can't run away. I can't even do it to keep you safe. Everybody's watching us. Not just the bad guys. Everybody's watching. They're counting on me, Benny. They're counting on us."

"Yeah. But I don't give a shit about anything but you," I confessed.

She shook her head, denying me. "That isn't true. You aren't like them. You aren't like Sal."

"You can tell yourself that, Baby Ruth. But you and I both know it's not true. I *am* like them. Everybody's rotten. And that's why you're crying."

"That's not why I'm crying!"

"What do you think this was? Tonight? Downstairs? That was me mobbing up. And you know it."

She hissed out a long, pent-up breath and glared at me. "That wasn't you mobbing up. That was you nailing yourself to the cross. That's what that was. And you've been doing it since we met. News flash, Benny. You aren't Jesus Christ, and you can't save me."

"Esther," I groaned.

"Everyone underestimates me. Even you." She swiped angrily at her tears and then wagged her dripping finger at me. "They always have. But I've never been a fool."

"I don't underestimate you, Baby Ruth. I overestimate my ability to keep up."

Her smile was tremulous, replacing her glower, and I wrapped her condemning finger in my fist and brought it to my chest.

"When did you learn 'Ave Maria'?" I asked.

"At Gene's bar in Detroit."

I stared at her, dumbfounded. She stared back at me, defiant, daring me to contradict her.

"Don't underestimate me, Benny Lament. Not again. I'm smart. And I know exactly who you are."

"Who am I?"

"You're my partner. My manager. My lover. My friend. We are friends, aren't we, Benny Lament?"

That day in Pop's apartment seemed like a lifetime ago.

"Yeah," I whispered. "We're friends, Baby Ruth. I'm your friend, I'm your man, and I'm your biggest goddamn fan."

I leaned down to kiss her, but she avoided my lips, dancing around the split edges and swollen places to save me from pain, but I needed her there most, and I gripped her hair, holding her still so I could taste her mouth and chase the new ache in the bottom of my belly. She opened sweetly, letting our tongues brush where our lips couldn't, and for a long time we simply kissed, seeking what we could not find. We needed peace. We needed safety. And there was none to be had.

So we found pleasure instead. Distraction. Communion. Everything that hurt became a distant hum, drowned out by the immediacy of her skin and her scent and her soft shudders. I was clumsy, playing her body the way I'd played the piano in the lounge, one-handed and wishful, wanting to do more than I was able, able to do more than I'd believed.

We loved each other for a long time, and we didn't talk about Rudolf Alexander or the outcropping of unknowns that waited for us in the morning. Esther fell asleep near dawn, her emotion spent, her passions sated. But I could not sleep. I had to stay alert. I had to stand guard. And I could not sleep in this room.

I groaned out loud, sickened again, and Esther stirred. I willed myself to be still. To think. To examine.

I wasn't even sure what it meant, the finger in the glass.

Was it a threat? Or a reminder. Or maybe . . . a settled debt.

An eye for an eye, a tooth for a tooth.

A finger for a finger. It was Sal who'd orchestrated it, I had no doubt. Rudolf Alexander had lost a finger, and I had another chain around my neck.

"We have an understanding," Sal had said, but I didn't understand any of it. They all had so much shit on each other that once something slipped, the whole house of cards would come down.

I knew one thing . . . and I'd always known it. You were either in or you were out. You couldn't do family halfway. If you tried, you just kept getting pulled in deeper and deeper until everyone shared the same sins, simply by sharing the same name.

Sal said it was finished, but it wasn't finished. None of it. Severed fingers and twisted arms only led to new bedfellows and old enemies waiting to pounce, and Bo Johnson was still out there. Bo Johnson and a thousand sins no one had ever paid for.

The Barry Gray Show

WMCA Radio

Guest: Benny Lament

December 30, 1969

"The night you performed at the Regal Theatre in Chicago there was a bomb threat," Barry Gray says.

"Yeah. A threat . . . but fortunately no bomb," Benny replies.

"But several people were injured trying to get out."

"Yeah. People were pushing and shoving. Scared to death. It was chaos."

"What happened?" Barry asks.

"It was toward the end of the night. The Miracles were getting ready to go on. The rest of the performers had finished. We sang 'The Bomb Johnson' to end our portion of the show, and all of a sudden, security swarmed the stage. Instead of a bomb threat, the papers the next day called it the 'Bomb Johnson threat.'"

"The threat was just a joke?"

"The police weren't joking, and it wasn't funny. Minefield was accused of inciting the crowd in Pittsburgh. In Chicago, our song apparently inspired a bomb threat."

"No evidence of a bomb was ever found, and the threat was eventually traced to someone who had a history of race baiting," Barry says.

"Yeah. Well . . . one person can do a lot of damage. I think about that all the time. How the things we do affect everyone else. That day is definitely one I won't forget."

"Tell us about it."

"Esther and I got married in the morning and performed at the Regal that night. Esther wore the same dress to both events. She wore black. Now there's an omen for ya." Benny Lament laughs a little, but it sounds forced, and Barry Gray stays silent, waiting for him to continue.

"We didn't have a party or flowers. We didn't celebrate with champagne or music. There wasn't any music at all. We made our promises and signed our names on the document in front of us. Money, Alvin, and Lee Otis were our witnesses and our only attendees. We were married, by the power of the State of Illinois, and we walked out the same way we'd walked in, somber and serious, a band in black. There was a photographer who offered to take our picture, and Esther and I took one, standing side by side, holding hands, staring at the camera like a couple of escaped convicts getting our mugshots."

"You took another picture that day. One with Alvin, Lee Otis, and Money. It's become iconic," Barry says.

"That picture was the cover for our first full-length album. We had intended to use something else . . . a picture we took at a Motown Christmas party. But I didn't like it. I looked like a gangster, and I didn't want that. I didn't want to look like a gangster."

"That album was released in 1961 and entitled *The Bomb*. It has a picture of Bo Johnson and Maude Alexander on one side and the picture of Minefield on the other. The group picture is especially powerful."

"It's powerful because it's real. You can see it on all of our faces. Even Alvin wasn't smiling."

"You look like you'd been in a fight," Barry says, as though he's studying the picture.

"I don't think I landed any punches. It definitely wasn't a fair fight, I'll tell ya that much."

"That was from the attack at the Fox Theatre?"

"Yes. I wore sunglasses, or it would have looked a lot worse. I had two black eyes and my nose was broken."

"You're standing behind Esther in that one. And your size difference is marked. It doesn't look like a wedding photo."

"It was a family photo."

"None of you are touching. No arms slung around shoulders or tight cluster. You look so grim . . . or maybe just determined. And Esther's standing right there in the middle with a droopy white daisy in her hand."

"It was fake. The woman with the camera insisted she have it. She was trying to make the picture look like a wedding shot. Instead, Esther looks like she is about to toss it on a grave."

25

Change

We married Friday morning, December 30, 1960, before we had to be at the Regal for sound check. It was a pretty grim affair, more like a funeral than a wedding. My face hurt worse than my finger. It looked worse too. I was the ugliest son of a bitch I'd ever seen, but Esther still went through with it.

She planted a careful kiss on my swollen lips and promised she would love me anyway. She was subdued—we all were—but when she said, "I will," she said it fiercely, like she'd come to terms with all of it. And all of me. We walked out of the municipal building with a fake flower and a receipt for a couple of wedding pictures on the courthouse steps. Then we grabbed a sandwich and arrived at the Regal just after noon.

Sound check was miserable. I hadn't slept, my mouth was too sore to eat, and I couldn't make it through a full show with one hand. My mitts had always been the size of ham hocks, but I'd grown into them over a span of years. The thick bandages on my left hand made it twice the size, and I had only hours until showtime. I made Esther cut off all her careful wrapping and put a single piece of tape over the stitches.

"It's going to hurt," she protested.

"I can play without one finger, but I can't play without five," I explained. "Not for an entire show, and not at the tempo we're going to have to keep."

The pain was biting, but the adjustment was worse. I kept trying to use a finger that wasn't there, and it threw off my rhythm. My hands couldn't do what my head said they could. I resorted to playing with three fingers on my left hand, keeping my stump and my pointer finger elevated above the others and just playing chords. I simplified every song, and Money picked up my slack, riffing where there was a hole and backing me up on my solos. It wasn't going to be my best performance—hell, it might be my worst—but I was determined to get through it.

I wore a pair of black glasses to hide my eyes, a hat to shadow my face, and a thick layer of stage makeup to cover my bruises. The makeup made me sweat and it stung my eyes, making it hard to see the keys. It was probably better that way. The trick to not panicking was to not look at my hands and ignore the crowd.

It didn't help that Sal sat in the front row, Theresa beside him, with the Tonys like mismatched salt and pepper shakers on either side. Theresa's brother, Mike, and his wife were in attendance too, sitting with a whole line of mob guys and their big-busted girlfriends in the row behind Sal. Half of them had seen her perform the night before, and they were smitten. When we sang "Beware" Esther wagged her finger at them in warning, and they all laughed like they suddenly preferred lithe singers with perfect curls and very high heels. I was just grateful she couldn't touch their hair.

"And how are you tonight, Benny Lament?" she asked, her hip popped in the glittery black dress she'd married me in only hours before.

"It's a little hot in here, Esther," I answered.

"It sure is, Benny." She fanned herself like she was the reason.

"You thinkin' what I'm thinkin'?" I asked, using one of our standard transitions.

"Well, I don't know. What are you thinking?"

"I'm thinking about something cold."

"Your heart?" Esther asked, deadpan.

"Nah."

"Your kisses?"

The audience hooted at her audacity.

"Now how would you know anything about my kisses?" I said, and Lee Otis played a little *ba DUM DUM* on his drums, underscoring the fact that it was a joke.

We launched into "Cold" like we'd done it a thousand times. "You're cold. So cold, and I'm standing here all alone. Wishing that you'd come home. But you're cold."

I wasn't cold. I was roasting. One song after another, I did my best to keep up, but it was Esther who carried us. Again. I was woozy by the end, heart pounding, hands sweating, eyes stinging, but as much as I wanted to finish, I was dreading the final song.

I didn't want her to sing it.

Maybe it was Sal in the front row or the fact that Bo Johnson was alive and well and I was not, but when the spotlight dropped on Esther for "The Bomb," I almost stood and pulled her back, the way I'd done the night we'd met, standing beneath the streetlight at the edge of Central Park.

"Before we go, I want to tell you a story," she began. "The story of my father and my mother and me."

Esther told the tale and sang the first verse while conducting the sighs and swells in the audience with her outstretched arms. I thought we had made it when we rounded the final chorus, and I held my breath through the last lines. When the spotlight suddenly shimmied away like a spooked cat, the audience gasped and my sweating hands slipped, glancing off the keys. Esther kept singing; the light was gone but her microphone wasn't.

"He's Bo 'the Bomb' Johnson, and you better watch out," Esther sang, but something was wrong in the theater. I stood, swaying, from the bench, but Money stepped forward and drew Esther back, his guitar squealing in protest, the song cut off on its last breath.

The lights came up abruptly, flooding the puzzled audience, and a handful of security guards and policemen walked out on stage.

"Folks," a police officer said, getting too close to the microphone, his hands upraised, palms out, urging calm. "Please make your way to the exits. Don't run. Don't push. We've had a bomb threat and we want to be cautious. Please . . . make your way to the nearest exit."

If he'd wanted people to stay calm, he shouldn't have said "bomb."

"Son of a bitch," I heard Money gasp. He wasn't the only one. Someone in the audience yelled that there was smoke, and the concern became instant panic.

"Folks. There is no smoke." The police officer made it worse again.

"Fire?" voices gasped.

"I smell smoke," someone screamed, and one scream set off another.

An officer motioned for us to get off the stage. I was only too happy to obey.

"The crew and other artists have already been told to exit," the officer explained to us. "Please make your way out the back."

I pulled off my glasses and mopped at my face with Pop's handkerchief. I must have swayed, because Alvin and Esther were immediately propped beneath my arms, keeping me upright.

"You okay, Benny?" Alvin said.

"I'm fine. I'm just glad it's over."

"It's never over," Money grunted. "It's never freaking over. A bomb threat? What next?"

"Just stay together," I begged. "Nobody goes anywhere alone." If they let go of me, I was going down.

The stairs feeding the three levels of the theater would be packed, and we veered down the long corridor that led to the rear staircase, similar to the one in the Fox Theatre in Detroit. We were parked across the street and would have to work our way around to the front and through the crowd to reach the car, but at least we would be out of the building.

"I don't like this," Money hissed. "Something is going down."

I didn't like it either, but I was in no condition to do anything but keep my feet moving. The halls were empty, and Esther's heels echoed like gunfire.

We huddled together, making our way out the emergency door. A blast of cold air greeted us, and I stopped, lifting my face in relief.

"My coat is in the dressing room. My hat too," Money said unhappily. "I wonder when they'll let us back in?" He wore his guitar slung across his back and Alvin had his bass, but we had all left personal items inside.

"Where are we?" Lee Otis asked. "This definitely isn't the way we came in."

The little emergency exit had spit us out in an alleyway, and we paused to get our bearings. The other performers must have taken a different route, or they were simply a few minutes ahead. The alley was strewn with boxes, and dim lights bracketed the rear doors of several businesses on either side. A car screeched past the end of the alleyway, backed up, and turned in, pinning us in its twin beams.

"Who is that?" Money whispered. I turned and yanked on the door we'd just exited, but it had locked behind us.

Fat Tony and Sticks stepped out of the car and slammed their doors in unison. Sal stepped out half a second later. They left the car running.

"Benny? You okay? We thought maybe you'd come out the back," Fat Tony called, approaching me slowly.

Relief as sweet as the cold air coursed through me.

"We're fine, Tony," I said. I began walking toward him, Esther and her brothers trailing me cautiously.

A moment later, Theresa climbed out too, swaying slightly, following her husband like she didn't want to be in the car alone. Her blonde hair was sprayed up into an unnatural dome, and her black fur coat was clutched so tightly around her neck that I pulled at my own tie in discomfort. She was wearing her favorite earrings too, the black diamond baubles that looked like Maude's.

"Bo Johnson's here, Benito," Sal said as they neared. His face was grim, his jaw was set, and there was a gun in his hand. "I saw him inside."

I pulled up abruptly. Esther was stone beside me, and Money, Alvin, and Lee Otis formed a wall at my back. Money's guitar sang as he shifted his weight, and Theresa whimpered and reached for Sal's arm.

The emergency door behind us whooshed and swung, and Bo Johnson, right on cue, stepped out into the dank alley, his gun drawn, his distinctive hat drawn low. His topcoat flapped around his legs, and his shiny black shoes reflected the moonlight overhead. We were caught in the space between them, Sal, Theresa, and the Tonys on one end, the long, bowler-hatted silhouette of Bo Johnson on the other.

The Tonys both drew their weapons.

"No," I shouted, stepping in front of Esther and warding the Tonys off. "Nobody needs to do that. He's with us. He's with me."

Sal's eyes flickered over Esther and back to the figure that advanced slowly, his gun in front of him, his stride long.

"Bo Johnson saved my life in Detroit," I said, my eyes clinging to Sal's pointed gun. "None of us are enemies," I said.

Bo stopped, but he didn't lower his gun. Nobody lowered their guns. Money began easing back, pulling his brothers and Esther out of the line of fire, but I stayed centered between the opposing sides, afraid that if I cleared the way, firing would commence, and there was no one there I could bear to lose. I was surrounded on all sides by pieces of my life. By members of my . . . family.

Johnson's stance was easy, the barrel in his left hand, the grip in his right, but the way Money had described his methodical execution of the four men who had attacked me left me little doubt that the Bomb Johnson would not hesitate to shoot.

"Go on now, Benny," Bo Johnson rumbled. "You all just keep on walking. Get outta here."

"And then what?" I said. "You all shoot it out?"

"Go, Benito. Take your aunt. Take your woman and her family. Let us finish this," Sal insisted.

"He is my family," Esther spoke up, trying to pull out of Money's grip. "Bo Johnson is my family."

"He killed your mother," Sal said to Esther, his eyes lingering on her before they slid back to Bo Johnson. "He killed Maude . . . and he left you. Surely you know this."

"I did not kill Maude," Bo Johnson said, every word an emphatic punch.

"You killed her," Esther said, pointing at Sal. "You killed my mother because you couldn't have her."

"Me?" Sal said, scoffing. "No. No." Sal shook his head. "I didn't kill her. I loved her."

It was what he'd said when I'd accused him of killing Pop, like love and violence could not exist in the same man.

Theresa laughed, incredulous, and all eyes swung to her.

I'd never heard Theresa laugh before. It was an odd sound, like someone was tickling her with a sharp knife and she was afraid to skewer herself.

And she kept laughing, tears beginning to stream down her cheeks as if the mirth had overcome her.

Sal winced. "Go back to the car, Theresa."

She opened her purse, fumbling for something to dry her eyes even as she cackled and cried.

"Go back to the car!" Sal barked. "Tony . . . take Theresa and go. Sticks, you stay with me."

"But boss," Fat Tony protested, his gaze swinging from Theresa to Bo Johnson. His gun hand twitched.

"Benny!" Esther screamed.

Somebody fired, and everyone dropped. I threw myself to the side, reaching for Esther, but her brothers had already pulled her to the ground, each of them trying to cover the other, their limbs and bodies piled together, their heads tucked beneath their arms.

"Theresa!" Sal bellowed.

She was waving a small white revolver like a child with a Fourth of July streamer.

Sal lunged for the tiny gun and she fired, the bullet whizzing past his head and pinging into the trash cans on the other side of the alley. Sal flinched and roared, and Theresa shot again, her aim swinging wildly like she wasn't sure who she wanted to kill.

Sticks dove toward her, tackling her to the ground, and the gun went off again.

Bo Johnson was running toward Sal, his gun out, and I scrambled, coming out of my crouch, knowing that he would kill or be killed, and I could not allow either of those things.

"Stop!" I yelled. "Don't shoot! Don't shoot."

Sticks was down, Fat Tony too, though I didn't know why. Salvatore Vitale and Bo Johnson stood a mere five feet apart, each gun pointed at the other man's head.

Sticks eased himself up off of Theresa, his arms extended like a cowboy at a rodeo, seeing if his calf would bolt. Her gun lay near Fat Tony's inert form.

"Tony?" I yelled.

"I'm good, Benny. I'm good," he groaned. He didn't sound good. Sticks crouched at his side, his eyes skittering from the showdown in front of them to the pale face of his longtime friend.

"Put your gun down, Uncle," I insisted. "Please."

"So Bo Johnson can shoot me, nephew? You would choose him over me? You would choose Bo Johnson over family? Jack chose him . . . and Jack died. Maude died. And still you choose him."

"She's gone, Uncle. Maude Alexander is gone. Pop's gone too. And nothing we do here is going to bring them back. Killing Bo Johnson won't bring them back."

"He's not going to kill me, Benny. I'm going to kill him," Bo Johnson said, his voice low and easy.

"She wanted me. She wanted me, and he couldn't handle it. So he killed her. He killed Maude," Sal said, his lips trembling over his clenched teeth.

"She didn't w-want you, Salvatore," Theresa moaned, trying to rise. She rolled to her knees and looked longingly toward her little gun. Her giant coat hung from her plump shoulders and her makeup was smeared across her face. She'd lost one of her shoes. "And Bo Johnson didn't kill her."

"Do you know what happened to her, Aunt Theresa?" I asked. "Do you know who did?"

Bo Johnson flinched like he'd been punched in the stomach, and his gun jerked. Sal's eyes widened, and he stared at me in angry bafflement.

"Maude Alexander killed herself," Theresa insisted. "She killed herself. She was a miserable woman. A terrible woman! She slept with everyone. She destroyed families. She destroyed her own family. And I'm tired of talking about her. She's gone!"

"Boss. Tony needs a doc," Sticks interrupted.

"I'm okay, Sticks. Help me up," Fat Tony insisted. "I hit my head. That's all. I'm okay."

Sticks didn't dare lower his gun. He was trying to cover Theresa while tending to his friend. She was fingering the baubles at her ears like they gave her courage.

"Were those Maude Alexander's earrings?" I asked softly, suddenly certain Esther was right.

"They're mine," Theresa said, but she shrank, pulling her ugly coat close and patting the concrete around her, in search of her shoe.

"Let me see them," Sal said, shooting his hand out. Theresa froze. Then she rose to her feet, swaying a little. She tugged the earrings from her lobes and set them in his hand.

He studied them, his palm flat, fingers extended, and then he raised his eyes to his wife.

"Where did you get these, Theresa?" he said.

"They're mine," she repeated, emphatic.

"Where did you get them?" he insisted again.

"I've been wearing them for twenty years. And you never noticed," Theresa said. "Or did you just never look at me long enough?" She flinched as if her bravery would cost her, and I felt a flash of sympathy for my skittish aunt.

"Where did you get them?" Sal asked, enunciating each word.

"They are mine!" Theresa screeched, and then she immediately cowered, like her own raised voice had scared her. "They are mine," she said again, softly. "I earned them."

"I gave those to Maude," Bo Johnson said. His attention had shifted to Theresa, but his gun had not.

"Maude took something of mine. So I took something of hers," Theresa said, her tone like a petulant child's.

"What did she take, Theresa?" Sal asked, his voice barely above a whisper.

"She took you."

"She didn't. I am still here," Sal argued, dismissive.

It was the same phrase I'd used several times with Esther and her brothers. *I'm still here.* Physical presence meant nothing when what mattered most—my heart, my commitment, my loyalty—was elsewhere.

Sal's defense—*I'm still here*—angered Theresa as well.

"You have NEVER been here." She stamped her foot. "You don't know me at all. You don't want to know me. But I know everything about you. You were going to leave me. You gave her everything . . . and I had nothing!"

"What did you do to Maude?" Bo Johnson interrupted, impatient. He'd had enough of the drama playing out before us.

"She did nothing," Sal said, his voice weary. He sighed heavily and lowered his gun, a signal of surrender. "They are simply earrings. Theresa admired Maude. Most women did. Giuliana did. Many women copied her style."

"I did not admire her!" Theresa cried. "I hated her."

Sal put a hand on his wife's arm, but she flung him off like she couldn't bear to be touched. He tried again, pulling her back from the edge she'd so obviously reached. He even leaned over and found her missing shoe, forcing it onto her foot. She almost fell, but he straightened and caught her.

"Let's go home, Theresa. Your daughters are waiting. Your granddaughter too." He had completely forgotten about Bo Johnson, about the odd standoff and the loaded guns that seemed far less dangerous than his wife's bubbling rage.

"It's all your fault, Salvatore," she insisted.

"Yes. I know, Theresa," Sal agreed, soothing her. But his mea culpa wasn't enough. She wanted to tell us all why he was to blame. She had cracked, and alcohol-induced confessions, bitter and bone deep, started oozing out the fissures.

"I thought . . . she took my baby," Theresa babbled. Tears had begun to stream down her face in black rivulets.

"Your baby?" Sal asked, disbelieving.

"I thought she was my baby." Theresa pointed at Esther, who had risen to her feet, and then she jabbed her finger at Sal. "I thought you gave her a baby. You hadn't given me a baby. And I'd been waiting so long."

"Let's go home, Theresa," Sal tried again, but he made no move to leave or to take her arm again.

"I thought she took my baby!" Theresa screamed.

"What is this nonsense?" Sal hissed. "You are drunk. You need to stop talking."

Sticks had helped Fat Tony to his feet, and he seemed dazed but not damaged. We were all frozen, like pieces on a game board, with nothing to do but wait for our turns.

Theresa did not stop talking. Her words were spilling out now with her tears, following the streaks of black that hid in the collar of her fur coat.

"I went to her house. To Maude's house. She was expecting Bo Johnson, and all the staff had been dismissed or sent out for the evening. I watched them all go. Then I knocked on the door. She opened it herself. She was all dressed up for him. A purple dressing gown. Red lipstick. Black diamond earrings. I knew you had given them to her. She wore them to taunt me."

"I didn't give them to her, Theresa," Sal interjected, but she wasn't listening anymore.

"The baby was sleeping, she said, but I told her I had to speak to her. I told her I knew she was sleeping with my husband."

Sal looked at Bo Johnson then, at the gun in his hands and the shadows obscuring his face, but Bo's eyes were riveted on Theresa. Theresa was the ringmaster for the first time in her life, and her voice rose to encompass her entire audience.

"She denied it. But I knew she was lying," Theresa said. "She was holding a glass of wine. So I asked for one too. She set her glass down and turned to make me a drink."

"Theresa . . . shut up," Sal said. "Shut up. We're done here. Sticks . . . let's go." Sal grabbed Theresa's arm but she ripped herself away, clawing at his hands and talking as fast as she could, desperate to keep us all listening.

"I was ready. I had my pills in my pocketbook. I thought maybe I would kill myself too. I was ready to die. But I wanted her to die more. I'd crushed a handful of pills into a powder, and I put the powder in her wine," Theresa said, and the odd, hysterical laughter bubbled up as she fought Sal's attempts to quiet her. "She drank it right down. She drank it all. And she fell . . . fast . . . asleep."

Theresa wasn't talking to Sal anymore. She wasn't even talking to us. She was remembering, and Sal's efforts to protect her—or protect himself—suddenly ceased. He simply listened with the rest of us in stupefied horror.

"I held a pillow over her face when she fell asleep. It smudged her lipstick, and she looked silly. That made *me* feel good, seeing her look so silly. I pulled off her earrings and messed up her hair. That made me feel good too. I put a handful of pills on the table. Some on the floor. Like she'd spilled them. Then I went to get the baby. All I really wanted was that baby. She was Sal's. And Sal is mine." She placed her hand on her chest as she said those last words, defending herself *to* herself.

"But she wasn't Sal's," Bo Johnson said, his voice a rumble of thunder that seemed to jar her back to the present.

"No." Theresa sighed, and she frowned. "She wasn't. She was a little colored baby."

Esther had begun to shake, her small frame trembling beside me, and I wrapped my arm around her, steadying us both.

"I heard him come in," Theresa said.

"Who?" Sal asked. "Who did you hear?"

"I heard you." Theresa pointed at Bo, who was so still in the darkened alley, he almost melded with the shadows.

"You found Maude," she said, addressing him, her voice triumphant like she reveled in knowing his secret. "You cried. I've never heard a man cry before. You cried for a long time, and I stayed hidden . . . watching you. Then you took the baby. And you left. And I . . . went home too." She shrugged. "And everyone thought someone else was to blame," she said, shaking her head.

"You killed her," Sal said, like he couldn't believe it.

"I killed her." Theresa sighed like it was a relief to say it. "And you all blamed yourselves for not protecting her. Poor Maude. Always so many men throwing themselves at her feet."

Bo Johnson was crying. It was soundless, but his tears caught the light as they dripped from his clenched jaw and darkened the gray of his topcoat.

"I was afraid for a long time," Theresa muttered. "I was sloppy, the pills were mine, and I drank from my glass. But no one even asked me about her." She unclenched Sal's fist, took the earrings from his hand, and brought them to her chest.

"I took her earrings. I wanted something to remind me of what I'd done. I put them on the stand next to my bed. And every day I looked at them. I was still as invisible to you as I've always been. But I was different too. I was . . . powerful. Something changed that night. In me. And I got pregnant. You gave me my babies. And I was not invisible to them."

There was a moment of silence in the alley, a settling, an acceptance. Not of what had been done, but what had been revealed.

"Did you kill Carla too, Theresa?" Sal asked, his voice soft.

She blinked. Once. Twice. And then she confessed to that too.

"You should not have brought her into my home," Theresa said, and Sal's shoulders fell forward as his chin hit his chest.

"And what about Jack . . . did you kill Jack?" he whispered. "Did you hire Mickey Lido?"

Theresa frowned and shook her head, adamant, and her bleached hair danced. But Sal didn't believe her denial.

"Mickey was a Reina man. One of your father's soldiers. I couldn't figure out why a Reina man would hurt Jack. I thought maybe Alexander got to him. But you got to him. You hired him . . . didn't you?"

"No," Theresa said.

"Yes!" Sal roared. "Tell me!"

My breath caught, and my legs buckled. *Oh God. Oh, Pop.*

"Jack was talking about her." Theresa pointed at Esther. "He was stirring up all the bad times again. He got Benny involved. And that night . . . they were on the radio . . . singing about Bo Johnson.

Jack wanted the whole world to know about Bo Johnson and Maude Alexander. He said he wanted justice for them. He wouldn't shut up about it. He got sick, and he got a conscience, I guess. I just . . . thought . . . if Jack died, Benny would let it go. He'd stop playing with them and go back to his old ways. Benny never made any fuss. It was Jack that was stirring it all up. It was Jack pushing that girl on him."

"You hired Mickey to kill Jack," Sal repeated, stupefied. "Jack . . . who . . . loved us."

"He was dying anyway," Theresa said, looking at me. "Did you know that, Benito? He was dying anyway. It was . . . an act of mercy."

It occurred to me then that the world of Murder Inc. and Albert Anastasia wasn't just my world. It was Theresa's world too. It'd been Theresa's world all her life. Mob daughter. Mob wife. And she'd learned how to navigate in it. Hired hitmen, intimidation, drive-by shootings, and sawed-off fingers. Theresa knew who to call.

"Go get in the car, Theresa," Sal said, his voice level. Quiet. Finished.

She looked stunned, as if she'd just performed a soaring aria and been told it was subpar. She'd been dismissed again, relegated back to her corner. Made to feel invisible.

"But . . . ," she stammered. "I . . . I am not finished."

"Go get in the car!" Sal bellowed, pointing toward the car with his loaded gun, his fury terrible to behold. But Theresa did not cower before him. Not this time. Not anymore.

She lunged at him, grasping for his gun, her fingers curled like claws, her face contorted with incensed intention. Sal staggered back against her furious weight, trying to keep the gun from her clutches while he pushed her away.

"Kill me," she shrieked. "Kill me, Salvatore, or I will kill you."

But it was Sticks who shot her.

He fired once, his arm extended, face expressionless. Then he lowered his gun and took off his hat, holding it over his heart.

Sal had fallen to his knees in the struggle, and he looked up at Sticks, dazed, his arms filled with his motionless wife. Blood soaked her fur.

Sticks waited, his hat doffed, his eyes flat.

"She's . . . dead," Sal said.

"I'm sorry, Boss," Sticks said. "I didn't see no other way to end it. It was like she said . . . you or her." He didn't sound sorry. He didn't sound sorry at all. He had loved my father, and in his mind, I'm sure justice had been served.

Sal nodded slowly, mouth pursed, accepting the apology. Then he eased Theresa off of him, rolling her to the side, and he stood, straightening his suit coat and brushing at the blood on his sleeves like it had suddenly begun to rain. He paused, his eyes on the ground, and bent to pick something up.

Fat Tony walked forward and hoisted Theresa up by the armpits. Sticks took her legs. Together they waddled toward the car, her body swinging between them. The lights were still on and the engine was still running.

Sal watched them for a moment, then he turned and walked toward us, halting in front of Esther. Blood spotted his face, but his hair was perfectly coiffed. He placed Maude Alexander's earrings in her hand.

"You should have these."

Then he looked at me.

"I'm sorry, Benito," he murmured, echoing Sticks. But he sounded more sincere.

"You're going to have trouble when old man Reina finds out your man shot his daughter," Bo Johnson said. "You gonna tell him it was me, Vitale?"

"No. I'm going to tell him the truth." Sal shrugged and looked at Bo Johnson. "It was his man that killed Jack. He'll be glad to have some answers. Reina loved Jack."

"Everybody loved Jack," Bo said.

"Everybody loved Jack," Sal repeated. Everybody loved Jack, and not many people loved Theresa. The truth hung in the air, tragic and terrible, and Sal didn't even have to say it.

"She was right, you know," Bo added.

Sal quirked an eyebrow, waiting for Bo to continue.

"This . . . this is on you." Bo Johnson made a circle in the air, indicating the scene around him. "This is your fault, Salvatore Vitale. All of it. But I'm not gonna kill you. Not tonight. Maybe not ever."

"I'm not going to kill you either, Bo Johnson. But I don't ever want to see you again." It was as much of a truce as there was ever going to be.

Sal shot his sleeves and buttoned his suit coat. He turned to go. "Are you coming, nephew?" he asked softly, looking back at me.

Money swore beneath his breath, and Esther was suddenly rigid in my arms.

"No, Uncle. I'm not."

Sal nodded once, his mouth twisting. "You know what this means, Benito?"

"I know what it means."

"Don't come to me."

"I won't."

"Don't expect me to fix the world and give me nothing in return."

"This is on you, Sal Vitale. All of this. On you," Bo repeated softly. "You ain't never fixed a mess you didn't make. Benny Lament don't owe you shit. You owe him. You owe Jack."

For a moment I thought Sal would lash out, that the declarations made only seconds before would be rescinded and guns would blaze, but Sal's eyes flicked over me again, soft, conciliatory. And then he walked away.

Sal didn't apologize to Esther or to Bo Johnson, or to the motionless men who stood behind me, their instruments slung across their backs, and their lives forever altered. He left the alley in the same way he'd entered it, in the long, black car Pop had once driven him around in. Snow had begun to fall, soundless flakes that flitted around our shoulders and came to rest on the blood-spattered ground. It reminded me of the night Pop died, the night Esther and I had left the WMCA studios, and Esther had laughed up at the sky, celebrating our triumph.

"We're good together," she'd said. Then she'd asked me if I was scared, and I'd admitted I was. I hadn't stopped being scared since that day. Not even once. But . . . I hadn't run, I hadn't buckled, and I hadn't mobbed up.

I wasn't going to either.

I knew where I belonged.

A security guard stuck his head out the emergency door, peering at us curiously. Bo Johnson still held his gun pointed in the direction of the now-empty alley, but his back was to the man.

"We're letting everybody back in. False alarm. Better safe than sorry," the guard said, chipper. He didn't appear at all suspicious or nervous.

"Thank you for the update," Bo Johnson said, his voice warm and low. Friendly. "We'll be right there."

When we didn't appear in any hurry to enter, the guard propped the door and told us to make sure we pulled it closed behind us. He whistled as he retreated, the sound echoing in the stairwell.

Bo Johnson tucked his gun in his coat and approached Esther, his gaze regretful, his skin still striped from his recent tears. He reached for Esther's hand and held it clasped in his.

"It's an honor to meet you, Miss Esther Mine."

"It's Mrs. Esther Lament," she whispered. "As of ten o'clock today." Her ring was on her finger. Mine was still in Detroit.

"Esther Lament," Bo repeated. "Well, what do you know? Congratulations. To both of you."

For a moment they just looked at each other, face-to-face, father to daughter.

"I can't stay with you, baby girl," he whispered, and I imagined they were words he'd said once before.

"I know," Esther answered.

"You got Lament to look after you. His daddy did a good job. Benny will too."

"He's the one who needs looking after," she said, wry. "And who's going to look after you, Bo Johnson?"

He shrugged and stuck out his chin.

"I'm used to being in the ring alone." He tried to smile, but his heart wasn't in it. He studied all of us then—Esther, Money, Lee Otis, Alvin, and me.

"Don't talk about any of this," he said. "It's like I told Benny a long time ago. You can sing all you want. Singing won't get you in trouble. But don't talk about me. Don't talk about this. It'll be better that way. Some things have a way of working themselves out. Even if it takes twenty years."

"Singing's gotten us into plenty of trouble," Lee Otis said.

I had the sudden urge to laugh. It wasn't funny. None of it was funny, but I wanted to laugh.

"Hell yes, it has," Money hooted, and Bo Johnson chuckled, the sound so rolling and wonderful, my swollen nose stung and my throat caught.

"I've gotta talk," Alvin argued. "I can't pray if I can't talk."

"You pray all you want. You sing and pray and you make better choices than old Bo Johnson and Sal Vitale."

"Alvin says violence isn't the answer," Lee Otis said. "But we're still grateful for you. We still prayed for you."

Bo Johnson straightened his bowler hat and wiped at his cheeks with the back of his sleeve. "Violence isn't the answer. Change is the answer. But that's hard. A whole lot harder than throwing a punch."

We watched him walk away, his stride long and his coat flapping. At the end of the alley he turned left, and he was gone.

"Change is the answer," Alvin said, sounding satisfied. "I knew there was one."

The Barry Gray Show

WMCA Radio

Guest: Benny Lament

December 30, 1969

"You were married in Chicago, but you didn't stay in Chicago," Barry Gray says.

"No. We didn't stay anywhere for long. But the invisible line was everywhere, and in some places the line wasn't invisible at all."

"There was prejudice everywhere you went?" Barry Gray asks.

"Sure. Prejudice is human nature, and it isn't always ugly or violent or even obvious. We all make judgments, some of them justified, some of them not. We're taught a certain way of thinking and doing, we're taught to blame or justify, and a lot of the time we don't even know we're doing it. And that's true of everybody. Not just white people. I told Esther she had a chip on her shoulder, and she told me I had a blind spot."

"Is that where the song 'A Chip and a Spot' came from?" Barry Gray asks, his interest piqued.

"You guessed it. We had a big fight and wrote a hit, which happened a lot. But Esther was right. I had a huge blind spot. I didn't know how deep the lines ran and how entrenched the system to keep people apart really was. The obstacles were real. They are real."

"Even here in New York?"

"Everywhere. Growing up in New York, I'd seen how people grouped up according to ethnicity, but I didn't know that it wasn't just preference, just families looking out for each other. It made sense to me that people wanted to live among people with similar customs and cultures and language. I thought people segregated themselves because they wanted to. Chinatown, Little Italy, Harlem—it didn't occur to me that many people didn't have an option."

"You toured with Motown for a while. What happened after that?"

"We strapped the instruments to the top of the car and we kept moving. We followed Route 66 from Chicago to LA, performing every place that would have us along the way."

"How were you received?"

"Most people didn't know what to think. Some had heard our songs. Some had heard of us. Most people aren't ugly right to your face. They just make life difficult when your back is turned. They complain or point fingers. They whisper about you or spread mistrust. But people are curious too. They wanted to see us. So we let them look."

"You've gotten used to that? People staring?"

"If you want people to change . . . ," Benny prods.

"You have to show them what it looks like," Barry finishes.

"Some places there was nowhere we could stop. Long stretches on 66 where there were no services for Negros. Whites-only establishments, stations, restaurants, hotels. I would drop off Esther and

the boys, gas up the car, buy some sandwiches, and go back and get them."

"You'd drive straight through?"

"We took turns driving—though I was the only one with a license. I couldn't relax when I wasn't at the wheel, so I ended up doing most of it."

"What was the goal?"

"Attention, I suppose. Even bad press is better than no press. If you want to make a name for yourself, you have to perform. You have to get your music to as many ears as possible."

"It worked."

"I spent every dime I'd saved, and Pop's money too, before we started making it back. But eventually, yeah. We made it back, and then some. But we worked our tails off."

"You were thrown in jail, run out of town, booed off the stage—"

"We weren't booed, we were bounced," Benny interrupts.

"Someone threw a glass jar at Money. It split his head open. Esther was dragged off the stage," Barry continues.

"That was the second time I was thrown in jail, but nobody touched Esther again. Not after that."

"You put a couple boys in the hospital."

"They weren't boys, and they started it."

"Your father was a fighter—"

"Something I never wanted to be. But I told you, the older I get, the more like him I am."

26

Together Forever

Esther and I were almost never alone that first year. That was the hardest part. I drove with her sitting beside me; we performed together, ate together, spent every waking minute together and slept beside each other almost every night, but depending on where we were, some nights we couldn't even sleep in the same hotel, and that was torture. *If a man can't protect and provide it'll make him mean or it'll drive him crazy.*

Sometimes I would miss her so much, even when she was sitting right next to me, that my hands would shake, my belly would ache, and my missing finger would throb like it was still attached and not lost somewhere in Detroit, a bit of bone in a dog's belly or a rat's nest. When we had those minutes or hours alone with a wall or a door between us and the rest of the world, I couldn't decide whether I wanted to kiss her or touch her or just talk without her brothers listening or ears judging.

The best part was that she felt the same way.

Esther liked to lie with her head on my chest and her legs tangled with mine and make me "play her back" like I'd done the first time we danced, my fingers finding the ridges in her spine like the keys on the piano. We wrote a few songs that way, but it usually ended up with her mouth on mine, her sighs in my throat, and our bodies intertwined.

It was exquisite agony, those days on the road, and when we finally found our way back to New York, back to Pop's apartment and to the streets where we'd both been born, it was hard for us to leave again. Arthur Avenue and the Belmont neighborhood was inhabited by Italians almost exclusively, until Esther Mine—Esther Lament—moved in, but it didn't take long until everyone knew she belonged with me.

"She married Lament's kid. The musician."

"Her father was Bo Johnson, the boxer."

Then someone else would say, "Didn't he beat Lament?"

"Yeah, I heard he beat Lament. Knocked him out cold," somebody would agree.

"Well whaddaya know? She's his kid?"

"Small world."

"Small world."

And it was. It was the smallest, strangest, most wonderful world. Ugly and beautiful. Ugly and hard. But times, they were a-changin'. It was in the air. It was in the neighborhoods and on the radio. We went to Augusta and sang for a segregated crowd because Ray told us we made a bigger statement on the stage than off. But after that performance, which made national news, we refused to do it again, though we performed in the South off and on throughout the next decade. It didn't help the situation in the South—not black or white—if no one stood up and said, "This is what it looks like. This is what love looks like. And it's okay."

I learned what Esther liked and what made her laugh—I couldn't get enough of her laugh. The first time I got her really laughing in bed, I almost came without sliding inside her, and I had to put my hand over her mouth and think about chords and progressions and minor keys so she had time to find her pleasure before I ruined all of our fun. I tried not to be too gentle.

Sometimes she snarled and snapped and pinched me in frustration. Sometimes she called me Benny Lament with the sass of those early days, the days when she didn't know if she could trust me and the days when I'd wanted nothing more than to run, hard and fast, from what I knew was my fate. But other times she stood in the open window of our Bronx apartment where my mother had sung Carmen for the neighborhood. She sang her own songs, in her own way, and the neighborhood fell in love with her too.

Not once did I regret my decision to marry Esther Mine. Not in '62 when she wanted to sing at a concert on the campus of Ole Miss to support James Meredith, the first black student enrolled at that school. Riots broke out all over the campus, but we raised ten thousand dollars for Meredith and for a Mississippi voter drive. I didn't regret my decision in '63 when Alabama's new governor, George Wallace, promised "segregation now, segregation tomorrow, and segregation forever"; we simply looked at each other and shook our heads.

"Together now, together tomorrow, together forever," Esther said, turning off the television.

A few months later, the Children's Crusade in Alabama was organized, and over a thousand kids were arrested over their three-day youth march. The images of dogs and fire hoses being turned on them sent Esther into a rage, and she vowed not to bring a "colored child into a world like this." She woke me two days later, happy tears streaming down her face, to tell me she was pregnant.

Esther and I attended the funeral of Rudolf Alexander in '64. We weren't certain if he'd ever done anything to make our road more difficult. We didn't know where his influence began and Theresa's ended. Their sins were knotted together, never to be unraveled. Sal believed he'd hired the men to shoot up the street corner that day in Harlem and take my finger in front of the Fox. And Sal knew everything. Almost.

We didn't ever know if he'd used his influence to get a warrant for our arrest in Pittsburgh or intimidate Ahmet Ertegun at Atlantic, but it made sense that he had. The truth is, he may not have cared about us at all, but an article in the *New York Times* claimed he had a falling out with Bobby Kennedy over the "Bo Johnson story," and he was removed from his cabinet position.

We didn't go to his funeral to pay our respects; we went for Maude Alexander. For a man with so much wealth and power, there were very few in attendance. His wife had died not long after Maude. His oldest son was killed in the last days of the Second World War. His youngest son, an ambassador to somewhere, didn't attend.

"He worked every day of his life," the pastor said in his eulogy. "Never has there been a harder working man or a man more committed to his country."

Maybe that was true. I didn't know. But if it was, he had so little to show for it.

No relationships. No mourners. No one to throw flowers on his grave. Our son, Bo Johnson Lament, was an infant in Esther's arms, and he would never know his great-grandfather. We left before they laid Rudolf Alexander in the ground, and I never got close enough to the casket to see whether he had all his fingers.

If there was wealth he'd left behind, I don't know what became of it. I'm sure his diplomat son received a handsome inheritance, but Esther wasn't ever openly acknowledged. We were visited a month after his death by his estate lawyer, though, and he informed us a scholarship had been created in Maude Alexander's name, and that it could be applied to any music program or college in the state. First consideration was to be made to Negro students or students with mixed heritage. He said Esther had been named an administrator and could choose the yearly recipients if she wished. It was a small concession to her identity, to her existence, and after some thought, she agreed to review the applicants and select the winners each year.

It occurred to me, sitting at the funeral service for Rudolf Alexander, that he'd rejected the things I too had once disdained. Family. Connection. Posterity. Responsibility. Like me, he was a man who had loved his work, but at the end of his life no one had loved him. Esther had saved me from that, and sadly, she could have saved Rudolf Alexander from the same thing had he chosen differently.

How could I have any regrets? We met Bobby Kennedy in '64 when the Civil Rights Act was passed, and we marked our five-year wedding anniversary by performing at the White House in '65. In '67, the Supreme Court ruled that the laws against interracial marriage were unconstitutional, but our celebrations were short-lived. In July of that same year, riots broke out in Detroit down Twelfth Street over housing, unemployment, and charges of citywide racial discrimination. The powder keg Mrs. Esther Gordy Edwards had warned about in '60 exploded after a police raid, and the resulting riots lasted five long, hot days.

The newscasts and papers reported breathlessly on the fallout with enough hate and destruction in the background to make people shake their heads and take sides. When the smoke cleared, a black deliveryman named Jack Lament was among the dead, and Esther and I knew it was him. We'd seen him a few times in the years after Chicago. He would show up unannounced and spend an hour or two. He never had much to say. He just wanted to check on us. He got to hold his grandsons.

No one else ever knew that Bo "the Bomb" Johnson had lost his final bout.

We went to Detroit to claim his body. Esther had to show her identification to establish a relationship. The name on her passport was "Esther Lament," and the shared name was proof enough for their purposes. Ironic that their names had matched for the first time.

"He was your father?" they asked her.

"He was my father," she said.

We took his body back to New York and buried him beside Maude Alexander in Woodlawn Cemetery. It was the only home they were ever going to have together.

In '68, Martin Luther King Jr. was murdered in Memphis, making us wonder if his dream would ever come to pass. Rumors of mob involvement, questions about politics and payoffs and inside deals abounded, just like they had when JFK was killed in '63. And like most things, I doubted that what we saw and what we were told was really the truth. I knew better. There were riots after King's death too, the bubbling cauldron spilling over in places that had welcomed us and a few that had run us off. Those were the darkest days for me, when the ugliness seemed to overwhelm the beautiful, where I was convinced my father was right and only the rotten survived.

"His dream will come true," Esther had reminded me then. "The biggest dreams always do. I dreamed of you, didn't I?"

She *had* dreamed of me, a mobster's kid who played piano and wrote songs, and for all his faults and failings, Pop had made that dream come true. Not one day, not one minute, not one hour did I ever regret the day I followed him to Shimmy's to hear Esther Mine sing. For better or worse, for richer or poorer, in sickness and health, in black and in white, we managed to build our *famiglia* with all the shards and pieces we brought with us.

I've come to terms with Pop and the choices he made. I'm done holding that grudge and asking those questions. Maybe his choices allowed me to make better ones, and that's all we can leave to our kids. A better choice.

The Barry Gray Show

WMCA Radio

Guest: Benny Lament

December 30, 1969

"Now folks, many of you are probably wondering why Esther Mine isn't with us tonight. We had planned to have her here, hoped to have her here. Benny and Esther don't typically do appearances without the other. But Christmas morning, Benny and Esther welcomed their third child into the world. A daughter?"

"That's right. We have two sons—Bo and Jack—and now, a daughter. We named her Giuliana Maude after our mothers," Benny says.

"I made history—talk-radio history—because of a call in to my radio program," Barry Gray says. "I held the phone right up to the mic and had a conversation on air. The technology has improved a little since then, but I think it only appropriate to end this decade with another call. Esther, are you with us?"

"I'm here, Mr. Gray," Esther Mine says. Her voice is a little tinny through the line, but it's unmistakably her.

"Welcome to *The Barry Gray Show*, Esther. We wish you were here, singing with Benny, but I guarantee my audience is listening with bated breath."

"I wish I could be there too, Barry. For old times' sake. You've been with us from the beginning," Esther says.

"I only have you for a few minutes, and Benny has told us so much—"

"I guarantee he hasn't told you the good parts," Esther interrupts, and Barry laughs.

"Tell us about your family. Where are your brothers now? We haven't talked much about Lee Otis, Alvin, and Money."

"We've got so much family, it's hard to keep track," she says.

"Lee Otis isn't playing the drums anymore?" Barry Gray asks.

"Not in the band. Not after the first couple of years. It wasn't his dream. It wasn't the life he wanted for himself. But it paid his way through college. He's Professor Mine now."

"But Money's still playing lead guitar," Barry Gray inserts.

"Playing lead guitar and busting my chops. He and Esther keep me humble," Benny Lament says.

"And Alvin? What about Alvin? I've never met a more likable guy," Barry says.

"Alvin's a reverend," Esther answers. "He marched to Selma and has his own church. The Change Baptist Church."

"Nobody prays like Alvin," Benny says.

"And nobody plays like Benny," Esther adds.

"Well, nobody sings like you do, Esther," Barry Gray says. "We have to hear you sing before we go. I know singing for your audience through a phone line isn't what you're used to, but you and Benny end every show with the same song."

"Yes, we do. We call it 'Bombing' the stage," Esther says.

"Will you sing us a few lines, Esther?" Mr. Gray asks.

"Only if Benny will sing it with me. You there, Benny?"

"I'm here."

"Don't let me down, Benny Lament," she says, and breaks into song.

"They call him the Bomb 'cause you never know when he'll go off," she croons.

"They call him the Bomb 'cause his swing makes the shingles blow off," Benny counters, dropping the last note an octave, the way he always does.

"They call him the Bomb 'cause he's big and loud," Esther sings.

"They call him the Bomb 'cause he can level a crowd." Benny's voice is so deep on "level a crowd" that it sounds like a foghorn.

"He's Bo 'the Bomb' Johnson, and you better watch out," they sing together, bringing the song to an end.

Barry Gray claps and everyone laughs.

"Watch out, world," Barry Gray says. "This duo isn't done yet. Benny Lament and Esther Mine, thank you for being with us tonight, and thank you for showing us what change looks like. I, for one, am grateful."

"Thank you, Barry," Esther says.

"Thank you, Barry," Benny echoes. "For everything."

"Hey, Benny?" Esther pipes up like she's going to finish the broadcast with a joke.

"Yeah?" Benny sounds as though he is braced for a punchline, a closing salvo, but instead Esther's voice is clear and sweet.

"I love you, Benny Lament."

"I love you too, Baby Ruth."

"And on that note, Happy New Year, one and all. May we love each other better in the decade to come. This is Barry Gray at WMCA in New York, signing off. Good night, everyone."

AUTHOR'S NOTE

I'm not going to lie: this story scared me. It felt big and unwieldy and fraught with land mines—which is why I called the band Minefield—that I wasn't sure I could navigate. It isn't history that took place that long ago, and there was no comfortable distance from the setting or the time. It's recent. It's ugly, and it's sensitive. Add to that, I wasn't alive in the sixties. I don't have any firsthand knowledge of the decade this story was set in—not the music scene, the Mafia life, the political world, or the civil rights movement. I was not there. But if storytellers wrote only about things they had personally experienced, it would be like musicians playing only music they had personally written.

I don't want to just sing my own songs; I want to sing the songs of many voices, even if the songs are painful and scary. I want to play all the chords. Like Benny said, you can't appreciate the resolution without the dissonance. I can only hope I played the right notes and struck the right balance. I tried very hard to do just that.

First off, a quick thank-you to Uncle Jack Lomento, my favorite Sicilian, for letting me use his name for Pop, and a thank-you to my Grandpa Frank, who was born and raised in the Bronx and never lost the accent. I thought of you on every page, Grandpa.

With every work of historical fiction, I always like to separate the fiction from the fact. Of course Benny Lament and Esther Mine are fictional, as is their story, but many of the characters in this story are real.

Bo "the Bomb" Johnson's character was loosely inspired by the real-life world heavyweight boxing champion Jack Johnson, who was jailed in 1920 for having a relationship with a white woman. It wasn't until recently that Jack Johnson received a presidential pardon. Jack Johnson wasn't perfect, but he *was* a champion, and he didn't deserve the treatment he got. It was his story that started me thinking about writing a character like him.

Ahmet Ertegun, Jerry Wexler, and engineer Tom Dowd of Atlantic Records were pioneers in the music industry and well-known advocates of Black artists and their music. Ahmet's desire to sign Benny and Esther would have been right in character with the real man.

Berry Gordy, founder of Motown Records, is not fictional. He's real, as is his family and his sister, Mrs. Esther Gordy Edwards, who played a small role in my story. I took pains to do my research, but I don't know Berry Gordy personally, nor did I know Esther Gordy Edwards, but I admire both greatly and hope I did them justice. Of course Smokey Robinson and Ray Charles are real as well. The recent documentary *Hitsville: The Making of Motown* is a great resource if you want to learn more about an amazing American success story and hear Berry Gordy tell the tale in his own words.

Barry Gray, known in some circles as the Father of Talk Radio, was also a real person who worked for WMCA radio in New York. He had a long and storied career. I was able to find an autobiography he published in 1975 called *My Night People* that I greatly enjoyed. He interviewed Malcolm X in 1960, and I would highly recommend listening to the interview. It is so telling of the era and their respective places in it.

Patrick Sweeney, the prosecutor killed by Salvatore Vitale, is fictional, as is Uncle Sal. Apparently, there was an actual gangster by the name of Salvatore Vitale, but my character was not inspired or based on him or any other real person. However, Albert Anastasia, Murder Inc., and many of the gangsters mentioned in the story are real. The story of "Kid Twist" Reles being pushed from the window of the hotel on Coney Island the day he was set to testify against Anastasia is true, as is the story of Albert Anastasia's murder in the barbershop at the Park Sheraton Hotel.

Politics and organized crime have a dirty history. There still exists some belief that the mob had a hand in JFK's death and in the death of Martin Luther King Jr. Don't go down the rabbit hole like I did, but just be aware that, like Pop tells Benny, everybody was a little bit rotten. The sixties were filled with some colorful characters, no doubt about it, and it was highly interesting, and sometimes discouraging, doing the research into so many of these intersecting worlds.

Finally, I am a huge fan of Gladys Knight. I was lucky enough to sing with her gospel choir for seven years. Those years are filled with moments I will never forget, but the thing I will most remember is listening to Gladys sing and tell her story. It is my hope that novels like *The Songbook of Benny Lament* echo some of the truths that I learned from Ms. Gladys. She said many times, "How can we ever learn to love each other if we don't know each other's stories?" And I took that to heart.

May we seek to learn each other's stories so that we might love each other a little better.

Amy Harmon

ACKNOWLEDGMENTS

Special thanks to my team at Lake Union, editor Jodi Warshaw and developmental editor Jenna Free, in particular. Your insight and suggestions made this process a joy, as usual.

To my personal beta readers and editors, Karey White, Amy Schmutz, Korrie Kelley, Renita McKinney, Alexandra Kane, Danielle Distler, and Jessica Teodoro. Thank you all for your love and input on this book. I am blessed to have been able to call on all of you. You made Benny better!

To my assistant, Tamara Debbaut, who always makes my work so much easier. Thank you for your friendship and steadiness. Your loyalty and love are irreplaceable.

To my agent, Jane Dystel, please don't ever leave me. You have been an ongoing blessing.

To my sweet daughter, Claire, who helped me talk through a difficult scene (for hours!) and saved my sanity right at the end.

And finally, to the people who love me most. I wouldn't be me without you. Thank you.

ABOUT THE AUTHOR

Amy Harmon is a *Wall Street Journal*, *USA Today*, and *New York Times* bestselling author. Her books have been published in two dozen languages—truly a dream come true for a little country girl from Utah. Harmon has written sixteen novels, including the *Wall Street Journal* and *Washington Post* bestseller *What the Wind Knows*; the *USA Today* bestsellers *The Smallest Part*, *Making Faces*, and *Running Barefoot*; and the #1 Amazon bestselling historical novel *From Sand and Ash*, which won a Whitney Award for Book of the Year in 2016. Her novel *A Different Blue* is a *New York Times* bestseller. Her *USA Today* bestselling fantasy *The Bird and the Sword* was a Goodreads Best Book of 2016 finalist. For updates on upcoming book releases, author posts, and more, go to www.authoramyharmon.com.